PENGUI[N CLASSICS]

AU BONHEUR DES DAMES

(The Ladies' Delight)

ÉMILE ZOLA, born in Paris in 1840, was brought up at Aix-en-Provence in an atmosphere of struggling poverty after the death of his father in 1847. He was educated at the Collège Bourbon at Aix and then at the Lycée Saint-Louis in Paris. He was obliged to exist in poorly paid clerical jobs after failing his *baccalauréat* in 1859, but early in 1865 he decided to support himself by literature alone. Despite his scientific pretensions Zola was really an emotional writer with rare gifts for evoking vast crowd scenes and for giving life to such great symbols of modern civilization as factories and mines. When not overloaded with detail, his work has tragic grandeur, but he is also capable of a coarse, 'Cockney' type of humour. From his earliest days Zola had contributed critical articles to various newspapers, but his first important novel, *Thérèse Raquin*, was published in 1867, and *Madeleine Férat* in the following year. That same year he began work on a series of novels intended to follow out scientifically the effects of heredity and environment in one family: the Rougon-Macquart. The work contains twenty novels which appeared between 1871 and 1893, and is the chief monument of the French Naturalist Movement. On completion of this series he began a new cycle of novels, the Trois Villes: *Lourdes, Rome, Paris* (1894–6–8), a violent attack on the Church of Rome, which led to another cycle, the Quatre Evangiles. He died in 1902 while working on the fourth of these.

ROBIN BUSS is a writer and translator who contributes regularly to *The Times Educational Supplement*, *The Times Literary Supplement* and other papers. He studied at the University of Paris, where he took a degree and a doctorate in French literature. He is part-author of the article 'French Literature' in *Encyclopaedia Britannica* and has published critical studies of works by Vigny and Cocteau, and three books on European cinema, *The French through Their Films* (1988), *Italian Films* (1989) and *French Film Noir* (1994). He is also part-author of a biography, in French, of King Edward VII (with Jean-Pierre Navailles, published by Payot, Paris, 1999). He has translated a number of other volumes for Penguin, including Jean Paul Sartre's *Modern Times* and, more recently, Zola's *L'Assommoir* for Penguin Classics.

AU BONHEUR DES DAMES
(The Ladies' Delight)

ÉMILE ZOLA, born in Paris in 1840, was brought up at Aix-en-Provence in an atmosphere of struggling poverty after the death of his father in 1847. He was educated at the Collège Bourbon at Aix and then at the Lycée Saint-Louis in Paris. He was obliged to exist in poorly paid clerical jobs after failing his *baccalauréat* in 1859, but early in 1865 he decided to support himself by literature alone. Despite his scientific pretensions Zola was really an emotional writer with rare gifts for evoking vast crowd scenes and for giving life to such great symbols of modern civilization as factories and mines. When not overloaded with detail, his work has tragic grandeur, but he is also capable of a coarse, 'Cockney' type of humour. From his earliest days Zola had contributed critical articles to various newspapers, but his first important novel, *Thérèse Raquin*, was published in 1867, and *Madeleine Férat* in the following year. That same year he began work on a series of novels intended to follow out scientifically the effects of heredity and environment in one family, the Rougon-Macquart. The work contains twenty novels which appeared between 1871 and 1893, and is the chief monument of the French Naturalist Movement. On completion of this series he began a new cycle of novels, the Trois Villes: *Lourdes*, *Rome*, *Paris* (1894–6–8), a violent attack on the Church of Rome, which led to another cycle, the Quatre Evangiles. He died in 1902 while working on the fourth of these.

ROBIN BUSS is a writer and translator who contributes regularly to *The Times Educational Supplement*, *The Times Literary Supplement* and other papers. He studied at the University of Paris, where he took a degree and a doctorate in French literature. He is part-author of the article 'French Literature' in *Encyclopaedia Britannica* and has published critical studies of works by Vigny and Cocteau, and three books on European cinema: *The French through Their Films* (1988), *Italian Films* (1989) and *French Film Noir* (1994). He is also part-author of a biography, in French, of King Edward VII (with Jean-Pierre Navailles, published by Payot, Paris, 1999). He has translated a number of other volumes for Penguin, including Jean Paul Sartre's *Modern Times* and, most recently, Zola's *L'Assommoir* for Penguin Classics.

ÉMILE ZOLA

AU BONHEUR DES DAMES

(*The Ladies' Delight*)

Translated and Edited by

ROBIN BUSS

PENGUIN BOOKS

PENGUIN BOOKS

Published by the Penguin Group
Penguin Books Ltd, 80 Strand, London WC2R 0RL, England
Penguin Putnam Inc., 375 Hudson Street, New York, New York 10014, USA
Penguin Books Australia Ltd, 250 Camberwell Road, Camberwell, Victoria 3124, Australia
Penguin Books Canada Ltd, 10 Alcorn Avenue, Toronto, Ontario, Canada M4V 3B2
Penguin Books India (P) Ltd, 11 Community Centre, Panchsheel Park, New Delhi – 110 017, India
Penguin Books (NZ) Ltd, Cnr Rosedale and Airborne Roads, Albany, Auckland, New Zealand
Penguin Books (South Africa) (Pty) Ltd, 24 Sturdee Avenue, Rosebank 2196, South Africa

Penguin Books Ltd, Registered Offices: 80 Strand, London WC2R 0RL, England

www.penguin.com

First published 1883
This translation first published in Penguin Classics 2001

012

Set in 10/12.5 pt PostScript Monotype Ehrhardt
Typeset by Rowland Phototypesetting Ltd, Bury St Edmunds, Suffolk
Printed in England by Clays Ltd, St Ives plc

ISBN-13: 978–0–140–44783–5

CONTENTS

INTRODUCTION

One of the more obvious pleasures of reading Émile Zola's novel-cycle, the Rougon-Macquart, is that each volume introduces you to a particular facet of life in the period in which the novels take place, that of the French Second Empire (1851–1870). The two best-known works in the series, *L'Assommoir* and *Germinal*, are set, respectively, in working-class Paris and in the mining area of Northern France; *Le Ventre de Paris* is a monument to the great central market of Paris, Les Halles, which was finally moved to the suburbs a hundred years after Zola's novel was published; *L'Oeuvre* reflects Zola's friendship with the painter Paul Cézanne, and the aesthetic and ideological struggles in the art world at the time of Impressionism; *La Bête humaine* portrays the life of workers in the early days of rail travel, while *L'Argent* dissects the operation of the Stock Market, at a time when fortunes were made and scandals flared in the financial world. This was to be a 'Natural and Social History of a Family Under the Second Empire', and in it Zola seeks to spotlight aspects of life that distinguish this period in French history from others, and to discover social institutions that are new or, for some other reason, reveal the inner political, financial and social workings of the imperial regime.

The department store was a phenomenon that peculiarly suited his purpose. It represented an innovation that, in Zola's view, would transform the commercial life of the country. It was also a microcosm of society, in which one could see the class system in operation and perhaps glimpse the model of some future, more just organization of social and industrial relations. The department store was also a site in which one could raise questions of fashion, advertising, architecture and town planning, as well as the role of women, the exploitation of women, changes in the structure of the family, the power of women as consumers and the new opportunities offered to them as workers. In the present novel, the eleventh in the cycle of twenty, *Au Bonheur des Dames* ('The Ladies' Delight'), named for the imaginary store in which it is set, Zola reaches for the very heart of Second Empire society, within the context of a Cinderella love story and against a background of frivolity and seduction, silks and satins and calico and lace.

Ceci tuera cela: the theme of 'this will kill that' in Victor Hugo's historical novel *Notre-Dame de Paris* – where 'this' is the printed book and 'that' the cathedral, the stone 'encyclopedia' of the Middle Ages – can also be seen as a guiding theme of *Au Bonheur des Dames* – though here it is a new consumerist religion, enshrined in its great department stores, that is killing off small family shops. It is often pointed out that, in fact, the arrival of the great stores did not result in the massacre of small tradesmen and family businesses that Zola foresaw. But to accuse him of simply being wrong is to miss the point. The department store, that great mechanism, taking goods in at one end, transmuting them into gold and delivering them to all parts of the city, is only one of the pillars around which capitalist society is built. Factories and plants of every sort operate in a comparable way to transform capital invested in raw materials into profit. Moreover, what is threatened, according to Zola, is not only the family business, but the family itself, as well as the small 'craftsman' (craftsmen either literally, like Bourras in the novel, who carves his own umbrella handles, or like Baudu, who sees himself as possessing special skills in the old 'art' of selling). The battle between the new form of commerce and the old reflects much wider social and industrial changes – and, in this sense, Zola was not altogether wrong in believing that 'this will kill that'.

The immediate enjoyment of reading his work, however, does not stem from any insights into the society of the Second Empire. He transports us inside this partly ostentatious, partly hidden world of the department store and reveals it in all its splendour – the description of the Great White Sale in the final chapter is a well-known *tour de force* – and in its petty miseries: the intrigues among the staff, the living conditions of the girls who boarded on the top floor of the shop, the acquisitive greed of the customers. The day that Denise, Pauline and Deloche spend in Joinville is a highlight of the novel, a vivid sketch of young Parisian shopworkers on a jaunt. There is much that we can still recognize and some things that have changed: the staff dining room, for example, with its 'grills large enough to grill martyrs, pots that would fricassé a sheep, a monumental plate-warmer and a marble basin filled by a continuous stream of water' (p. 282), the male assistants carrying their trays and collecting their bottles of wine, the vocal complaints about the quality of the fish, the loaf of bread down the centre of the table with a knife stuck in it and the 'shining zinc counter on which the portions of wine were set out in rows – little bottles without corks, still damp from washing' (p. 160). He recaptures for us the feel of moments in the past, such as 'the tender hour of dusk, that minute of discreet sensual pleasure in Parisian apartments, between the dying of the light from outside and the coming of the lamps that the servants are still lighting in the pantry' (p. 77). And in this novel, in particular, he glories in the 'tide of guipure, Mechlin, Valenciennes and Chantilly' (p. 108), in the 'light satins and soft silks: royal satins, renaissance satins, with pearly shades of spring water; and featherweight silks, crystal clear, Nile green, sky blue, blush pink, Danube blue' (p. 102); and in 'camisoles, little bodices, morning dresses, dressing gowns, linen, nansouk, lace, long white clothes, free and thin, in which one could feel the stretching and yawning of idle mornings after amorous evenings' (p. 399). The wares of *Au Bonheur des Dames* are displayed for us as they were to the pampered bourgeoises of the Second Empire, who would frequent the department stores to meet one another, buy clothes and materials, or simply to enjoy the sensual pleasure of touching all these silks and satins and lace – perhaps before going up to the reading room thoughtfully provided by the management of this store, to leaf through the fashion magazines or write a letter, 'heads down, as if hiding the paper beneath the flowers on their hats' (p. 408). The book is a display case where we can enjoy such vignettes from a vanished past.

There is clearly the fruit of direct observation in it, as well as documentation. In December 1882, when Zola had almost finished writing the novel, the journalist Alfred Douane reported in *Gil Blas* that for a whole month in the preceding winter the writer had spent five or six hours in the afternoons either at the *Bon Marché* or at the *Louvre* or at the *Place Clichy* – where Madame Zola was a regular customer. Lucky Madame Zola: not every wife can persuade her husband to come shopping for five or six hours in her favourite store on successive afternoons. The personal visits to the best-known emporia of Zola's time, and the imaginative effort to weld all together into a novel about a department store some fifteen years earlier, were the final stage in a long process of preparation and research. The result is a worthy tribute to this phenomenon of the age.

In fact, he had included a novel about trade as one of the 'fundamental worlds of modern society' in his preliminary outline for the Rougon-Macquart cycle, having been struck ever since his first arrival in Paris in 1858 by the new department stores, in particular by the advertisements for them in the press, and by the changes in the shape of the city as a result of the replanning under the aegis of Baron Haussmann. While many of the individual novels highlight one aspect or theme connected with Second Empire society, 'Haussmannization', as it is now called, is a recurrent topic in most of the Parisian novels; it is referred to particularly in *L'Assommoir*, *Le Ventre de Paris* and *La Curée*. Baron Georges Haussmann, Prefect of Paris from 1853 to 1869, undertook a massive programme of clearance in the capital, demolishing much of the old, overcrowded centre and pushing through the great boulevards that we now think of as characteristic of Paris: the Boulevard Saint-Michel and the Boulevard Saint-Germain on the left bank, the Boulevard de Strasbourg and the Boulevard de Sébastopol on the right. Under his aegis, three new bridges were built across the Seine and great crossroads were created at Place de l'Étoile, Place de la République (then Place du Château d'Eau) and Place d'Italie. Les Halles were reconstructed in the modern materials of glass and iron, a wing was added to the Louvre, the Opéra was started, new parks were opened and improvements were made to the sewage and water systems. Zola generally approved of these changes, but he was aware of their effects on the working-class inhabitants of the areas demolished for slum clearance. In *Au Bonheur des Dames,* the writer's attitude to the changes is positive, seeing them as progressive and necessary for the creation of a modern city.

The novel started to take shape during the late 1860s, the period when its action is set, and early in the next decade Zola had decided that it would revolve around the activities of Octave Mouret, linked through his paternal grandmother (Ursule Macquart) and his mother (Marthe Rougon) to the dynasty of the Rougon-Macquarts (the idea of the whole cycle was to study the effects of heredity in two families with a common ancestor). By February 1880, the periodical *Le Voltaire* was already announcing the writer's plan to dedicate a novel to 'those great modern emporia which have, in the past few years, transformed the habits of Parisians'. But the announcement was premature. To begin with, Zola suffered a series of personal disasters in the year 1880 which seriously interrupted his work. In April, his close friend Edmond Duranty died, followed in May by the death of another friend and literary mentor, Gustave Flaubert. These two events left him feeling that 'there is nothing but sadness and life is not worth living'. Worse was to come: in October, these deaths were followed by another still more grievous loss, when his mother, whom he adored, died of a heart attack at the age of sixty-one. He continued with journalism, theoretical writings on Naturalism and an adaptation of his novel *Nana* for the theatre, but he was unable to turn to the next planned volume in his great project, the Rougon-Macquart cycle.

Moreover, before he could begin *Au Bonheur des Dames*, he had to write the novel that precedes it in the life of Octave Mouret, *Pot-Bouille*, the tenth in the series. Set in a Parisian middle-class apartment block, this was to be his 'pessimistic' analysis of the bourgeois mentality: Mouret, the ambitious seducer, reveals the shallowness and hypocrisy behind the building's respectable façade. Zola started to write this novel in February 1881 and it appeared in instalments in *Le Gaulois* from April 1882. Some months earlier, as we have seen, he was haunting the department stores of Paris for material and by February 1882 was at last writing the first draft of *Au Bonheur des Dames*.

Despite the presence of Octave Mouret as a central character in both novels, *Au Bonheur des Dames* is not, in a real sense, a sequel to *Pot-Bouille*; more a corrective, a counterpart, the other side of a coin.

Pot-Bouille had shown the dark side of the bourgeoisie under the Second Empire, *Au Bonheur des Dames* reveals the positive side of the same class, its energy, its ability to create wealth and prosperity. Despite the terrible personal blows Zola had suffered in 1880, by two years later he had recovered some of his energy and optimism, allowing him to exorcize some of his earlier feelings of despair through the marginal character of Paul de Vallagnosc, Mouret's friend and former school-mate. Vallagnosc has no ambition, despite a brilliant school career (Octave, like Zola himself, did not shine at school); life, he feels, is pointless. Octave starts at the bottom of the ladder and works his way up, by charm, drive and effort, to become director of his mighty emporium, while Vallagnosc is stuck in a tedious, if respectable, bureaucratic post. Where Vallagnosc represents the decaying upper class, so exhausted that it has lost faith even in itself, Mouret is the force of the new age, open to every kind of change and driven by an irresistible lust for life and power.

Indeed, this – the 'optimistic' view of the bourgeoisie – is the only novel in the Rougon-Macquart cycle that can definitely be said to have a happy ending. 'A complete change of philosophy,' Zola wrote in his notes before starting work. 'No more pessimism. Don't conclude that life is stupid and sad; on the contrary, conclude that it is constantly at work, that its bringing to birth is powerful and joyful. In a word, go with the century, express the century, which is a century of action and conquest.'

This was the intention, but it is so far from Zola's habitual cast of mind that we should not be surprised to find it tempered by less sanguine ideas. As well as being the playground in which the bourgeoisie can express its joyful creativity, the world is a Darwinian jungle in which the fittest, the Mourets, can only survive at the expense of weaker competitors. As Zola saw it, the dodos of the new commerce were the old-fashioned shopkeepers, and the model for these was provided in the work of Honoré de Balzac, whose *Comédie Humaine* had offered a panorama of French society in the earlier part of the nineteenth century. Two books by Balzac dealt specifically with trade: *La Maison du Chat-qui-pelote*, a short novella published in 1830; and, more importantly, the novel *Histoire de la grandeur et de la décadence de*

César Birotteau, maître-parfumeur, published in 1837, the story of a perfumer who invents a cure for baldness, but is brought to bankruptcy by a dishonest and embittered former employee.[1] The character of Baudu, the shopkeeper in *Au Bonheur des Dames*, proud, stubborn, narrow-minded, owes a great deal to César Birotteau.

Retail trade in France had been strictly controlled under the Ancien Régime, and during the first half of the nineteenth century the typical outlet was still the *boutique*, specializing in only one variety of product and with no fixed prices: bargaining was the rule. Advertising was in its infancy: César Birotteau's lengthy 'prospectus' for his Cephalic Oil is presented by Balzac as a curious innovation. Gradually, however, from the 1820s onwards, the supremacy of the *boutique* in Paris was challenged by the arrival of the *magasin de nouveautés*, selling a wider variety of goods (for example, different kinds of clothing, plus umbrellas, furs, cottons and so on), as well as the novelty goods known as *articles de Paris*. César Birotteau's wife had been an assistant in just such a place,

> the first of those shops that have since opened all over Paris, bearing a greater or lesser number of painted signs, hanging streamers, displays full of shawls on swinging racks, cravats arranged like card-houses and a host of other commercial attractions, fixed prices, little ribbons, posted bills, illusions and optical effects taken to such a degree of perfection that their shop-fronts have become poems to trade.[2]

It is not hard to see, in these *magasins de nouveautés*, the infant precursors of the great department stores of the second half of the century – and in Balzac's description of this 'poem to trade', the literary germ of Octave Mouret's mighty emporium.

Fixed prices – Mouret stresses these as one of the principles on which his business is founded – were crucial to the new type of commerce. Aristide Boucicaut, founder of the *Bon Marché* in 1852, was responsible for this innovation which we now take for granted. Customers no longer had to haggle, manufacturers and retailers knew their costs and margins of profit, stores could offer bargains which were seen to be a reduction on the previous price. Boucicaut was a former pedlar who introduced commission on sales, participation in profits, a policy of returns, free entry (encouraging customers to browse at will) and regular clearance sales – all part of Octave Mouret's policy at *Au Bonheur des Dames*. He shared with Mouret, too, the idea that the customers should be encouraged to get lost in the store, both to make it seem more crowded, and in the hope that they would be tempted unexpectedly on their way around.

The director of the *Bon Marché* eventually married one of his own assistants and Madame Boucicaut, who would run the store by herself after his death, was even more active than he had been in arranging social security and leisure facilities for staff, including music and language classes. Other models for Mouret include H. A. Chauchard, the son of a restaurant owner who founded the *Louvre* department store in 1855 with help from the financier Périer, and Ernest Cognacq, founder of the *Samaritaine*, another former shop assistant who married Louise Jay, an assistant from the dress department of the *Bon Marché*. Together, Cognacq and Jay became famous as art collectors, though they seem to have been interested in art as an investment rather than for its own sake – and, as Louise Jay said, it kept her husband from spending his wealth on other women. They specialized in paintings and *objets d'art* of the eighteenth century (the women of Boucher and Fragonard were to be Ernest Cognacq's substitute for living mistresses), and their collection can be visited in the Musée Cognacq-Jay, in the Hôtel Denon, near the Métro station of Saint-Paul.

The basic principle behind the department store was to sell cheaply and in bulk, while the 'art' of selling in the old-fashioned shop, as we learn from Baudu, had been to talk up the price as high as possible. At first sight, everyone stands to gain from the change: the large shop makes greatly increased profits, can operate economies of scale and provide benefits to its staff, while giving the customers the goods that they want at cheaper prices. In reality, as Zola discovered in the course of his research, the picture was not quite so rosy. Cognacq at the *Samaritaine* subjected his staff to a host of petty regulations governing their dress and behaviour. He gave them a free lunch, but insisted that everyone should sit at the same place in the dining room, for example.

Any 'indecency' in dress was strictly punished. There was no job security: as we learn from Zola's novel, mass dismissals were common in the low season and it was widely assumed that female assistants would be worn out by the age of forty. Since they were not allowed to marry and keep their jobs, this left them with little alternative, Zola concluded, but to go on the streets.

He got his information about life in the department stores from three main informants: Léon Carbonneaux, a head of department in the *Bon Marché*, Beauchamp, an employee at the *Louvre* and Mademoiselle Dulit, a sales assistant at the store *Saint-Joseph* – it was Dulit, for example, who told him that it was almost impossible for a young woman assistant to remain 'honest'; she would have to take a lover if she was to survive. The novelist also went to considerable lengths to check other details, some of which are indicated in the notes, with the help of specialists in various fields, such as the architect Frantz Jourdain[3] and the lawyer Émile Collet. He visited the shops and made notes and sketches, which can still be seen among his papers in the Bibliothèque Nationale. He read articles in the press, noting in particular one in *Le Figaro*, in March 1881, which talked about the 'neurosis' that was supposed to afflict some women in these large shops, leading to a 'mania for theft'. But the most interesting aspect of this article is the fact that it suggests that the department store reflects the views of the social theorist Charles Fourier. Zola also refers directly in the novel to the Fourierist community (or 'phalanstery'), in passages that carry the perspective forward from the past of the old-fashioned *boutique*, through the present of the vibrant modern department store towards a possible future for social, industrial and human relations.

The present, in this 'poem of modern activity' (as Zola describes the novel in his outline plan), is harsh and inhuman; time and again, he refers to the store as a 'machine', impersonal and efficient – 'real steam engines', he calls the large shops in his plan, crushing the small shopkeepers. Characteristic of this stage is the figure of Octave Mouret, the exploiter of women, unscrupulous, energetic. And, like all seducers, he is himself seduced, enraptured by the very scent of the female customers whom he elevates to make them the queens of his empire. Only when the one woman arrives who can enchant and tame Octave, and make him suffer in his turn for the suffering that he has imposed on other women, will justice – personal and social – be achieved.

The instrument of this conversion through love is to be the humble figure of Denise Baudu, the focus of the romance around which the novel is built. Denise is another version of all those poor girls in the fairy tales who succeed by winning the love of powerful men: Cinderella, the original of them all, but also Richardson's Pamela and other eighteenth-century heroines, or Jane Eyre (who refuses to compromise with Mr Rochester and is driven into the wilderness, until circumstances put him in her power). She is comparable even to the heroine of the film *Pretty Woman*, who wins the heart of the asset stripper and converts him to better ways – with the difference, of course, that where Denise seduces her man by refusing him her body, in *Pretty Woman* the prostitute begins by offering her favours, only to have them rejected by the businessman, who is too jaded to care. Times have changed, but the fundamental story remains the same. This is the *conte bleu* aspect of the novel, which, for some readers, is another of the novel's pleasures, and for others its greatest weakness.

However, it is a mistake to see the love story as something merely tacked on to the novel. For a start, the romance between Denise and her boss is not implausible. Given that two of the directors of Parisian stores had married shop assistants (Boucicaut at the *Bon Marché* and Cognacq at *La Samaritaine*), the odds on this happening were a good deal better than those on a match between a prince and a scullerymaid, even with the help of a pumpkin and a fairy godmother. More important still is the centrality of Denise's role to the overall scheme of the novel. On one level, she serves as the reader's point of view, conveying the experience of the department store through the eyes of a naive young provincial and enlisting our sympathy for the hard-worked, often ill-treated young women behind the counters. At the same time, she is a necessary counterweight to Octave, bringing a human face to the impersonal operation of the machine and convincing him that his staff need good treatment if they are to give of their best.

Denise, breaking away from her roots in her uncle's old-fashioned *boutique*, allies herself with the forces of progress and bows to the inevitable, but without losing her humanity: 'She no longer fought against it, but accepted this law of struggle, though her woman's soul filled with anguished compassion and sympathetic tenderness at the idea of suffering humanity . . .' (p. 380). And, while Mouret himself represents the present, with its necessary mission to sweep away the past, Denise suggests a Utopian vision of the future, in which the harshness of the machine will be tempered by notions of co-operation and mutual help: 'she would get excited, seeing the huge, ideal store, the phalanstery of trade [*see below*], in which everyone would have a precise share of the profits according to his or her deserts, as well as security for the future, ensured by a contract' (p. 348).

Throughout Europe, the nineteenth century was the great age of social reform and visions of social reform. Charles Fourier (1772–1837) was a brilliant, often eccentric and sometimes erratic social theorist, whose writings were to have an understandable appeal to the twentieth-century Surrealists; and some of his writings on sex were not published until the 1960s. Fourier believed that a harmonious society could be achieved, provided the basic human passions were gratified, and that the ideal site for this would be a new social unit, which he called a 'phalanstery'. It would consist of around 1,620 members and have a complex internal organization, involving people with different professions or skills in various relationships and hierarchies. Like most Utopian theorists, Fourier entered into quite minute descriptions of the organization and running of these communities, in his book *Le Nouveau monde industriel* (1829).

At several points in *Au Bonheur des Dames*, Zola picks up the suggestion in the article from *Le Figaro* that the modern department store, with its one or two thousand employees, some living on the premises, and the range of skills and services it requires, is a kind of Fourierist phalanstery. Zola must have remembered the article a year later when he wrote his outline of the book, which he said was to 'embody the whole materialistic and phalansterian century'. There are several references to 'phalansteries' in the novel, as well as to the department store as a world in itself: in Chapter 12, Mouret, inspecting his empire, finds that his staff could populate a small town: he had fifteen hundred sales assistants, and a thousand other employees of every kind, including forty inspectors and seventy cashiers; the kitchens alone employed thirty-two men; there were ten people in advertising, three hundred and fifty porters in livery, twenty-four permanent fire wardens . . . (p. 331)

This is something so much greater in scale than the small family shop that it becomes qualitatively different – and, as the 'dynasty' of the Lhommes shows, it threatens the traditional family.

Yet this reflection on the size of Mouret's achievement comes at the very moment when he feels most strongly how meaningless it all is. The only thing that he wants now is the one woman who refuses to give herself to him, the woman who will also supply the machine with warmth and humanity. And when, on the last page, she does finally declare her love and accept his proposal, we are looking not only towards the traditional ending in which this couple live happily ever after – though that is also in view, presumably in a new, more harmonious version of the family – but towards a future for *Au Bonheur des Dames* and its staff of prosperity and good working relations. A happy ending all round, with Denise and Octave's marriage as 'a symbolic union of the capitalist and the worker'.[4]

Of course, there are elements in the portrayal of Denise herself and her relations with Mouret that reveal nineteenth-century attitudes and assumptions about women, sex and love that are no longer generally held. Mouret's womanizing, in this and the previous novel, does not seem to damage his suitability as a mate for our heroine, though it is precisely her 'purity' that makes her worthy of him. Indeed, this saintly figure manages to combine the characteristics of the Virgin Mary, being at once a virgin and a 'mother' (the word is used repeatedly) to her two brothers. She rejects Pauline's friendly suggestion that, if she is to survive as a shopgirl, she must take a lover; she rejects the love of Deloche; and, most of all, she consistently refuses even to declare her love, let alone to become the mistress of the man she really adores, Octave Mouret. Like Jane Eyre, she would rather leave and risk losing him than betray her principles. Assuming that one is prepared to believe Denise's insistence that she is not in any way calculating in her tactics, the moral standard set for our heroine is far above that required of our hero – and not only in matters of sex. Zola does not condemn him, for example, when he unjustly turns on his staff for trivial offences, merely because of the turmoil in his private life (Chapter 12), or for his exploitation of Madame Desforges as a means to reach Baron Hartmann. His attitude towards his female customers is contemptuous; cynicism and egotism are the qualities that more obviously characterize him in his human relations, and it requires a leap of faith to believe that, abruptly, his love for Denise and the suffering that it induces can purge him of these qualities. This, rather than the romance itself, is the fairytale aspect of the novel that stretches credibility.

However, in another sense, Mouret already seems, in some curious way, 'pure', almost devoid of sexual desire. The eroticism in the novel is not attached to the romantic couple at its centre, but to the garments and fabrics in the store, in an almost fetishistic transference:

> the heaviest stuffs reposed as though in a basin: the thick weaves, the damasks, the brocades and the silks decorated with pearls or gold and silver threads, in the midst of a deep velvet bed – every sort of velvet, black, white and coloured, embossed on silk or satin, its shimmering patches forming a motionless lake in which reflections of landscapes and skies seemed to dance. Women, pale with longing, leaned over as though to see their own reflections in it . . . seized by a vague fear that they might be swept up in the torrent of such luxury and by an irresistible desire to leap and to lose themselves in it. (p. 102)

The customers are dehumanized, while the goods on display become human: Denise sees

> women who had stopped and were pressing one another against the panes, a whole crowd brutalized by greed. And, in this passion sweeping along the street, the clothing materials came to life: lace shivered, fell back and hid the depths of the shop behind a disturbing veil of mystery; even the lengths of cloth, thick, square-cut, exhaled tempting breaths, while the coats on the dummies threw out their chests, endowing them with souls, and the great velvet overcoat swelled, warm and supple, as though across living shoulders with a beating breast and swaying hips. (p. 16)

The assistants, too, are desexed, partly because of the management's ban on relations between them, and partly for reasons of class. If shop assistants dress smartly, 'above their station', because they must deal with women of a higher class, this is all the more reason for these bourgeoises to treat them as they do servants, as invisible, not-quite-humans. So, when Mignot is fitting gloves on Madame Desforges, he is surprised not to see any sign of sensual pleasure on her face, unaware that for her 'he was not a man; she employed him for these intimate tasks with her usual scorn for servants, without even looking at him' (p. 99).

This transfer of desirability from the human beings in the novel to the garments and to the store itself – that impersonal machine – sets up a divide between eroticism (associated with what is impersonal, mechanical) and love. Yet one may well ask oneself again what, underneath, is this love that Mouret feels for Denise. The more he comes to respect her, the more he wants to possess her; and the more she refuses to yield, the more obsessed he becomes with having her. Will they be happy together? According to the brief summary of their fate in the last novel in the Rougon-Macquart cycle, *Le Docteur Pascal*, Octave 'had two children with his wife Denise, a boy and a girl, and, though he adored his wife, he started to go off the rails again'. The happy ending was perhaps not so happy after all.

The critics were, on the whole, favourable to the novel when it appeared, though it was noticeable that some of the better-known ones, for example Fernand Brunetière and Henri Fouquier, chose not to review it. Brunetière, originally an admirer of Zola and of Naturalism, had turned against both a few years earlier, and Fouquier had published a harsh review of *Pot-Bouille* in the periodical *Gil Blas*. Some of the favourable critics liked the romantic plot, while many stressed the documentary value of the novel.[5] Later writers, admirers of Zola, have suspected that praise for the novel's 'human' qualities – the ending was 'simple, true and touching' according to the review *Le Mot d'ordre* – was motivated by all the wrong reasons. The Zola who had shocked the middle-class reading public with *L'Assommoir* and *Nana*, who had held a mirror up to it in *Pot-Bouille*, had at last written a book that was optimistic, pleasant, honouring capitalist enterprise and the profit motive. Doesn't the touching final scene, in which Denise at last declares her love, take place beside the desk in Mouret's office, loaded with the coins and banknotes from the store's first million-franc sale?

In fact, only the most naive person would be taken in by the rosy ending and believe that this represents the 'optimistic' view of the modern world that Zola originally intended. Not only is it hard to believe in Mouret's conversion from cynical exploiter to warm humanitarian, but every other character in the novel apart from the saintly Denise is in some way pitiful or despicable. Can one really disagree with Mouret's judgement on the old shopkeeper, Bourras, that he is an old fool for not having accepted the compensation he is offered? As for the Baudus, they are pathetic in their inability to change with the times. The shop assistants are engaged in a vicious struggle for position (this is perhaps the first novel to show 'office politics' operating in such a setting); Madame Desforges is odious in her snobbery; and her friends and fellow-shoppers, 'these ladies', are so powered by impulses of greed and acquisitiveness that modern feminists have seen them as a 'female mob', perhaps reflecting Zola's fear of the growing power of women.[6] The store, that impersonal mechanism, in its great iron and glass building, is like a hothouse, with its own seasons (selling winter coats in summer, and so on), cultivating a jungle the denizens of which are engaged in a vicious struggle to survive and to acquire.

Some admirers of Zola, including Henri Guillemin, have found this novel deficient in terms of character and plot – though, as Guillemin says, 'one never wastes one's time reading Zola';[7] others have stressed the 'documentary' value of Zola's work, based as it is on extensive research in the department stores themselves and information supplied by expert witnesses. Such attitudes do less than justice to the novel. As I said earlier, to treat the story of Denise and Mouret as merely incidental is to overlook how profoundly the meaning of the whole is embodied in these two characters and their contrasting aspirations for the future; while to reduce the interest of the novel merely to its documentary elements is to ignore the creative use that Zola has made of his research.

He realized, in particular, that the change from the old *boutique* to the new *grand magasin* was not merely a matter of consumer convenience and economies of scale. The customer of the small, specialized shop would go there in order to buy a particular item: an evening gown, a coat, a hat, an umbrella . . . She would call on the shopkeeper, express her desire and bargain with him over the price. But with the arrival of the large department store, shopping became one of the middle-class woman's chief activities, as well as a recreation and entertainment: the store was a theatre in which the goods were set out in alluring tableaux, the customer was part of the audience for all that the store had to offer. She could go inside without any precise idea of what she wanted, wander round, enjoy the displays and allow herself to be tempted into unplanned purchases. She entered into a new relationship not only with the seller of the goods, but also with the very activity of shopping.

'The ladies' – *ces dames*, as Zola repeatedly refers to the group around Madame Desforges – were members of the middle and upper bourgeoisie whose needs and tastes the early department stores tried to reflect. But the commodities that defined their lifestyle and their membership of this social group were now more cheaply and more widely available to those who merely aspired to belong to that social group: it was possible henceforth to buy into the bourgeoisie; and the objects needed to accede to the class became themselves the focus of desire. The 'young ladies' behind the counter – *ces demoiselles* – were the forerunners and the symbols of such social mobility, working-class girls whose employment meant that they had to adopt clothing and manners above their station (which is why they seem such a threat to Madame Desforges and her circle).

The department store was selling far more than just a few essential consumer goods, as the successive sales at *Au Bonheur des Dames* demonstrate; it was selling aspirations, status, dreams and yearnings. This 'quasi-public world', Elaine Adelson writes in her perceptive study of shoplifting in the nineteenth-century American department store, was 'an arena' in which 'relationships of women, gender, and class were vividly exposed';[8] 'the large stores educated people to want things, and they played a crucial role in determining the essentials of middle-class life and aspirations'.[9] It was Zola's genius to conceive the operation of this process primarily in erotic terms, to observe not only that women were the main consumers of the goods offered by the department stores, not only that the bright, subtly designed emporia 'seduced' them into buying the goods on offer, but that there was a transfer of erotic desire on to the goods themselves, so that these objects become, in the novel, endowed with sensual properties capable of making good wives squander their husbands' wealth and respectable ladies turn to thieving. The store itself is made, if anything, more alluring by the contrasting presence, at the centre of the story, of the calculating, bloodless seducer, Mouret, and the virginal heroine, Denise.

Of course, what Zola sees as a phenomenon characteristic of the French Second Empire was, in fact, an international one: Selfridges and Whiteley's in London, Macy's in New York, Marshall Field in Chicago and others were adopting techniques and playing social roles very similar to those of the *Bon Marché* and *Au Printemps* in Paris; one has only to recall one's own earliest visits to such places, the aura surrounding their names, the excitement aroused by their seemingly endless displays of toys, clothes and other goods, to acknowledge the power of the great department store. And this was not something that ended with the collapse of the Second Empire; on the contrary, the phenomenon of the consumer society, obsessed with image, fashion and gratification, is one that, a century after Zola's death, we are only beginning to understand. Of all Zola's novels, this is surely the one that has most relevance for our time. The mining community of *Germinal*, the working-class Paris of *L'Assommoir* and *Le Ventre de Paris*, are fascinating, but they belong to the past, while the greed and the illusions that were nurtured under the glass roofs of *Au Bonheur des Dames* are part of a world that we can easily recognize, since it was the birthplace of so much in our own.

NOTES

1. See Honoré de Balzac, *César Birotteau*, translated by Robin Buss, Penguin Classics, 1994.
2. Ibid., p. 24.

3. The design for a new shop that Jourdain showed Zola was eventually used in *La Samaritaine*.
4. Rachel Bowlby, *Just Looking: Consumer Culture in Dreiser, Gissing and Zola* (New York/London: Methuen, 1985), p. 67.
5. Apparently an American management consultancy produced a limited edition of one nineteenth-century translation, recommending Mouret's ideas to its readers as a guide to sales techniques. See Kristin Ross's introduction to the nineteenth-century translation re-issued by University of California Press in 1992: E. Zola, *The Ladies' Paradise* (Berkeley: University of California Press, 1992), p. xxii.
6. See Susanna Barrows, *Distorting Mirrors: Visions of the Crowd in Late Nineteenth-Century France*, Yale University Press, 1981.
7. See Henri Guillemin, *Présentation des Rougon-Macquart* (Paris: Gallimard, 1964).
8. Elaine Abelson, *When Ladies Go A-Thieving* (Oxford: Oxford University Press, 1989), p. 4.
9. Ibid., p. 5.

CHRONOLOGY

1840 (2 April). Émile Zola born in Paris, the son of an Italian engineer, Francesco Zola, and of Françoise-Emilie Aubert.

1843 The family moves to Aix-en-Provence, which will become the town of 'Plassans' in the Rougon-Macquart novels.

1847 Francesco Zola dies, leaving the family nearly destitute.

1848 The rule of King Louis-Philippe (the July Monarchy, which came to power in 1830) is overthrown and the Second Republic declared. Zola starts school.

1851 The Republic is dissolved after the *coup d'état* of Louis-Napoleon Bonaparte who in the following year proclaims himself emperor as Napoleon III. Start of the Second Empire, the period that will provide the background for Zola's novels in the Rougon-Macquart cycle.

1852 Zola is enrolled at the Collège Bourbon, in Aix, where he starts a close friendship with the painter Paul Cézanne. Aristide Boucicaut founds the *Bon Marché*, the first of the Parisian department stores.

1855 Founding of the *Grands Magasins du Louvre*.

1858 The family moves back to Paris and Zola is sent to the Lycée Saint-Louis. His school career is undistinguished and he twice fails the baccalaureate.

1860 The start of a period of hardship as Zola tries to scrape a living by various kinds of work, while engaging in his first serious literary endeavours, mainly as a poet. These years saw the height of the rebuilding programme undertaken by Baron Haussmann, Prefect of Paris from 1853 to 1869, which is reflected in several of Zola's novels, including *Au Bonheur des Dames*.

1862 Zola joins the publisher Hachette, and in a few months becomes the firm's head of publicity.

1863 Makes his début as a journalist.

1864 Zola's first literary work, the collection of short stories, *Contes à Ninon*, appears.

1865 Meets his future wife, Gabrielle-Alexandrine Meley; they marry in 1870.

1866 Leaves Hachette. From now on, he lives by his writing.

1867 Publication of *Thérèse Raquin*, the story of how a working-class woman and her lover kill her husband, but are afterwards consumed by guilt. In the Preface to the second edition, Zola declares that he belongs to the literary school of 'Naturalism'.

1868 Zola develops the outline of his great novel-cycle, the Rougon-Macquart, which he subtitles 'The Natural and Social History of a Family Under the Second Empire'. It is founded on the latest theories of heredity. He signs a contract for the work with the publisher Lacroix.

1870 The outbreak of the Franco-Prussian War leads in September to the fall of the Second Empire. Napoleon III and Empress Eugénie go into exile in England and the Third Republic is declared. Paris is besieged by Prussian forces. *La Fortune des Rougon* starts to appear in serial form.

1871 Publication in book form of *La Fortune des Rougon* and *La Curée*, the first novels in the Rougon-Macquart cycle. After the armistice with Prussia, a popular uprising in March threatens the overthrow of the government of Adolphe Thiers, which flees to Versailles. The radical Paris Commune takes power until its bloody repression by Thiers in May; the events would have great importance for the Socialist Left. Zola was shocked both by the anarchy of the Commune and by the savagery with which it was repressed.

1872 Publication of *Le Ventre de Paris*, the third of the Rougon-Macquart novels, set in and around the market of Les Halles.

1874 Publication of *La Conquête de Plassans*.

1875 Publication of *La Faute de l'Abbé Mouret*.

1876 *Son Excellence Eugène Rougon* follows the career of a minister under the Second Empire. Later in the same year, the seventh of the Rougon-Macquart novels, *L'Assommoir*, appears in serial form and immediately causes a sensation with its grim depiction of the ravages of alcoholism and life in the Parisian slums.

1877 *L'Assommoir* is published in book form and becomes a best-seller. Zola's fortune is made and he is recognized as the leading figure in the Naturalist movement.

1878 Zola follows the harsh realism of *L'Assommoir* with a gentler tale of domestic life, *Une page d'amour*.

1879 *Nana* appears in serial form, before publication in book form in the following year. The story of a high-class prostitute; the novel was to attract further scandal to Zola's name.

1880 Zola expounds the theory of Naturalism in *Le Roman expérimental*. In May, Zola's literary mentor, the writer Gustave Flaubert, dies; in October, Zola loses his much-loved mother. A period of depression follows and he suspends writing the Rougon-Macquart for a year.

1882 Zola's next book, *Pot-Bouille*, centres on an apartment house and the character of the bourgeois seducer, Octave Mouret. The novel analyses the hypocrisy of the respectable middle class.

1883 Mouret reappears in *Au Bonheur des Dames*, which studies the phenomenon of the department store.

1884 *La Joie de vivre*. Towards the end of the year, *Germinal* starts to appear in serial form. Set in a northern French mining community, this powerful novel is Zola's most politically committed fictional work.

1886 *L'Oeuvre* gives a fascinating insight into Parisian and literary life, as well as a reflection of contemporary aesthetic debates, drawing on Zola's friendship with many leading painters and writers. However, Cézanne reacts badly to Zola's portrait of him in the novel, and ends their friendship.

1887 *La Terre*, a brutally frank portrayal of peasant life, causes a fresh uproar and leads to a crisis in the Naturalist movement when five young writers, calling themselves disciples of Zola, sign a manifesto against the novel.

1888 The 'scandalous' *La Terre* is followed by another sentimental work, *Le Rêve*. Zola meets Jeanne Rozerot, the mistress with whom he will have two children.

1890 *La Bête humaine*, the story of a sadistic killer, is set against the background of the railways. Though not the best novel in the cycle, it is to be one of the most popular.

1891 *L'Argent* dissects the world of the Stock Exchange.

1892 *La Débâcle* analyses the French defeat in the Franco-Prussian war and the end of the Second Empire.

1893 The final novel in the cycle, *Le Docteur Pascal*, develops the theories of heredity that have guided *Les Rougon-Macquart*.

1894 With *Lourdes*, Zola starts a trilogy of novels, to be completed by *Rome* (1896) and *Paris* (1898), about a priest who turns away from Catholicism towards a more humanitarian creed. In December, a Jewish officer in the French Army, Captain Alfred Dreyfus, is found guilty of spying for Germany and sentenced to life imprisonment in the penal colony on Devil's Island.

1897 New evidence in the case suggests that Dreyfus' conviction was a gross miscarriage of justice, inspired by anti-Semitism. Zola publishes three articles in *Le Figaro* demanding a retrial.

1898 Zola's open letter, *J'Accuse*, in support of Dreyfus, addressed to Félix Faure, President of the Republic, is published in *L'Aurore* (13 January). It proves a turning-point, making the case a litmus test in French politics: for years to come, being pro- or anti-Dreyfusard will be a major component of a French person's ideological profile (with the nationalist Right leading the campaign against Dreyfus). Zola is tried for libel and sentenced to a year's imprisonment and a fine of three thousand francs. In July, waiting for his appeal to be heard, he leaves for London, where he spends a year in exile.

1899 Zola begins a series of four novels, *Les Quatre Évangiles*, which would remain uncompleted at his death. They mark his transition from Naturalism to a more idealistic and utopian view of the world.

1902 On 29 September, Zola is asphyxiated by the fumes from the blocked chimney of his bedroom stove, perhaps by accident, perhaps (as is still widely believed) assassinated by anti-Dreyfusards. His remains were transferred to the Pantheon in 1908.

FURTHER READING

Abelson, Elaine S., *When Ladies Go A-Thieving. Middle-Class Shoplifters in the Victorian Department Store* (Oxford: Oxford University Press, 1989).

Bohme, Margarete, *The Department Store. A Novel of Today* (New York: Appleton, 1912).

Bowlby, Rachel, *Just Looking: Consumer Culture in Dreiser, Gissing and Zola* (New York/London: Methuen, 1985).

Brown, Frederick, *Zola. A Life* (New York: Macmillan, 1995).

Hemmings, F. W. J., *The Life and Times of Émile Zola* (London: Paul Elek, 1977).

Lancaster, Bill, *The Department Store. A Social History* (Leicester: Leicester University Press, 1995).

Miller, Michael B., *The Bon Marché. Bourgeois Culture and the Department Store, 1869–1920* (Princeton: Princeton University Press, 1981).

Williams, Rosalind, *Dream Worlds. Mass Consumption in Late Nineteenth-Century France* (Berkeley: University of California Press, 1982).

Wilson, Angus, *Émile Zola. An Introductory Study of His Novels* (London: Secker and Warburg, 1952).

Zeldin, Theodore, *France, 1848–1945. Ambition and Love* (Oxford: Oxford University Press, 1979).

A NOTE ON THIS AND SOME OTHER TRANSLATIONS

The text used for this translation is the one published in the third volume of the edition of the Rougon-Macquart in the Bibliothèque de la Pléiade (Paris: Gallimard, 1964) under the direction of Armand Lanoux, with notes by Henri Mitterand; I am grateful to Mitterand for some of the information used in the notes here.

Au Bonheur des Dames was the first of Zola's novels to be translated into English. Even as he was writing the book, he was in touch with Frank Turner, an English translator living in France, to whom he sent a summary of the novel, then sections of the text.[1] The translation, published by Tinsley Brothers in November 1883, was quite heavily expurgated, but ironically, what the publisher cut out were specific references to sexual matters, for example to Jean's mistresses, while the atmosphere of eroticism that envelops so much of the novel, in its references to clothing, to the sensual textures of materials, to the power of Mouret over women or to the desires and pleasures of the female customers, was allowed to stand. A fuller version was the one published by Henry Vizetelly in 1886; Vizetelly was to go to prison two years later for bringing out a translation of *La Terre*.

There have been three films of *Au Bonheur des Dames*: a German film of 1922, *Des Paradies des Damen*; Julien Duviver's film of 1929; and André Cayatte's of 1943. Alfred Machin's 1913 film *Au Ravissement des Dames*, though the title suggests Zola's novel, is said to be about how the poor, tubercular shopgirls in a large store infect their rich customers, which is a long way from Zola's novel. By far the most interesting work to have been inspired by it, however, is Grigori Kosintsev and Leonid Trauberg's *Noviy Vavilon ('New Babylon')*, a masterpiece of Soviet silent cinema, which tells the story of the

Franco-Prussian war and the Paris Commune through the eyes of Louise, a shop assistant in a store called 'The New Babylon' (played by Elena Kuzmina, in her screen début). This is also slightly remote from the plot of Zola's novel, but faithful to the project of showing the department stores as the cathedrals of modern capitalism.

NOTES

1. See E. Zola, *Correspondance*, vol. IV, 1880–1883 (Éditions du CNRS, Presse de l'Université de Montréal, under the direction of B. H. Bakker, 1983).

AU BONHEUR DES DAMES

CHAPTER 1

Denise had come by foot from the Gare Saint-Lazare, where she had got off a train from Cherbourg with her two brothers, after a night spent on the hard bench of a third-class carriage. She was holding Pépé's hand and Jean followed behind; all three were exhausted by the journey, startled and lost in the immensity of Paris, looking up at the houses and stopping at every crossroads to ask for the Rue de la Michodière, where their Uncle Baudu lived. But when she finally arrived at the Place Gaillon, the girl stopped dead in surprise:

'Oh!' she exclaimed. 'Take a look at that, Jean!'

They stayed, rooted there, pressed against one another, dressed entirely in black: they were using up the old clothes that they had worn in mourning for their father. She was small for her twenty years and looked impoverished, carrying her light parcel, while her little brother, five years old, was hanging on her other arm and, behind her, the elder one, splendid in the full bloom of his sixteen years, stood with swinging arms.

'Well I never,' she continued, after a pause. 'Now that is a shop!'

At the corner of the Rue de la Michodière and the Rue Neuve-Saint-Augustin, was a fashionable draper's with brightly coloured displays gleaming in the soft, pale October light. The clock on the Église Saint-Roch was sounding eight and there was no one on the street except the Parisian early birds: office workers on their way to work and housewives shopping. In front of the door, two employees up a double ladder had just hung out some knitwear, while another was kneeling, with his back turned, in a window on the Rue Neuve-Saint-Augustin, delicately folding a length of blue silk. The shop was still empty of customers, the staff had barely arrived, but it was buzzing inside like an awakening beehive.

'Crikey!' said Jean. 'It's a darned sight better than Valognes ... Yours wasn't as smart as that.'

Denise nodded. She had spent two years back there at Cornaille's, the top ladies' wear shop in the town; and coming suddenly across this shop, this building that seemed so enormous to her, brought a lump to her throat and left her standing, shaken, engrossed, forgetting everything else. The high door on the angle overlooking the Place Gaillon, entirely made of glass, rose as far as the mezzanine, surrounded by a mass of heavily gilded ornamental mouldings. Two allegorical figures, a pair of laughing women, leaning backwards with naked breasts, held between them the sign: *Au Bonheur des Dames*. From there, the windows stretched away along the Rue de la Michodière and the Rue Neuve-Saint-Augustin, where they occupied another four buildings apart from the one on the corner, two on the left, two on the right, all recently bought and done up. The perspective made the whole complex seem endless to her, with its ground-floor displays and the spotless windows on the mezzanine behind which one could see all the inner life of the shop floor. Upstairs, a lady wearing a silk dress was sharpening a pencil while two others beside her were unfolding velvet robes.

'*Au Bonheur des Dames*,' Jean read, with the gentle laugh of a handsome young man who had already been involved with a woman in Valognes. 'That's nice, isn't it? It ought to bring the customers running!'

But Denise was still contemplating the display at the main door. Out in the open, even on the pavement, an avalanche of cheap goods had spilled out – the bait at the doorway, the bargains which halted the customer as she went past. It started high with woollens and linen items, merino, Cheviot and flannelette, hanging down from the mezzanine floor, waving like flags, their neutral shades, slate grey, navy blue or olive green, interrupted by white price tags. Beside them, also hanging and framing the doorway, were strips of fur, narrow bands to trim dresses, squirrel like fine ash, swans' down like driven snow, and imitation ermine and sable, made of rabbit. Below this, in racks and on tables, in the midst of a pile of remnants, was a profusion of hosiery, selling dirt cheap, gloves and knitted woollen scarves, hoods, cardigans, a winter display of variegated colours, mottled, striped, with patches of bleeding red. Denise saw a tartan for forty-five centimes, strips of American mink for a franc, mittens for five *sous*.[1] It was an enormous, fairground display, as though the shop were bursting and the excess pouring into the street.

Uncle Baudu was forgotten. Even Pépé, not letting go his sister's hand, was staring wide-eyed. A carriage obliged all three of them to move from the middle of the square and, mechanically, they started up the Rue Neuve-Saint-Augustin, walking alongside the windows and pausing afresh at each new display. To begin with they were enchanted by a complicated piece of window-dressing: at the top were umbrellas, arranged at an oblique angle so that they seemed to form the roof of a rustic hut; below them were silk stockings, hanging on rails to show the rounded forms of calves, some dotted with bunches of roses, others in every shade, the black ones netted, the red ones with embroidered corners, and flesh-coloured stockings whose satin texture was as soft as the skin of a blonde; and, finally, on cloth at the back of the display, there were symmetrically arranged gloves, with the long, outstretched fingers and narrow palms of a Byzantine Madonna, which had that stiff, almost pubescent grace of women's accessories when they have never been worn. But it was the last window that really caught their eye. The most delicate flower colours radiated from a display of silks, satins and velvet in a fluid, shimmering range of tones. At the top were the velvets, deep black or white as curds; lower down were the satins, pink, blue, sharply creased, shading off into infinitely softer tones; and, lower still, the silks, in the full panoply of a rainbow, with lengths of cloth twisted into the shape of shells or folded as if around a curving waist, brought to life by the shop assistants' agile fingers; and, between each motif, each coloured statement, ran a light, gathered ribbon of cream-coloured foulard as a discrete trimming. There, at either end, could be seen huge piles of the two silks exclusive to the shop: Paris-Bonheur and Cuir-d'Or, two exceptional items that were to revolutionize the drapery business.

'Oh! Look at that faille[2] for five francs sixty,' Denise murmured in astonishment, pointing to the Paris-Bonheur.

Jean was starting to get bored. He stopped a passer-by.

'Please, sir, for the Rue de la Michodière?'

After it had been pointed out to them – first on the right – all three retraced their steps, turning back round the corner of the shop; and, as she was starting down the street, Denise was stopped again by a window displaying ladies' clothes. At Cornaille's, in Valognes, ladies' wear had been her particular responsibility, but she had never seen anything like this. She stood and admired it, rooted to the spot. At the back, a large, expensive scarf in Bruges lace was spread out like an altar cloth, its two wings extended, in white tinged with red. There were garlands scattered around, made of flounces of Alençon lace; and then, by armfuls, a cascade of every kind of lace: Mechlin, Valenciennes, Venetian and appliqué from Brussels, like falling snow. To right and left, lengths of cloth rose in dark columns, which had the effect of thrusting the altar still futher back, and all around, in this chapel dedicated to the worship of womanly charms, were the clothes: in the centre, a velvet coat trimmed with silver fox, a unique piece; on one side, a silk cloak lined with squirrel; and on the other, a linen coat edged with cockerel's feathers; and finally evening wraps in white cashmere or white quilting, trimmed with swans' down or chenille. There was something for every taste, from wraps at twenty-nine francs to the velvet coat priced at eighteen hundred francs. The material swelled across the round bosoms of the tailors' dummies, broad hips emphasized their slender waists and where the head should be, there was a large price tag, stuck into the red flannel of the neck with a pin; and mirrors on either side of the display were carefully positioned to reflect the dummies and multiply them endlessly, peopling the street with these beautiful women, all for sale, who bore their prices in fat figures in place of heads.

'They're terrific!' Jean muttered, finding no other word to express his feelings.

He had suddenly become motionless in his turn, his jaw dropping. So much feminine luxury made him blush with pleasure. He had the beauty of a young girl, a beauty that he seemed to have stolen from his sister, with his radiant skin, his ginger curls, his lips and eyes moist and full of feeling. Beside him, his sister seemed more slender than ever in her amazement, her mouth too big for her long face and her complexion already dulled beneath her pale hair. And Pépé, who was also blond, but with the fair hair of childhood, pressed closer to her, as though overwhelmed by an anxious need to be hugged, at once enchanted and disturbed by the lovely ladies in the window. There was something so unusual and so fetching about the three light-haired children on the pavement, poorly dressed in black, the sad-looking girl between the pretty child and the proud youth, that passers-by turned round and smiled.

A fat man with grey hair and a broad, sallow face had been watching them for some time, standing at the doorway of a shop on the far side of the street. He had been there, raging inside himself at the window displays of *Au Bonheur des Dames*, with bloodshot eyes and tight lips, when the sight of the girl and her brothers finally drove him to exasperation. What were they doing, the three nitwits, gawping in that way at such a mountebank's display?

'What about our uncle?' Denise said suddenly, as though waking up with a start.

'We are in the Rue de la Michodière,' said Jean. 'He must live somewhere around here.'

They looked up and turned round. And there, right in front of them, above the fat man's head, they saw a green sign, its yellow lettering washed out by the rain: *Au Vieil Elbeuf, drapery and flannelling, Baudu, formerly Hauchecorne*. The house, behind its ancient coating of discoloured whitewash, dull and squat beside the large Louis XIV mansions surrounding it, had only three windows in its façade; and these square windows, without shutters, were plainly decorated with an iron grill of two crossed bars. But what struck Denise most forcibly in this bare frontage, her eyes still dazzled by the bright displays at *Au Bonheur des Dames*, was the ground-floor shop, low-ceilinged beneath a very low mezzanine floor, with bays like prison windows, in a half-circle. Woodwork, in the same colour as the sign, a bottle green that wind and rain had streaked with ochre and pitch, framed two deep-set shop windows to right and left, black, dusty, behind which one could faintly make out piles of materials. The door was open, disclosing what seemed like the dank blackness of a cellar.

'There it is,' Jean said.

'Well, we've got to go in,' Denise declared. 'Come on, Pépé.'

All three of them were nervous, however, overcome with shyness. When their father had died, succumbing to the same fever that had carried off their mother a month earlier, Uncle Baudu had indeed written to his niece, in the emotional aftermath of this double bereavement, to say that there would always be a place for her with him whenever she wanted to seek her fortune in Paris. But this letter was now nearly a year old, and the girl was starting to regret having left Valognes on the spur of the moment, without warning her uncle. He didn't know them at all, having not been back there himself since the day he had set out as quite a young man to take up a position as junior assistant with the draper Hauchecorne, before eventually marrying the boss's daughter.

'Monsieur Baudu?' Denise asked, finally plucking up courage to address the fat man, who was still looking at them, surprised at their behaviour.

'That's me,' he answered.

At this, Denise blushed purple and stammered:

'Oh, I'm so glad! I'm Denise, this is Jean and this is Pépé . . . You see, Uncle, we came . . .'

Baudu seemed overcome with amazement. His fat red eyes swam in his sallow face and he spoke slowly, stumbling over his words. He was quite clearly at a loss to comprehend this family which had fallen on him out of the blue.

'What! What! You? Here?' he said, over and over again. 'But you were in Valognes! Why aren't you in Valognes?'

She had to explain it to him in her soft, slightly tremulous voice. After the death of their father, who had poured every last farthing into his dye-works, she had been left to bring up the two children. What she earned at Cornaille's was not enough to feed all three of them. Of course, Jean had been working for a cabinet-maker who repaired old furniture, but he wasn't paid anything. However, he did develop a liking for old things and he would carve figures in wood. One day, finding a piece of ivory, he even amused himself carving a face in that and a gentleman had seen it, who happened to be there, and it was this same gentleman who had made up their minds to leave Valognes, by finding Jean a position in Paris with a craftsman in ivory.

'You see, Uncle, Jean is to start as an apprentice with his new master from tomorrow. They are not asking me for any money and he will get his bed and board. So I thought that Pépé and I would always manage somehow. We can't be worse off here than in Valognes.'

What she had not mentioned was Jean's love affair: letters written to the young daughter of a noble family in the town, kisses exchanged over a wall – and the outraged reactions that had made up her mind to leave; so, if she was accompanying her brother to Paris, it was chiefly to keep an eye on him: she was full of maternal anxieties for this great boy, so handsome and merry, who won every woman's heart.

Uncle Baudu was still quite overcome. He started asking her more questions – though, now that he had heard her speak of her brothers, he did revert to the familiar form.[3]

'So your father left you penniless? I thought he had a little bit left. Oh, I warned him in my letters not to take over that dye-works! A big heart, but no head for business! And you were left with these two lads to look after; you had to feed this little family, did you?'

The bilious look had vanished from his face and the blood had cleared from the eyes with which he had been staring at *Au Bonheur des Dames*. He suddenly realized that he was blocking the entrance.

'Come on in,' he said. 'As you're here . . . Come on, it's better than hanging around next to that nonsense.'

And, after scowling angrily one more time at the windows across the street, he led the way into the shop, calling to his wife and daughter.

'Élisabeth, Geneviève! Come here, we have company!'

But Denise and the two boys paused before plunging into the darkness of the shop. Blinded by the bright light of the street, they blinked as though on the threshold of some unfamiliar pit and tested the ground with their feet, instinctively fearing that they might meet an unexpected step. So it was that, drawn still closer together by this vague unease and pressing even more tightly against one another, with the youngest still clinging to the girl's skirts and the elder boy behind, they made their entrance, smiling with engaging timidity. The early sunshine emphasized the black outlines of their mourning dress and a shaft of slanting light gilded their blond hair.

'Come on in,' Baudu said again.

In a few brief words he described the situation to Madame Baudu and her daughter. The first of these was a little woman consumed by anaemia, completely white, with white hair, white eyes and white lips. Geneviève, in whom her mother's degeneration[4] was still more pronounced, had the debility and discolouration of a plant that has grown away from the light. And yet, the magnificent black hair, thick and heavy, that had somehow sprouted from this impoverished flesh, gave her a certain sad charm.

'Come in,' the two women said in their turn. 'You are welcome.'

They sat Denise down behind a counter. Pépé immediately got up on his sister's knees, while Jean, leaning back against a wooden panel, stayed close to them. As they looked round the shop, their eyes becoming accustomed to the dark, they were reassured. Now they could see it, with its low, smoke-stained ceiling, its oak counters shiny with use, and its ancient display racks with their heavy ironwork. Bales of dark merchandise were piled up to the beams. The smell of cloth and dyes, an acrid chemical smell, seemed to be intensified by the damp of the floor. At the back of the shop, two male assistants and a young lady were putting away lengths of white flannel.

'Perhaps this little gentleman would like something to eat or drink?' Madame Baudu asked Pépé, with a smile.

'No thank you,' Denise replied. 'We had a cup of milk in a café opposite the station.'

And, since Geneviève was staring at the light parcel that she had put down on the floor, she added: 'I left our trunk there.'

She blushed, realizing that it wasn't the done thing to land on people's doorsteps like that. Even as the train was leaving Valognes, she had felt full of misgivings about it; and that was why, when they arrived, she had deposited the trunk and given the children breakfast.

'Come, now,' said Baudu, suddenly. 'Let's talk and talk seriously . . . I did write to you, it's true, but that was a year ago, and I must tell you, my poor child, that business over the past year has not been good . . .'

He stopped, with a lump in his throat from a feeling that he did not want to show. Madame Baudu and Geneviève had lowered their eyes with an air of resignation.

'Oh, it's only a temporary setback,' he went on. 'I'm not worried . . . But I have had to reduce my staff: there are only three people here now and it's not yet the right time to be taking on a fourth. So I can't give you the work I offered, my poor girl.'

Denise listened to him and was so upset that she turned quite pale. He pressed the point home, saying:

'It wouldn't be worth it, for you or for us.'

'That's all right, Uncle,' she managed to say at last. 'I'll try to get by even so.'

The Baudus were not bad people, but they did complain that they never had any luck. In the days when their business was going well, they had to bring up five boys, three of whom died by the age of twenty; the fourth had gone to the bad and the fifth had just left for Mexico as a captain in the army.[5] Geneviève was all they had left. Bringing up this family had been expensive and Baudu had brought about his own downfall by purchasing a huge pile of a house in Rambouillet, where his wife's father came from; so there was a growing tide of bitterness rising in the faithful old tradesman's stubborn heart.

'One should let people know,' he went on, gradually becoming irritated at his own unkindness. 'You might have written to me, I should have told you to stay there. Goodness! When I heard of your father's death, I said what people usually say. And now you drop in, without a word of warning. It's most inconvenient.'

He was raising his voice, getting it all off his chest. His wife and daughter stayed there, staring at the floor, the sort of submissive creatures who never ventured to interrupt. Meanwhile, Jean went pale and Denise was clasping the terrified Pépé to her. Two large tears ran down her cheeks.

'It's all right, Uncle,' she repeated. 'We'll leave.'

Suddenly, he calmed down. There was an embarrassed silence. Then he continued in a gruff voice:

'I'm not sending you away . . . Now that you're here, you can always sleep upstairs for tonight; then we'll see.'

At this, Madame Baudu and Geneviève exchanged a glance that meant they could start sorting it all out. Everything was arranged. There was no need to bother about Jean. As for Pépé, he would be just fine with Madame Gras, an old lady who lived in a large ground-floor flat in the Rue des Orties, where she boarded young children for forty francs a month. Denise announced that she had enough to pay for the first month; all that was left was to find somewhere for her. There must surely be a job for her in the neighbourhood.

'Wasn't Vinçard looking for a salesgirl?' Geneviève said.

'Yes! That's right!' Baudu exclaimed. 'We'll go and see him after lunch. We must strike while the iron is hot.'

Not a single customer had come to interrupt this family discussion. The shop was as dark and empty as ever. At the back of it, the two assistants and the young lady carried on with their work, exchanging the odd whisper in hissing tones. Then three ladies did arrive, and Denise was left on her own for a moment. She gave Pépé a kiss, with a lump in her throat at the idea that they were soon to be parted. The child, as affectionate as a kitten, hid his face and said nothing. When Madame Baudu and Geneviève came back they decided he was very well-behaved and Denise assured them that he never made any more noise than this: he would stay quiet for whole days on end, nourished by caresses. So, until lunchtime, the three of them talked about children, about housekeeping, and about life in Paris and the provinces, making brief, vague remarks, in the manner of relatives who are slightly awkward at not knowing one another. Jean had gone out to the door of the shop and stayed there, taking an interest in the life of the streets and smiling at the girls as they went by.

At ten o'clock, a maid appeared. Usually, Baudu, Geneviève and the first assistant took their meal, then the table was laid again at eleven o'clock for Madame Baudu, the other male assistant and the young lady.

'Time to eat!' the draper exclaimed, turning towards his niece. And since they were all already sitting in the narrow dining room behind the shop, he called to the first assistant, who had still not joined them. 'Colomban!'

The young man made his excuses: he wanted to finish putting away the flannels. He was a large lad, twenty-five years old, thick-set and crafty, with cunning eyes in his otherwise open face, with its soft mouth.

'For goodness' sake! There's plenty of time for that,' Baudu said, seated squarely in front of the table on which he was cutting up a piece of cold veal with the skill of a cautious employer who could weigh each thin slice to the nearest gramme just by looking at it.

He served everyone and even cut up the bread. Denise had sat Pépé down beside her so that she could make sure he ate decently. But she was worried by the dark room: looking round it, she had an oppressive feeling, being used to the broad, well-lit, bare rooms of her native province. A single window opened on a little inner courtyard which communicated with the street through a dark alleyway at the side of the house; and the courtyard, damp and filthy, was like the bottom of a well, with only a round patch of murky light shining on it. In winter, they must have to keep the gas lit from morning to evening. When the weather was good enough to make that unnecessary, it was still more gloomy. It took a moment for Denise's eyes to become accustomed enough to the light for her to see the food on her plate.

'There's a chap with a healthy appetite,' Baudu announced, observing that Jean had finished his veal. 'If he works as hard as he eats, he'll make a fine figure of a man. But what about you, lass, aren't you hungry? And, tell me, now that we have a chance to talk, why didn't you get married, there in Valognes?'

Denise put down the glass from which she was about to drink.

'Marry, Uncle? Me, get married? You can't be serious? What about the children?'

She began to laugh, the idea was so outlandish to her. In any case, would any man want her, penniless, as thin as a rake and still with no hint of beauty? No, no, she would never get married; two children were enough for her.

'You are wrong there,' said her uncle. 'A woman always needs a man. If you'd got yourself some decent fellow, you and your brothers wouldn't have landed up like gypsies on the streets of Paris.'

He paused again: the maid had brought in a plate of roast potatoes and he shared them out with the most parsimonious impartiality. Then, pointing his spoon at Geneviève and Colomban, he went on: 'Take those two! They'll be married next spring, if we have a good winter season.'

This was the custom in a patriarchal firm. Its founder, Aristide Finet, had given his daughter Désirée to his head clerk Hauchecorne; and Baudu himself, having arrived in the Rue de la Michodière with seven francs to his name, married Élisabeth, the daughter of Old Hauchecorne – and now intended to hand over his daughter, Geneviève, together with the shop, to Colomban, as soon as business picked up. The only reason for delaying this marriage, which had been decided upon three years ago, was his scruples, his unshakeable probity: he had taken over the firm as a prosperous business and did not want to pass it on to his son-in-law with fewer customers and worse prospects.

Baudu went on, introducing Colomban, who came from Rambouillet, like Madame Baudu's father. They were even distantly related. He was a hard worker who had slaved away in the shop for ten years now and really earned his promotions. Beside which, he was not just anybody! His father was that merrymaker Colomban, a veterinary surgeon known throughout the Seine-et-Oise,[6] an artist in his profession, but such a lover of the good life that it devoured all his wealth.

'Thank heavens,' the draper said, summing up. 'Even though the father drinks and runs after women, the son came here and learned the value of money.'

While he was speaking, Denise examined Colomban and Geneviève. They were sitting next to one another, but remained quite calm, without a blush or a smile. The young man had been counting on this marriage since he first entered the shop. He had worked his way up from junior assistant to salesman, patiently, step by step, until at last he was taken into the family's confidence, its secrets and its pleasures. All the while he led a life like clockwork and considered Geneviève a fine, respectable match. The certainty of having her kept him from desiring her; and the girl, similarly, had grown accustomed to loving him, but with the seriousness of her repressed being and with a deep passion that she was unaware of herself, in her dull, well-ordered everyday existence.

'When two people like one another and when they can . . .' Denise felt obliged to say, smiling, to be agreeable.

'Yes, that's how it always ends,' said Colomban, chewing slowly; he had not previously uttered a word.

Geneviève gave him a long look, then said in her turn:

'As long as you get on together, it all comes naturally.'

Their affection had grown in this ground-floor shop in its old quarter of Paris like a flower in a cellar. For the past ten years, he had been all that she knew, spending whole days by his side, behind the same piles of cloth in the dark corners of the shop; and morning and evening, the two of them would meet, elbow to elbow, in the narrow dining room that was as chilly as the bottom of a well. They could not have been better hidden away had they been lost in the undergrowth, miles out in the country. Only the shadow of a doubt, a jealous fear, would reveal to the young woman that, in the midst of this conniving darkness, she had given herself forever through emptiness of the heart and boredom of the mind.

Meanwhile, Denise thought that she noticed a hint of some burgeoning anxiety in the look that Geneviève gave Colomban, so she replied good-naturedly:

'Oh! When two people love one another, they always get on together.'

Baudu, meanwhile, was presiding over the table. He had handed round slivers of Brie and, to celebrate the arrival of his relatives, ordered a second dessert, a pot of gooseberry jam. This extravagance seemed to surprise Colomban. Pépé, who had behaved very well up to this point, became over-excited when the jam appeared. Jean, whose interest had been held by the talk about marriage, was staring at his cousin Geneviève, finding her too soft and too pale: deep down, he thought she looked like a little white rabbit, with black ears and red eyes.

'Enough chatter!' said the draper, giving the signal to get up from the table. 'We must make way for the others. Just because we've given ourselves a treat, that's no reason to go entirely overboard.'

Madame Baudu, the other assistant and the young lady arrived to sit down in their turn. Once again, Denise was left alone, sitting by the door, waiting for her uncle to take her round to see Vinçard. Pépé was playing at her feet, while Jean had gone back to his observation post at the door. For almost an hour, she watched what was happening around her. Occasionally, customers came in: a lady appeared, then two more. The shop still smelled musty and, in the half-light, the old-fashioned business, straightforward and unassuming, seemed to be weeping at its neglect. But what fascinated her, on the other side of the street, was *Au Bonheur des Dames*: she could see the windows through the open door. The sky was still overcast, the air was warmed by a rainy softness despite the time of year and, in this white light, where the sun's rays seemed to be dispersed like powder, the store was coming to life and business was flourishing.

Watching, Denise had the impression of a machine working at high pressure, its thunderous power extending even into the displays. These were no longer the cold windows that she had seen that morning; now they seemed vibrant, warmed up by the shuddering life within. People were looking at them, women who had stopped and were pressing one another against the panes, a whole crowd brutalized by greed. And, in this passion sweeping along the street, the clothing materials came to life: lace shivered, fell back and hid the depths of the shop behind a disturbing veil of mystery; even the lengths of cloth, thick, square-cut, exhaled tempting breaths, while the coats on the dummies threw out their chests, endowing them with souls, and the great velvet overcoat swelled, warm and supple, as though across living shoulders with a beating breast and swaying hips. But if the building exuded the warmth of a factory, it was chiefly because of the commerce inside it and the jostling around the counters that one could sense behind its walls. Here, there was the continuous purring of a machine at work, the customers shovelled in, heaped in front of the displays and dazzled by the goods, before being hurled against the cash desks. And it was all organized and regulated with mechanical precision, a whole nation of women caught up in the power and logic of the turning cogs.

Denise had been feeling its pull since the morning. She was amazed and attracted by this store, which seemed so huge to her, as she watched more people go into it in an hour than used to come to Cornaille's in six months; and, in her longing to go inside, there was a vague sense of fear that completed her seduction. At the same time, her uncle's shop made her uneasy; she felt an unreasoning contempt, an instinctive repugnance for this icy backwater of old-fashioned business. All that she had gone through, her timid entrance, her relatives' sour welcome, the dreary luncheon in the half-light of a dungeon and the waiting in the dozy solitude of this moribund old place, culminated in a vague sense of protest, a yearning for life and light. And, despite her inherent good nature, she kept constantly turning back towards *Au Bonheur des Dames*, as though the salesgirl in her needed to be warmed by the blaze of all that trade.

'People are going in there, at least,' she let slip.

But she immediately regretted the remark when she saw the Baudus beside her. Madame Baudu, who had finished lunch, was standing there, her face white, her pale eyes staring at the monster; resigned to their fate. She could not see it or pass it on the far side of the street without her eyes filling with a dumb sense of despair. As for Geneviève, she was keeping an increasingly anxious watch on Colomban who, not realizing he was being observed, was looking enraptured at the girls selling ladies' wear in the department which one could see through the windows of the mezzanine floor. Baudu, with a bilious expression, merely remarked:

'All that glitters is not gold. Just wait!'

Clearly, the members of the family were holding down the flood of resentment that welled up in their throats. A feeling of pride would not allow them to reveal their true feelings to these children, who had only just arrived. At length, the draper made an effort and turned round, dragging himself away from the spectacle of the shop across the street.

'Very well,' he said. 'Let's go and talk to Vinçard. Jobs are in short supply, tomorrow it may be too late.'

But before going out, he instructed the second assistant to go to the station and fetch Denise's trunk. Meanwhile, Madame Baudu, to whom the young woman had entrusted Pépé, decided that she would take advantage of the lull and take the child round to the Rue des Orties, to Madame Gras, so that they could chat and make arrangements. Jean promised his sister not to move from the shop.

'We'll only be a moment,' Baudu explained as he was going down the Rue Gaillon with his niece. 'Vinçard has specialized in silk, where there is still good business to be done. Oh, he's in trouble like everyone else! But he's a sly dog who manages to make ends meet by sheer meanness . . . though I think he wants to retire, because of his rheumatism.'

The shop was in the Rue Neuve-des-Petits-Champs, near the Passage Choiseul. It was clean and bright, fashionably luxurious, but small and sparsely stocked. Baudu and Denise found Vinçard conferring with two gentlemen.

'Don't worry,' the draper exclaimed. 'We're in no hurry, we can wait.'

And returning discreetly to the door, he bent over and whispered in the girl's ear:

'The thin one is under-buyer for silks at the *Bonheur* and the fat one is a manufacturer from Lyon.'[7]

Denise understood that Vinçard was promoting his business to Robineau, the representative from *Au Bonheur des Dames*. He was giving his word, with a frank, open expression and easy manner, like a man who was not afraid to swear by something. According to him, his business was a goldmine; and, glowing with rude health, he broke off to curse the confounded pains that were forcing him to abandon his fortune. But Robineau, twitching with anxiety, interrupted him impatiently: he knew all about the crisis in the trade; and he mentioned the name of a shop specializing in silks which had already gone under because of the proximity of the *Bonheur*. Vinçard, roused to anger, raised his voice:

'Good Lord! That great booby Vabre was bound to crash! His wife devoured everything . . . Apart from which, we're more than half a kilometre away, while Vabre was right next door to the place.'

At this, Gaujean, the silk manufacturer, put in a word. Once more, the voices were lowered. He was accusing the large stores of ruining the French silk industry: three or four of them dictated to him and dominated the market; and he was implying that the only way to combat them was to encourage small businesses, particularly specialist shops, who were the way of the future. This is why he was prepared to offer Robineau very generous credit terms.

'Look how the *Bonheur* has treated you,' he went on. 'No consideration for services rendered – they're machines for exploiting people! You had been promised the chief buyer's job for ages when Bouthemont came in from outside, with no claim on it, and was given it there and then.'

This injustice was still a sore point with Robineau. Even so, he was hesitating to set himself up and explained that the money was not his own: his wife had inherited sixty thousand francs and he was full of scruples about it, saying that he would prefer to cut both his hands off at once rather than risk it in a bad business deal.

'No, I haven't made up my mind,' he said eventually. 'Give me time to think it over and we'll have another talk about it.'

'As you wish,' said Vinçard, concealing his disappointment behind an air of good humour. 'It's not in my interest to sell. Now, if it weren't for my pains . . .'

Then, coming back to the centre of the shop: 'What can I do for you, Monsieur Baudu?'

The draper, who had been listening with one ear, introduced Denise, described as much of her background as he thought appropriate and said that she had worked for two years in the provinces.

'And, since they tell me you're looking for a good sales assistant . . .'

Vinçard pretended to be overcome with despair.

'Oh, what a cruel twist of fate! I have indeed been looking for a salesgirl for a week, but I've just engaged one, not two hours ago.'

There was a silence. Denise appeared quite dismayed, so Robineau, who had been looking at her with interest, no doubt touched by her impoverished appearance, offered the following piece of information:

'I know that they need someone at our place, in the ladies' wear department.'

Baudu could not repress a heartfelt cry:

'At your place! Oh, no, not that!'

Then he fell into an embarrassed silence. Denise had gone quite red: the idea of going to that great store – she would never dare! The thought filled her with pride.

'But why not?' Robineau asked, in surprise. 'On the contrary, it would be an opportunity for the young lady. I advise her to come tomorrow morning and introduce herself to Madame Aurélie, the chief buyer. The worst that can happen is that they don't take her on.'

To disguise his inner revulsion, the draper resorted to vague generalities: he knew Madame Aurélie, or at least her husband, the cashier Lhomme, a fat man who had lost his right arm under an omnibus. Then, suddenly coming back to Denise, he said: 'In any case, it's her business, not mine . . . She's quite free . . .'

He went out, nodding to Gaujean and Robineau. Vinçard accompanied him to the door, repeating his regret. The young woman was left behind in the middle of the shop, intimidated, though anxious to get more details from Robineau; but she didn't dare. She, too, took her leave, with a simple 'Thank you, Monsieur.'

Outside on the pavement, Baudu said nothing. He was walking quickly, as if driven forward by his thoughts, forcing her to run after him. In the Rue de la Michodière, he was about to go indoors when a neighbour, standing at the door of his own shop, gestured to him to come over. Denise stopped to wait for him.

'What do you want, Bourras, my friend?' the draper asked.

Bourras was a tall old man with a beard and long hair, who looked like an Old Testament prophet; he had piercing eyes beneath his great bushy eyebrows. He traded in walking-sticks and umbrellas, did repairs and even carved handles, which had earned him the reputation of an artist in the neighbourhood. Denise glanced at the windows of his shop, in which the umbrellas and sticks were set up in regular lines. But when she looked up higher, it was the house itself that astonished her the most: a hovel squeezed between *Au Bonheur des Dames* and a large Louis XIV mansion, its two storeys shoved into this narrow gap by some means or other and now crushed inside it. Without support from the buildings on either side, it would have collapsed: the slates on its roof were twisted and rotten, its two-windowed façade was lined with cracks, marked by long streaks of rust running down the half-decayed woodwork of the shop sign.

'You know he wrote to my landlord to buy the house,' said Bourras, staring at the draper with his fiery gaze.

Baudu went pale and his shoulders slumped. There was a silence and the two men stayed face to face, staring intently.

'You must be ready for anything,' he said eventually.

At this, the old man flew into a rage, shaking his flowing locks and beard.

'Let him buy the house, he'll pay four times what it is worth! But I swear to you that so long as I live, he shan't touch a stone of it. My lease still has twelve years to run . . . We shall see, we shall see!'

It was a declaration of war. Bourras turned towards *Au Bonheur des Dames*, which neither man had mentioned. For a moment, Baudu shook his head in silence; then he crossed over the street to his own house, his legs shaking, merely repeating: 'My God! Oh, my God!'

Denise, who had heard all this, followed her uncle. Madame Baudu was also returning with Pépé and said straightaway that Madame Gras would take the child when they wanted. But Jean had just vanished and his sister was anxious. When he came back, his face lit up, chattering excitedly about the boulevard, she gave him a sad look that made him blush. Their trunk had been brought and they would be sleeping upstairs, under the roof.

'So what about Vinçard's?' Madame Baudu asked.

The draper described his unsuccessful approach, adding that a job had been pointed out to his niece; and, extending his arm in a gesture of contempt towards *Au Bonheur des Dames*, he spat out the words: 'Yes! There!'

The whole family was hurt. In the evening, the first dinner was served at five o'clock, so Denise and the two children resumed their places, with Baudu, Geneviève and Colomban. The little dining room was lit by a gas lamp and smelled strongly of food. They ate in silence; but when it came to the dessert Madame Baudu, who had been unable to stay still, came in from the shop and sat down behind her niece. And then the torrent that had been held back since the morning burst and each of them poured out their feelings about the monster.

'It's your business, you are free to do as you like,' Baudu repeated, for a start. 'We're not trying to influence you . . . But, if you only knew what kind of a place it is!'

Curtly he told the story of that Octave Mouret.[8] What luck he had! Here was a lad who had arrived in Paris from the south with the charming audacity of an adventurer and had immediately been involved in love affairs and had exploited countless women; one scandal where he had been caught in the act was still the talk of the neighbourhood. And, after that, the sudden and inexplicable conquest of Madame Hédouin, which had brought him *Au Bonheur des Dames*.

'That poor Caroline!' Madame Baudu added. 'She was distantly related to me. Oh, if she had lived, things would have been very different. She wouldn't allow us to be slaughtered . . . He was the one who killed her, yes! With that building work of his! One morning, when she was looking round the site, she fell into a hole in the ground and three days later, she died. And she had never had a day's illness; she was so fit and so beautiful! Her blood is under the stones of that shop.'

Through the wall, she pointed her pale, trembling hand at the store. Denise, who had been listening as one listens to a fairy tale, gave a slight shudder. The fear that had been lurking since that morning behind the temptation that she felt, might perhaps come from the blood of that woman which she imagined she could see now in the red cement of the basement.

'It seems to be bringing him luck,' Madame Baudu added, without naming Mouret.

The draper shrugged his shoulders, scorning such old wives' tales. He carried on with his story, explaining the situation in commercial terms. *Au Bonheur des Dames* had been founded in 1822 by the Deleuze Brothers. When the elder one died, his daughter, Caroline, married the son of a cloth-maker, Charles Hédouin, and later, after she was widowed, became the wife of that Mouret. In this way she brought him half the shop. Three months after the wedding, the other brother also died, childless, so that when Caroline perished in the foundations, Mouret remained as sole heir and sole owner of the *Bonheur*. What luck!

'He's a man of ideas, dangerously addle-headed: he'll turn the whole neighbourhood upside-down, if no one stops him!' Baudu went on. 'I think Caroline, who was a bit of a dreamer herself, must have been carried away by that gentleman's wild schemes . . . In short, he decided to buy the house on the left, then the one on the right; and, when he was left alone, a couple more, so that the shop went on growing and growing, until it now threatens to swallow us all up!'

Though he was addressing Denise, he was really talking for his own benefit, going over and over the story that obsessed him, with a feverish need for satisfaction. He was the one with the temper in the family, always ready to break out, his fists always clenched. Madame Baudu did not interrupt, sitting motionless on her chair; Geneviève and Colomban had their eyes lowered and were distractedly picking up and eating some crumbs of bread. It was so hot and stuffy in the little room that Pépé had fallen asleep across the table and even Jean's eyes were shutting.

'Just wait!' Baudu went on, his temper suddenly flaring. 'The schemers will come a cropper! Mouret is in difficulty, I know he is. He has had to plough all his profits back into his crazy plans for expansion and advertising. Moreover, in order to raise capital, he's come up with this idea of persuading most of his employees to invest their money with him.[9] So he hasn't got a penny just now and, failing a miracle, if he doesn't manage to triple his sales as he hopes, you see what a crash there'll be! Oh, I'm not vindictive, but I promise you when that day comes, we'll be hanging out the lights.'

He carried on talking, in vengeful tones, as though the collapse of *Au Bonheur des Dames* would restore the slighted dignity of his own business. Had anyone ever heard of such a thing? A ladies' shop that sold everything – that made it a bazaar! And the staff were a fine bunch, a load of popinjays who handled everything as though they were in a railway station, treating the goods and the customers like parcels, dropping their employer or being dropped by him at the slightest word, with no feeling, no manners and no skills! Suddenly, he called on Colomban to support him: he, Colomban, surely, having been brought up in the old school, knew the slow but sure means by which one picked up the subtleties, the tricks of the trade. The art was not to sell a lot, but to sell it dear.[10] And, apart from that, he could say how they had treated him, how he had become one of the family, cared for when he fell ill, his linen laundered and darned, how they had kept a paternal eye on him and, in short, loved him!

'Of course, of course,' Colomban repeated, after each of his boss's utterances.

'You are the last, old chap,' Baudu finally said, getting sentimental.

'They won't make any more after you . . . You are my only consolation, because if this shoving and pushing is what they call trade nowadays, I don't understand it, I'd rather pack it in.'

Geneviève, her head bent over one shoulder as though her thick mass of black hair were too heavy for her pale forehead, was watching the assistant with a smile; and in her look, there was a hint, a tiny wish to see whether Colomban might feel a pang of guilt and blush at such praise. But the lad had been trained in the playacting of old-fashioned business practice and maintained a calm front and pleasant manner, with a wily twist to his lips.

Meanwhile, Baudu was shouting still louder, accusing that jumble sale opposite, those savages who were slaughtering each other in their struggle for life, of eventually undermining the family itself. He mentioned their neighbours in the country, the Lhommes, mother, father and son, all three of them now working in that dump, people with no real home, always out, only eating at home on Sundays – in short, a hotel and restaurant life! Admittedly, his own dining room was not large and you might even have wished that it had more light and air; but at least he had lived here, a life surrounded by his family's affection. As he spoke, his eyes travelled round the little room and he started to shake, at the unadmitted thought that one day, if they finally destroyed his business, these savages might force him out of this hole where he was so comfortable, alongside his wife and his daughter. Despite his pretended confidence, when he spoke about the final collapse, he was full of terror underneath and could really feel the area being invaded and eaten up, bit by bit.

'I'm not trying to put you off,' he went on, trying to remain calm. 'If it's to your advantage to take a job there, I'll be the first to say: go on.'

'I'm sure you will, Uncle,' Denise muttered, bewildered, but with a growing desire, in the midst of all this excitement, to be in *Au Bonheur des Dames*.

He had his elbows on the table now and was making her uncomfortable with his stare.

'Come, now. You're in the business. Do you consider it reasonable that a simple draper's shop should start to sell everything? In the old days, when there was plain dealing, a draper's meant cloth and nothing else. Nowdays, their only idea is to trample over the other man and grab everything. This is what people round here don't like about it, because the small shops are really starting to feel the pinch. That Mouret is ruining them. Take Bédoré and Sister, at the hosiery shop in the Rue Gaillon: they've lost half their customers already. Mademoiselle Tatin, the lady who sells lingerie in the Passage Choiseul, has had to lower her prices and try to undercut him. And the effect of this scourge, this plague, extends as far as the Rue Neuve-des-Petits-Champs, where I've been saying that Vanpouille Brothers, the furriers, won't be able to hold out. What! Drapers selling furs! It's ridiculous! Another of Mouret's notions!'

'What about gloves?' said Madame Baudu. 'Isn't it atrocious! He has dared to set up a glove department! Yesterday, when I was walking along the Rue Neuve-Saint-Augustin, Quinette was standing at his door, looking so miserable that I didn't like to ask if business was good.'

'And umbrellas,' Baudu continued. 'That's the end! Bourras is convinced that Mouret quite simply wants to bankrupt him. I mean, what sense is there in having umbrellas with materials? But Bourras is tough, he won't let his throat be cut. We'll be laughing, one of these days.'

He talked about other tradesmen, going through the whole neighbourhood. From time to time, he let something slip: for example, if Vinçard was trying to sell up, then the rest of them might as well start packing, because Vinçard was like those rats which leave a house when it is about to fall down. Then he would immediately contradict himself, dreaming of an alliance, an understanding between the small retailers to challenge the giant. For a while, he deliberately avoided speaking about himself, his hands shaking, his mouth twitching nervously. At last, he decided to go ahead.

'As for myself, so far I can't complain too much. Oh, he has harmed me, the scoundrel! But up to now he has only stocked ladies' materials, light fabrics for dresses and heavier ones for coats. People still come here to buy men's wear, velvet and corduroy for shooting jackets and livery, not to mention flannels and felts – I defy him ever to have such a wide selection of those. But he does needle me. He thinks he's got under my skin by putting his ladies' department there, directly opposite. You saw his window, didn't you? He always puts his finest articles out, with materials arranged around them, in a veritable fairground display to catch the girls' eyes. No, honestly! I wouldn't stoop to such tactics! The *Vieil Elbeuf* has been around for almost a hundred years and doesn't need such con tricks at the front door. As long as I'm alive, the shop will remain as it was when I took it over, with its four sample pieces to right and left, and nothing else!'

The whole family was affected. Geneviève ventured to say something, after a pause.

'Our customers like us, Papa. We must hope. Why, only today, we had Madame Desforges and Madame de Boves in and I'm expecting Madame Marty for some flannel.'

'And yesterday,' Colomban announced, 'I had an order from Madame Bourdelais. Though I have to say that she mentioned an English tweed on sale opposite for ten *sous* less, which appears to have been just the same as the one we are selling.'

'To think,' Madame Baudu murmured in her tired voice, 'that we saw that business when it was no bigger than a pocket handkerchief! Honestly, my dear Denise, when the Deleuzes started it, it had only one window on the Rue Neuve-Saint-Augustin, a broom cupboard where you could hardly fit two lengths of Indian cloth with three lengths of calico. The shop was so small that you couldn't turn around in it. At that time, *Le Vieil Elbeuf*, which had been in business for more than sixty years, was already what you see here today. Oh, it's all changed, utterly changed.'

She shook her head and, speaking slowly, described the central drama of her life. She had been born in the *Vieil Elbeuf* and actually loved its damp stones. She lived through it and for it; and, having once gloried in this business as the most prosperous and richly stocked shop in the neighbourhood, she had endured the lasting agony of seeing its once despised rival grow gradually larger until it outstripped her own shop and threatened its existence. For her, this was an ever-open wound: she was dying from the humiliation of her *Vieil Elbeuf*, still surviving as it did from accumulated momentum, feeling in herself that the shop's death would be her own and that she would perish on the day that it closed down.

There was a silence. Baudu was beating the retreat with his fingers on the oiled tablecloth. He had a feeling of weariness, almost of regret, now that he had once more poured out his feelings. But in its despondency, the whole family continued to stare into the distance, pondering its bitter fate. They never had had good fortune. The children had grown up and wealth was within their grasp when suddenly competition had brought ruin. Moreover, there was the house in Rambouillet, a country house where for ten years the draper had dreamed of retiring, a real bargain, he said, an ancient pile that he had constantly to keep repairing, until he decided to rent it out, though the tenants didn't pay him. His last profits were going into it – though it was the only little foible he had indulged, in his scrupulous probity and obstinate attachment to the old ways.[11]

'Come on, now!' he suddenly exclaimed. 'We must leave the table for others . . . This is just a lot of pointless chatter.'

It was as though they had been woken up. The gaslight hummed, in the dead air of the little room. They all leaped to their feet, breaking the melancholy silence. Meanwhile, Pépé was so fast asleep that they laid him on some pieces of flannel. Jean, yawning, had already gone back to the street door.

'So, to sum up, you'll do as you like,' Baudu said again to his niece. 'We're telling you how it is, that's all. But it's up to you.'

He looked at her inquiringly, expecting a final answer. Denise, who had been still more attracted to *Au Bonheur des Dames* by these stories, instead of being turned against it, remained calm and sweet as ever with, underneath, the obstinate will of a Norman woman. She replied only:

'We'll see, Uncle.'

And she mentioned having an early night, as well as the children, all three of them being very tired. But six o'clock had hardly struck and she wanted to stay a moment longer in the shop. Night had fallen and she went back to the dark street, soaked by a fine, steady rain, which had been falling since sunset. This was a surprise for her: a few moments had been enough for the street to be full of puddles, for filthy water to pour down the gutters and for the pavements to be sticky with thick, well-trodden mud. Under the drenching shower, she could see only a chaotic parade of umbrellas, jostling one another and swelling out in the darkness like great sombre wings. At first, she shrank back, struck by the cold and made to feel even more gloomy by the ill-lit shop, which was positively dismal at this time of day. A damp wind, the breath of the old quarter, came in from the street; it was as though the water pouring off the umbrellas ran as far as the counter or that the street with its mud and its puddles was coming in and putting the final touches to the mildew on the ground floor, white with saltpetre.[12] She shuddered at this vision of Old Paris, soaked through, and was astonished to find the great city so icy and so ugly.

But on the far side of the road, shone the deep rows of gaslights at *Au Bonheur des Dames.* She went closer, attracted to it once more, feeling as though warmed at this hearth of blazing light. The machine was still growling, still bustling, letting off its steam in a final roar as the salespeople folded up the materials and the cashiers counted their takings. Through windows pale with condensation, she could make out a vague swarming of lights, like the confusion inside a factory. Behind the curtain of falling rain, the spectacle, blurred and distant, took on the appearance of a giant fire chamber in which the dark shadows of the stokers could be seen passing across the red glow from the boilers. The windows faded away and you could only see opposite the snowy lace, its whiteness heightened by the frosted glass of a row of gaslights. It was like a chapel; and against this background, the clothes stood out in even sharper relief: the great velvet coat trimmed with silver fox became the silhouette of a headless woman dashing through the rain to some party in the mysterious depths of Paris after dark.

Giving way to the temptation, Denise had come as far as the door, unconcerned by the splashes of rain that soaked her. At this time of the night, blazing like a furnace, *Au Bonheur des Dames* finally seduced her altogether. In the great metropolis, dark and silent under the rain, in this Paris that she did not know, it shone like a beacon, seeming by itself to give light and life to the city. She dreamed of her future there: a lot of work bringing up the children, and other things as well, she didn't know what, distant things that made her shudder with desire and fear. The idea of the woman dead in the foundations came back to her and she was afraid: she thought she could see blood in the bright patches; the whiteness of the lace calmed her again and a feeling of hope rose in her breast, a certainty of joy to come – while the spray of water made her hands cold and cooled her feverish excitement from the journey.

'That Bourras,' said a voice behind her.

She leaned out and saw Bourras standing motionless at the end of the street, in front of the shop window in which, that morning, she had noticed a great, ingenious structure built out of umbrellas and walking sticks. The tall old man had slipped out into the darkness to fill his eyes with this triumphant display; and now, with a look of pain on his face, he did not even feel the rain hammering against his bare head and streaming off his grey hair.

'He's crazy,' said the voice. 'He'll catch his death.'

Turning, Denise saw that the Baudus were behind her once more. Despite themselves, like Bourras whom they thought crazy, they kept coming back to this spectacle which broke their hearts. They had a furious need to suffer. Geneviève was very pale. She had noticed that Colomban was looking at the shadows of the salesgirls moving in front of the window on the mezzanine; and while Baudu was stifled with repressed rancour, Madame Baudu's eyes had quietly filled with tears.

'You'll be going there tomorrow, I suppose?' the draper asked eventually, tormented by uncertainty, yet realizing quite well that his niece had been won over like the rest of them.

She hesitated, then said gently:

'Yes, Uncle, unless it upsets you too much.'

CHAPTER 2

The next day, at half past seven, Denise was in front of *Au Bonheur des Dames.* She wanted to present herself there before taking Jean to his master, who lived some way off at the top of the Faubourg du Temple. But she was so used to getting up early that she had come down too soon: the shop assistants had only just started to arrive and, fearing that she might look ridiculous, she stayed kicking her heels for a while on the Place Gaillon, overcome by shyness.

A cold wind had already dried the pavements. Lit by the pale early light beneath an ashen sky, the male employees were hurrying out of all the adjoining streets, their coat collars turned up, their hands in their pockets, caught unexpectedly by this first shudder of winter. Most were on their own and disappeared into the depths of the store without a word or even a look in the direction of their colleagues walking along beside them; others were coming in twos and threes, speaking rapidly, spread across the whole width of the pavement; and all of them before going inside, performed the same action of throwing their cigarettes or cigars into the gutter.

Denise noticed that several of these gentlemen stared at her as they went by. Her shyness only increased, she could not find the strength to follow them now, and decided that she would only go in when the procession stopped, blushing at the idea of being jostled in the doorway among all these men. But the procession did not stop; so, to escape their looks, she went for a slow walk around the square. When she came back she found a tall lad, pale and lanky, standing in front of *Au Bonheur des Dames* where, for the past quarter of an hour, he seemed to have been waiting like herself.

'Mademoiselle,' he asked eventually, in a stammering voice, 'are you by any chance an assistant in the store?'

At first, she was so overcome at hearing this stranger speaking to her that she did not answer.

'You see,' he said, becoming still more flustered, 'it's because I thought I might find out whether they could take me on, and hoped you might have been able to tell me something.'

He was as shy as she was and only dared to approach her because he felt her trembling like himself.

'I should be happy to, Monsieur,' she finally replied. 'But I know no more than you do. I'm here to apply, just as you are.'

'Oh, I see,' he said, now quite disconcerted.

And they both blushed deeply, the two of them remaining face to face for a moment in their shyness, touched by the kinship of their situation, yet neither one daring to wish the other good luck out loud. Then, since they apparently had nothing to add and were both increasingly embarrassed, they separated awkwardly and started to wait on different sides, a few steps from one another.

The staff were still going in. Now Denise could hear them joking when they passed close to her, casting a sidelong glance. Being an object of attention made her even more ill at ease and she was deciding to go for half an hour's walk around the quarter when the sight of a young man hurrying towards them along the Rue Port-Mahon made her pause for a minute longer. He was obviously a head of department, because all the assistants greeted him respectfully. He was tall, with pale skin and a well-kept beard; and his eyes were the colour of old gold, as soft as velvet; they settled for a moment on her as he was crossing the square. He was already going inside the shop, with no sign of interest, while she stood motionless, quite overwhelmed by that look, full of some unusual feeling in which there was more unease than charm. Really, she was afraid; and she began to walk slowly down the Rue Gaillon, then the Rue Saint-Roch, until she got her courage back.

The man was something more than a head of department, it was Octave Mouret himself. He had not slept the previous night, because, after spending the evening at a stockbroker's, he had gone to have supper with a friend and two ladies who had been picked up backstage at a small theatre. He went quickly up to his apartment, had a wash and changed; and when he sat down at his desk, in his study on the mezzanine floor of the shop, he was fit, bright-eyed and clear-skinned, ready for work as though he had spent ten hours in bed. The study was huge, furnished in old oak and green rep,[1] and had no ornament except a portrait, the portrait of that Madame Hédouin about whom people still spoke. Since her passing, Octave had kept fond memories of her and shown his gratitude to her memory for the fortune she had bestowed on him at their marriage. So before he got down to signing the bills waiting on his blotter, he gave the portrait the smile of a contented man. Did he not always return here to work in front of her, after his young widower's adventures, when he emerged from the boudoirs where he had been led astray by pleasure?

There was a knock and, without waiting, a young man came in. He was tall and lean, with thin lips and a pointed nose – in fact, very well turned-out, with his smooth hair already streaked with grey. Mouret looked up and, still signing, asked: 'Did you sleep well, Bourdoncle?'

'Very well, thank you,' the young man replied, strutting around, entirely at home.

Bourdoncle, the son of a poor farmer near Limoges, had started at *Au Bonheur des Dames* at the same time as Mouret, when the shop only occupied the corner of the Place Gaillon. Very bright and energetic, it seemed likely at the time that he would easily take the place of his friend, who was less serious-minded and got up to all sorts of escapades, made careless mistakes and was involved in worrying affairs with women; but he did not have the genius of the ardent Provençal, nor his daring, nor his all-conquering charm. In any case, with the instinct of a prudent man, he had ceded obediently to the other from the start, without a struggle. When Mouret advised his employees to invest their money in the firm, Bourdoncle had been one of the first to do so, even handing over an unexpected legacy from an aunt. And, gradually, after rising up through the ranks, as a sales assistant, then under-buyer and finally buyer in the silk department, he had become one of the boss's right-hand men, one of the six investors who helped him to run *Au Bonheur des Dames* in what was much like a ministerial cabinet under an absolute monarch. Each one of them supervised a particular area, with Bourdoncle as general overseer.

'What about you?' he went on, in a familiar tone. 'Did you sleep well?'

When Mouret replied that he had not been to bed, the other shook his head, muttering: 'It's not healthy.'

'Why?' Mouret said merrily. 'I'm less tired than you are, my good friend. Your eyes are all puffy with sleep, you're dragging yourself down with too much prudent living . . . Have a bit of fun, it will stir up your ideas!'

This was always a friendly quarrel between them. At one time, Bourdoncle had beaten his mistresses because, so he said, they kept him awake. Now, he pretended to hate women, while no doubt having casual encounters outside which he did not mention, so small was the part they played in his life; while in the shop he was content to exploit the customers, greatly despising their frivolous need to spend a fortune on their silly rags. Mouret, by contrast, put on an enchanted air, was enraptured and cajoling when there was a woman about, and was constantly swept up in some new love affair. And his passions were like an advertisement for the shop: you might have thought that he was embracing the whole of the fair sex in a single caress, the better to bewitch them and keep them at his mercy.

'I saw Madame Desforges last night,' he went on. 'She was delectable at that ball.'

'She isn't the one you had supper with afterwards?' his partner asked.

Mouret protested.

'Oh, no! The idea of it! She's very respectable, old chap . . . No, I took supper with Héloïse, the little piece from the Folies . . . Such a silly goose, but so amusing!'

He took another bundle of bills and went on signing. Bourdoncle continued to strut. He went to glance out into the Rue Neuve-Saint-Augustin, through the high windows, then came back, saying: 'You know they will have their revenge.'

'Who's that?' Mouret asked, not paying attention.

'These women, of course.'

This made Mouret even jollier, his fundamental brutality breaking through the façade of sensual adoration. A shrug of the shoulders seemed to indicate that he would discard them all like empty wrapping paper, once they had helped him to make his fortune. Bourdoncle repeated stubbornly, in his cold manner:

'They'll get their own back . . . There will be one who'll have revenge for them all, it's bound to happen.'

'Dinna fear!' Mouret exclaimed, exaggerating his Provençal accent. 'That one's not yet born, my good fellow. And if she does turn up, you know . . .'

He had picked up his penholder, which he brandished, stabbing it into the air as though trying to pierce an invisible heart with a knife. His deputy resumed his walk, bowing as ever to the boss's superiority, though disconcerted by the flaws in his genius. Clear-minded, logical, passionless, immune to temptation, he still had to understand the feminine side of their success. Paris yielded in a kiss to the bolder man.

There was a silence. The only thing that could be heard was Mouret's pen. Then, in answer to his brief questions, Bourdoncle told him about the great launch of winter goods that was to take place the following Monday. It was a matter of the greatest importance and the firm's success was tied up in it, because there was an element of truth in the rumours: Mouret was speculating with poetic fervour, but so extravagantly and with such an urge to outdo himself that a collapse seemed imminent. He had a new approach to business, a sort of commercial imagination that had once worried Madame Hédouin and which now, despite its early successes, dismayed those involved. They muttered that the boss was going too fast; they accused him of expanding the business too hastily, without being able to count on a large enough growth in customers; and most of all they shuddered as they watched him gamble all the cash in the till on a single turn of the cards and piling the counters with goods while not keeping a *sou* in reserve. Hence, after a considerable amount of money had been paid to builders, all the firm's capital was tied up in this launch – once again, it was victory or death. And, in the midst of all this commotion, his triumphal good humour never faltered, being that of a man adored by women who never can be betrayed. When Bourdoncle dared to express some anxieties about the over-expansion of this department or that, where the turnover was shaky, he gave a fine, confident laugh and said: 'Forget it, my dear man! The shop is too small!'

Bourdoncle seemed totally bewildered, no longer trying to hide his fear. The shop too small! A draper's shop with nineteen departments and a staff of four hundred and three!

'Of course, it is,' Mouret went on. 'We'll have to expand within the next eighteen months . . . I'm seriously considering it. Last night, Madame Desforges promised to introduce me to someone at her house tomorrow . . . Well, we'll talk about it when the idea is ripe.'

And, having finished signing the bills, he got up and went over to his associate, who was having difficulty in recovering, and gave him a few friendly pats on the shoulder. He found it very amusing, this alarm among the cautious folk all round him. In one of those fits of coarse frankness that he sometimes inflicted on his friends, he announced that underneath he was more of a Jew than all the Jews in the world: he took after his father, a fellow who knew the value of money, whom he resembled in mind as well as physically; and, if he had inherited a hint of nervous imagination from his mother, this was perhaps his greatest fortune because he felt an invincible power to do and dare anything.

'You know we'll stick by you to the end,' Bourdoncle said eventually.

Then, before going down to the shop for their usual look around, the pair still had certain small matters to clear up. They examined the sample of a little book with counterfoils which Mouret had just devised for debit notes. Having observed that the larger the commission given to the assistants, the faster outdated goods, the 'turkeys' of the trade, disappeared from the shelves, he had thought up a new scheme by which the sales staff could gain by the sale of all goods: he gave them a certain percentage on every last piece of material or item that they sold. The system had revolutionized the drapery business, creating a struggle for survival,[2] from which the bosses gained. Moreover, in his hands, this struggle became his favourite formula, an organizing principle that he applied constantly. He released passions, made opposing forces confront one another, allowed the big fish to swallow up the small and grew fat on this rivalry. The sample of the book was approved: at the top, on the stub and on the detachable debit note, it showed the department and the assistant's number; then, also repeated on both sides, were columns for measurements, description of the items and price. The assistant had merely to sign the slip before handing it to the cashier. In this way, checking was as simple as could be: one had only to collate the slips which the cashier delivered to the counting-house with the stubs retained by the assistants. In this way, every week, they would get their percentage and bonus, without any confusion.

'People will steal less from us,' said Bourdoncle, with satisfaction. 'You've got a really good idea there.'

'And last night I thought of something else,' said Mouret. 'Yes, my good fellow, last night, at that supper . . . I want to give the staff in the counting-house a little bonus for every mistake that they find in the debit notes as they are collating them . . . You see: that way we shall be certain that they will not overlook a single mistake, but will rather be inclined to invent them.'

He began to laugh, while the other man looked at him with admiration. He was delighted by this new application of the principle of the struggle for survival, because he had a genius for administrative systems and dreamed of exploiting the appetites of others, so that he could satisfy his own, quietly and utterly. When one wanted to get the most out of people, he would often say, and even to get a bit of decency out of them, one first had to confront them with their own needs.

'Well, then, let's go down,' Mouret said. 'We must look to this sale . . . The silk arrived yesterday, didn't it? And Bouthemont must be in reception.'

Bourdoncle followed him. The reception was in the basement, on the side facing the Rue Neuve-Saint-Augustin. Here, on a level with the pavement, was a glass cage where the lorries unloaded their goods. These were weighed, then tipped down a fast chute, of oak and metal which had been rubbed by bales and packing cases until it shone. All deliveries came through this gaping trap door, continually swallowed up, a cascade of materials falling with a roar like a river. Particularly at peak periods, the chute poured an endless stream into the basement: silk from Lyon, woollen cloth from England, Flanders linen, calico from Alsace, cotton prints from Rouen. At times, the lorries had to queue up; and the bundles, as they slid down to the bottom of the hole, made the dull noise of a pebble thrown into deep water.

As he went by, Mouret stopped for a moment in front of the chute. It was working, with a line of cases coming down under their own steam: you couldn't see the hands of the men who were shoving them from above, so they appeared to be falling by themselves, a shower pouring out of a spring on high. Then, bales came into view, tumbling over and over like rolling stones. Mouret looked on without a word, but this downpour of goods falling into his shop, this flood worth thousands of francs a minute, lit a brief flame in his clear eyes. Never before had he had such a sharp awareness of the challenge: it was this great heap of merchandise that he had to launch to every corner of Paris. He kept his mouth shut and went on with his inspection.

In the grey light from the wide cellar windows, a team of men was taking in the deliveries, while others unnailed the packing cases and opened the bales in the presence of the heads of department. The bustle of a building yard filled this cellar, this basement with its vaults resting on cast-iron pillars and its concreted walls.

'Have you got everything, Bouthemont?' Mouret asked, going up to a broad-shouldered young man who was checking the contents of a packing case.

'Yes, it should all be here,' he replied. 'But it will take me the rest of the morning to count it.'

The head of department looked over the invoice while standing in front of a large counter on which one of his assistants was placing the lengths of silk, one by one, as he took them out of the case. Behind them there were other counters, also covered with goods, being examined by a whole little tribe of assistants. There was a general unpacking amid an apparent confusion of materials being scrutinized, turned over and marked, in the midst of a hum of voices.

Bouthemont, who was getting to be well known in the trade, had the round face of a merry fellow, with a pitch-black beard and fine brown eyes. A native of Montpellier, loud-mouthed and fond of having fun, he was not much of a salesman, but unequalled when it came to buying. He had been sent to Paris by his father, who had a draper's shop in his home town, but he had absolutely refused to return when the old man decided that the lad knew enough to take over the business; and since then a rivalry had grown up between father and son, the former tied up in his little provincial shop and outraged at seeing a mere assistant earning three times what he was making himself, while the other poked fun at the old man's habits, trumpeting his own wages and turning the shop upside-down every time he came to see him. Like the other departmental managers, he had a fixed salary of three thousand francs and, in addition to that, a percentage on sales. Montpellier, amazed and full of respect, said that Bouthemont's lad had taken home nearly fifteen thousand francs the year before; and this was only a start: to the annoyance of his father, people predicted that the figure would rise even further.

Meanwhile, Bourdoncle had picked up one of the pieces of silk and was examining the grain with the attentive look of an expert. It was a faille with a blue and silver selvage, the famous Paris-Bonheur with which Mouret intended to strike a decisive blow.

'It really is very good,' said his associate.

'And it looks even better than it is,' said Bouthemont. 'Only Dumonteil can make it for us . . . On my last trip, when I fell out with Gaujean, he was willing to put a hundred looms on this pattern, but he was asking for twenty-five centimes more per metre.'

Almost every month, Bouthemont made these factory visits, lived for days in Lyon, staying at the best hotels and with a free hand when he was negotiating with the manufacturers. In any case, he enjoyed complete freedom and could buy whatever he liked, provided that he increased the turnover of his department every year by a ratio fixed in advance. Indeed, the increase was the amount on which he got his percentage bonus. His position in *Au Bonheur des Dames*, in short, like that of his colleagues, all the other managers, was that of a special trader in an assemblage of different shops, a sort of vast trading city.

'So, that's settled,' he went on. 'We'll price it at five francs sixty . . . You know that's barely the cost price.'

'Yes, yes: five francs sixty,' Mouret said eagerly. 'And if I was on my own, I'd sell it at a loss.'

The department head gave a hearty laugh.

'Oh, I'm quite happy with that! It would triple our sales and since all that matters to me is the size of the turnover . . .'

But Bourdoncle pursed his lips and didn't smile. He would be getting his percentage on the total profit and it was not in his interest to cut prices. His job as supervisor was actually to keep an eye on the price ticket to see that Bouthemont did not give way to the urge to increase the sales figures and sell the goods for too little profit. Moreover, he was still a prey to his old anxieties when confronted with publicity schemes that were beyond him. He dared to express his misgivings:

'If we sell it at five francs sixty, it's as though we were selling at a loss, since we shall have to deduct our expenses, which are quite considerable . . . Everywhere else they'd be selling at seven francs.'

Suddenly, Mouret lost his temper. He slapped his open hand down on the silk and shouted out in irritation:

'I know *that*, and that's why I want to make a present of it to our customers . . . Honestly, my dear fellow, you'll never understand women. Don't you see that they'll be falling over each other to get at this silk!'

'I'm sure they will,' Bourdoncle interrupted, obstinately. 'And the more they grab hold of, the more it will cost us.'

'We'll lose a few centimes on each item, I admit. So what? A fine disaster *that* will be if we attract all those women and have them at our mercy, enthralled, driven crazy by the profusion of merchandise and emptying their purses without pausing to count. All that matters, my dear friend, is to excite them, and for that we need one item which cajoles them and causes a stir. After that, you can sell the rest as dear as it is elsewhere and they'll still think they are getting it cheaper from you. For example, our Cuir-d'Or, that taffeta for seven francs fifty, which sells at that price everywhere, will also be considered an extraordinary bargain and be enough to make up for the loss on Paris-Bonheur. You see, you see!'

He was waxing eloquent.

'You understand: in a week's time, I want Paris-Bonheur to revolutionize the market. It is our stroke of luck, the one that will save us and launch us. That's all anyone will be talking about and the blue and silver selvage will be known from one end of the country to the other. And you just listen to the savage way our competitors will moan. The small businesses will be further crippled by it. They'll be sunk, all those rag-and-bone men dying of rheumatism in their cellars.'

The assistants who were checking the deliveries all round where the boss was standing listened and smiled. He loved to talk and get his way. Once more, Bourdoncle gave in. Meanwhile, the packing case had been emptied and two men were taking the nails out of another one.

Then Bouthemont said: 'It's the manufacturers who aren't laughing! In Lyon, they're furious with you. They claim that your bargains are ruining them. You know Gaujean gave me a positive declaration of war. Yes, he swore he would give long credits to the small shopkeepers, rather than accept my prices.'

Mouret shrugged his shoulders.

'If Gaujean is going to be unreasonable,' he replied, 'Gaujean will be left stranded. What are they complaining about? We pay them immediately, we take everything they make, so the least they can do is to work for less . . . In any case, what matters is that the public should benefit.'

The assistant was emptying the second case, while Bouthemont had gone back to checking the items against the invoice. Then another assistant, at the end of the counter, would make them up and, once they had been checked, the invoice, signed by the head of department, had to be taken up to the central counting-house. Mouret watched the work for a moment longer – all the activity occasioned by the deliveries which were mounting up and threatening to flood the basement – then, without another word, like a captain pleased with his troops, he went off, followed by Bourdoncle.

The pair walked slowly through the basement. At intervals, the cellar windows cast a pale light and in the depths of dark corners, along narrow corridors, gas mantles burned constantly. In these corridors they kept the reserves, in vaults behind wooden fences, where the different departments piled their excess stock. As he went by, the boss glanced at the heating stove that was to be lit for the first time on Monday, and at the little firemen's post guarding a giant gas metre enclosed in an iron cage. The kitchen and the dining rooms, old cellars that had been transformed into little rooms, were on the left at the corner of the Place Gaillon. Finally, at the far end of the basement, he arrived at the despatch department. Parcels that the lady customers did not want to carry away were taken down here, sorted out on tables and put into compartments, each of which represented a district in Paris. Then, by a wide stairway which came out just opposite *Le Vieil Elbeuf*, they were taken up to the vans parked near the pavement. In the mechanical operation of *Au Bonheur des Dames*, this staircase on the Rue de la Michodière constantly discharged the goods that had entered by the chute in the Rue Neuve-Saint-Augustin, after they had passed through the cog-wheels of the different departments upstairs.

'Campion,' Mouret said to the head of despatch, a retired sergeant with a lean face. 'Why were six pairs of sheets, purchased by a lady around two o'clock yesterday, not delivered in the evening?'

'Where does the lady live?' the employee asked.

'In the Rue de Rivoli, at the corner of the Rue d'Alger – Madame Desforges.'

At this early hour, the sorting tables were bare and the compartments held only the few parcels that remained from the evening before. While Campion was rummaging among these parcels, after consulting a register, Bourdoncle looked at Mouret, thinking that this devil of a man knew everything and took care of everything, even at the table of a late-night restaurant or in his mistresses' boudoirs. At length, the head of department discovered the mistake: the cash desk had given an incorrect number and the parcel had been returned.

'Which cash desk invoiced it?' Mouret asked. 'Huh? Did you say it was number ten?'

And, turning towards his associate, he said:

'Number ten is Albert, I think? We'll go and have a word with him.'

But before going round the shop, he wanted to visit the mail order department which occupied several rooms on the second floor. It was here that they received all the orders from outside Paris and abroad, and every month he went there to examine the post. Over the past two years, this had been increasing daily and already the service which had started with about ten employees now needed more than thirty. Some opened the letters, others read them, sitting on either side of a single table. Still others classified them, giving each an order number which corresponded to a pigeon-hole. Then when the letters had been distributed to the various departments and they had brought up the items, each of these items was put into a pigeon-hole as it arrived according to its number. All that remained was for them to be checked and packed, in the room next door where a team of workers nailed and tied from morning to evening.

Mouret asked his usual question:

'How many letters this morning, Levasseur?'

'Five hundred and thirty-four, Monsieur,' the head of mail order replied. 'After the sale on Monday, I'm afraid I may not have enough hands. We found it very hard to manage, yesterday.'

Bourdoncle nodded in satisfaction. He hadn't been expecting five hundred and thirty-four letters on a Tuesday. Around the table, the staff were cutting and reading, in a continual noise of crumpled paper, while the coming-and-going of those carrying the goods had started in front of the pigeon-holes. This was one of the most complicated and important of the departments in the store, where the staff lived in a constant fever, because it was mandatory that orders received in the morning must all be despatched by the same evening.

'We'll give you as many people as you need, Levasseur,' Mouret said eventually, after verifying that the department was running smoothly. 'You know, when there's work, we never refuse extra staff.'

Upstairs, under the roof, were the rooms where the salesgirls slept. But he came back down and went into the central counting-house, close to his study. It was a room behind a glass partition with a brass window in it, behind which could be seen a huge safe, fixed to the wall. Here, two cashiers combined all the takings which were brought up each evening by Lhomme, the chief cashier in the store; they would then take charge of expenses, paying the manufacturers, the staff and the rest of the tribe that lived off the store. The counting-house opened on another room where ten employees checked the invoices. Then there was another office, the clearing-house: six young clerks, bent over black desks with shelves of registers behind them, calculated the percentages due to the sales staff and collated the debit notes. This was a brand new service, and it was running badly.

Mouret and Bourdoncle had walked through the counting-house and the verification office. When they entered the other room, the young clerks, whose heads were tossed back with laughter, started in surprise. Mouret didn't tell them off, but explained the system that he had thought up for them, giving a little bonus for each mistake that they found in the sales invoices. And when he went out, the clerks stopped laughing and went eagerly back to work, hunting for mistakes, as though someone had cracked a whip over them.

On the ground floor, in the shop, Mouret went directly to cash desk number ten, where Albert Lhomme was polishing his nails while waiting for the customers to arrive. People talked about 'the dynasty of the Lhommes', since Madame Aurélie, the buyer in ladies' wear, after manoeuvring her husband into the post of chief cashier, had managed to get a job as retail cashier for her son, a tall, pale lad of dubious morals, unable to stay long anywhere and a source of acute anxiety to his parents. But when he was face-to-face with the young man, Mouret kept in the background, not wanting to tarnish his reputation for charm by acting like a policeman and, for reasons of tactics and personal preference, kept to his role as a benevolent deity. He nudged Bourdoncle, the faceless cypher, whom he usually entrusted with dealing out punishments.

'Monsieur Albert,' Bourdoncle said sternly. 'You've taken down an address incorrectly again and the parcel came back to us. This is intolerable.'

The cashier saw fit to protest and called on the porter who had made up the parcel in his defence. This chap, whose name was Joseph, also belonged to the Lhomme dynasty, being Albert's foster-brother and owing his job to Madame Aurélie's influence. Albert was trying to get him to say that the mistake was due to the customer, but he stammered and tugged at the little beard that hung from his scarred face, torn between his conscience as an old soldier and his gratitude to his patrons.

'You leave Joseph alone!' Bourdoncle shouted eventually. 'And stop arguing. Oh, it's lucky for you that we appreciate the good work that your mother does for us!'

At that moment, Lhomme ran up. From his own desk, close to the door, he could see his son's, in the glove department. Already grey and puffy because of his sedentary occupation, he had a soft, shapeless face that seemed to have been worn away in the glare of the money which he endlessly counted. His amputated arm was no hindrance to him in this task and people even went out of curiosity to watch him check the takings, so quickly did the coins and banknotes slip through his left hand, the only one that remained to him. The son of a tax collector from Chablis, he arrived in Paris as bookkeeper for a merchant at the Port-aux-Vins.[3] Then living in the Rue Cuvier, he married the daughter of his concierge, a little tailor from Alsace; since that day he had been subject to his wife, whose commercial ability commanded his respect. She made more than twelve thousand francs in ladies' wear, while he earned only a fixed salary of five thousand francs. And his deference towards a wife who could take home such an amount extended to the son, who also belonged to her.

'What is it?' he muttered. 'Has Albert done something wrong?'

At this point, as usual, Mouret arrived on the scene, playing the good prince. Where Bourdoncle had instilled fear, he took care to remain popular.

'A silly mistake,' he murmured. 'My dear Lhomme, your Albert is a nincompoop who should model himself on you.'

Then, changing the subject, he became even more agreeable:

'What about that concert, the other day? Did you have a good seat?'

A blush rose to the old cashier's white cheeks. He had only one weakness, which was music, a secret vice for which he sought solitary satisfaction, going to theatres, concerts and recitals. Despite his amputated arm, he played the horn, thanks to an ingenious system of clips, and since Madame Lhomme hated the noise, he wrapped cloth round his instrument, in the evenings, ecstatically pleased in spite of everything by the peculiar, dull sounds that emerged. In the unavoidable disarray of the household, he had made a little refuge for himself in music – that and the money in his till: this was all he knew, apart from his admiration for his wife.

'A very good seat,' he replied, with shining eyes. 'You are too kind, Monsieur.'

Mouret, who took personal pleasure in satisfying people's desires, sometimes gave Lhomme tickets that lady patrons had forced on him; and he completely charmed Lhomme by exclaiming: 'Ah, Beethoven! Ah, Mozart! What music!'

Without waiting for a reply, he went off to join Bourdoncle, who was already going round the various departments. The silks were in the central hall, an inner court where the roof had been glazed. Both of them first followed the gallery along the Rue Neuve-Saint-Augustin, which was occupied by white linen from one end to the other. Nothing unusual caught their eye and they passed slowly among the respectful assistants. Then they turned into furnishing fabrics and hosiery, equally well ordered. But in woollens, along the gallery which ran at right angles to the Rue de la Michodière, Bourdoncle resumed his role of high executioner when he saw a young man sitting on a counter, looking exhausted after a night out; and the young man, who was called Liénard, son of a rich draper in Angers, hung his head beneath the reprimand, fearing nothing, in a carefree life of idleness and pleasure, except that he might be called back to the provinces by his father. From then on, criticisms fell like hailstones, the gallery of the Rue de la Michodière taking the full force of the storm. In drapery, an apprentice salesman, one of those who are not paid, but sleep in the department, had come back after eleven o'clock; in haberdashery, the under-buyer had just been caught at the back of the basement, finishing a cigarette. But the full force of the tempest fell on the glove department over the head of one of the few Parisians in the store, Handsome Mignot, as they called him, though he had come down in the world, being the illegitimate son of a lady who taught the harp. His crime was to have caused an uproar in the dining room by complaining about the food. As there were three sittings, one at half-past nine, the next at half-past ten and the third at half-past eleven, he was trying to point out that since he was in the third sitting, he always got the remnants of the sauces and the left-overs.

'What! The food isn't good?' Mouret asked, with an innocent air, opening his mouth for the first time.

He only allowed one franc fifty per day per person to the chef, a frightful Auvergnat,[4] who still found the means to line his own pocket; and the food was truly awful. But Bourdoncle shrugged his shoulders:

a chef who had four hundred luncheons and four hundred dinners to serve, even in three sessions, could hardly be expected to concern himself with the refinements of the culinary art.

'No matter,' the boss said, good-naturedly. 'I want all our employees to have plenty of good, wholesome food. I'll talk to the chef.'

And Mignot's complaint was swept under the carpet. Then, coming back to their point of departure, standing near the door in the midst of the ties and umbrellas, Mouret and Bourdoncle heard the report of one of the four inspectors whose job it was to keep an eye on the store. Old Jouve, a former army captain, decorated at Constantine[5] – still a handsome man with his large, sensual nose and magnificent bald pate – mentioned that a sales assistant had called him 'an old booby', after a simple reprimand, and the assistant was sacked on the spot.

Meanwhile, the shop was empty of customers. Only housewives from the neighbourhood were making their way through the empty aisles. At the door, the inspector who checked the staff in had just closed his register and was separately writing down the names of the latecomers. This was the moment when the sales people settled into their departments, which the porters had been sweeping and dusting since five o'clock. Each of them hung up his hat and coat, stifling a yawn, faces still white from sleep. Some said a few words to one another and looked around, as if loosening up for a day's work. Others, without hurrying, took off the green baize cloths with which, the previous evening, they had covered the goods, after folding them up; and the heaps of materials emerged, symmetrically laid out; the whole shop was clean and tidy, shining calmly in the pleasant early morning light, while waiting for the pushing and shoving of buying and selling to choke it once more and somehow shrink it beneath the chaos of linen, cotton, silk and lace.

In the bright light of the central hall, in the silk department, two young men were talking in low voices. One, small and attractive, sturdily built and pink-skinned, was trying to match some coloured silks for a counter display. He was called Hutin, the son of a café owner in Yvetot, who had managed in only eighteen months to become one of the top salesmen, because of his flexible nature and the continual smoothing touch of flattery behind which he concealed his raging appetites, consuming everything and devouring the world, hungry or not, for the simple pleasure of doing it.

'Listen here, Favier, in your place I'd have slapped his face, I swear I should!' he told the other man, a tall, bilious lad, dry and yellow-skinned, a native of Besançon from a family of weavers, devoid of charm but concealing a disturbing force of will beneath his offhand manner.

'It doesn't achieve anything, slapping people,' he muttered coolly. 'It's better to wait.'

They were talking about Robineau, who kept an eye on the assistants while the head of department was in the basement. Hutin was surreptitiously undermining the under-buyer, because he wanted his job. Already, to damage him and make him leave, on the day when the chief buyer's post which he had been promised became vacant, he had the idea of bringing in Bouthemont from outside. But Robineau was holding his ground and now it was an hourly battle. Hutin dreamed of stirring up the whole department against him and driving him out with bad feeling and minor irritations. In any case, he adopted his usual pleasant manner, particularly exciting Favier, who was just behind him among the salesmen, and appeared to let himself be led on, but with sudden changes of heart in which one could sense a whole personal campaign being carried on in silence.

'Hush! Seventeen!' he said sharply to his colleague, using a well-established signal to warn him that Mouret and Bourdoncle were coming.

The pair were, indeed, carrying on with their inspection across the hall. They stopped and asked Robineau to explain about a consignment of velvet, the boxes from which were piled up on a table. And when Robineau answered that they were short of space, Mouret exclaimed, with a smile:

'I told you so, Bourdoncle: the shop is too small already! One day we shall have to knock down the walls to the Rue de Choiseul . . . Wait and see what a crush there'll be, next Monday!'

He questioned Robineau some more and handed out orders to do with the sale for which every department was preparing. But for a few minutes, though he carried on speaking, he had been watching what Hutin was up to: lingering over the placing of blue silks next to grey and yellow ones, then stepping back to judge how the shades harmonized with each other. Suddenly, Mouret interrupted him:

'Now why are you trying to spare their eyes?' he asked. 'Don't be afraid, blind them! Come on! Red! Green! Yellow!'

He picked up the pieces and was throwing them around, crumpling them, to make startling combinations of colours. Everyone agreed, the boss was the finest display artist in Paris, a revolutionary indeed, who had introduced the brutal and the colossal into the science of window-dressing. He wanted landslides of cloth tumbling as though it had been accidentally emptied out of the boxes, blazing with the most intense colours, each striking sparks from its neighbours. When they left the store, he would say, his customers ought to have eye strain. Hutin, on the other hand, belonged to the classical school which believed in symmetry and harmony achieved through subtle variation of shades, and watched him light up this blaze of materials in the middle of the table without venturing the merest hint of criticism, but with his lips pursed into the pout of one whose artistic principles are outraged by such excess.

'There!' Mouret exclaimed, when he had finished. 'Leave it, and tell me if it pulls the women in, on Monday.'

In point of fact, just as he was going back to Bourdoncle and Robineau, a woman came up and stayed standing for a few moments in front of the display, which quite took her breath away. It was Denise. After dithering for almost an hour in the street, torn by a dreadful fit of shyness, she had finally plucked up her courage. The problem was that her head was spinning to such an extent that she couldn't understand the clearest directions, and even though the assistants, whom she had stammeringly asked for Madame Aurélie, had pointed out the stairs to the mezzanine, she thanked them, then turned left where she had been told to turn right, so that for the past ten minutes she had been wandering around the ground floor, going from one counter to the next, amid the malevolent curiosity and sullen indifference of the sales staff. Inside her, at one and the same time, there was a desire to escape and a restraining urge to admire. She felt lost, very small inside this monster, this still resting machine, afraid of being caught up in its movement, which had already started to make the walls shake. The thought of the shop at *Le Vieil Elbeuf*, narrow and black, made her see this huge store as even greater than it was, gilded it with light, like a whole city, with its monuments, squares and streets, through which it seemed impossible that she should ever find her way.

Up to now, however, she had not dared to venture into the silk hall, intimidated by its high ceiling, its opulent counters and its church-like atmosphere. Then, when she finally fled there to escape the laughter of the salesmen in white linen, she had, so to speak, run straight into Mouret's display and, despite her confusion, the woman in her awoke and blushed suddenly as she forgot herself on seeing the blaze of silks.

'What's this?' Hutin said coarsely in Favier's ear. 'The slut from Place Gaillon.'

Mouret, pretending to listen to Bourdoncle and Robineau, was actually flattered by the poor girl's obvious fascination, just as a countess may be stirred by the animal desire of a passing coachman. But Denise had looked up and was still more disturbed when she recognized the young man whom she had taken for a buyer; she imagined that he was looking sternly at her. At this, not knowing how to leave and completely bewildered, she turned again to the nearest member of staff, standing beside her, who was Favier.

'For Madame Aurélie, please?'

Favier was unpleasant and replied briefly: 'On the mezzanine.'

And Denise, trying to escape as quickly as she could from the eyes of all these men, thanked him and was once more turning away from the staircase when Hutin instinctively gave way to his gentlemanly nature. He had called her a slut but he summoned her back in his most agreeable salesman's manner.

'No, no, this way, Mademoiselle . . . If you would be so good . . .'

He even took a step or two ahead of her, leading her to the foot of the staircase which was on the left of the hall. There he bowed and favoured her with the smile that he gave all women.

'At the top, turn left. Ladies' wear is opposite.'

Denise was deeply stirred by this polite behaviour, which seemed to reach out like a hand of friendship. She looked up and examined Hutin.

Everything about him appealed to her: his handsome face, his smiling look which dispelled her fear and his voice which struck her as soft and reassuring. Her heart welled with gratitude and she expressed her feelings in the few disjointed words that she managed to stammer out:

'You are too kind . . . Don't bother . . . Thank you, Monsieur, thank you.'

Hutin was already rejoining Favier and coarsely whispering, under his breath: 'What a beanpole! Huh?'

Upstairs, the young woman walked straightaway into ladies' wear. This was a huge room surrounded by high, carved, oak wardrobes, with clear glass windows overlooking the Rue de la Michodière. Five or six women, in silk dresses and looking very pert with their curled chignons and their crinolines swept back, were busying themselves there as they chatted. One, tall and slim, with an elongated head and the appearance of a bolted horse, was leaning back against a wardrobe, as though already exhausted.

'Madame Aurélie?' Denise repeated.

The assistant looked at her without answering, with a look of contempt at her humble outfit, then turned to one of her colleagues – a small girl with an unhealthy, pale complexion – and asked, in an artless, world-weary voice:

'Mademoiselle Vadon, do you know where the buyer is?'

The other, who was sorting cloaks by size, did not even bother to look up.

'No, Mademoiselle Prunaire, I have no idea,' she said primly.

There was silence. Denise remained standing where she was and no one took any further notice of her. However, after waiting for a short while, she plucked up enough courage to ask a further question.

'Do you think that Madame Aurélie will be back soon?'

At this, the under-buyer in the department, a thin, ugly woman whom she had not noticed, a widow with a jutting jaw and wiry hair, called out to her from a wardrobe where she was checking price tickets:

'Wait here, if you want to talk to Madame Aurélie herself.'

And, turning to another sales assistant, she added:

'Might she not be at reception?'

'No, Madame Frédéric, I don't think so,' the girl replied. 'She didn't say anything, she can't have gone far.'

With this information, Denise stood where she was. There were in fact a few chairs for the customers, but as no one told her to sit down, she did not dare take one, even though she was so nervous that her legs were giving way. Naturally, the young ladies had guessed that she was a sales assistant looking for a job, and they were staring at her, undressing her out of the corner of their eyes, with no leniency, but the secret hostility of diners unwilling to move over to make way for hungry new arrivals from outside. Her feeling of embarrassment was growing and she strolled across the room to look out of the window, just to save face. Directly in front of her was the *Vieil Elbeuf*, with its rusty façade and lifeless windows, seeming so ugly and miserable when seen from the lively, luxurious surroundings around her, that she felt a kind of remorse tugging at her heart.

'I say,' whispered the tall girl, Prunaire, to little Vadon. 'Have you seen her boots?'

'What about her dress!' the other answered quietly.

For Denise, still looking out across the street, it was as though she were being eaten up. But she felt no anger: she didn't consider either of them pretty: the tall one with her hank of red hair falling across her horse's neck, or the little one, with her complexion like sour milk, which made her flat face look soft and boneless. Clara Prunaire, the daughter of a clog-maker in the Bois de Vivet, debauched by the footmen at the Château de Mareuil where the Countess took her in to do the darning, had later worked in a shop in Langres and, now in Paris, was avenging herself on men for the kicks that Old Prunaire had landed on her bruised behind. Marguerite Vadon was born in Grenoble where her family traded in cloth and had to be sent up to *Au Bonheur des Dames* to disguise a lapse, a child accidentally conceived. If she remained on her best behaviour, she was to go back home to run her parents' shop and marry a cousin who would wait for her.

'Well, well!' Clara went on, softly. 'There's one who won't cut much ice here!'

Then they fell silent, as a woman of around forty came in. This was Madame Aurélie, heavily built and tightly laced into her black silk dress, the upper part of which, stretched over the vast roundness of her shoulders and bosom, shone like armour. Under her dark ringlets she had big, unblinking eyes, a stern mouth and wide, somewhat sagging cheeks. The majesty of her position as chief buyer was starting to give her face the puffiness of a Roman Emperor's bloated visage.

'Mademoiselle Vadon,' she said, in a tetchy voice. 'Didn't you take the model of the waisted coat to the workshop yesterday?'

'There was an alteration that needed to be made, Madame,' the salesgirl answered. 'Madame Frédéric kept it.'

At this, the under-buyer took the model out of a cupboard and the discussion continued. Nothing could withstand Madame Aurélie, when she felt obliged to defend her authority. So vain that she preferred not to be called by her real name, Lhomme, which she disliked, and denying that her father was a concierge, speaking of him as a tailor with his own shop, she was only affable to those young ladies who bent easily and mildly to her will, falling over in admiration before her. Previously, in the dressmaker's workshop that she had tried to set up on her own account, she had become bitter, constantly dogged by ill luck and irritated at the idea that she had it in her to achieve her ends, but never seemed to manage anything except disaster. Now, even though she had been a success at *Au Bonheur des Dames,* where she earned twelve thousand francs a year, she still seemed to bear a grudge against everyone and was particularly hard on beginners, just as life had been hard on her at the start.

'Enough talk!' she snapped at last. 'You are no more sensible than the rest, Madame Frédéric. Have the alteration done at once.'

While all this was going on, Denise had stopped looking out of the window. She guessed that this lady must be Madame Aurélie, but she was upset by the shouting and stayed there, still waiting. The assistants, delighted at having caused a row between the buyer and her second-in-command, had gone back to their work with an air of the most utter indifference. A few minutes went by, but no one was kind enough to save the young woman from her embarrassment. Finally, it was Madame Aurélie herself who noticed her and, amazed at seeing anyone not moving around, asked what she wanted.

'Please, are you Madame Aurélie?'

'I am.'

Denise's mouth had gone dry and her hands were cold: she felt the same fear as she used to as a child when she expected to be whipped. She stammered out her request and had to start again before it could be understood. Madame Aurélie's large, still eyes looked at her, without the softening of a single fold in her imperial visage.

'How old are you?'

'Twenty, Madame.'

'Twenty, you say! You don't look sixteen!'

Once more, the assistants looked up. Denise hastened to add: 'Oh, but I'm very strong!'

Madame Aurélie shrugged her broad shoulders, then announced:

'Heavens above, I'm ready to put your name down! We write in whoever applies. Mademoiselle Prunaire, give me the register.'

They could not find it straightaway, it must be with Inspector Jouve. While Tall Clara was off looking for it, Mouret came in, still followed by Bourdoncle. They were completing their tour of the departments on the mezzanine; they had been through lace, shawls, furs, furnishings and lingerie, and now they were ending with ladies' wear. Madame Aurélie went to one side and talked to them for a while about an order for coats that she meant to give to one of the main Parisian suppliers. Usually, she bought direct, on her own responsibility, but when it was a large purchase, she preferred to consult the management. After this, Bourdoncle told her about her son Albert's latest mistake, which seemed to plunge her into despair: the boy would kill her; at least, his father, though no genius, knew how to behave. The whole dynasty of the Lhommes, of which she was the unchallenged head, was often a source of considerable worry to her.

Meanwhile, Mouret, surprised at seeing Denise again, leaned over to Madame Aurélie to ask her what the girl was doing there; and when the chief buyer replied that she was asking to be taken on as a salesgirl, Bourdoncle, with his contempt for women, was outraged at such presumption.

'Come now,' he muttered. 'It must be a joke! She's too ugly.'

'I admit she's no beauty,' Mouret said, not daring to defend her, though still moved by the enchantment she had shown downstairs, in front of his display.

However, they brought the register and Madame Aurélie went back to Denise. The girl certainly made no good impression. She was very clean, in her slender black woollen dress, and they did not bother about the simplicity of her outfit, since she would be provided with a uniform, the regulation silk dress; but she looked quite puny and had a sad face. While not requiring their girls to be beautiful, they did like them pleasant on the sales floor. Beneath the stares of these ladies and gentlemen who were studying her and weighing her up like peasants haggling over a mare in the market, Denise finally lost her composure.

'What's your name?' the head buyer asked, pen in hand, ready to write at the end of a counter.

'Denise Baudu, Madame.'

'Age?'

'Twenty and four months.'

And she repeated, daring to look up at Mouret, this man she believed to be a head of department, whom she kept on meeting and whose presence disturbed her:

'I may not look it, but I'm quite sturdy.'

They smiled. Bourdoncle looked impatiently at his fingernails. In fact, the remark had met with a discouraging silence.

'Which store did you work in, in Paris?' the buyer went on.

'But, Madame, I've just come up from Valognes.'

Another catastrophe. Generally, *Au Bonheur des Dames* demanded that its salespeople should have served an apprenticeship of a year in one of the smaller firms in Paris. At this, Denise was in despair and, had she not thought about the children, she would have left, to bring an end to this useless interrogation.

'Where were you in Valognes?'

'At Cornaille's.'

'I know it – good firm,' Mouret remarked.

Normally, he never interfered with the taking-on of staff, the heads of department being responsible for their own people. But with his acute sensitivity to women, he perceived in this girl a hidden allure, a power of charm and tenderness of which even she was unaware. The reputation of the previous firm carried considerable weight and was often decisive. Madame Aurélie continued in a gentler voice:

'Why did you leave Cornaille's?'

'For family reasons,' Denise replied, blushing. 'Our parents died and I had to come here with my brothers . . . Here's a reference.'

It was excellent. Her hopes were starting to revive, when one last question caused her further embarrassment.

'Do you have any other references in Paris? Where are you living?'

'With my uncle,' she muttered, hesitating to name him because she was afraid that they would never want the niece of one of their competitors. 'My uncle Baudu, there, across the street.'

At this, Mouret interrupted again.

'What! You're Baudu's niece! Did he send you?'

'Oh, no, Monsieur!'

She couldn't help laughing, the idea seemed so peculiar. And the laugh transformed her. She blushed and the smile, on her slightly too large mouth, was like a blossoming of the whole face. Her grey eyes were lit with a soft fire, her cheeks dimpled adorably and even her fair hair seemed to take flight in the fine, brave merriment of her whole being.

'But she's pretty!' Mouret whispered to Bourdoncle.

His associate refused to accept this, with a bored gesture. Clara had pursed her lips and Marguerite turned her back. Only Madame Aurélie nodded her approval when Mouret went on:

'Your uncle was wrong not to bring you, his recommendation would be enough. They say that he resents us. We are more generous than that, and if he cannot find work for his niece in his own business, well, we shall show him that she only has to knock on our door to be welcome here. Tell him that I am still very fond of him and that his resentment should not be turned against us but against the new commercial climate. And tell him that he will finally go under if he insists on his heaps of ridiculous, old-fashioned goods.'

Denise's face went from pink to white. This was Mouret. No one had spoken his name, but he had revealed himself, and now she guessed it, understanding why, in the street, in the silk department and now once again, this young man stirred such feelings in her. These feelings, which she could not interpret, were pressing more and more heavily on her heart, like an excessive weight. All the stories that her uncle had told her returned to her mind, made Mouret seem larger, surrounding him with myth and making him the master of the awesome machine that, since early that morning, had held her in the iron teeth of its cogs. And, behind his fine head with its trim beard and eyes the colour of old gold, she saw the dead woman, this Madame Hédouin, whose blood had cemented the stones of the business. At this, she shuddered as she had done the previous day and decided that she was quite simply afraid of him.

Meanwhile Madame Aurélie was closing the register. She only needed one assistant and already had six applicants. But she was too keen to please her employer to hesitate. Despite that, the application would follow the usual course, Inspector Jouve would make inquiries and write a report, and the buyer would make her decision.

'Very well, Mademoiselle,' she said, grandly, to leave no doubt about her authority. 'We shall be writing to you.'

For a moment, Denise remained standing there, awkwardly. She did not know which foot to put first, surrounded by all these people. At last, she thanked Madame Aurélie and, when she had to pass in front of Mouret and Bourdoncle, bade them farewell. By now they were too busy to bother with her any more and did not even return her greeting, taken up with examining the model of the waisted coat with Madame Frédéric. Clara made a gesture of annoyance to Marguerite, as if to predict that the new salesgirl would not be very welcome in the department. Denise must have felt this indifference and hostility behind her, because she went down the stairs with the same unease as she had felt in going up them, seized by a peculiar sense of anxiety and wondering if she should be glad or otherwise that she had come. Could she count on getting the job? Her discomfort, which had prevented her from understanding clearly, was once more sowing doubts in her mind. Two feelings dominated all the rest, gradually sweeping the others away: there was the effect that Mouret had had on her, which was so profound as to make her afraid; and there was the friendliness of Hutin, the only pleasant moment in the morning, a delightfully sweet memory which filled her with gratitude. As she was crossing the shop towards the exit, she looked around for the young man: she would like to be able to thank him again with a look and she was quite sad at not seeing him.

'Well, Mademoiselle, were you successful?' a trembling voice asked her as she finally stepped out on to the pavement.

She turned round and recognized the tall, lanky young man with the pale face who had talked to her that morning. He, too, was coming out of *Au Bonheur des Dames* and seemed more intimidated than herself, quite overcome by his recent interview.

'Goodness me! I don't know at all, Monsieur,' she replied.

'Same here. They have such a way of looking at you and speaking to you in these . . . I'm going for lace, I've just come from Crèvecoeur's in the Rue du Mail.'

They were standing in front of one another again, and not knowing how to take their leave, started to blush. Then the young man, who was so shy that he felt he had to say something, plucked up his courage and asked, in his gentle, awkward manner:

'What is your name, Mademoiselle?'

'Denise Baudu.'

'And I'm called Henri Deloche.'

Now they were smiling. Accepting that they were in the same situation, they shook hands.

'Good luck, then!'

'Yes, good luck!'

CHAPTER 3

Every Saturday, from four to six, Madame Desforges offered a cup of tea and some cakes to those of her intimate friends who wished to visit her. Her apartment was on the third floor, between the Rue de Rivoli and the Rue d'Alger, and the windows of the two drawing rooms opened on the Tuileries gardens.

That Saturday, it happened that, as a servant was about to show him into the main drawing room, Mouret caught sight of Madame Desforges crossing the little drawing room through a door of the antechamber which had been left open. She stopped when she saw him and he went through, greeting her ceremoniously. Then, when the servant had shut the door, he quickly clasped the young woman's hand and kissed it tenderly.

'Careful, there are people there,' she said softly, nodding towards the door of the main drawing room. 'I went to find this fan so that I could show it to them.'

And she tapped him merrily on the face with the tip of the fan. She was auburn-haired, with quite a full figure and large, jealous eyes. Not letting go of her hand, he asked:

'Is he coming?'

'Surely,' she replied. 'He promised me.'

They were speaking of Baron Hartmann, director of the Crédit Immobilier. Madame Desforges, whose father had been a member of the Council of State, was the widow of a stockbroker who had left her a fortune (though some exaggerated its size, while others denied its existence altogether). Even while her husband was alive, so it was said, she had shown her gratitude to Baron Hartmann, a leading financier whose advice was valuable to the family; and later, after her husband's death, the liaison was assumed to have continued, still prudently, without any indiscretion or scandal. Madame Desforges never put herself forward and was received everywhere among the upper bourgeoisie into which she had been born. Even now, when the passion of the banker, that sharp-witted and sceptical man, was becoming more of a paternal affection, while she did allow herself to take lovers – which he tolerated – she was so measured, considerate and tactful in her affairs, with such a fine understanding of society and such skill in applying it, that appearances were kept up and no one would have dared openly to challenge her reputation. At first, after meeting Mouret at the house of some mutual acquaintances, she hated him, only to give herself to him later, carried away by the urgent passion with which he assailed her; and, all the time that he was manoeuvring to reach the Baron through her, she gradually found herself developing a genuine, deep affection for him and loved him with the ardour of a woman who was already thirty-five – though she would only admit to twenty-nine – and was in turmoil at the idea that he was younger than her, terrified that she might lose him.

'Does he know?' he asked her.

'No, you can explain the matter to him yourself,' she said, dropping the familiar form.[1]

She looked at him, thinking that he really did not know anything, if he used her in this way with the Baron and pretended to consider him merely as an old friend of hers. But he was still holding her hand and calling her his 'dear Henriette', and she could feel her heart melting. Saying nothing, she leaned across and pressed her lips to his, then said quietly:

'Hush, they're expecting me. You come in behind me.'

Soft voices could be heard in the large drawing room, muffled by the hangings. She pushed the double door, leaving both sides open and gave the fan to one of the four ladies who were seated in the middle of the room.

'Here it is!' she said. 'I'd mislaid it and my chambermaid would never have found it.'

Then, turning round gaily, she added:

'Come in, Monsieur Mouret, come through the little drawing room. That will be less formal.'

Mouret greeted the ladies, whom he knew. The room with its Louis XIV furniture and brocade embroidered with flowers, its gilded bronzes and its great green plants, had a soft, feminine intimacy despite the high ceilings; and through the two windows, you could see the chestnuts in the Tuileries, their leaves blown about by the October winds.

'But this Chantilly lace is not at all bad!' exclaimed Madame Bourdelais, who was holding the fan.

She was a small, blonde woman of thirty, with a delicate little nose and bright eyes, who had been at boarding school with Henriette, then married a deputy head of department at the Ministry of Finance. She came from an old bourgeois family, and ran her own household and her three children with energy, good grace and a fine sense of the practicalities of life.

'And you paid twenty-five francs for this piece?' she went on, studying each mesh of the lace. 'What? In Luc, did you say? From a local lacemaker? No, no, it's not expensive. But you had to have it made up.'

'Naturally,' said Madame Desforges. 'The frame cost me two hundred francs.'

At this, Madame Bourdelais started to laugh. So that was what Henriette called a bargain! Two hundred francs for a simple ivory mounting with a monogram! All that for a scrap of Chantilly that had saved her at most five francs! You could find just the same fans, ready mounted, for a hundred and twenty francs; and she mentioned a shop in the Rue Poissonnière.

Meanwhile, the fan was going from one lady to the next. Madame Guibal hardly glanced at it. She was tall and thin, with red hair and a face bathed in indifference, out of which, from time to time, her grey eyes exhibited dreadful pangs of egoism behind her air of detachment. She was never seen in the company of her husband, a lawyer who was well known in the courts and said to enjoy free living, being entirely devoted to his briefs and his pleasures.

'Oh!' she exclaimed, handing the fan on to Madame de Boves. 'I've only ever bought two in my life. People always give you too many.'

The Countess replied in an ironic tone:

'My dear, you're lucky to have a considerate husband.'

And, leaning over to her daughter, a tall girl of twenty-one-and-a-half, she added:

'Look at the monogram, Blanche. What lovely work! It must have been the monogram that put up the price.'

Madame de Boves had just passed forty. She was a splendid woman, with a neck like a goddess, a large face, regular features and full, languorous eyes; her husband, the general inspector of the Stud,[2] had married for her beauty. She seemed quite moved by the delicacy of this monogram, as though overcome by a feeling of desire that had drained the blood from her cheeks. Suddenly, she said:

'Tell us what you think, Monsieur Mouret. Is two hundred francs excessive for such a frame?'

Mouret had been standing, surrounded by the five women, smiling and taking an interest in what interested them. He took the fan, looked carefully at it and was about to pronounce when the servant opened the door and announced:

'Madame Marty.'

A thin woman came in, ugly, ravaged by smallpox, but turned out with studied elegance. She was ageless, her thirty-five years seeming forty or thirty, according to her mood of the moment. A red leather bag, which she did not let go, hung from her right hand.

'Dear lady,' she said to Henriette. 'Pray excuse me with my bag . . . Just imagine: I was on my way to see you and I went into the *Bonheur* and spent far too much again; I didn't want to leave this downstairs in the cab, for fear of having it stolen.'

She gave a laugh because she had just seen Mouret.

'Oh, Monsieur, I'm not trying to advertise for you, since I hadn't noticed that you were here . . . But you do have some extraordinary lace at the moment.'

This had distracted attention from the fan, which the young man put down on a table. These ladies were now consumed by the need to see what Madame Marty had bought. She was famous for her spending sprees, unable to resist temptation, so virtuous that she would never give in to a lover, yet utterly faint-hearted and yielding when confronted with a tiny piece of chiffon. The daughter of a humble civil servant, she was now ruining her husband, a teacher in the second year at the Lycée Bonaparte who had constantly to be looking for extra work, so that he could double his salary of six thousand francs and meet the household's constantly rising expenses. And she didn't open the bag, hugging it on her knees, but talked about her daughter Valentine, now fourteen and one of her most expensive follies, because she dressed her as she did herself, giving way to the temptation of all the latest fashions.

'You know,' she went on, 'this winter they're making dresses trimmed with a little lace for young girls . . . And of course when I saw such a pretty Valenciennes . . .'

At last, she decided to open the bag. The ladies were just peering inside when the ringing of the bell in the antechamber broke the silence.

'It's my husband,' Madame Marty stammered, quite overcome. 'He was meant to fetch me on his way back from school.'

She had quickly closed the bag and, instinctively, concealed it under a chair. All the ladies began to laugh. At that she started to blush at her haste, took the bag back on her knees and remarked that men would never understand and did not need to know.

'Monsieur de Boves, Monsieur de Vallagnosc,' the servant announced.

Amazement! Even Madame de Boves was not expecting her husband. He was a handsome man, with moustaches and a goatee beard, who adopted the military bearing favoured at the Tuileries; he kissed Madame Desforges' hand: he had known her at her father's when she was a girl. Then he stood back to allow the other visitor, a tall, pale fellow with a distinguished, thin-blooded look, to greet the mistress of the house in his turn. But the conversation had hardly resumed before two faint cries were heard above it:

'What! Is it you, Paul?'

'Well, well! Octave!'

Mouret and Vallagnosc were shaking hands while Madame Desforges exclaimed in surprise: were the two of them acquainted? Indeed they were: they had grown up together in school at Plassans. The surprising thing was that they had never met in her house before.

Still clasping hands, they joked as they made their way into the small drawing room just as the servant was bringing tea, in a china service on a silver tray, which he put down beside Madame Desforges, in the middle of the marble-topped table with its little brass edging. The ladies came over and their chatter got louder, with remarks half-finished and interrupted, while M. de Boves, standing behind them, leaned over from time to time and added something with the good manners of a polished public servant. The huge room, so bright and softly furnished, became even more joyful at the sound of these chattering voices, mixed with laughter.

'If it isn't old Paul!' Mouret said again.

He had sat down beside Vallagnosc on a sofa. Alone at the far end of the small drawing room, a very pretty little room hung with buttercup-coloured silk, far from the ears of the ladies and only seeing them through the wide-open door, they sniggered and giggled, looking into each other's eyes and tapping each other on the knees. Their whole youth came back to them: the old boarding school in Plassans, with its two courtyards, its damp classrooms, the refectory where they ate so much cod and the dormitory where pillows flew from bed to bed as soon as the monitor started to snore. Paul came from an old family of parliamentarians belonging to the minor aristocracy, now reduced to sulking poverty; he was good at school work, always first in class and constantly held up as an example by the master, who predicted a bright future for him. As for Octave, languishing at the bottom of the class among the dunces, plump and happy, he would expend his energies outside school on violent pursuits. Despite this difference of temperament, they became inseparable until the *baccalauréat*, from which one emerged crowned with glory, while the other just scraped by after two unsuccessful attempts. Then life had carried them their separate ways, only to meet again now after ten years, already aged and different.

'Tell me,' Mouret asked. 'What has become of you?'

'Nothing has become of me.'

Even in the joy of their reunion, Vallagnosc had maintained his weary and disillusioned manner. His friend was astonished and insisted:

'Well, you must be doing something . . . What is it?'

But he replied: 'Nothing.'

Octave started to laugh. Nothing was not enough. Eventually, word by word, he dragged Paul's story out of him, the familiar story of one of those poor boys whose birth makes them feel they should remain in the liberal professions and who bury themselves in the depths of their proud mediocrity, considering themselves lucky if they do not starve to death with their desk drawers full of diplomas. Paul had taken law in deference to family tradition, then continued to be supported by his widowed mother, who already had enough worry trying to marry off her two daughters. He had finally succumbed to shame and left the three women to struggle by on the remnants of their fortune while he took up a junior post in the Ministry of the Interior, where he was buried like a mole in its hole.

'So what do you earn?' Mouret asked.

'Three thousand francs.'

'But that's a pittance! Oh, my poor chap, my heart bleeds for you . . . Why, you were such a brainbox! You smashed the lot of us! And all they're giving you is three thousand francs, after knocking you on the head for five years already. No, it's not fair!'

He broke off and returned to himself.

'I took my leave of them all . . . You know what happened to me?'

'Yes,' said Vallagnosc. 'They told me you were in trade. You have that big store on the Place Gaillon, don't you?'

'That's it . . . Calico, old boy!'

Mouret was looking up and once again slapped Paul's knee with the hearty good humour of a man who was not ashamed of the work that has made him rich.

'Calico, by the ton! Good lord, you remember, I didn't fit in with their system, even though I never thought I was any stupider than the next man. When I did pass the *bac* to please my folks, I could quite well have become a lawyer or a doctor like my friends, but those jobs scared me stiff – you see so many people just twiddling their thumbs in them . . . So, by jove, I kicked over the traces – and I didn't regret it – and dived straight into trade.'

Vallagnosc gave an embarrassed smile. Eventually, he said:

'It's a fact, your *baccalauréat* can't be much use to you for selling cloth.'

'I'll say!' Mouret replied, merrily. 'All I ask is that it shouldn't get in my way. And, you know, when you've been daft enough to tie that round your neck, it's no easy job to shake it off. You go through life at a snail's pace, while the others, those who have nothing to hold them back, run on ahead like madmen.'

Then, noticing that this appeared to be giving pain to his friend, he took his hands before continuing:

'Come, now, I don't want to upset you; but admit that your qualifications have not satisfied any of your needs . . . Do you know that the head of my silks department will be earning more than twelve thousand francs this year? Precisely! A boy of very moderate intellect, whose education amounted to some spelling and the four rules of arithmetic.[3] The ordinary sales staff in the firm make three or four thousand francs, more than you do, and their education never cost anything, unlike yours, they were never sent out into the world with a signed guarantee that they would conquer it. Of course, earning money is not everything. All I can say, though, is that between the poor devils with a veneer of education who clutter up the liberal professions and don't have enough to fill their bellies, and practical chaps, well prepared for life, who know their job from top to bottom – darn it, I know which I'd choose: I'm for the second against the first, because I think that these are the ones who really understand the times we live in.'

He had raised his voice and Henriette, serving tea, looked round. When he saw her smile, from the back of the large drawing room, and noticed that two other ladies were listening, he was the first to laugh at his own phrase-making.

'In short, old chap, any calico-seller who starts in the business today is a potential millionaire.'

Vallagnosc leaned back feebly on the sofa, adopting a pose of tiredness and contempt, with his eyes half-closed, adding affectation to the genuine exhaustion of his breed.

'Puh!' he murmured. 'Life's not worth the trouble. There's nothing amusing about it.'

And when Mouret looked at him with shocked amazement, he added:

'Everything happens and nothing happens. One might as well just stay out of it altogether.'

He went on to talk about his pessimism, about the mediocrity and disillusionment of life. At one time, he had dreamed of being a writer, but associating with poets had left him with a sense of universal despair. He had repeatedly come to the conclusion that all effort was wasted, all time equally boring, however spent, and the world ultimately futile. Pleasure was bound to fail and there was none to be had even in wrongdoing.

'Come, do you enjoy yourself?' he asked in the end.

Mouret, astonished and indignant, exclaimed: 'What! Do I enjoy myself! What are you blathering about? My dear chap, have you fallen so low? Of course I enjoy myself – and even when things are going wrong, because I go crazy at seeing them go wrong. I'm a passionate man, I don't just sit back and let life go by – which may be why it interests me.'

He glanced towards the drawing room and lowered his voice.

'Oh, there are some women who have given me headaches, that I do admit. But when I have hold of one, by God I hold on to her! It doesn't always fail and I don't share her with anyone, believe me . . . Then it isn't always a matter of women, because they don't mean that much to me, after all. It's wanting something and acting on it, you see, creating something, in short. You get an idea and you fight for it, you hammer it into people's heads, you see it grow and triumph . . . Oh, yes, my good fellow, I enjoy it right enough!'

His words resonated with the joy of action and the pleasure of being alive; he said it again: he belonged to his age. Honestly, you had to have something wrong in your make-up, some weakness in your head and limbs, to shrink from action at a time when so much was being done, when the whole century was thrusting forward into the future. And he mocked all those people without hope, the disillusioned, the pessimists, all those who were sickened by the new sciences and who adopted the tearful pose of poets or the tight lips of sceptics, in the midst of this vast workshop of the modern world. A nice way to behave, it was, very decent and intelligent, yawning with boredom when you saw others at work!

'That's the only pleasure I have, yawning at others,' Vallagnosc said, giving a cold smile.

Suddenly, Mouret's anger subsided and he became once more the affectionate friend.

'That's my old Paul, always the same, always talking in paradoxes. What? We haven't met up again just to quarrel. Everyone has his own views, and just as well. But I must show you my machine in operation and you'll see, it's not so silly. Come, now, tell me your news. I hope your mother and sisters are well. And weren't you due to get married in Plassans, six months ago?'

He stopped, at a sudden movement from Vallagnosc; and, since the other man glanced round the room anxiously, Mouret also turned and noticed that Mademoiselle de Boves was staring at them. Tall, heavily built, Blanche took after her mother, with this difference, that in her the face was already growing puffy, thickened by unhealthy fat. On his discreet inquiry, Paul replied that nothing was yet settled and perhaps never would be. He had met the young lady at Madame Desforges', where he had been a regular visitor last winter, but had lately seldom come, which explained how he had managed not to meet Octave here before now. The Boves invited him in their turn and he was especially fond of the father, an old rake now retired, but working for the civil service. In any case, there was no money there: Madame de Boves had only brought her husband her Junoesque beauty and the family lived off the mortgaging of their one remaining farm, the slender income from which was luckily supplemented by the nine thousand francs which the Count made as general inspector of the Stud. He kept the ladies, mother and daughter, very short of money, which he still dissipated on his amours away from home, and they were sometimes reduced to mending their own dresses.

'So, why?' Mouret asked, simply.

'My God, just to get it over with,' said Vallagnosc, with a weary movement of his eyelids. 'And we do have expectations: there's an aunt who ought to die soon.'

Meanwhile, Mouret was keeping a close watch on Monsieur de Boves, who was sitting next to Madame Guibal, attentive and laughing with the affectionate laugh of a man bent on seduction. He turned to his friend and winked in such a significant way that Paul said:

'No, not her . . . At least, not yet . . . The trouble is that his department sends him to every corner of France to stables where they keep stud horses, and in that way he always has an excuse for his absences. Last month, when his wife thought he was in Perpignan, he was living in a hotel with a piano teacher in some godforsaken part of town.'

There was a pause. Then the young man, who had also been keeping watch on the Count's wooing of Madame Guibal, went on softly:

'By golly, you're right . . . Particularly since the dear lady is no shrinking violet, or so they say. There's a very funny story about her and some officer . . . But just look at him! Isn't he a scream, the way he mesmerizes her out of the corner of his eye! My dear chap, that's the Old France for you! I just adore the man: he could quite well say that he's the reason I'm marrying his daughter.'

Mouret laughed, finding this very amusing. He asked Vallagnosc some more questions and when he learned that the first idea of his marriage to Blanche came from Madame Desforges, he thought the story was better than ever. Dear Henriette took a widow's pleasure in marrying people off, so much so that when she had provided for the daughters, she might even on occasion let the fathers choose their mistresses among her acquaintance; but it was all so natural and done in such a proper manner that no one ever found anything scandalous in it. And Mouret, who loved her as a busy, active man who was in the habit of measuring out his affections, put aside any idea of seduction and felt a purely comradely feeling for her.

At that moment, she appeared at the door of the little drawing room, followed by an old man of around sixty, who had come in without the two friends noticing. At times, the ladies' voices took on a shriller note, accompanied by the faint tinkling of spoons in china teacups; and, occasionally, there would be a brief silence in the midst of which you could hear the sound of a saucer put down too heavily on the marble top of the side table. A sudden ray of the setting sun, which had just appeared beside a large cloud, gilded the crowns of the chestnut trees in the garden and streamed through the windows in a dust of red gold, setting the brocading and brass on the furniture ablaze.

'Come over here, my dear Baron,' Madame Desforges was saying. 'Let me introduce you to Monsieur Octave Mouret, who has the most heartfelt desire to express his warmest admiration to you.'

And, turning to Octave, she added:

'Baron Hartmann.'

The old man's lips were drawn in a shrewd smile. He was a small, energetic person, with the large head of a man from Alsace, whose heavy features were lit with a spark of intelligence at every twist of the mouth and every merest flicker of an eyelid. For a fortnight, he had been resisting Henriette's wish for him to meet Octave; it was not that he felt any excessive jealousy, being an intelligent man resigned to his paternal role, but because this was the third of her men friends that Henriette had introduced him to, and in the long run he was rather afraid of looking ridiculous. So as he approached Octave, he gave the quiet chuckle of a rich patron who, while quite ready to be charming, was not willing to be taken for a ride.

'Oh, Monsieur!' Mouret said, with a Provençal's enthusiasm. 'The Crédit Immobilier's last operation was astonishing! You cannot imagine how happy and proud I am to shake your hand.'

'Too kind, too kind,' the Baron said, still smiling.

Henriette looked at them brightly, without a blush. She was standing between them, her pretty head lifted and turning from one to the other; and, in her lace dress, open to reveal her wrists and her delicate neck, she seemed delighted at seeing them get on so well.

'Gentlemen,' she said eventually. 'I'm going to leave you to talk.'

Then, turning to Paul, who had stood up, she asked him: 'Would you like a cup of tea, Monsieur de Vallagnosc?'

'I should indeed, Madame.' And the two of them went back into the drawing room.

When Mouret was seated on the sofa beside Baron Hartmann, he once again expressed his admiration for the way that the Crédit Immobilier was run. Then he turned to the matter that really interested him, which was the new road, an extension of the Rue Réaumur, part of which was to be opened under the name of Rue du Dix-Décembre,[4] between the Place de la Bourse and the Place de l'Opéra. Planning permission had been given eighteen months earlier, the expropriation panel had just been appointed and the whole neighbourhood was excited about this huge thoroughfare, wondering when the work would begin and showing an interest in the condemned houses. Mouret had been waiting for the project for almost three years, at first because he thought it would encourage business, then with an ambition to expand which he did not dare admit openly, because his plans were getting so large. Since the Rue du Dix-Décembre would cut across the Rue de Choiseul and the Rue de la Michodière, he could imagine *Au Bonheur des Dames* spreading into the whole area of housing surrounded by these streets and the Rue Neuve-Saint-Augustin: he could see it already, with a palatial façade on the new street, triumphal, master of a conquered city. And from this came his urgent desire to meet Baron Hartmann, when he learned that the Crédit Immobilier, under a contract with the authorities, had undertaken to demolish the way and lay down the Rue du Dix-Décembre, provided that it was granted ownership of the adjacent sites.

'It is true?' he remarked, trying to appear naive. 'You will hand over the street, ready-made, with its drains, pavements, gas lights? And the adjacent sites will be enough to compensate for the expense? That's fascinating, quite fascinating.'

Finally, he turned to the delicate topic. He had found out that the Crédit Immobilier was secretly buying up the houses in the block that included *Au Bonheur des Dames*, not only the ones that were due to be demolished, but others, too, those that were to be left standing. To him, this hinted at some plan of future rebuilding and he was very concerned for the fate of his own dreams of expansion, fearful that he might one day find himself up against a powerful enterprise, owning buildings which it would certainly not give up. Indeed, it was this anxiety that had made him resolve to establish a link between himself and the Baron, a friendly link through a woman, the kind that is so close between men of an amorous disposition. Of course, he might have gone to see the financier in his office to discuss the proposal that he had to offer him at their ease. But he felt stronger at Henriette's, knowing how the possession of a shared mistress brings men together and softens their hearts. That the two of them should be there, wrapped in her beloved scent, having her to hand ready to persuade them with a smile, seemed to him a guarantee of success.

'Aren't I right in saying that you have bought the former Hôtel

Duvillard, that old building adjoining my store?' he eventually asked, out of the blue.

Baron Hartmann hesitated briefly, then denied it. But, looking him straight in the face, Mouret started to laugh, henceforth playing the role of a decent young man, open in business, hand on heart.

'I say, Monsieur le Baron! Since I have the unexpected honour of meeting you, I have a confession to make . . . Oh, I'm not asking you to let me into your secrets! But I should like to confide my own in you, because I am convinced I could not be entrusting them to a wiser head. In any case, I need your advice and I have been plucking up courage to come and see you for some time.'

Indeed, he did make his confession, starting with his early years and not even disguising the financial crisis that he was experiencing in the midst of his triumph. He covered it all: the successive expansions, profits constantly ploughed back into the business, the money invested by his staff; the firm risking its very existence at each new launch, with all the capital being gambled as though on the turn of a card. However, it was not money that he was asking for, because he had a fanatical faith in his customers. His ambitions were rising and he suggested to the Baron that they should establish a partnership in which the Crédit Immobilier would contribute the huge palace that he could already see in his dreams, while he from his side offered his genius and the business that he had already established. They would assess the respective contributions: nothing seemed to him easier to achieve.

'What are you going to do with your land and your buildings?' he asked insistently. 'No doubt, you must have some idea, but I am sure that your idea is not as good as mine. Think of this: we shall build a shopping arcade on the site, pull down or do up the existing buildings and open the largest store in Paris, an emporium that will make millions.'

And he gave a heartfelt exclamation: 'Oh, if only I could do it without you! But you have everything, now. And then I would never raise the necessary advances . . . Come, we must do a deal! We'll make a killing!'

'My dear sir, how worked up you are getting!' Baron Hartmann said simply. 'What an imagination you have!'

He shook his head, still smiling, making up his mind not to return one confidence for another. The Crédit Immobilier's plan was to set up a rival to the Grand-Hôtel on the Rue du Dix-Décembre, a luxury establishment with a central location that would attract foreign visitors. As it happened, since the hotel was only to occupy the sites on the edge, the Baron might have considered Mouret's idea even so, and come to a deal over the rest of the block, which still represented a huge area. But he had already sponsored two of Henriette's friends and was growing tired of his fine role as a compliant patron. Then, despite the passion for activity that made him open his purse to all young men with intelligence and daring, he was more astonished than beguiled by Mouret's commercial genius. Was this gigantic shop not a rash and fantastic undertaking? Surely, he would be risking certain disaster, trying to expand the ladies' wear business beyond all reasonable measure? In short, he did not believe in it, and refused.

'No doubt,' he said, 'there is something attractive about the notion; but it belongs in the imagination of a poet. Where would you find the customers to fill this commercial cathedral?'

Mouret looked at him for a moment in silence, as though struck dumb by his refusal. Could it be possible? A man with such flair? And suddenly, with a superbly eloquent gesture, he indicated the ladies in the drawing room, exclaiming:

'But there are the customers!'

The sun was fading and the dusting of red gold was now just a pale yellow light, expiring in farewell in the silk of the fabrics and the panels of the furniture. As dusk approached, a feeling of intimacy filled the large room with sweet warmth. While Monsieur de Boves and Paul de Vallagnosc were talking by one of the windows, gazing out over the garden, the ladies had drawn closer together and there, in the middle of the room, made a narrow circle of dresses, out of which rose laughter, whispers, eager questions and answers – all the passion of women for spending money and for fabrics. They were talking clothes and Madame de Boves was describing a ball gown.

'First of all, a transparent dress in mauve silk, with over it flounces of old Alençon lace, thirty centimetres across . . .'

'Oh, would you believe it!' Madame Marty interrupted. 'Some women are lucky!'

Baron Hartmann, having followed Mouret's hand, looked at the ladies through the wide-open door. He continued to listen to them, with one ear, while the young man, spurred on by the urge to convince him, confided further in him, explaining how the ladies' wear business worked nowadays, at a time when it was based on a continuous and rapid renewal of capital, which had to be converted into goods as often as possible in a single year. In that way, in the current year, his capital of only five hundred thousand francs had been converted four times and had thus produced a turnover of two million francs. A pittance, as it happened, which they would increase tenfold, because he insisted that he was certain eventually to turn over the capital fifteen or twenty times in some departments.

'Do you see, Monsieur le Baron, that's how the whole thing works. It's very simple, but someone had to think of it. We don't need great amounts of working capital. We concentrate on getting rid of the merchandise we have bought very fast, allowing us to replace it with more goods, so that the capital earns interest every time. In this way, we can be satisfied with small profits; as our general expenses amount to the huge figure of sixteen per cent and we hardly ever take more than twenty per cent profit on the stock, this means an overall profit of at the most four per cent – yet it will add up to millions when you are dealing with large amounts of goods, constantly replaced . . . You understand, don't you? Nothing could be clearer.'

The Baron shook his head once again. Even though he had welcomed the most daring schemes – people still talked about how ready he had been to take risks when the first gas lights were being tested – yet now he remained uneasy and stubbornly opposed.

'I understand quite well,' he said. 'You sell cheap in order to sell a lot, and you sell a lot in order to sell cheap. But you still have to sell and I come back to my question: to whom will you sell? How do you expect to keep on selling such quantities?'

Mouret's answer was interrupted by a sudden chatter of voices from the drawing room. It was Madame Guibal, who would have preferred the flounces of Alençon only on the front.

'But my dear,' Madame de Boves was saying, 'the front was covered in it, too. I've never seen anything so extravagant.'

'Well, now! You've given me an idea,' said Madame Desforges. 'I've got a few metres of Alençon . . . I must look some out as a trimming.'

And the voices fell until they were no more than a murmur. Figures were flung about, there was some proper bargaining to inflame desires and the ladies bought lace by the handful.

'There, what?' said Mouret when he was able to speak. 'You can sell what you want, when you know how to sell! That's the secret of our success.'

So, with his Provençal's eloquence, using warm language that painted pictures in the mind, he showed how the new sort of trade worked. First of all, there was the hugely increased power of accumulation, with all the merchandise concentrated on one point, each item supporting and promoting the rest. Nothing was ever idle, the season's special item was always there and, from one counter to the next, the customer was entrapped, buying materials here, cotton there, the coat somewhere else, dressing herself, then stumbling across something unexpected and giving way to her need for things that were pretty, but useless. Finally, he praised the system of brands with known prices.[5] The great revolution in ladies' wear had started with this invention. If old-fashioned business and small tradesmen were on their last legs, it was because they could not keep up with price-cutting on marked prices. Nowadays, competition took place under the very eyes of the public: just walking past the shop windows revealed the prices and each shop made reductions, content with the smallest possible profit; there was no trickery, no carefully planned windfall on some material sold at twice its real value, but continuing business, a regular so much per cent on every item and a fortune invested in the smooth running of a sale which was all the greater because it took place in the open. Wasn't this an astonishing invention? It was revolutionizing the market, it was transforming Paris, because it was created out of women's flesh and blood.

'The women are mine, I don't care about the rest!' he said, with brutal honesty, in the heat of the moment.

At this exclamation, Baron Hartmann seemed deeply moved. His smile lost its little ironic twist and he gazed at the young man, progressively won over by his faith and starting to feel almost affectionate towards him.

'Hush!' he murmured, with paternal anxiety. 'They'll hear you.'

But the ladies were now all speaking at once and so excited that they were no longer listening even to one another. Madame de Boves was completing her description of the evening's dresses: a tunic of mauve silk, draped and held by lace bows, the bodice with a very low décolleté and still more lace bows on the shoulders.

'You see,' she said. 'I'm having a similar bodice made for myself with a satin . . .'

'And what I wanted,' Madame Bourdelais interrupted, 'was some velvet – such a bargain!'

Madame Marty asked:

'What? How much was the silk?'

Then, all the voices started up simultaneously. Madame Guibal, Henriette and Blanche were measuring, cutting and throwing aside. It was a pillage of materials, a sacking of shops, a hunger for luxury that gorged itself on dresses, dreamed of and coveted, such a joy in clothes that they lived smothered in chiffon as they did in the warm air they needed to survive.

Mouret, meanwhile, had cast an eye towards the drawing room and, in a few words whispered in Baron Hartmann's ear – as though entrusting him with one of those amorous confidences that men sometimes venture between themselves – he completed his explanation of the system of modern large-scale trading. Here, more significantly than any of the facts he had previously given, at the apex, emerged the exploitation of women. Everything led to this point: the capital which was constantly being renewed, the system of concentrating the merchandise, the low prices to attract the customers, the fixed prices to reassure them. Woman was what the shops were fighting over when they competed, it was woman whom they ensnared with the constant trap of their bargains, after stunning her with their displays. They had aroused new desires in her flesh, they were a huge temptation to which she must fatally succumb, first of all giving in to the purchases of a good housewife, then seduced by vanity and finally consumed. By increasing their sales tenfold and democratizing luxury they became a dreadful agent of expense, causing ravages in households and operating through the madness of fashion, which was constantly more expensive. And if in store woman was queen, adulated in herself, humoured in her weaknesses, surrounded by every little attention, she reigned as a queen in love, whose subjects were swindling her so that she paid for each of her whims with a drop of her own blood. Thus, behind the eloquence of his love of the fair sex, Mouret displayed the brutality of a Jew selling a woman's flesh by the pound: he raised a temple to her, had a legion of servants to perfume her with incense and devised the ritual of a new religion. He thought only of her and sought constantly to invent more powerful means of seduction; and, when her back was turned, when he had emptied her pockets and unhinged her nerves, he was filled with the secret contempt of a man whose mistress has just been stupid enough to give herself to him.

'Just get the women,' he said softly to the Baron, with a suggestive laugh. 'And you will sell the world!'

Now, the Baron had understood. A few sentences were enough, he guessed the rest; but the idea of this sort of amorous exploitation stimulated him and stirred the old rake's past. He winked knowingly and came to admire the inventor of this system for consuming women. It was clever, very clever. He made the same remark as Bourdoncle, drawing on his past experience:

'They'll get their own back, you know.'

But Mouret shrugged his shoulders in a gesture of haughty contempt. They all belonged to him, they were his *thing* and he belonged to none of them. When he had taken his fortune and his pleasure from them, he would cast them aside for anyone who could still derive some profit from them. It was the calculated contempt of a Southerner and a speculator.

'Well, my dear sir,' he asked, in conclusion. 'Do you want to come in with me? Does a deal over the land seem feasible to you?'

The Baron was half won over, but still shrank from committing himself to that extent. The charm which was gradually having its effect on him left a shred of doubt at the back of his mind. He was about to reply with an evasive remark when an urgent call from the ladies spared him the trouble. In the midst of their laughter, voices were calling: 'Monsieur Mouret! Monsieur Mouret!'

And as Mouret, irritated by this interruption, pretended not to have heard them, Madame de Boves, who had been on her feet for a short while, came to the door of the little drawing room.

'They're asking for you, Monsieur Mouret . . . It is quite unmannerly of you to bury yourself away in a corner so that you can talk business.'

At this, with obvious good grace and an air of delight, which astonished the Baron, he obeyed. The two men rose and crossed into the main drawing room.

'But I am at your disposal, Mesdames,' Mouret said, with a smile, as he came in.

He was greeted with a clamour of triumph, and had to go still further into the room, because the ladies were making a place for him among them. The sun had just set behind the trees in the garden, night was falling and a gentle darkness was spreading little by little across the huge drawing room. It was the tender hour of dusk, that minute of discreet sensual pleasure in Parisian apartments, between the dying of the light from outside and the coming of the lamps that the servants are still lighting in the pantry. Monsieur de Boves and Vallagnosc, still standing by one of the windows, cast a pool of shadow on the carpet, while Monsieur Marty, who had slipped in quietly a few minutes before and was now standing motionless in the last ray of light from the other window, exhibited his impoverished profile, his clean, but worn topcoat and the classroom pallor of his face; these ladies' discussion about dresses had left him quite shattered.

'And is the sale for next Monday?' Madame Marty happened to be asking.

'Yes, indeed, Madame,' Mouret replied, in a musical tone, the actor's voice that he put on when speaking to women.

Henriette broke in.

'You know, we'll all be there. I'm told that you have wonderful things prepared for us.'

'Yes, wonderful things,' he said with an air of modest self-satisfaction. 'I simply try to be worthy of the confidence you show in me.'

But they kept questioning him. Madame Bourdelais, Madame Guibal and even Blanche wanted to hear more.

'Come, now, give us some details,' Madame de Boves insisted. 'You're killing us.'

They were gathering round when Henriette pointed out that he had not even had a cup of tea. At this, there was consternation and four of them set about serving him, but only on condition that he would answer their questions. Henriette poured and Madame Marty held the cup, while Madame de Boves and Madame Bourdelais argued over who should have the honour of putting sugar in it. Then, after he had declined to sit and had begun slowly to drink his tea, standing among them, they all came closer, imprisoning him in the circle of their skirts and smiling up at him with heads raised and shining eyes.

'Your silk, your Paris-Bonheur, which all the newspapers are talking about?' Madame Marty said impatiently.

'Ah!' he replied. 'An extraordinary line, a coarse-grained silk which is sturdy and supple . . . You'll see, ladies. And ours is the only place where you can find it, because we have purchased exclusive rights to it.'

'Really! A fine silk at five francs sixty!' Madame Bourdelais said enthusiastically. 'It's incredible.'

Since the publicity for it had started, this silk had played a considerable role in their daily lives. They spoke about it and promised it to themselves, driven by desires and doubts. And, behind the talkative curiosity that they heaped upon the young man, one could distinguish the peculiar temperament of each one as a shopper: Madame Marty, carried away by her passion for spending, taking everything in *Au Bonheur des Dames*, without discrimination, as she chanced to encounter the displays; Madame Guibal, strolling around for hours without ever making a purchase, happy and contented at simply giving her eyes a treat; Madame de Boves, stretched for cash, constantly tortured by excessive desires and bearing a grudge against goods that she could not take away with her; Madame Bourdelais, with a sensible and practical bourgeois flair which took her straight to a bargain, using department stores with the skill of such a good housewife, quite dispassionate, that she made considerable savings out of them; and, finally, Henriette who, with her high dress sense, only bought certain items there: gloves, hosiery, household linen.

'We have other materials, amazing bargains, astonishingly good quality,' Mouret went on in his singsong voice. 'For example, I recommend our Cuir-d'Or, a taffeta of incomparable sheen . . . In fancy silks, we have some delightful arrangements, with designs picked from hundreds by our buyer; and, when it comes to velvet, you will find the fullest possible range of tones . . . I must warn you that people will be wearing woollens a lot this year. You must see our quilted materials and our Cheviots.'

They no longer interrupted, but pressed still closer in around him, mouths half open in a faint smile, their faces bent forward, as though their whole being was craning towards the tempter. Their eyes paled and a light shudder ran across their necks. And he maintained the calm of a conqueror, amid the unsettling scents that rose from their hair. He continued to take a little sip of tea between each sentence, and its perfume cooled that of those other, more pungent scents in which there was a hint of animal musk. Baron Hartmann, his eyes fixed on Mouret, and confronted with a self-possessed seduction which was strong enough to manipulate women in this way without succumbing to the intoxicating charms that they exhaled, felt his admiration grow.

'So we'll be wearing woollens?' Madame Marty said, her ravaged features softened by the eagerness of her vanity. 'That I must see.'

Madame Bourdelais, not dazzled by all this, took her turn to say: 'So must I. Your remnant sale is on Thursday . . . I'll wait; I've got the whole family to clothe.'

And, turning her elegant blonde head towards the mistress of the house: 'Does Sauveur still dress you?'

'Good heavens, yes!' Henriette replied. 'Sauveur is very expensive but she's the only person in Paris who knows how to make a bodice . . . And then, whatever Monsieur Mouret says, she has the prettiest designs, prints that you don't see anywhere else. I simply can't bear to see every woman around wearing my dress.'

At first, Mouret gave a quiet smile. Then he gave them to understand that Madame Sauveur bought her materials from him. Of course, she did get certain designs directly from the manufacturers, reserving the rights for herself, but when it came to black silks, for example, she waited for a bargain to come up at *Au Bonheur des Dames*, then bought up a considerable amount of it which she resold at two or three times the price.

'That's why I'm quite sure that her people will take our Paris-Bonheur. Why should she go to the manufacturer and buy it for more than she would have to pay us? On my honour, we're selling at a loss.'

For the ladies, this was the *coup de grâce*. The idea of having the merchandise at a loss stirred the callous side of their feminine nature, which means that a woman's pleasure in buying something is doubled when she thinks she is robbing the person who sells it to her. He knew that they were unable to resist a bargain.

'But we're selling everything for nothing!' he exclaimed merrily, picking up Madame Desforges' fan which was behind him on the little table. 'Here! What about this fan . . . How much would you say?'

'The lace twenty-five francs and the mounting two hundred,' said Henriette.

'Well, the Chantilly lace is not expensive, though we have the same at eighteen francs . . . As for the mount, my dear lady, it's a frightful theft. I shouldn't dare to sell one like it at more than ninety francs.'

'I told you so!' cried Madame Bourdelais.

'Ninety francs!' muttered Madame de Boves. 'You'd really have to be penniless to miss such an opportunity.'

She took the fan and was examining it once again with her daughter Blanche; and into her great regular features, into her wide sleepy eyes, rose the desperate, repressed desire that she could not satisfy, for some whim. The fan was now passed for a second time around the ladies, accompanied by comments and exclamations. Monsieur de Boves and Vallagnosc, meanwhile, had left the window. The former came and stood behind Madame Guibal, running his eyes across her bodice – in his prim, superior manner – while the young man leaned over Blanche, trying to find something agreeable to say to her.

'It's a trifle sad, don't you think, Mademoiselle, that white mount with the black lace?'

'Oh! I've seen one in mother of pearl and white feathers,' she said, solemnly, without the trace of a blush on her puffy cheeks. 'Something quite virginal.'

Monsieur de Boves, who had doubtless caught the covetous look with which his wife's eyes were following the fan, finally made his contribution to the conversation.

'They break so easily, those little things.'

'Don't tell me about it!' that handsome redhead Madame Guibal said with a pout, pretending not to care. 'I'm quite sick of having mine stuck back together.'

For some while, Madame Marty, getting very worked up by the conversation, had been fiddling madly with the red leather bag on her knees. She had not yet been able to show off her purchases and she was tormented by a sort of sensual need to expose them to view. Suddenly, forgetting her husband, she opened the bag and brought out a few metres of narrow lace wound round a cardboard tube.

'Here's the Valenciennes for my daughter,' she said. 'It's three centimetres wide and delightful, don't you think? One franc ninety.'

The lace passed from hand to hand. The ladies let out exclamations. Mouret remarked that he sold such small trimmings at the manufacturer's cost price. Meanwhile, Madame Marty had closed the bag, as one does to hide things that should not be displayed. But seeing the success of the Valenciennes, she could not resist the temptation to pull out a handkerchief.

'There was this handkerchief, too. Brussels work, my dears. Oh, a real find! Twenty francs.'

After which, the bag became inexhaustible. She blushed with pleasure, the modesty of a woman unclothing herself made her charming and self-conscious, at each new item that she brought out. There was a cravat in Spanish bobbin-lace for thirty francs; she hadn't wanted it but the assistant swore to her that the one she was holding was the last and that the price was about to go up. After that, there was a small veil in Chantilly, rather dear at fifty francs, but if she didn't wear it, she would make something out of it for her daughter.

'My, oh my! Lace is so pretty!' she kept saying, with a nervous smile. 'When I get in there, I could buy the whole shop.'

'And this?' asked Madame de Boves, studying a remnant of guipure.[6]

'That,' she replied, 'is for an insert. There are twenty-six metres – at one franc a metre: do you see?'

'Well, I never!' said Madame Bourdelais in surprise. 'What can you do with it?'

'Heavens, what do I know? But the pattern was so amusing.'

At that moment, she looked up to see her husband's horrified face in front of her. He had gone even paler and his whole body expressed the resigned anguish of a poor man watching his hard-earned salary withering away before him. Each new piece of lace was a disaster for him: bitter days of teaching swallowed up, humiliating searches for extra work thrown away and the constant effort of his life amounting to this concealed torment, the hell of a needy household. Confronted with the growing terror in his eyes, she tried to take back the handkerchief, the little veil, the cravat, her hands darting about feverishly, while she repeated, with an embarrassed laugh:

'My husband will be telling me off . . . I promise you, dearest, that I was very sensible, because there was a large mantilla for five hundred francs which was, oh, truly wonderful!'

'Why didn't you buy it, then?' Madame Guibal asked calmly. 'Monsieur Marty is the most gracious of men.'

The teacher was forced to bow and say that his wife was quite free to do as she pleased. But the mere thought of the danger of this large mantilla had sent a shiver down his spine; and, when Mouret just happened to be saying that department stores increased the well-being of middle-class households, he gave him a fearsome look, the flash of hatred from a timid man who would not dare to strangle somebody.

In any case, the ladies had not let go of the lace. They were intoxicated by it. The pieces were unwrapped, and passed back and forth, making the circle tighter still, linking the ladies with slender threads. On their knees, they felt the caress of a miraculously fine cloth and their guilty fingers lingered on it. They were hemming Mouret in more closely, bombarding him with fresh questions. As the light was still fading, there were times when he had to bend forward, let his beard lightly touch their hair, so that he could examine a piece of needlework or point out a design. But, in this soft sensuous dusk, surrounded by the warm scent rising off their shoulders, he still remained their master, for all the rapture that he feigned. He was Woman: they felt penetrated and possessed by that delicate sense he had of their innermost beings, and they abandoned themselves, seduced by him; while he, now certain that he had them at his mercy, enthroned as conqueror above them, seemed like the despotic clothing king.

'Oh, Monsieur Mouret! Oh, Monsieur Mouret!' murmured whispering, swooning voices out of the darkness of the room.

The dying whiteness of the sky was extinguished on the bronze fittings on the furniture. Only the lace preserved a snowy glimmer on the dark knees of the ladies, a confused mass that seemed to surround the young man with half-visible, kneeling devotees. A last gleam of light shone on the side of the tea pot, the brief, bright glow of a night-light burning in an alcove, warmed by the scent of tea. Then, suddenly, a servant came in with two lamps and the charm was broken. The drawing room awoke, bright and merry. Madame Marty put the lace back at the bottom of her little bag; Madame de Boves was eating one last rum baba; and Henriette, who had stood up, was speaking in low tones to the Baron, in the recess by a window.

'He is charming,' said the Baron.

'Yes, isn't he?' she let slip, with the involuntary exclamation of a woman in love.

He smiled and looked at her with paternal indulgence. This was the first time that he had felt her so deeply attracted; and, while he was above experiencing any pain at this, he did feel compassion at seeing her in the hands of this gentle, but entirely cold young man. For that reason, he felt he should warn her and murmured, in a light-hearted tone of voice: 'Take care, my sweet, he will devour you all.'

A flame of jealousy lit Henriette's lovely eyes. No doubt, she had guessed that Mouret was merely using her to approach the Baron, so she swore that she would make him crazy with affection for her – he whose love was that of a busy man and had the facile charm of a song carried away by the breeze.

'Oh, no!' she said, pretending to be joking in her turn. 'It's always the lamb which ends up eating the wolf.'

Very interested by this remark, the Baron encouraged her with a nod. Here perhaps was the woman who was destined to come and avenge all the rest.

When Mouret, after repeating to Vallagnosc that he would like to show him his machine in full swing, came up to bid them farewell, the Baron kept him back in the window recess, overlooking the darkness of the garden. He was finally giving in to the seducer, he had found faith, seeing him in the midst of all those ladies. The two men spoke in hushed voices for a moment. Then the banker declared:

'Very well, I shall look into the matter. If your sale on Monday reaches the figure that you expect, then we have a deal.'

They shook hands and Mouret, with a delighted look, took his leave; because he did not digest his dinner properly unless he could go every evening and review the day's takings at *Au Bonheur des Dames.*

CHAPTER 4

That Monday, 10 October, a bright sun victoriously broke through the grey clouds that had been hanging over Paris for the previous week. All night, a drizzle of fine rain had continued to make the streets damp and dirty; but at first light the pavements were swept by the fresh breeze that carried the clouds away and the blue sky had a joyful, spring-like clarity.

So it was that, from eight o'clock, *Au Bonheur des Dames* blazed under this bright sunlight, in all the glory of its great winter sale. Flags fluttered by the door, while woollens flapped in the crisp morning air, rousing the Place Gaillon with the clatter of a fairground and along both streets the windows composed symphonies of displays, their shining hues enhanced by the polished glass. It was like a riot of colour, a joy of the street bursting out here, in this wide open shopping corner where everyone could go and feast their eyes.

At this hour, however, few people were going in, only a few busy customers, housewives from the neighbourhood or women wishing to avoid the afternoon crush. The shop felt empty behind the lengths of cloth that bedecked it, armed and ready for action, with its waxed floors and counters overflowing with goods. The morning crowd, hurrying by without slowing down, hardly glanced at the shop windows. In the Rue Neuve-Saint-Augustin and the Place Gaillon, where the carriages would park, there were, by nine o'clock, just two cabs. Only the inhabitants of the neighbourhood, especially small trades people, roused by this display of banners and plumes, were gathering in groups by the doors and at the corners, looking up and passing bitter comments. Their indignation was excited by one of the four vans that Mouret had recently launched in Paris which was standing in the Rue de la Michodière in front of the despatch office. These vans were painted green, with yellow and red trim, and highly varnished panels that shone gold and purple in the sunlight. This particular example, in its brand new paintwork, emblazoned with the name of the shop on each of its four sides and additionally capped by a placard announcing the day's sale, eventually set off at a trot, drawn by a magnificent horse, when they had finished loading it with the parcels left over from the previous day. And Baudu, the colour draining from his face as he stood at the door of the *Vieil Elbeuf*, watched it drive off as far as the boulevard, parading the hated name of *Au Bonheur des Dames* around the town in starry radiance.

Meanwhile, a few cabs arrived and took their place in the line. Whenever a customer appeared, there was a movement in the group of boys under the main door of the shop who were dressed in livery: jacket and trousers of light green, a striped yellow and red waistcoat. The old retired captain, Inspector Jouve, was there, too, with his decoration, like a time-worn token of honest dealing, greeting the ladies with solemn courtesy and stooping to point out the departments. Then, they vanished into the hall, which had been converted into an oriental salon.

So, each and every one, as she entered, was carried away in wonder and surprise. This was Mouret's idea. He had been the first to buy a collection of old and new carpets in the Near East, at a very favourable price – those rare carpets that, until then, only antique dealers sold for high price; and he was going to flood the market with them, selling them almost at cost, simply so that he could create a splendid décor that would attract real connoisseurs to the shop. This oriental salon could be seen from the centre of the Place Gaillon; it was composed solely of carpets and door-curtains which some men had put up according to Mouret's directions. Firstly, hanging from the ceiling, were Smyrna carpets with complex patterns picked out on a red background. Then, on all four sides, were door-curtains – door-curtains from Kerman and Syria, striped with green, yellow and vermilion; coarser door-curtains from Diarbekir, rough to the touch, like a shepherd's cloak; and still more carpets which could be used as wall hangings, long carpets from Isphahan, Tehran and Kermanshah, the wider carpets of Shumaka or Madras, strange flowerings of peonies and palms where the imagination was let loose in the garden of dreams. On the floor, which was strewn with thick fleeces, there were more carpets: in the centre, an Agra, an astonishing piece with a wide, soft blue border against a white background, on which were exquisitely imagined patterns in a blueish violet. After that, wonders were displayed on all sides: velvet-sheened carpets from Mecca, prayer carpets from Daghestan with symbolic designs, carpets from Kurdistan spread with blossoming flowers. Finally, in a corner, there was a cut-price heap of carpets from Gurdis, Kula and Kircheer, starting at fifteen francs. This sumptuous pasha's tent was furnished with chairs and divans, made out of camelhair bags, some ornamented with particoloured diamond shapes and others with naive pictures of roses. Here were Turkey, Arabia, Persia and India: palaces had been emptied, mosques and bazaars ransacked. Tawny gold was the dominant hue in the old worn carpets where the faded colours preserved a dark warmth like the residue of a burnt-out furnace, the fine, deep shade of an old master painting. Visions of the East hovered beneath the extravagance of this savage art amid the strong scent that this ancient wool had kept from lands of sun and vermin.

At eight o'clock in the morning that Monday, the day when Denise happened to be starting work, she crossed the oriental salon and remained thunderstruck, no longer recognizing the entrance to the store and losing what remained of her composure in this harem right in front of the door. After a boy had led her up to the attic floor and handed her over to Madame Cabin, who was in charge of cleaning and looking after the employees' rooms, this lady settled her into number seven, where someone had already brought up her trunk. It was a narrow cell with a mansard ceiling opening on the roof through a skylight and furnished with a little bed, a walnut cupboard, a dressing-table and two chairs. Twenty similar rooms extended along a monastic corridor, painted yellow; and here lodged the twenty out of the thirty-five young ladies in the store who had no family in Paris, while the remaining fifteen stayed outside, some with occasional aunts or cousins. At once, Denise took off the thin woollen dress, worn with brushing and darned at the elbows, which was the only one she had brought from Valognes, and put on the uniform of her department, a dress of black silk, altered to fit her, which had been left on her bed. It was still a little big, too wide across the shoulders. But she was so agitated that she hurried on without her vanity hesitating over such details. She had never before worn silk. When she went downstairs again, done up in her new finery – and awkward about it – she was aware of the skirt shining and felt ashamed at the noisy rustling of the material.

Downstairs as she came into the department, a row was going on. She heard Clara saying in a shrill voice:

'Madame, I was here before her!'

'That's not true,' Marguerite retorted. 'She pushed past me at the door, but I already had my foot inside.'

All this revolved around who should come first on the order board, which determined who served the first customer. The sales girls wrote their names on a slate, in the order in which they arrived; and each time one of them had a customer, she put her name back at the bottom of the list. Madame Aurélie eventually took the side of Marguerite.

'It's always so unfair!' Clara muttered angrily.

But the two young ladies were reconciled by the arrival of Denise. They looked at her and exchanged a smile. Just look how she was turned out! The girl went awkwardly to put her name at the bottom of the order board, while Madame Aurélie scrutinized her, pursing her lips. She felt obliged to say:

'My dear, two of you would fit into that dress. You'll have to have it taken in . . . And what's more, you don't know how to dress yourself. Come here and let me tidy you up a bit.'

She led her in front of one of the tall mirrors which alternated with the panelled doors of the cupboards where they kept the clothes. The huge room, surrounded by these mirrors and this carved oak woodwork, trimmed with red moquette in a large pattern of leaves, looked like the plain drawing room of a hotel, in which guests were constantly crossing back and forth. The young ladies added to the impression, dressed in their silk uniforms and behaving in their most alluring manner, while never sitting down on the dozen or so chairs which were reserved for customers alone. Each of them had a large pencil sticking up with its point in the air between two buttons on her bodice, as though piercing her breast; and one could see, half emerging from a pocket, the white shape of the credit-note book. Several of them had ventured to put on jewellery: rings, brooches, chains; but, in the uniformity imposed by their clothing, their vanity and the one extravagance in which they tried to rival one another, was their hair, uncovered, luxuriant, supplemented by plaits and chignons if not sufficient in itself, combed, curled and paraded.

'Pull in the belt at the front,' Madame Aurélie was saying. 'There, at least you don't have a hump at the back. And your hair: how can you make such a mess of it! If you wanted, it could be splendid.'

Indeed, her hair was Denise's only attractive feature. Ash blonde in colour, it fell to her ankles; and when she was doing it up, it was so awkward that she would merely roll it around and pin it up in a bun, held by the strong teeth of a horn comb. Clara was most put out by this hair and pretended to find it funny, so clumsily was it fixed, in its wild beauty. She had motioned to a sales girl from lingerie to come over, a girl with a broad face and pleasant manner. The two departments were adjacent and at constant war with each other, but the young ladies might sometimes reach an understanding if it was to make fun of people.

'Mademoiselle Cugnot, just look at that great mane of hair,' said Clara, while Marguerite elbowed her, also pretending to be choking with laughter.

However, the girl from lingerie did not feel like joking. She had been looking at Denise for a while and remembered what she herself had to endure for the first months in her department.

'So what?' she said. 'Not everyone has a mane like that!'

And she went back to lingerie, leaving the other two slightly put out. Denise, who had heard this, followed her with a grateful look while Madame Aurélie gave her a credit-note book in her name saying: 'Come, now, tomorrow you must get yourself up better . . . For now, just try to learn the routine of the shop and wait for your turn to sell. Today is going to be a hard one, so we can see what you're made of.'

Yet the department was empty: few customers came up to ladies' wear at this early hour. The young ladies were conserving their energy, standing straight, moving slowly, getting ready for the exhaustion of the afternoon. So Denise, cowed by the idea that they were all watching her debut, sharpened her pencil, to have something to do; then, like the others, she stuck it into her breast between two buttonholes. She commanded herself to be bold, because she had to make her way here. The day before, they had told her that she would be joining the firm *au pair*, which meant without a fixed salary: she would have only the percentage and commission on whatever she sold. But she hoped to reach twelve hundred francs, because she knew that a good assistant could go as high as two thousand when she tried. Her budget was worked out: a hundred francs a month would allow her to pay Pépé's rent and to keep Jean who was not earning, and she could buy some clothes and linen for herself. However, if she was to achieve such a high figure, she would have to be strong and hard-working, not arouse resentments around her, stick up for herself and, if necessary, tear her share away from her companions. As she was nerving herself for the fight, a tall young man, walking past the department, smiled at her; and when she recognized Deloche, who had joined the day before in the lace department, she smiled back, happy at finding a friend and seeing his greeting as a good omen.

At half past nine a bell rang for the first session of lunch, then a fresh peal called the second session. The customers had still not appeared. Madame Frédéric, the under-buyer and a widow of unbending pessimism who enjoyed looking on the dark side, briefly swore that the sale was a disaster: they would see no more than four cats, they could close up their cupboards and go home. This prediction cast a cloud over the dull face of Marguerite, ever eager to make money, while Clara, who had the manner of a bolted horse, was already dreaming of an eligible party in the Bois de Verrières, should the store collapse. As for Madame Aurélie, silent and unsmiling, she paraded her Caesar's mask around the empty department like a general accepting responsibility for victory or defeat.

At around eleven o'clock, a few ladies appeared. Denise's turn came to sell and a customer was announced.

'The fat provincial, you know,' Marguerite murmured.

She was a woman of forty-five who came very occasionally to Paris from the depths of some remote *département*. There, for months on end, she would put her money aside; and no sooner was she out of the train than she would rush to *Au Bonheur des Dames* and spend everything. Only very seldom did she order by post, because she wanted to see, to have the joy of touching the goods and even going so far as to stock up on needles which, according to her, cost a fortune in her little town. The whole shop was acquainted with her, knew that she was called Madame Boutarel and that she lived in Albi, without bothering about the rest, what or who she was.

'Are you well, Madame?' Madame Aurélie asked graciously coming over to her. 'And what would you like? We shall be with you immediately.'

Then she turned round and called: 'Girls!'

Denise was going over, but Clara had dashed in front of her. She was usually quite lazy about selling and not bothered about money since she earned more elsewhere, with less effort. However, she was spurred on by the idea of snatching a good customer from the new girl.

'Excuse me, it's my turn,' said Denise, in disgust.

Madame Aurélie sent her back with a stern look and muttered: 'There are no turns, I'm the only boss here . . . Just wait until you know something before you serve a regular customer.'

Denise shrank back, the tears rising to her eyes, but, wanting to hide this excessive sensitivity, she turned her back and stood in front of the plate-glass window, pretending to look into the street. Were they going to stop her from selling? Perhaps they were conspiring together to deprive her of any serious sales. She was seized by a fear of the future and felt herself crushed by so many unbridled interests. Giving way to the bitterness of her rejection, her forehead against the cold window pane, she looked across at the *Vieil Elbeuf*, and thought that she should perhaps have begged her uncle to keep her; perhaps he too wished to go back on his decision, because he had seemed very upset to her on the previous day. Now she was all alone in this huge place where no one liked her and she felt lost and wounded. Pépé and Jean, who had never been away from her before, were living with strangers. It was a wrench, and the two big tears that she was holding back were making her see the street through a mist.

All this time, there was a hum of voices behind her.

'This one clumps me up,' Madame Boutarel was saying.

'Madame is wrong,' Clara said. 'The shoulders are perfect . . . Unless, of course, Madame would prefer a pelisse to a coat.'

But Denise shuddered. A hand was placed on her arm and Madame Aurélie was admonishing her severely.

'So now you're not doing anything but watch the world go by? Oh, no, this is just not good enough!'

'But since I'm not allowed to sell, Madame.'

'There's plenty of other work to do, my girl. Begin at the beginning. Put the clothes back in the cupboards.'

In order to satisfy the few customers who had arrived, they had already had to turn the cupboards upside-down and, to the left and the right of the room, on the two long oak tables, there was a jumble of coats, pelisses, cloaks and other clothes of every size and material. Without answering, Denise started to fold them carefully and arrange them back in their cupboards. This was the most lowly beginner's work. She made no further protest, knowing that what was demanded was passive obedience and waiting for the buyer to let her sell something, as she had at first seemed prepared to do. She was still folding when Mouret appeared. It was a shock for her, she blushed and felt herself succumbing to her strange fear when she thought he might speak to her. But he didn't even notice her, no longer recalling this little girl whom he had backed up because of a momentary impression of charm.

'Madame Aurélie!' he called curtly.

He was slightly pale, though his eyes were clear and resolved. Going round the departments, he had just found them empty and suddenly the possibility of a disaster had reared its head, despite his stubborn faith in luck. Admittedly, it was barely eleven o'clock and he knew from experience that the crowds only came in the afternoon. But there were other disturbing signs: at previous sales, there had been some activity even in the morning, but now he could not even see the women with no hats, the customers from the surrounding streets who came along as neighbours. Like all great commanders on the point of commencing battle, he had been seized with a superstitious weakness, despite his usual quality as a man of action. It was not going to work, he was lost and he could not say why; he thought he could read his defeat on the very faces of the women walking past.

And, in point of fact, Madame Boutarel, who always bought something, was going, with the parting remark:

'No, you haven't anything that I like . . . I'll see, I'll have to make up my mind.'

Mouret watched her go. And, when Madame Aurélie ran to answer his call, he took her to one side and they exchanged a few brief words. She gave a despairing gesture, clearly telling him that the sale was not catching. For a moment they stayed face to face, overcome by the kind of doubts that generals hide from their men. Then, he said aloud, in his rousing voice:

'If you need more people, take a girl from the workshop . . . She might be able to help a bit.'

In despair, he went on with his inspection. He had been avoiding Bourdoncle since the morning, irritated by the other man's anxious remarks; but he ran into him coming out of lingerie, where business was even less brisk, and had to endure all his misgivings. At this, he told him frankly to go to hell, with a savagery that did not even spare his closest colleagues when things were bad.

'Leave me alone! Everything's all right . . . I'll be kicking out the lily-livered among you before long.'

Mouret took up his stand, alone, by the hall banisters. From here he could oversee the whole shop, with the mezzanine counters around him and the ground-floor departments down below. Upstairs, the emptiness bothered him: in lace, an old woman was having all the boxes brought out, without buying anything, while three good-for-nothings, in lingerie, were spending an age over some collars for less than a franc. Downstairs, under the covered galleries, in the shafts of light coming in from the street, he noticed that the customers were starting to become more numerous. There was a slow procession, a stroll along the counters, patchy, full of gaps. Women in tight jackets were crowding into haberdashery and hosiery, but there was almost no one in linen and woollens. The boys, in their green coats and big shiny buttons, were simply waiting, with their hands dangling at their sides. From time to time, an inspector passed by, stiff and ceremonious in his white tie. But Mouret's heart bled chiefly at the sight of the dead silence of the hall: the light was falling on it from above, through a frosted glass roof which diffused the light into a white dust and seemed to leave it in suspension above an apparently sleeping silk counter, in the midst of the chill silence of a chapel. A clerk walking past, some whispered words or the rustling of a passing skirt, broke it with only minute sounds, muffled by the heat from the boiler. However, carriages were drawing up: one could hear the horses coming to a sudden stop, and the sound of doors slamming. From outside, came a distant rumble of noise, from inquisitive passers-by pushing and shoving in front of the windows, cabs parking on the Place Gaillon and all the movement of an approaching crowd. But when he saw the idle cashiers leaning back in their chairs and noted that the packing tables remained empty, with their boxes of string and reams of blue paper, Mouret, indignant at being nervous, thought he could feel his great machine coming to rest and going cold beneath him.

'I say, Favier,' Hutin muttered. 'Look at the boss, up there. He doesn't look as though he's enjoying himself.'

'What a lousy dump this is!' Favier replied. 'Just think: I haven't sold a thing yet!'

The two of them, keeping an eye out for customers, conversed in short sentences, without looking at one another. The other staff in the department were piling up lengths of Paris-Bonheur, under Robineau's orders, while Bouthemont, deeply engaged in conversation with a thin young woman, seemed to be taking an important order in a hushed voice. Around them, on shelves of fragile elegance, the silks, wrapped in long sleeves of cream paper, were piled like booklets of some unusual shape. Then, cluttering the counters, fancy silks, moires, satins and velvets resembled beds of cut flowers, a harvest of delicate and precious materials. This was the really elegant department, a veritable salon in which the goods, light as air, were like its luxurious furnishings.

'I must have a hundred francs for Sunday,' Hutin went on. 'If I don't average my twelve francs a day, I'm done for . . . I was counting on this sale of theirs.'

'Crikey! A hundred francs is a bit steep,' said Favier. 'I'll be happy with fifty or sixty . . . Are you buying classy women now, then?'

'No, old chap, I'm not. But I did something silly: I made a bet and I lost. So I've got to buy dinner for five people, two men and three women. What a ghastly morning! The first woman that goes by, I'll flatten her with twenty metres of Paris-Bonheur!'

They continued chatting for a while longer, saying what they had done the day before and what they intended to do next week. Favier bet on the horses, Hutin went boating and entertained girls who sang in cafés. But they were driven by a similar need for money, they thought only of money, they struggled for money from Monday to Saturday, then they spent it all on Sunday. In the shop, this was their driving thought, a struggle without quarter or pity. And that sly fellow Bouthemont had just grabbed for himself the messenger from Madame Sauveur, the thin woman who was chatting with him! A fine catch, two or three dozen items, because the great dressmaker bought in bulk. And a moment ago, Robineau had also done Favier out of a customer!

'We'll have to get even with that one!' said Hutin, taking advantage of the slightest thing to turn the department against the man whose job he was after. 'Is it right for buyers and under-buyers to be selling? On my word, my friend, if I were ever to become an under-buyer, you see how well I'd treat you all.'

And every fibre of his small Norman body, plump and friendly, was devoted to an energetic display of good-naturedness. Favier could not restrain himself from a sidelong glance, but he remained phlegmatic in his bilious way and merely answered:

'Yes, I know . . . I couldn't wish for anything better.'

Then, seeing a lady coming their way, he added in a lower voice:

'Look out! Here's one for you.'

It was a florid woman with a yellow hat and red dress. Hutin immediately guessed that she was not going to be a customer. He quickly dipped below the counter, pretending to tie up his shoelaces and, from his hiding-place, snarled:

'Oh, no! Not likely! Let someone else take her on. Thanks very much – and waste my turn!'

Meanwhile, Robineau was calling for him:

'Who's first, gentlemen? Is it Monsieur Hutin? Where is Monsieur Hutin?'

When Hutin stubbornly refused to reply, the next assistant in line got the florid lady. And, sure enough, all she wanted were some samples with prices. She kept the assistant for more than ten minutes, plying him with questions. But the under-buyer had seen Hutin get up from behind the counter, so when a new customer arrived, he stepped in severely and stopped the young man, who was hurrying up to serve her.

'Your turn has gone. I called you and since you were behind there . . .'

'But, Monsieur, I didn't hear you.'

'That's enough! Put yourself down at the end. So, Monsieur Favier, it's your turn.'

Favier, who was secretly very amused by the whole episode, gave his friend an apologetic look. Hutin, his lips pale, had turned away. What infuriated him was that he knew the customer well, a delightful blonde who often came to the department and whom the assistants among themselves referred to as 'the pretty woman', not knowing anything about her, not even her name. She bought a lot, had it taken to her carriage, then vanished. Tall, elegant, but with exquisite charm, she appeared to be very rich and to belong to the best society.

'So, what about your trollop?' Hutin asked Favier when he came back from the cash-desk where he had taken the lady.

'Trollop, no,' he said. 'She's too smart. She must be the wife of a stockbroker or a doctor – anyway, I don't know, something of the sort.'

'Forget it! She's a trollop. Who can tell nowadays with the distinguished airs they put on!'

Favier looked at his credit-note book.

'Who cares!' he said. 'I took her for two hundred and ninety-six francs. That gives me nearly three francs.'

Hutin scowled and vented his anger on the credit-note books – another silly idea for cluttering up their pockets! There was a silent struggle going on between them. Normally, Favier pretended to take second place, recognizing Hutin's superiority, while secretly undermining him. So Hutin keenly felt those three francs made so easily by a salesman whom he considered inferior to himself. A fine day, indeed! If it went on like this, he would not make enough to buy seltzer water for his guests. And as the battle heated up, he walked back and forth in front of the counters, teeth sharpened, wanting his share of the spoils and jealous even of his boss, who was leading the thin young lady off, saying:

'That's understood. I shall do all I can to obtain this favour from Monsieur Mouret.'

It was already some time since Mouret had left the mezzanine, where he stood near the banister overlooking the hall. Suddenly, he appeared at the top of the main staircase leading down to the ground floor and from here he still dominated the whole shop. The colour was returning to his face and his confidence was returning, making him taller at the sight of the crowd of people gradually filling the store. Here at last was the rush he had been expecting, the afternoon crush which, for a short time in his anxiety, he had thought would never come. The staff were all at their posts and a final bell had sounded the end of the third session for lunch. They might still recover from the disastrous morning, which had no doubt been due to a shower that fell around nine o'clock, because the sky had resumed its bright hue of victory. Now the mezzanine-floor departments were livening up and he had to step aside to let the ladies go by in little groups on their way up to lingerie and ladies' wear, while behind him, in lace and shawls, he could hear large figures being called. But what mainly reassured him was the sight of the galleries on the ground floor: there was a crush in front of haberdashery, even linens and woollens were swamped and the line of customers had closed up, almost all of them now wearing hats,[1] with a few bonnets of late-coming housewives. In the silk hall, under the pale light, ladies had removed their gloves so that they could gently feel the lengths of Paris-Bonheur while talking quietly to one another. And he was not mistaken in the sounds coming from outside, carriage wheels, slamming doors and the swelling hubbub of the crowd. He could feel the machine start working beneath his feet, warming up, reviving, from the cash-desks with the ringing of gold, to the tables where the boys were rushing to pack up the goods, and right down to the basement, in the despatch department, which was filling with parcels that had been sent down and shaking the whole building with its subterranean rumbling. In the midst of the bustle, Inspector Jouve was walking solemnly up and down, keeping an eye open for thieves.

'Why, it's you!' Mouret exclaimed suddenly, recognizing Paul de Vallagnosc, whom a boy was bringing to him. 'No, no, you're not disturbing me . . . And in any case, if you want to see everything you have only to follow me, because today I'm manning the fort.'

He was still anxious. Certainly, people were coming, but would the sale be the triumph they hoped? Even so, he laughed with Paul and led him off merrily.

'It looks as though it's warming up a bit,' Hutin told Favier. 'Only, I've got no luck. There are some days like that, by Jove! I've just scored another zero, that bitch didn't buy a thing from me.'

And he nodded towards a lady who was leaving, curling her nose at all the materials. He would not get fat on his thousand francs' salary if he sold nothing. Normally, he made seven or eight francs in percentage and commission which, with his fixed earnings, gave him around ten francs a day on average. Favier never got beyond eight, and now the blighter was snatching the best bits from his plate, because he had just sold another dress – a cold fish, who never did learn to butter up a customer! It was infuriating!

'The bonneteers and bobbineers seem to be raking it in,' muttered Favier, referring to the staff in hosiery and haberdashery.

But Hutin, who had been casting an eye around the store, suddenly said:

'Do you know Madame Desforges, the boss's girlfriend? That's her: the brunette in the glove department who's trying on some gloves with Mignot.'

He fell silent before resuming in a low voice, as though speaking to Mignot and keeping his eyes fixed on him:

'That's right, old chap, give her fingers a good rub, and see how far it gets you! We know about your conquests!'

There was rivalry between him and the assistant on the glove counter, both handsome men who pretended to flirt with their customers. Actually, neither one could boast of any real success. Mignot lived on the myth of a police commissioner's wife who was supposed to have fallen in love with him, while Hutin really had made the conquest of a lace trimmer who was tired of hanging around the low-class hotels in the neighbourhood. But they lied, giving the impression that they were involved in mysterious affairs, making rendezvous with countesses between sales.

'You should have her,' said Favier, poker-faced.

'That's a thought!' Hutin exclaimed. 'If she comes over here, I'll twist her round my finger – I need five francs!'

In the glove department a whole line of ladies were seated in front of the narrow counter covered in green baize, with nickel corners. And the smiling assistants were heaping in front of them the flat, bright pink boxes which they extracted from the counter itself, like the labelled drawers of a filing cabinet. Mignot in particular leaned over with his pretty doll-like face, cooing softly in his Parisian voice, with its rolled *r*s. He had already sold Madame Desforges a dozen pairs of kid gloves, Bonheur gloves, a speciality of the house. After that, she had asked for three pairs of suede gloves and she was now trying on some Saxon gloves, afraid that the size might not be correct.

'Oh, they fit Madame perfectly!' said Mignot. 'The six-and-three-quarters would be too large for a hand such as yours.'

Half lying on the counter, he held her hand and took her fingers one by one, sliding the glove on with a well-rehearsed caress, long and emphatic; and he looked at her as though expecting to see on her face the surrender of sensual pleasure. But she leaned with her elbow on the edge of the baize, her wrist lifted, and entrusted her fingers to him as calmly as she would give her foot to the chambermaid who was buttoning her boots. He was not a man; she employed him for these intimate tasks with her usual scorn for servants, without even looking at him.

'I'm not hurting you, Madame?'

She shook her head. Usually, she found the smell of the Saxon gloves unsettling – that wild animal smell sweetened as it were with a hint of musk; sometimes she would laugh about it, confessing her liking for this ambiguous scent where one can detect the raging beast lashing around in a young girl's box of rice powder. But sitting next to this ordinary counter she did not smell the gloves and they created no sensual warmth between her and this unremarkable salesman doing his job.

'Anything else, Madame?'

'Nothing, thank you. Please take this to cash desk number ten, for Madame Desforges . . . All right?'

As a regular customer, she would give her name to a cash desk and send each of her purchases there, without being followed by an assistant. When she had left, Mignot turned to his neighbour with a wink, trying to make out that something extraordinary had taken place.

'What about her?' he muttered coarsely. 'I could glove her all over.'

Meanwhile, Madame Desforges was carrying on with her shopping. She came back to the left and paused in linen to buy some napkins, then carried on round until she reached woollens, at the end of the gallery.

Since she was pleased with her cook, she wanted to give her a dress. A dense crowd was bursting out of the woollen department, all the middle-class housewives had come and were feeling the material, absorbed in silent computations. She had to sit down for a moment. Large bolts of cloth were stacked in compartments on the wall and the assistants brought them down one by one with a sudden heave of their arm. So they were starting to lose their way on the buried counters, where the materials spread, jumbled together. There was a rising tide of neutral shades, dull woollen tones, iron greys, yellow greys, slate greys, with here and there the burst of a Scottish tartan or a blood-red flannel. And the white labels on the items were like a sparse scattering of snowflakes dotting the black December ground.

Behind a pile of poplin, Liénard was joking with a tall, bare-headed girl, a worker from the neighbourhood, sent by her employer to match some merino wool. He hated these special sale days: there was too much heavy work, so he tried to get round it, being mainly supported by his father and not giving a fig for selling: he contrived to do just enough of it to avoid getting the sack.

'Listen, Mademoiselle Fanny,' he said. 'You're always in a hurry . . . Did the mixed vicuna go well the other day? You know I'm coming to get my commission from you.'

But the girl ran away laughing and Liénard found himself face-to-face with Madame Desforges, unable to avoid asking her:

'How can I help Madame?'

She wanted a dress, inexpensive but well made. Liénard, in the hope of sparing his arms – that being his sole concern – tried to persuade her to take one of the materials already spread out on the counter. There were cashmeres, serges and vicunas, and he swore to her that nothing better was to be found, they never wore out. But none of these seemed to satisfy her. She had noticed a blueish coarse serge on a shelf. So eventually he saw nothing for it but to take down the length of cloth, which she decided was too rough. After that, she tried a Cheviot, some cross-striped and some greys, every variety of wool, which she was curious to feel, just for the pleasure of it, having made up her mind that in the end she would take whatever came to hand. So the young man had to get down samples from the very top shelves; his shoulders were aching and the counter had vanished under the soft grain of cashmeres and poplins, the rough wool of Cheviots and the fluffy down of vicuna. Every sort of cloth and every shade of colour took its turn. She even had him bring up some grenadine silk and Chambéry gauze, though she did not have the least intention of buying any. Finally, when she had had enough:

'Oh, for goodness' sake! The first one is still the best. It's for my cook. Yes, that serge with the little dots costing two francs.'

And when Liénard had measured it out, pale with suppressed anger:

'Be good enough to take it to cash desk number ten . . . It's for Madame Desforges.'

As she was leaving, she noticed Madame Marty near by, with her daughter Valentine, a tall young lady of fourteen, slim and quite forward, who was already casting a guilty woman's eyes over the merchandise.

'Why! It's you, my dear!'

'Yes, indeed, my dear . . . What a crowd, no?'

'Oh, don't tell me about it, I'm stifling. Such a success! Have you seen the oriental salon?'

'Superb! Incredible!'

And, amid elbowings and shoves from the swelling crowd of small spenders who were descending on the cheap woollens, they swooned over the display of carpets. Then Madame Marty explained that she was looking for material for a coat, but had not yet made up her mind and wanted to examine something in padded wool.

'Oh, please, mother,' Valentine whispered. 'That's so common.'

'Come to the silks,' said Madame Desforges. 'We must see their famous Paris-Bonheur.'

For a moment, Madame Marty hesitated. It would be very expensive and she had formally promised her husband that she would be sensible! She had been shopping for an hour and already a whole train of things was following behind her: a muff and some gathers for herself, stockings for her daughter. Eventually, she told the assistant who was showing her the padded coat:

'After all, no. I'm going to the silks . . . That's not really what I want.'

In the silk department, a crowd had also gathered. They were pressing in particular around the interior display which Hutin had put up, Mouret adding the final touches. At the back of the hall, around one of the little iron pillars that supported the glass roof, there was a sort of cascade of material, a frothy sheet falling from above and spreading out as it descended towards the floor. First of all, a spring of light satins and soft silks: royal satins, renaissance satins, with pearly shades of spring water; and featherweight silks, crystal clear, Nile green, sky blue, blush pink, Danube blue. Then came the heavier fabrics, the duchess silks, the wonderful satins, with warm colours, tumbling in swollen waves. And down below the heaviest stuffs reposed as though in a basin: the thick weaves, the damasks, the brocades and the silks decorated with pearls or gold and silver threads, in the midst of a deep velvet bed – every sort of velvet, black, white and coloured, embossed on silk or satin, its shimmering patches forming a motionless lake in which reflections of landscapes and skies seemed to dance. Women, pale with longing, leaned over as though to see their own reflections in it. All, confronted by this bursting cataract, stopped in their tracks, seized by a vague fear that they might be swept up in the torrent of such luxury and by an irresistible desire to leap and to lose themselves in it.

'There you are!' said Madame Desforges, coming across Madame Bourdelais sitting in front of a counter.

'Why, hello!' she replied, shaking hand with the ladies. 'Yes, I came in to take a look round.'

'What do you think? Isn't this display amazing? It's a dream . . . And the oriental salon, have you seen the oriental salon?'

'Yes, yes, it's extraordinary!'

However, beneath this enthusiasm, which was undoubtedly to be the fashionable response for the day, Madame Bourdelais preserved the cool head of a practical housewife. She carefully examined a piece of Paris-Bonheur, because she had come solely to take advantage of the exceptionally good price on this one silk, if she really considered it such. She must have been happy with it because she ordered twenty-five metres, reckoning on cutting a dress out of it for herself and a jacket for her little daughter.

'What! Are you going already?' Madame Desforges asked. 'Won't you walk round with us?'

'No, thank you. I'm expected at home. I didn't want to risk bringing the children into this throng.'

And she left, preceded by the assistant carrying her twenty-five metres of silk and leading her to cash desk number ten, where young Albert was going out of his mind, bombarded by all the requests for invoices. When the assistant was able to approach, after debiting his sale with a pencil mark on his book of counterfoils, he called out the sale which the cashier wrote down in the register; then it was double-checked and the sheet from the book was fastened on an iron spike near the stamp for receipts.

'One hundred and forty francs,' said Albert.

Madame Bourdelais paid and gave her address, because she was on foot and did not want her arms encumbered. Behind the cash desk, Joseph was already taking the silk and wrapping it up; then the parcel was thrown into a basket on wheels and sent down to the despatch department where all the goods from the shop now seemed to be trying to pour down with a noise like a sluice.

Meanwhile, the crowd pressing around the silk counter was so dense that Madame Desforges and Madame Marty could not at first find a free assistant. They stayed there amid a throng of ladies looking at materials, feeling them, stationed here for hours without being able to make up their minds. But Paris-Bonheur seemed destined for particular success: around it was developing one of those crazes, those sudden feverish infatuations that decide a fashion in a single day. All the assistants were engaged solely in measuring out lengths of this material. Above the hats, the unfolded lengths of silk glimmered palely as the fingers ran continually up and down the oak rulers hanging from brass rods and one could hear the sound of scissors biting into the cloth; there was no end to all this, as successive lengths of material were unwrapped, as though there were not enough arms to satisfy the greedy hands of the customers reaching across the counter.

'It really is not bad for five francs sixty,' said Madame Desforges, who had managed to catch hold of a piece at the edge of a table.

Madame Marty and her daughter Valentine were disillusioned. The newspapers had spoken so much about it that they expected something stronger and more brilliant. But Bouthemont had just recognized Madame Desforges and, wishing to get on the right side of an attractive lady who was said to have great influence over the boss, he came forward, with a rather coarse display of affability. What! Was no one serving her! This was outrageous! She must forgive them, because they really didn't know if they were coming or going. And he looked for some chairs among the surrounding dresses, laughing with his good-natured laugh in which there was a crude fondness for women, which did not seem to displease Henriette.

'I say,' Favier muttered to Hutin's back, on his way to take a length of velvet off a shelf. 'Now Bouthemont is doing your special.'

Hutin had forgotten about Madame Desforges, driven to distraction by an old lady who, after keeping him for a quarter of an hour, had just bought one metre of black satin for a corset. When there was a rush on, they no longer paid any attention to the order list: the assistants took the customers as they came. And he was just going to serve Madame Boutarel, who was ending her afternoon at *Au Bonheur des Dames*, where she had already spent three hours that morning, when Favier's warning made him jump. Was he going to miss the boss's lady friend, when he had sworn to get five francs out of her? This would be the height of bad luck, because he hadn't yet made three francs, despite the rush of skirts all over the place.

Bouthemont happened to be saying loudly:

'Come, now, gentlemen, can we have someone here!'

So Hutin handed Madame Boutarel to Robineau, who was not busy.

'There, now, Madame. Let the under-buyer look after you. He will be able to assist you better than I can.'

And he hurried over, getting the salesman on woollens, who had been accompanying the ladies, to hand over Madame Marty's purchases to him. A fit of nervous excitement must have upset his fine instinct that day. Usually, at the first glance at a woman, he could tell if she would buy and how much. Then he would master his customer, hurrying to deal with her and send her on to the next assistant, making her mind up for her and persuading her that he knew better than she did which material she needed.

'What kind of silk, Madame?' he asked, in his most courteous manner.

Madame Desforges had barely opened her mouth, before he continued:

'I know: I have just the thing.'

When the length of Paris-Bonheur was unfolded, on a narrow corner of the counter between heaps of other silks, Madame Marty and her daughter came up. Hutin, who had been a little anxious, realized that it was first of all a matter of buying something for them. Words were exchanged under their breath and Madame Desforges advised her friend.

'Oh, of course,' she said quietly. 'A silk at five francs sixty will never be as good as one for fifteen francs, or even one for ten.'

'It's very flimsy,' Madame Marty said. 'I'm afraid that it doesn't have enough body for a coat.'

At this, the salesman intervened. He had the exaggerated politeness of a man who cannot be mistaken.

'But, Madame, pliability is the chief quality of this silk. It does not crease. It is precisely what you need.'

Impressed by such self-assurance, the ladies fell silent. They had picked the material up again and were examining it when they felt someone touch them on the shoulders. It was Madame Guibal, who had been walking around the shop for an hour at an easy pace, feasting her eyes on the assembled riches without buying so much as a metre of calico. And at this there was another outburst of chatter.

'Why! It's you!'

'Yes, it's me, though somewhat jostled around.'

'Oh, don't I know! There are so many people, you can't walk along. And what about the oriental salon?'

'Delightful!'

'Goodness me, what a success! Stay with us and we'll go up there together.'

'Thank you, no. I've just been there.'

Hutin waited, hiding his impatience beneath a smile that never left his lips. Would they keep him here for much longer? Nothing seemed to bother women, but it was as though they had stolen money out of his purse. Finally, Madame Guibal left, continuing her slow progress around the display of silks, turning her head with an air of delight.

'In your place,' Madame Desforges said, turning back to the Paris-Bonheur, 'I should buy the coat ready-made; it will be cheaper.'

'It's true that with the accessories and the making-up . . .' Madame Marty said thoughtfully. 'Then, you do have a choice . . .'

All three had stood up. Madame Desforges addressed herself to Hutin and said:

'Would you take us to ladies' wear?'

He was thunderstruck, unused to such failure. What, the dark-haired lady was not going to buy anything! His instinct had let him down! He gave up Madame Marty and pressed on with Henriette, exercising all his powers of salesmanship.

'And you, Madame, wouldn't you like to see our satins and velvets? We have some remarkable bargains.'

'No, thank you, some other time,' she replied calmly, no more looking at him than she had at Mignot.

Hutin had to pick up Madame Marty's purchases and walk ahead of these ladies, taking them to the ladies' wear department. But he had the further irritation of seeing that Robineau was selling a large quantity of silk to Madame Boutarel. Obviously, he had lost his touch: he wouldn't make two pennies. Beneath the charming politeness of his manners seethed the anger of a man who has been deprived of his booty by others.

'To the first floor, ladies,' he said, still smiling.

It was no easy matter to reach the staircase. A tight surge of heads was flowing beneath the galleries, expanding into a flood in the middle of the hall. A commercial battle was underway, in which the sales assistants had this army of women at their mercy and were passing them from one to the other, as fast as they could. The moment had come for the fearsome afternoon rush, when the super-heated machine led the customers round the floor, squeezing the money from their very flesh. In silks especially madness was in the air and Paris-Bonheur had attracted such a crowd that for several minutes Hutin could not take a step. Henriette, gasping for breath, looked up and saw Mouret at the top of the stairs in the place to which he always returned and from which he could see his triumph. She smiled, hoping that he would come down and release her; but he could not even make her out in the crowd; he was still with Vallagnosc, busy showing him the shop, his face radiant with victory. Now, the noise inside drowned the sounds from outside. One could no longer hear the wheels of the cabs or the slamming of doors. All that was left, above the great hum of the sale, was a sense of the vastness of Paris, a vastness that would supply more and more customers. In the still air, where the stifling central heating fanned the smell of materials, the hubbub increased, a compound of every noise: the constant padding of feet, the same phrases repeated a hundred times across the counters, the gold clinking on copper cash desks under siege from a throng of purses and baskets on wheels constantly emptying their load of parcels into the gaping cellars. And, in the fine dust, everything seemed to mingle, so that one could no longer distinguish one department from another. Over there, haberdashery appeared to be swamped; further on, in linens, a ray of sunlight shining through the window on the Rue Neuve-Saint-Augustin was like a golden arrow in the snow; here, in gloves and woollens, a thick bunch of hats and hair hid the distant reaches of the shop. One could no longer even see the women's dresses; only their heads or head-coverings floated on the surface, a patchwork of feathers and ribbons, while here and there a man's hat made a black patch and the pale faces of the women, hot and tired, were taking on the transparency of camellias. At last, thanks to vigorous use of his elbows, Hutin cleared a path for the ladies by walking in front of them. But when she reached the top of the stairs, Henriette found that Mouret was no longer there: he had just plunged Vallagnosc into the midst of the crowd, hoping to stun him once and for all – and himself seized with a physical need for this bath of triumph. He gasped for breath, feeling as it were a long embrace of all his customers deliciously against his limbs.

'To the left, ladies,' said Hutin, in his considerate voice, despite his growing sense of exasperation.

The crowds were just as great upstairs. Even the furniture department, usually the calmest, was being invaded. Scarfs, furs and lingerie were teeming. While the ladies were crossing the lace department, another encounter took place. Madame de Boves was there with her daughter Blanche, both surrounded by things that Deloche was showing them. And Hutin had to come to a halt again, the parcel in his hand.

'Hello! I was thinking about you!'

'And I was looking for you. But how can you find anyone, with all these people?'

'Splendid, don't you think?'

'Dazzling, my dear. We can hardly stand.'

'Are you going to buy anything?'

'Oh, no, just looking. We're sitting here so we can take a rest.'

So it was: Madame de Boves, who had barely enough money in her purse for her cab fare, was having boxes brought out and all kinds of lace, for the sheer pleasure of seeing and touching them. She had sensed that Deloche was new to the job, slow and awkward, unable to resist a lady's whims, so she was taking advantage of his obliging timidity and had kept him for half an hour, constantly asking for different items. The counter was overflowing and she plunged her hands into this mounting tide of guipure, Mechlin, Valenciennes and Chantilly, her fingers trembling with desire and her face gradually warming with sensual pleasure, while Blanche, beside her, in the throes of the same passion, was very pale, her flesh soft and bloated.

Meanwhile, the conversation went on. Hutin, standing quite still, awaiting their pleasure, could have slapped their faces.

'Well, now!' said Madame Marty. 'You are looking at cravats and scarfs like mine.'

This was true. Madame de Boves, who had been obsessed with Madame Marty's lace since the previous Saturday, had been unable to resist the urge at least to stroke the same designs, since the little money her husband gave her did not allow her to take them away. She blushed slightly and explained that Blanche had wanted to see the Spanish blond cravats, adding:

'You are going to ladies' wear . . . Very well, we'll see you soon. In the oriental salon, perhaps?'

'Yes, indeed, in the oriental salon. Splendid, what?'

They took their leave, delighted with themselves, amid the jumble created by the sale of cut-price trimmings and edgings. Deloche, happy to be working, had gone back to emptying the boxes for the mother and daughter. And, slowly, among the groups crowding around the counters, Inspector Jouve walked by with his military step, exhibiting his decoration and keeping watch over these fine and precious goods which were so easy to hide in a sleeve. When he passed behind Madame de Boves, surprised at seeing her up to her elbows in such a flood of lace, he cast a sharp eye on her feverish hands.

'Turn right, Madame,' said Hutin, walking on again.

He was beside himself. Wasn't it enough to have lost him a sale, back there? Now they were stopping at every turn! And what fed his irritation most of all was the hostility that materials felt for tailored clothes, the departments being in continual conflict, fighting each other for customers, to get their hands on the percentage and the commission. Even more than woollens, assistants in the silk department grew angry when they had to take a lady to ladies' wear, where she would opt for a coat, after getting them to show her taffetas and failles.

'Mademoiselle Vadon!' said Hutin, in a voice showing increasing signs of irritation, when he finally reached the department.

But she swept past without listening, entirely taken up with a sale that she was rushing through. The room was full, with a line of people crossing it at one end, entering and leaving through the doors of lace and lingerie, which were opposite one another, while at the back, customers were trying on clothes, arching their backs in front of the mirrors. The red carpet deadened the sound of footsteps, the high, distant noise from the ground floor faded and there was only the discreet murmur and warmth of a drawing room, weighed down by a great crush of women.

'Mademoiselle Prunaire!' Hutin shouted.

And, when she too refused to stop, he added under his breath, so as not to be heard:

'You old bags!'

He disliked them particularly, his legs aching from climbing up the stairs in order to bring them paying customers, angry at what he considered was the way they took the earnings out of his pocket. It was a silent struggle, in which they engaged with equal determination; and in their mutual exhaustion, always on their feet, with aching limbs, differences of gender vanished and all that was left, face-to-face, were contrary interests, driven by the fever of commerce.

'So, won't anyone do it?' Hutin asked.

Then he caught sight of Denise. Since the morning she had been kept at tidying away and they had only given her a few dubious sales which, in any case, she had failed to pull off. When he recognized her, busy clearing a huge pile of clothes off a table, he ran over.

'Here, Mademoiselle! Aren't you going to serve these ladies? They are waiting.'

He quickly handed her Madame Marty's purchases, which he was tired of carrying around. His smile was coming back and in it was the hidden malice of an experienced sales assistant guessing the awkward situation into which he was about to plunge the ladies and the young woman. She meanwhile was quite overcome by this unexpected sale that had come her way. For the second time, he seemed to her to be an unknown friend, brotherly and affectionate, ever hovering in the shadows, waiting to save her. Her eyes shining with gratitude, she stayed looking after him while he was elbowing his way through the crowd, trying to get back to his department as quickly as possible.

'I should like a coat,' said Madame Marty.

At this, Denise questioned her: what kind of coat. But the customer didn't know, she had no idea, she wanted to see the firm's models. And the young woman, already very tired and dazed by the crowds, lost her head. She had only ever served the occasional customer at Cornaille's in Valognes and she still had no idea of the number of models or where they were kept in the cupboards. So she kept on questioning the two friends, who were getting impatient, when Madame Aurélie saw Madame Desforges, and must have known about her affair with Mouret, because she hurried over and asked:

'Are these ladies being looked after?'

'Yes, the young lady who is looking over there,' Henriette answered. 'But she doesn't seem very knowledgeable, she can't find anything.'

At once, the buyer completed Denise's discomfiture by going over and telling her in an undertone:

'You can see you don't know what you're doing. Please don't interfere.'

And she called out:

'Mademoiselle Vadon, a coat!'

She stayed behind while they were shown the coats by Marguerite, who adopted a drily polite tone with customers, the unpleasant attitude of a young woman dressed in silk and rubbing shoulders with the most elegant women while even unwittingly feeling jealousy and bitterness towards them. When she heard Madame Marty say that she did not want to go beyond two hundred francs, she gave her a pitying look. Oh, Madame would spend more than that! It wasn't possible for Madame to find anything decent with two hundred francs. And she threw down the ordinary coats on a counter with a gesture that meant: 'Just look how shoddy they are!' Madame Marty did not dare to approve of any of them. She leaned across to whisper in Madame Desforges' ear:

'I say, don't you prefer to be served by a man? One does feel more at ease.'

At length, Marguerite brought a silk coat trimmed with jet, which she treated with respect. And Madame Aurélie called Denise over:

'At least do something useful . . . Put that on.'

Denise, quite overwhelmed, despairing of ever succeeding in the store, had remained motionless, with her arms dangling. No doubt, they were going to dismiss her and the children would have nothing to eat. The noise of the crowd rang in her head and she felt herself swaying, her muscles aching from lifting and carrying whole armfuls of clothes, a kind of exercise that she had never done before. However, she had to obey, letting Marguerite put the coat on her as on a model.

'Stand up straight,' Madame Aurélie said.

Almost immediately, however, Denise was forgotten. Mouret had just come in with Vallagnosc and Bourdoncle. He greeted the ladies and accepted their compliments on his magnificent show of winter fashions. Inevitably, there were admiring remarks about the oriental salon. Vallagnosc, who was coming to the end of his walk round the departments, expressed more surprise than admiration – because, after all, he thought in his dismissive, pessimistic way, it was only a heap of calico. As for Bourdoncle, he quite forgot that he belonged to the firm and joined in congratulating his boss, so as to make him forget the doubts and anxieties he had expressed that morning.

'Yes, yes, it's going quite well, I'm pleased,' said Mouret, radiant and smiling in response to an affectionate look from Henriette. 'But I mustn't interrupt you, ladies.'

So all eyes returned to Denise. She abandoned herself to Marguerite who got her to turn around slowly.

'There. What do you think?' Madame Marty asked Madame Desforges.

The latter, as supreme arbiter of fashion, made the final decision.

'Not bad, an unusual cut . . . But the waist is not very elegant.'

'Oh, you must see it on Madame herself,' Madame Aurélie interjected. 'You understand, it doesn't come across on this young lady who is not at all shapely . . . Now, Mademoiselle, stand up straight and show it off to advantage.'

They smiled. The colour drained from Denise's face. She felt ashamed at being turned into a machine which they felt free to scrutinize and laugh at. Madame Desforges, annoyed by the young woman's gentle face, added cruelly:

'Of course, it would look better if the young lady's dress was a size smaller.'

She gave Mouret the mocking look of a Parisian amused at the ridiculous get-up of a provincial girl. He felt the loving caress behind the look, the triumph of a woman enjoying her beauty and her skill. So, with the gratitude of an adored man, he felt he should add some mockery of his own, despite his goodwill towards Denise, whose secret charm had touched his amorous nature.

'And then, her hair should be combed,' he said quietly.

That was the end. Since the director deigned to mock, all the young ladies burst out laughing. Marguerite gave the quiet chuckle of a distinguished young woman restraining herself; Clara had left a sale, so that she could relish the fun without distraction; and even some girls from lingerie had come across, attracted by the noise. As for the ladies, they were enjoying it more discreetly, with an air of worldly wisdom; while only the imperious profile of Madame Aurélie was not laughing, as though the beautiful wild hair and fine virginal shoulders of the new assistant had dishonoured her in the proper management of her department. Denise had gone paler still, surrounded by all these mocking people. She felt as though she had been raped, stripped bare, left defenceless. What had she done wrong, for them to attack her in this way for her too thin waist and her too heavy hair? But, most of all, she suffered from the laughter of Mouret and Madame Desforges, instinctively aware of the understanding between them, her heart stabbed by some unknown pain. The lady was very unkind, picking like that on a poor girl who had said nothing; and he, surely, chilled her with a fear in which all other feelings were submerged before she could analyse them. So, a lonely pariah, intimately stricken in her sense of feminine modesty and disgusted by the injustice of it, she stifled the sobs rising in her throat.

'Yes, indeed. Make sure she's combed tomorrow, it's not decent,' the terrible Bourdoncle told Madame Aurélie, who had damned Denise from the start and was full of contempt for her small limbs.

And finally the under-buyer took the coat off her and muttered quietly:

'Well, Mademoiselle, that's a fine start. Really, if you were trying to show what you can do . . . No one could be more silly.'

Denise, afraid that tears were about to pour from her eyes, hurried back to the pile of clothes that she was moving and classifying on a counter. There at least she was lost in the crowd and tiredness stopped her thinking. Then she noticed that the salesgirl from lingerie, the one who had already come to her defence that morning, was beside her. She had seen what happened and whispered in Denise's ear:

'You poor thing, you mustn't be so sensitive. Hide it, or else they won't let up on you . . . You know, I come from Chartres. Yes, honestly – Pauline Cugnot. My parents are millers there. Well, they would have eaten me alive in the early days if I hadn't faced up to them. Come on, cheer up! Give me your hand and we'll have a friendly chat whenever you like.'

Denise was even more disturbed by the proffered hand. She squeezed it furtively and quickly picked up a heavy bundle of jackets, afraid that she might put a foot wrong again and be told off if they knew she had a friend.

Meanwhile, Madame Aurélie herself had just put the coat on Madame Marty's shoulders, amid exclamations of approval: Oh, yes! Very good! Straightaway, it took on some shape. Madame Desforges announced that she would not find anything better. Greetings were exchanged, Mouret took his leave and Vallagnosc, who had spotted Madame de Boves and her daughter in the lace department, hurried over to offer the mother his arm. Already, Marguerite, standing in front of one of the cash desks on the mezzanine, was calling out the various purchases of Madame Marty, who paid for them and gave orders for the parcel to be taken to her carriage. Madame Desforges had met up with all her items at cash desk number ten. Then, the ladies gathered once more in the oriental salon. They were leaving, but in a chattering chorus of admiration. Even Madame Guibal was ecstatic.

'Oh, how delicious! You might imagine you were actually there!'

'It's a real harem, isn't it? And not expensive.'

'Those Smyrna carpets! Oh, those carpets! What shades, what delicacy!'

'And that Kurdistan! Have you seen it? A Delacroix!'[2]

Slowly, the crowd was dispersing. Bells had already been rung, an hour apart, to announce the first two sittings for the evening meal. The third was about to be served and in the departments, now more or less deserted, none but a few last customers remained, whose urge to spend had made them oblivious to the time. Now, from outside, came only the grumbling of the last cabs, against a background of the thick voice of Paris, the snoring of an overfed ogre, digesting the linens and sheets, the silks and lace with which he had been stuffed since that morning. Inside, under the flaring of the gaslights which, burning in the dusk, had lit the last throes of the sale, it was like a battlefield still hot from the massacre of the materials. The sales staff, haggard with tiredness, were holding their positions amid the rout of their counters and their shelves, which seemed to have been blown apart by the fierce breath of a hurricane. It was hard to make one's way along the ground-floor galleries, so obstructed were they by the scattering of chairs; in gloves, one had to climb across a barricade of boxes piled around Mignot; in woollens, there was no getting by at all: Liénard was dozing above a sea of objects among which some heaps, left upright, though half destroyed, looked like the ruins of houses washed by a flooded river. And, further on, the white linens had snowed on the ground, so that one stumbled against drifts of napkins and walked across the light flakes of handkerchiefs. The same devastation upstairs, in the mezzanine departments: furs were strewn across the floor, ready-made clothes were heaped up like the greatcoats of wounded soldiers, lace and lingerie, unfolded, crumpled and heedlessly cast aside, suggested a whole army of women who had hurriedly undressed there in the heat of passion, while downstairs, in the depths of the store, the despatch department was still working away, bursting with parcels which it was discharging for the carriages to take away in a final shudder of the overheated machine. But in silks, especially, the customers had made a mass assault, they had stripped the place bare and one could walk through freely: the hall was empty and the whole massive supply of Paris-Bonheur had just been torn up and swept away, as though by a swarm of locusts. And, in the midst of this emptiness, Hutin and Favier were leafing through their credit books and calculating their percentages, breathless from the fray. Favier had made fifteen francs, Hutin had only managed thirteen, beaten for once and furious at his bad luck. Their eyes shone with the lust for profit, while the whole shop around them was also totting up figures and burning with the same fever, in the brutal merriment of a night of carnage.

'Well, Bourdoncle,' Mouret exclaimed. 'Are you still worried?'

He had gone back to his favourite position at the top of the mezzanine stairs by the banister; and, looking at the wreckage of materials spread out below him, he gave a victorious laugh. His fears of the morning, that moment of unpardonable weakness that no one would ever know about, gave him a violent need for triumph. The campaign had been decisively won, the small traders in the neighbourhood cut down and Baron Hartmann, with his millions and his building sites, convinced. As he watched the cashiers bending over their registers, adding up long columns of figures, as he listened to the little tinkle of gold falling through their fingers into the copper bowls, he could already see *Au Bonheur des Dames* growing out of all proportion, its hall widening, its galleries extending as far as the Rue du Dix-Décembre.

'And now,' he went on, 'are you persuaded that the store is too small? We could have sold twice as much.'

Bourdoncle ate humble pie, delighted at having been in the wrong. But one sight made them serious once more. As every evening, Lhomme, the chief cashier, had just accumulated the different takings from each cash desk. After adding them all up, he wrote up the total amount, sticking the sheet of paper on which it was written on his iron spike. After that, he would carry the takings to the central cash desk, in a portfolio or bags, according to the type of currency. That day, most consisted of gold and silver. He slowly came up the stairs carrying three huge bags. Not having a right arm – it had been cut off at the elbow – he pressed them with his left arm against his chest, supporting one with his chin so that it would not slip off. His heavy breathing could be heard from some distance away; he went by, proud and heavily burdened, between ranks of respectful assistants.

'How much, Lhomme?' Mouret asked.

The cashier replied:

'Eighty thousand seven hundred and forty-two francs and ten centimes!'

A roar of joyous laughter rose up in *Au Bonheur des Dames*. The figure was passed around. The takings were the highest that a ladies' wear shop had ever made in a single day.

That evening, when Denise went up to bed, she supported herself on the walls of the narrow corridor under the zinc roof. In her room, with the door shut, her feet hurt so much that she flung herself down on the bed. She stayed for a long time staring dully at the dressing-table, the wardrobe and all the bareness of the rented room around her. So this is where she would live; and her first day burrowed into her brain, dreadful, endless. Then she noticed that she was wearing silk. The uniform depressed her, so she had the childish idea, as she set about unpacking her trunk, of putting on her old woollen dress, which she had left on the back of a chair. But when she was back inside this wretched dress of hers, she was choked with emotion and the sobs that she had been holding back since the morning suddenly burst out in a flood of warm tears. She had fallen back on to the bed, where she wept at the thought of her two children, and wept on without having the strength to take off her shoes, drunk with tiredness and woe.

CHAPTER 5

The following day, Denise had hardly been on the floor for half an hour before Madame Aurélie snapped at her: 'Mademoiselle, you are wanted in the director's office.'

The young woman found Mouret alone, seated in the large office hung with green rep. He had just remembered 'Shockhead', which is how Bourdoncle referred to her; and, though normally he disliked laying down the law, he thought he might call her in and shake her up a bit, if she was still dressed like a provincial. The day before, though he had joked about it, his self-respect had been wounded at seeing the appearance of a member of his staff discussed in front of Madame Desforges. His feelings were a mixture of sympathy and anger.

'Mademoiselle,' he began. 'We took you on out of respect for your uncle and you must not put us in the unpleasant position of having . . .'

Then he stopped. Opposite him, on the far side of the desk, Denise was standing upright, serious and pale. Her silk dress was not too big, but hugged her shapely figure, fitting against the pure lines of her maidenly shoulders. And, though her hair, knotted in great braids, was still wild, she had at least tried to hold it in. After falling asleep fully dressed, unable to cry any longer, the young woman had woken at about four o'clock, feeling ashamed at this hysterical outburst. At once she set about taking in the dress and spent an hour in front of the narrow mirror putting the comb through her hair, without managing to flatten it as she wished.

'Ah! Thank heavens!' said Mouret. 'You are better this morning. It's just that confounded mop still!'

He stood up and tried to adjust her hair with the same familiar gesture that Madame Aurélie had tried on it the day before.

'There! Put that behind your ear . . . The bun is still too high.'

She said nothing, letting him put it right. Though she had sworn to be strong, she had felt cold all over as she entered the room, certain that she had been called up so that they could dismiss her. And Mouret's obvious good will did not reassure her: she still feared him and when she was near him felt this discomfort, which she explained as a quite natural anxiety when faced with the powerful man who held her fate in his hands. When he saw how she trembled as his hands touched the nape of her neck, he regretted his thoughtful gesture, being chiefly afraid that he might lose his authority.

'Anyway, Mademoiselle,' he said, once more putting the desk between himself and her, 'try to pay attention to your appearance. You are not in Valognes any longer, study our Parisian women . . . While your uncle's name may have been enough to open the door of our firm to you, I would like to think that you will live up to the standard that you seemed to promise. The trouble is that not everyone here shares my opinion. So, you have been warned, haven't you? Don't prove me wrong.'

He was treating her like a child, with more pity than kindness, his curiosity merely stirred by the desirable woman whom he could sense emerging from this poor, awkward child. And she, while he was lecturing her, noticed the portrait of Madame Hédouin whose handsome, regular face was smiling gravely in a gold frame, and started to tremble again despite his encouraging words. This was the dead lady, the one that people in the neighbourhood accused him of killing so that he could establish his firm on the blood from her veins.

Mouret was still speaking.

'Off you go,' he said finally, sitting down and carrying on with his writing.

She left and, in the corridor, gave a sigh of profound relief.

From that day on, Denise showed great courage. Beneath her emotional crises, there was an intellect always at work and the bravery of someone weak and alone who was cheerfully determined in pursuit of the tasks she had set herself. She made little fuss, but went directly ahead towards her goal, taking any obstacles in her stride – and she did all this simply and naturally, because her whole nature was in this invincible gentleness.

First of all, she had to overcome the dreadful tiredness of work in the department. The parcels of clothes made her arms ache so much that during the first six weeks she would cry out when she turned over in her sleep, her joints were so stiff and her shoulders so bruised. But she suffered still more from her shoes, the heavy shoes she had brought from Valognes, which she could not afford to replace with light boots. Constantly standing or walking up and down from morning to night, and reprimanded if she was caught leaning for a minute against the cupboards, she had swollen feet, a little girl's feet which seemed to have been broken in some implement of torture; the ankles throbbed and the soles were covered with blisters, the naked flesh sticking to her stockings. Then she felt a deterioration of her whole body, her limbs and organs strained by the exhaustion of her legs, together with sudden disturbances of a womanly nature, indicated by the pallor of her skin. Yet she, so thin, seemingly so delicate, carried on, while many of the girls had to leave ladies' wear, suffering from illnesses brought on by the work. Her willingness to endure pain and her dogged determination kept her upright and smiling even when she was on the point of collapse, entirely exhausted by work that would have finished many men.[1]

Beyond that, she had to endure the agony of having the department against her. The furtive persecution of her colleagues was added to her physical martyrdom. After exercising patience and gentleness for two months she had still not won them over. There were hurtful remarks and cruel tricks, and a rejection that struck her to the heart, needing affection as she did. They teased her for a long time over her unfortunate start: words like 'clog' and 'broom head' did the rounds, anyone who failed to make a sale was 'sent to Valognes' . . . In short, she was considered the departmental idiot. Then, when she later turned out to be a remarkable sales assistant, once she had got to know how things worked, there was indignant amazement; and from then on the young ladies combined to prevent her from ever serving a serious customer. Marguerite and Clara pursued her with instinctive hatred, closing ranks to avoid being devoured by this new arrival whom they feared behind their pretended contempt. As for Madame Aurélie, she was hurt by the young woman's proud reserve: here was one who didn't cluster round her with fawning admiration, so she left her to the spite of the favourites at her court, those who were always on their knees, feeding her with the unremitting flattery that her large, authoritarian person needed to flourish. For a short time, the under-buyer, Madame Frédéric, seemed not to be part of this conspiracy; but it must have been an oversight, because she turned out to be no less hard as soon as she became aware of the problems that behaving agreeably might cause her. So Denise's rejection was complete: they all fell on 'Shockhead' and she lived in a state of constant struggle, only managing to stay in the department with great difficulty, despite her courage.

This was her life, now. She had to smile, put a brave and pleasant face on everything, in a silk dress that did not belong to her; and she ached with tiredness, was ill-fed, badly treated, constantly under threat of summary dismissal. Her room was her sole refuge, the only place where she could still give way to floods of tears when she had had too much to bear during the day. But a dreadful cold invaded it from the zinc roof, covered with the December snow; she had to huddle in her bed, pull all her clothes around her and weep under the blanket to prevent the frost from chapping her face. Mouret no longer spoke a word to her. When she met Bourdoncle's stern eye while she was on duty, she would start to shake, because she felt he was a natural enemy who would not pardon her the slightest mistake. What surprised her in the midst of this general hostility, was the strangely benevolent attitude of Inspector Jouve. If he found her by herself, he would smile at her and try to say a kindly word. Twice he had saved her from a reprimand, though she had shown him no gratitude, more troubled than touched by his protection.

One evening, after dinner, as the young ladies were tidying away, Joseph came to tell Denise that a young man was asking for her downstairs. She went down feeling very anxious.

'Well, well!' said Clara. 'So Shockhead has a lover, does she?'

'He must be desperate,' said Marguerite.

Downstairs, by the door, Denise found her brother Jean. She had expressly forbidden him to come to the shop in this way, because it gave a very bad impression. But he seemed so beside himself, hatless and breathless after running from the Faubourg du Temple, that she hadn't the heart to scold him.

'Have you got ten francs?' he stammered. 'Give me ten francs – or I'm done for!'

The great scallywag was so funny declaiming this melodramatic phrase, with his tousled blond hair and his pretty, girlish face, that she might have laughed, were it not for her anxiety at the demand for money.

'What!' she said. 'Ten francs? What's wrong?'

He blushed, explaining that he had met the sister of a friend. Denise hushed him, becoming as embarrassed as he was and not needing to know more. Twice before he had come to request similar loans, but it had only been a matter of one franc twenty-five the first time and one franc fifty the next. It was always a question of some woman.

'I can't give you ten francs,' she told him. 'I still haven't paid Pépé's fees this month and I have barely enough. I will hardly have the money left to buy some boots that I badly need . . . It's quite unreasonable of you, Jean; it's very bad.'

'Then I'm done for,' he repeated, with a tragic gesture. 'Listen, little sister: she's a big brunette, we went to the café with her brother, but I never imagined that the drinks . . .'

She had to interrupt him again, and as tears were welling up in the dear fathead's eyes, she reached for her purse, took out a ten-franc piece and slipped it into his hand. Immediately, he began to laugh.

'I knew you would . . . But on my honour – never again! I'd have to be a real cad.'

And he rushed off, after kissing her on both cheeks like a madman. The staff, inside the shop, were amazed.

That night, Denise slept badly. Since her arrival at *Au Bonheur des Dames*, money had been a terrible worry. She was still a probationer with no fixed salary; and as the young ladies in the department prevented her from selling, she only just managed to pay Pépé's board and lodging, thanks to the negligible customers which they passed over to her. For her, it was dire penury, penury in a silk dress. Often she had to stay awake all night, maintaining her tiny wardrobe, mending her linen and darning her nightdresses like lace. In addition, she had patched her shoes as skilfully as a cobbler could have done. She risked doing her washing in her wash-basin. But her old woollen dress bothered her most of all; it was the only one she had and she was forced to put it on each evening when she took off her silk uniform, so it was getting dreadfully worn. A stain made her frantic and the slightest tear was a catastrophe. She had nothing of her own, not a penny, nothing with which to buy the little things that a woman needs; she had to wait a fortnight to buy more needles and thread. And then there were disasters, when Jean with his love affairs suddenly descended on her and caused havoc in her budget. Remove a one-franc piece and there was a gaping hole in it; but as for finding ten francs from one day to the next, it was quite out of the question. She had nightmares until daybreak, seeing Pépé thrown out into the street, while she was turning over the paving-stones with her torn fingers to see if there was any money underneath.

The very next day, she had to smile and play her part as a well-dressed young lady. Familiar customers came into the department and Madame Aurélie called her over several times, draping coats over her shoulders so that she could show off the new styles. And, even as she was bending this way and that, adopting the poses laid down by the fashion plates, she was thinking about the forty francs for Pépé's rent, which she had promised to pay that evening. She could easily manage without the boots for another month; but even if she were to add the four francs that she had saved up, *sou* by *sou*, to the thirty francs that she had left, it would still only make thirty-four francs. Where could she find the six francs to complete the amount? She felt quite faint with worry.

'As you see, the shoulders are free,' Madame Aurélie was saying. 'It's very distinguished and very convenient. You can cross your arms, Mademoiselle.'

'Oh, yes, easily,' said Denise, not letting her pleasant manner slip. 'You can't feel it. Madame will be delighted with it.'

Now she reproached herself with having gone, the other Sunday, to collect Pépé from Madame Gras, to take him for an outing to the Champs-Elysées. The poor child so seldom came out with her! But she had to buy him some gingerbread and a spade, then take him to see Punch-and-Judy, and in no time she had spent twenty-nine *sous*.[2]

Honestly, Jean was not considering the child when he did these foolish things. And then, everything would come back on her.

'Of course, if Madame doesn't like it . . .' the under-buyer was saying. 'I know! Mademoiselle, put the cloak on so that Madame can see for herself . . .'

Denise, mincing round with the cloak on her shoulders, said:

'It is warmer. It's the fashion this year.'

All day long, while putting on a good show for her work, she was agonizing over where to find the money. The young ladies, rushed off their feet, let her take an important sale; but it was only Tuesday and she would have to wait four days before she would get her pay. After dinner, she decided to put off her visit to Madame Gras until the next day. She would use the excuse of having been kept behind, and perhaps, between now and then, she might get the six francs.

As Denise was trying not to spend any money, she went up to bed early. What would she be doing out on the street, without a penny, shy as she was and still scared of the big city where she only knew the streets around the shop? After venturing as far as the Palais-Royal to get a breath of air, she would hurry back, shut herself in and start sewing or washing. All along the corridor outside the rooms there was a sort of barrack-room promiscuity and the girls were often unkempt; there was gossip over slops and dirty linen and a lot of bitterness that flared up into constant quarrels and reconciliations. Moreover, they were not allowed to go there during the day. This was not where they lived, but where they spent the night, not going back until the last moment in the evening, and escaping in the morning, still half-asleep, only partly woken by their hurried wash; so, with the draught that blew continually along the corridor and the weariness of thirteen hours work which made them fall on their beds without a murmur, the attic area came to resemble an inn housing the ill-tempered exhaustion of a band of travellers. Denise had no friends. Only one of those young ladies, Pauline Cugnot, showed her some kindness; and even then, since ladies' wear and lingerie were next to each other, and openly at war, the mutual sympathy of the two salesgirls had so far had to be restricted to the occasional, hurriedly exchanged word. Pauline did have the room next to Denise's, though since she vanished immediately after supper and did not return until after eleven o'clock, Denise only heard her getting into bed, but never actually met her outside working hours.

That night, Denise was resigned to playing cobbler again. She picked up her shoes, examined them and studied how she could get them to the end of the month. Finally, with a strong needle, she decided to resew the soles which were threatening to part with the uppers. Meanwhile, a collar and some sleeves were soaking in the basin which was full of soapy water.

Every evening, she heard the same sounds, the young ladies coming back one by one, brief whispered conversations, laughter and sometimes stifled arguments. Then the beds creaked, there were yawns and the rooms fell into a deep sleep. Her neighbour to the left often talked in her sleep, which at first frightened Denise. Perhaps there were others, like herself, who stayed awake to darn and mend, despite the rules, but if so they were taking the same precautions as she did: doing everything surreptitiously, avoiding any sudden movement, because only a chilly silence emerged from behind the closed doors.

It was ten past eleven when the sound of footsteps made her look up. Another of the young ladies coming back late! She recognized Pauline when she heard her open the door to the next room, but to her astonishment, the girl from lingerie came out into the corridor again and knocked quietly on Denise's door.

'Hurry up! It's me!'

The sales staff were not allowed to visit one another in their rooms, so Denise turned the key quickly in case her neighbour was spotted by Madame Cabin, who enforced this rule strictly.

'Was she there?' she asked, closing the door.

'Who? Madame Cabin?' said Pauline. 'Oh, I'm not scared of her. Five francs will see her off.'

Then she added:

'I've been wanting to talk to you for a long time. We never can, downstairs. And you looked so sad at supper this evening.'

Denise thanked her and asked her to sit down, touched by her good-natured manner. However, so upset was she by this unexpected visit that she had not put down the shoe she was mending – and Pauline happened to glance at that shoe. She shook her head, looked around the room and noticed the sleeves and collar in the basin.

'My poor girl, I guessed as much,' she said. 'My, oh my! I know all about that. You don't know how many of those nightdresses I washed, at first, when I was fresh up from Chartres and the old man wasn't sending me a penny! Yes, really, even my nightshirts! I had two and you could always find one of them soaking.'

She sat down, out of breath after hurrying there. Beneath the heavy features, there was something attractive about her broad face with its bright little eyes and big, soft mouth. And, without further ado, she told Denise her story: how she grew up in a mill, how Old Cugnot was ruined by a law suit and how he sent her to Paris to make her fortune with twenty francs in her pocket. After that, she started as a salesgirl, a humble job first of all in a shop in Batignolles,[3] then at *Au Bonheur des Dames* – a really hard beginning, with every sort of suffering and privation; and finally, how she lived now, earning two hundred francs a month, enjoying herself, with no worries, just letting the days go by. Jewels, a brooch and a watch chain shone on her rough blue linen dress, which was provocatively tight around the waist; and she smiled under her velvet toque,[4] which sported a large grey feather.

Denise had gone very red because of her shoe, and tried to stammer out an explanation.

'But, I tell you, I've done the same myself!' said Pauline. 'Come, now, I'm older than you are, I'm twenty-six-and-a-half, even though I don't look it. Tell me all about yourself.'

So, faced with such a candid offer of friendship, Denise gave in. She sat down, in her petticoat, with an old crocheted shawl around her shoulders, beside Pauline, who was fully dressed, and they had a good chat. It was freezing in the room, the cold seemed to be running off the mansard roof and the walls which were as bare as in a prison; but they didn't notice that their fingers were numb with cold, so absorbed were they in exchanging confidences. Bit by bit, Denise opened up: she spoke about Jean and Pépé and admitted how much she was worried about the question of money – which led the two of them to say just what they thought about the young ladies in the department. Pauline got it off her chest.

'Oh, the lousy bitches! If they behaved like proper colleagues, you could be making more than a hundred francs.'

'Everyone has it in for me, though I don't know why,' said Denise, bursting into tears. 'So Monsieur Bourdoncle is constantly keeping an eye on me, hoping to catch me out, as though he had something against me . . . Only Old Jouve . . .'

The other girl interrupted her:

'That old fox, the inspector! My dear girl, don't you trust him . . . You know, men with large noses like that . . . It's all very well him showing off his decoration, but there's a rumour of some trouble he had in our department, in lingerie . . . But what a child it is to get so upset! It's dreadful to be so sensitive! Good gracious! What you're getting happens to everybody: this is their idea of a welcome.'

She grasped Denise's hands and kissed her, carried away by the goodness of her heart. The matter of money was more serious. Undoubtedly, a poor girl could not support her two brothers, paying the board and lodging of the younger and treating the elder one's mistresses, with the few meagre pennies that the others didn't want; because it was probable that she wouldn't get a salary until business started to pick up in March.

'Listen, you won't be able to survive any longer,' said Pauline. 'Now, if I were you . . .'

But a noise in the corridor made her stop. It might have been Marguerite, who was accused of wandering around in her nightdress, spying on the others as they slept. The girl from lingerie, still holding her friend's hands, looked at her for a moment in silence, her ears pricked. Then she resumed, in a very low voice, with a look of gentle persuasion:

'If I were you, I'd get someone.'

'How do you mean, someone?' Denise whispered, not at first understanding.

When she did realize what was meant, she withdrew her hands and remained for a moment quite stupefied. The advice upset her like an idea that had never occurred to her and in which she could not see any advantage.

'Oh, no!' she replied simply.

'Well then,' Pauline said, 'you won't manage, I'm telling you. Just add it up: forty francs for the little boy, five francs from time to time for the big one; and you, after that – you can't go around all the time dressed like a pauper, with the young ladies making fun of your shoes – oh, yes, believe me, your shoes let you down. Get someone, it would be much better.'

'No,' Denise repeated.

'Well, you're not being reasonable. It's necessary, my dear girl, and it's so natural! We've all been there. Take me, for example. I was a probationer like you, without a farthing. Of course, they feed you and give you somewhere to sleep; but there are clothes to think of, and then it's not possible to stay penniless, shut up in your room, counting the flies. So, God knows, you've got to do it.'

She told Denise about her first lover, a solicitor's clerk whom she met on a trip to Meudon. After him, she went with a man from the post office. And now, since the autumn, she had been going out with a sales assistant from the *Bon Marché*, a really nice, tall boy with whom she spent all her spare time. She only had one at a time, incidentally. She was a decent girl and got quite indignant when she heard about those girls who gave themselves to the first comer.

'I'm not telling you to behave badly, at any rate!' she said, emphatically. 'That's why I don't want to be seen around your Clara, in case someone accuses me of painting the town as she does. But when you're quietly going with someone and have nothing to reproach yourself with ... Does it seem so bad to you?'

'No,' Denise replied. 'It's just that it doesn't suit me.'

There was a further silence. In the icy little room, the pair smiled at one another, touched by this whispered conversation.

'Besides, you'd have to be friends with someone first,' she said, blushing.

The girl from lingerie was quite astonished. Eventually, she laughed and kissed her again, saying:

'But, my dear thing, when you meet someone and you both fancy one another! How odd you are! No one's going to force you. Come on, why not let Baugé take us somewhere in the country? He'll bring along one of his friends.'

'No,' said Denise again, gentle, but stubborn.

So Pauline did not insist. Everyone was entitled to do as she pleased. She said what she did out of the goodness of her heart, because it upset her to see a colleague in such distress. And, as it was about to strike twelve, she got up to leave, but first of all forced Denise to accept the six francs that she needed, imploring her not to trouble herself about them and not to give them back until she was earning more.

'Now,' she whispered. 'Put out your candle so that no one can know which door is opening. You can relight it afterwards.'

When the candle was out, the two of them shook hands again and Pauline slipped quietly away to go back to her own room, adding no louder noise than the rustling of her skirt to the exhausted sounds of sleep coming from the other little rooms.

Before going to bed, Denise wanted to finish mending her shoe and to do her washing. The air grew colder as the night went on, but she did not feel it: the conversation had stirred all the blood in her heart. She was not shocked. She felt that one had every right to order one's life as one wished when one was alone and free on this earth. She had never followed conventional ideas; her common sense and her wholesome nature were enough to ensure that she lived a decent life. At around one o'clock she finally went to bed. No, she was not in love with anyone. So why should she disrupt her life and spoil the maternal affection that she felt for her two brothers? Yet she could not get to sleep; warm shivers ran up her spine and vague shapes passed before her sleepless eyes, then vanished into the night.

From that moment on, Denise took an interest in the romantic affairs of her colleagues in the department. When the work was not heavy, they had a constant preoccupation with men. Gossip abounded and the young ladies were kept amused by some tales for as much as a week. Clara's behaviour was scandalous: she had three gentlemen friends, they said, as well as a string of occasional lovers trailing behind her. And the only reason she still stayed in the shop, where she worked as little as possible, with the contempt of someone who could earn her money more pleasantly elsewhere, was to cover herself where her family was concerned – she lived in constant fear of Old Prunaire, who threatened to turn up in Paris and break her arms and legs with his clogs. Marguerite, on the other hand, was well-behaved and no one knew of her taking any lover; this was surprising, because they all talked about her adventures, how she had come to Paris to have a child in secret; but how did she come by a child, if she was so chaste? Some of them spoke of an accident, adding that she was now keeping herself for her cousin in Grenoble. The young ladies also joked about Madame Frédéric, alleging that she had discreet liaisons with important people; but the fact was that no one knew anything about her love affairs: she would vanish in the evening, tense in her widow's sullen silence, dashing off somewhere, though no one could say where she was going in such a hurry. As for Madame Aurélie's passions, her alleged desire for submissive young men, all this was certainly untrue: dissatisfied salesgirls had made it up among themselves, just for a laugh. It could be that the chief buyer had at some time past shown too much maternal feeling towards a friend of her son's, but nowadays she had a job to do in fashion, the job of a serious woman who no longer trifled with such childish things. Then came the herd, the evening stampede, nine out of ten of them having lovers waiting at the door: on the Place Gaillon, all along the Rue de la Michodière and the Rue Neuve-Saint-Augustin, there was a whole army of men standing still and looking expectantly out of the corners of their eyes; and when the exodus began, each of them would offer an arm to lead his girl away and they would disappear, chatting with the easy calm of a married couple.

However, what disturbed Denise the most was discovering the secret of Colomban. At all hours of the day, she could see him on the far side of the street in the doorway of the *Vieil Elbeuf*, looking up and staring at the young ladies in ladies' wear. When he felt that she was watching him, he blushed and looked away, as though afraid that she might report him to her cousin Geneviève, even though there had been no contact between the Baudus and their niece since Denise had gone to *Au Bonheur des Dames*. At first, she thought he was in love with Marguerite, in view of his bashful air, like a lovelorn suitor, because Marguerite was sensible and slept in the shop, which was not at all convenient. Then she was quite astonished when she became sure that the young man's ardent gaze was fixed on Clara. He had been consumed by love in that way for months now on the opposite pavement, without plucking up enough courage to declare himself; and all that for a free-living young woman who had her own place in the Rue Louis-le-Grand and whom he could have approached any evening before she went off on the arm of some new man! Clara herself seemed unaware of the conquest she had made. Denise's discovery filled her with pain. Was love so stupid then? What! Here was a young man who had such happiness within his grasp yet was ruining his life, worshipping this hussy as though she were the holy sacrament! From that day onwards, she felt a pang every time she saw Geneviève's pale, suffering silhouette behind the greenish windows of the *Vieil Elbeuf*.

This is how Denise thought in the evening as she watched the young ladies go off with their lovers. Those who did not sleep at *Au Bonheur des Dames* vanished until the next day, coming back to their departments with a smell of the outside on their skirts – an unsettling aura of mystery. And Denise had sometimes to smile in reply to the friendly nod that she got from Pauline, whom Baugé waited for regularly from half past eight onwards, standing on a corner of the Gaillon fountain. Then, the last to go out, she would stealthily take her walk around, always alone, before being the first to return and then work or go to bed, her head full of dreams, full of curiosity about all the life in Paris that she did not know. Not that she was at all jealous of the young ladies: she was happy in her solitude, living enclosed in her wild animal's existence as though in a den: but her imagination would get carried away, trying to guess at things and conjuring up the delights that were constantly described to her – cafés, restaurants, theatres or Sundays spent on the water and in dance halls. It left her with a sort of tiredness of the mind, a mixture of desire and lassitude; and she felt as though already satiated with these entertainments that she had never enjoyed.

However, there was little place for dangerous reveries in her hard-working life. In the shop, crushed by thirteen hours of labour, there was hardly any thought of love affairs between the salesmen and women. Even if the continual battle for money had not abolished all idea of gender, the constant rushing to-and-fro would have been enough to kill desire, occupying the mind and exhausting the limbs. People could mention only a very few, rare liaisons which survived the hostilities and the comradeship between men and women, and the endless pushing and shoving from one department to another. They were mere cogs, carried along by the march of the machine, abdicating their personalities and simply adding their individual strength to the raw sum of the phalanstery.[5] Only outside did individual life resume, with a sudden flaring of awakened passions.

However, one day Denise did see Albert Lhomme, the chief buyer's son, slip a note into the hand of a young lady from lingerie, after walking up and down the department several times with an air of unconcern. They were coming into the off season of the winter, which lasts from December to February; and she had some moments of rest, hours spent on her feet staring into the depths of the shop waiting for customers. The salesgirls from ladies' wear associated particularly with the salesmen from lace, though this forced intimacy did not go beyond jokes exchanged in a whisper. In lace, there was another joker who was after Clara, confiding dreadful secrets to her, just for a laugh, and in reality so little interested that he did not even try to meet her outside; and there were also, from one department to the next, between the gentlemen and the young ladies, knowing glances, remarks that they alone understood and occasionally surreptitious conversations, with backs half turned to one another and a distracted air, to fool the frightful Bourdoncle. As for Deloche, he was satisfied for a long time with merely smiling when he looked at Denise; then he grew bolder and murmured a friendly word as he went past her. The day that she saw Madame Aurélie's son give his missive to the girl from lingerie, Deloche happened to ask if she had enjoyed her lunch, wanting to show an interest in her and finding nothing more agreeable to say. He also noticed the white flash of the passing letter and looked at Denise; the pair of them blushed at this intrigue going on before their eyes.

But Denise, under these warm breezes that were gradually rousing the woman inside her, still retained a child's peace of mind. Her heart missed a beat only when she saw Hutin. In any case, as she saw it, this was merely gratitude; she felt only that she was touched by the young man's good manners. Every time he brought a customer to the department, she was quite overcome; and often, coming back from a cashier's desk, she found herself making a detour and unnecessarily going through the silk department, breathless with emotion. One afternoon, she found Mouret there, apparently watching her go past with a smile on his lips. He no longer paid any attention to her, only occasionally addressing a word to her to advise her on her appearance and laugh at her for being a tomboy, a wild thing, more like some lad whom he would never be able to turn into a smartly dressed woman despite his craft as a ladies' man; he would even laugh about it and condescend to tease her, while not wanting to admit how much this little salesgirl, with her funny hair, got under his skin. When he smiled like that, without speaking, Denise shuddered, as though she had done something wrong. Perhaps he realized why she was going through the silk department, even though she herself could not have explained what led her to make the detour.

Hutin, as it happened, did not seem even to notice the girl's grateful looks. The young ladies did not appeal to him and he pretended to despise them, while boasting more than ever about his amazing escapades with his female customers: a baroness had developed an instant passion for him at the counter and an architect's wife had fallen into his arms one day when he had gone to her house because of an error of measurement. This Norman bragging served to disguise the plain reality of girls picked up in bars and music-halls. Like all the young gentlemen in ladies' wear he had a mania for spending money, battling away all week through in his department with the determination of a miser, yet wanting nothing more than to squander his money on Sunday at the racecourse, in restaurants and dance halls – never saving, never borrowing, spending his earnings as soon as he got them with an utter indifference to the morrow. Favier was not included in these outings. Hutin and he, such close friends in the store, said goodbye at the front door and did not speak to each other again – many of the sales staff, who were in constant contact, became strangers to one another in this way, with no idea of how they lived, just as soon as they stepped into the street. But Hutin was close to Liénard. The two of them lived in the same hotel, the Hôtel de Smyrne in the Rue Sainte-Anne, a dark building entirely occupied by workers in the retail trade. They came in together in the morning; then, in the evening, the first to be free when the stock in his department was put away went and waited for the other in the Café Saint-Roch, in the Rue Saint-Roch, a little café where the assistants from *Au Bonheur des Dames* were in the habit of meeting, for an evening of drinking, brawling and playing cards in clouds of pipe smoke. Often, that's where they would stay, only leaving at around one o'clock when the landlord of the place got tired and threw them out. In fact, for the past month they had been going three times a week to spend the evening in a dive in Montmartre where there was music; they would take their friends there to applaud Mademoiselle Laure, a powerful singer, who was Hutin's latest conquest. They would express their appreciation of her talent with such violent thumpings of their canes and such loud exclamations that the police had already twice been obliged to interrupt the proceedings.

So the winter went by. Denise was finally granted a salary of three hundred francs. It was about time: her heavy shoes were barely holding together. For the last month, she even stopped going out, in case they suddenly fell to pieces.

'My goodness, Mademoiselle! What a noise those shoes of yours are making!' an irritated Madame Aurélie said several times. 'It's unbearable . . . What have you got on your feet?'

On the day when Denise came down wearing some fabric boots which had cost her five francs, Marguerite and Clara expressed their astonishment under their breath, though loud enough to be heard.

'Well, well! Shockhead has taken off her clogs,' one of them remarked.

'It must have been a wrench,' the other said. 'They were her mother's.'

In fact, there was a general antipathy towards Denise. The department had eventually found out about her friendship with Pauline and saw this liking for a girl from a rival department as an act of defiance. The young ladies talked about treason, accusing her of reporting every little thing they said to the next department. The war between lingerie and ladies' wear reached new heights; never had there been such hostility. Words as sharp as bullets were exchanged and there was even a slap one evening, behind the boxes of nightdresses. This long-standing dispute may have derived from the fact that in lingerie they wore woollen dresses, while the girls in ladies' wear were dressed in silk.

However it was, the lingerie assistants spoke of their neighbours with the outraged expressions of respectable young women – and the facts supported them, because it had been noticed that wearing silk seemed to affect the loose behaviour of the assistants in ladies' wear. Clara was slapped down for her flock of lovers, even Marguerite had her child thrown in her face and Madame Frédéric was accused of secret passions – and all this because of that Denise!

'Now then, young ladies, no unpleasant remarks, behave yourselves!' said Madame Aurélie, with a solemn air, amid this outburst of anger that had swept through her little tribe. 'Show us the sort of people you are!'

She preferred not to get involved. As she remarked one day in answer to a question from Mouret, the young ladies were each as bad as the other. But suddenly she flared up when she learned from Bourdoncle that he had just come across her son at the back of the basement kissing a girl from lingerie, the same assistant to whom the young man had been passing letters. It was atrocious and she accused lingerie straight out of having laid a trap for Albert; yes, it was a conspiracy against her: they were trying to dishonour her by destroying an inexperienced boy, once they discovered that her department was immune to attack. She only made such a fuss about it in order to confuse the issue, because she had no illusions about her son, knowing that no stupidity was beyond him. For a short while, the affair risked taking on serious proportions, because Mignot from the glove department was involved. He was Albert's friend and would favour the mistresses that Albert sent him, hatless girls who rummaged around for hours in the boxes; and, on top of all that, there was some story which no one ever got to the bottom of, about the lingerie assistant being given some Swedish gloves. In the end, the scandal was hushed up out of consideration for the chief buyer in ladies' wear, whom even Mouret treated with respect. All that happened was that a week later Bourdoncle found some excuse to sack the assistant who was guilty of having let herself be kissed. They might turn a blind eye to the dreadful goings-on outside, but the gentlemen would not put up with the slightest indecency in the store.

And it was Denise who bore the brunt of the affair. Well-informed as she was, Madame Aurélie nourished a vague grudge against her; she had seen her laughing with Pauline and believed it was some act of defiance or gossip about her son's love affairs. The result was that she isolated the young woman even more in the department. For some time, she had been planning to take the young ladies to spend one Sunday near Rambouillet at Les Rigolles, where she had bought a house with her first hundred thousand francs of savings; and she suddenly decided as a way to punish Denise that she would exclude her. Denise alone was not invited. A fortnight before it took place, the department was talking about nothing but this outing: they looked at the sky, warmed by the May sun, and discussed what they would do at each hour through the day, promising themselves every kind of delight – donkey rides, milk, brown bread – and only women, which was more fun! Usually, Madame Aurélie would get through her free days in this way by going for walks with some ladies, because she was so little used to finding herself with her family, and felt so uneasy and out-of-place on the rare evenings when she could dine at home with her husband and her son, that she preferred even on those evenings to abandon the household and go out for dinner in a restaurant. Lhomme went off on his own, delighted to resume his bachelor existence, and Albert sighed with relief and returned to his trollops; so that now, unaccustomed to home life, embarrassed and bored when they spent Sundays together, all three of them did little more than pass through their apartment, as if it were merely a hotel in which to spend the night. As for the outing to Rambouillet, Madame Aurélie simply announced that propriety forbade Albert to join them and it was tactful of the father, too, to decline to come. The two men were delighted. Meanwhile, the happy day approached and the young ladies did not stop talking about it, describing the clothes they were getting ready, as though they were leaving for a six-month journey. And all the time, Denise had to listen to them, rejected, pale and silent.

'What about that? Don't they make you mad?' Pauline said to her one morning. 'If I was in your place, I'd get them! They're having fun, but I'd be deadly serious, by golly! Come with us on Sunday, Baugé is taking me to Joinville.'

'No, thank you,' the young woman said, with calm determination.

'Why not? Are you still afraid you will be taken by force?'

Pauline gave a hearty laugh. Denise smiled, too. She knew quite well how things went: each of the young ladies had met her first lover – a friend invited by chance – on just such an outing, and she didn't want that.

'Look,' Pauline said. 'I promise you that Baugé will not bring anyone. It will just be the three of us. Since you're not keen on the idea, of course I won't marry you off.'

Denise hesitated, tormented by such desire that the blood rushed to her cheeks. All this time, when the other girls were talking about their trips to the country, she had felt stifled, consumed by a need for the open sky and dreaming about long grass coming up to her shoulders or the shade of giant trees pouring across her like cool water. Memories awoke of her childhood in the lush greenery of the Cotentin,[6] and with them a longing for the sun.

'All right, then, yes,' she said at last.

It was all arranged. Baugé would pick up the two young ladies at eight o'clock on the Place Gaillon and from there they would go by cab to the Gare de Vincennes. Denise, whose twenty-five francs' salary was all spent every month on the children, had only been able to smarten up her old black woollen dress by trimming it with fine-checked poplin; and she even made a hat for herself, shaped like a bonnet covered in silk and decorated with a blue ribbon. In this simple outfit she looked very young, like a little girl who has grown up too quickly; and she had the cleanliness of the poor, slightly ashamed and embarrassed by the excessive luxury of her hair which burst out of the plainness of her hat. Pauline, on the other hand, gloried in a silk spring dress, striped in white and violet, a matching toque laden with feathers and jewellery on her hands and around her neck – the extravagance of a well-heeled tradesman's wife. Silk on Sundays was a compensation for the week, when in her department she was forced to wear wool; while Denise, who had to put up with her silk uniform from Monday to Saturday, when Sunday came reverted to the thin wool of her poverty-stricken childhood.

'There's Baugé,' Pauline said, pointing out a tall lad standing beside the fountain.

She introduced her lover and Denise at once felt as ease, because he seemed such a decent sort. Baugé was huge, with the slow strength of an ox at the plough and a long Flemish face in which his vacant eyes laughed with childlike innocence. He was the younger son of a grocer; born in Dunkirk, he had come to Paris after being more or less turned out by his father and brother, who considered him a dimwit. At the *Bon Marché*, however, he was making three thousand five hundred francs. He was stupid, but very good with linen. Women found him rather sweet.

'What about the cab?' Pauline asked.

They had to walk to the boulevard. The sun was already getting warmer, the lovely May morning was smiling on the streets and there was not a cloud in the sky; a feeling of merriment hovered in the blue air, as clear as crystal. An involuntary smile crossed Denise's lips; she breathed deeply and felt that her chest was emerging from six months' suffocation. At last, she no longer sensed around her the enclosed atmosphere and heavy stones of *Au Bonheur des Dames*! And she had a whole day in the open countryside before her! It was an infinite joy, as though she had regained her health and could relish it with the brand new feelings of a young girl. However, in the cab, she averted her gaze in embarrassment when Pauline planted a big kiss on her lover's lips.

'Look!' she said, still turning towards the door. 'That's Monsieur Lhomme over there . . . How fast he's walking!'

'He's got his horn with him,' Pauline remarked leaning across. 'What an idiot! Honestly, you might think he had a rendezvous with some woman!'

Lhomme, with his instrument case under his arm, was indeed marching briskly along beside the Gymnase,[7] his head thrust forward, laughing merrily to himself at the idea of the treat that awaited him. He would spend the day with a friend, a man who was a flautist in a little theatre where on Sundays amateurs played chamber music from breakfast onwards.

'At eight o'clock! What a madman!' Pauline went on. 'And you know Madame Aurélie and all her gang must have taken the train for Rambouillet which left at six twenty-five. The husband and wife won't meet, that's for sure!'

The pair of them talked about the outing to Rambouillet. They did not wish rain on the others, because they would get drenched as well; but if there could just be a cloudburst there, without it splashing as far as Joinville, that would be a good joke. Then they turned on Clara, a good-for-nothing who had no idea how to spend the money she got from her lovers: didn't she go and buy three pairs of boots at a time, then throw them away the next day after cutting them with scissors because her feet were covered in corns? In any case, the young ladies in drapery were no more sensible than the young gentlemen: they devoured everything, never saving a penny and spending two or three hundred francs a month on frivolous clothes and sweets.

'But he only has one arm!' Baugé remarked suddenly. 'How does he manage to play the horn?'

He had been staring after Lhomme. Pauline, who sometimes had fun at the innocent lad's expense, told him that the cashier put the instrument up against a wall and he believed her implicitly, thinking the solution very ingenious. And when, afterwards, in a fit of remorse, she explained to him how Lhomme had adapted a system of pincers to his stump so that he could use it like a hand, he shook his head, suddenly mistrustful, saying that they wouldn't get him to swallow that one.

'You're so silly!' she said eventually, laughing. 'It doesn't matter, I love you all the same.'

The cab bowled along and they reached the Gare de Vincennes, just in time for a train. Baugé paid, but Denise had announced that she intended to contribute her share of the expenses; they would settle up in the evening. They got into the second class, hearing a buzz of merriment from the other carriages. At Nogent, a wedding party got out, to a burst of laughter. Finally, the train stopped at Joinville and they went directly to the island to order lunch; and they stayed there, on the river bank, under the tall poplars lining the River Marne. It was cold in the shade and a sharp breeze was blowing in the sunshine while on the far bank the clear purity of open farmland extended into the distance. Denise lingered behind Pauline and her boyfriend, who walked along with their arms around one another. She had plucked a handful of buttercups and was watching the water run past, so happy

– though her heart sank and she lowered her head whenever Baugé leaned across to kiss his friend's neck. Tears welled up in her eyes. Yet she was not miserable. Why did she have this lump in her throat? Why did this open countryside, where she had expected to feel so light-hearted, fill her with some vague sense of loss that she could not account for? Then, at lunch, she felt deafened by Pauline's raucous laughter. Pauline, who loved the suburbs with the same passion as a performer used to gaslight and the thick air of a crowded music hall, wanted to eat outside, despite the cold wind. She found the sudden breezes amusing when they lifted the tablecloth and thought the still naked arbour was a big joke, with its repainted trellis throwing diamond-shaped shadows on the table. And moreover, she stuffed herself, with the greedy hunger of a girl who did not have enough to eat in the shop and would gorge herself on what she liked once she got outside. This was her weakness; all her money went on it, on cakes, on salads and on little dishes that she would polish off in her free time. As Denise seemed to have had enough with eggs, fried fish and sauté of chicken, she restrained herself, not daring to order strawberries, since they were not yet in season and still dear and it would put the bill up too much.

'Now what shall we do?' Baugé asked, when coffee was served.

Usually in the afternoon Pauline and he went back to Paris for dinner and finished the day in a theatre. But at Denise's request they decided to stay in Joinville – it would be fun, they would really have their fill of the country. So for the whole afternoon they tramped the fields. At one moment, they did discuss hiring a boat, then they gave up the idea, because Baugé was too bad at rowing. But their walk, by chance, led them back even so to the Marne and they took an interest in the life of the river, the squadrons of skiffs and other craft, and the crews of rowers who manned them. The sun was going down and they were returning to Joinville, when from two skiffs which were racing each other downstream, came an exchange of volleys of insults, in which the repeated terms 'gowns' and 'hand-me-downs' were prominent.

'Look!' Pauline said. 'It's Monsieur Hutin.'

'Yes,' replied Baugé, holding out his hand to shield his eyes from the sun. 'I recognize that mahogany skiff. The other one must be rowed by a team of students.'

And he explained the long-standing rivalry between young scholars and shop assistants. When Denise heard the name of Hutin, she stopped and stared closely after the narrow boat, looking for the young man among the rowers, but unable to make out anything except the blurred white shapes of two women, one of whom, seated by the rudder, had a red hat. The voices were lost in the great sound of rushing water.

'Drown, drown the scholar's gowns!'

'Drown the hand-me-downs! Sink and drown!'[8]

In the evening, they went back to the restaurant on the island. But the air was too chilly, so they had to eat in one of the two inside rooms where the winter humidity made the tablecloths as damp as though they were freshly washed. By six o'clock, there was a shortage of tables; walkers hurried in, looking for a place to sit, while the waiters brought more chairs and benches, putting the plates closer together and squeezing people in. Now it was stifling and they had the windows opened. Outside, the daylight was fading and a greenish dusk descended from the poplar trees so fast that the restaurant owner, who was not properly equipped with lamps for these inside diners, had to put a candle on each table. The noise was deafening, as people laughed and called out and dishes clattered. The candles took fright and ran, flaring and spluttering in the breeze from the open windows, while moths flapped their wings in the warm, odorous air rising from the meat, broken by icy little draughts.

'They're enjoying themselves, I should say,' Pauline remarked, from the middle of a fish stew which she pronounced 'extraordinary'. And she leaned forward to ask:

'Did you notice Monsieur Albert over there?'

It was indeed the younger Lhomme, surrounded by three women of dubious appearance: an old lady in a yellow hat, with the face of a low bawd, and two minors, girls of thirteen or fourteen, lounging about with an embarrassing lack of modesty. He was already very drunk and banging his glass on the table, saying that he would box the waiter's ears if he didn't bring them their liqueurs at once.

'Well, well,' Pauline went on. 'What a family! The mother's in Rambouillet, the father's in Paris and the son's in Joinville . . . They won't be treading on one another's toes.'

Denise, who hated noise, smiled even so, enjoying the pleasure of not having to think in the midst of all this din. But suddenly, from the room next door, there was a burst of voices that drowned all the rest. The yells must have been followed by blows, because one could hear pushing and shoving, chairs knocked over and regular struggle, mingled with the same shouts they had heard on the river:

'Drown the hand-me-downs!'

'Sink and drown the scholars' gowns!'

And, when the cabaret owner's loud voice had calmed the opposing forces, Hutin suddenly appeared. Wearing a red jersey, with a cap, peak reversed, on the back of his head, he had the tall white girl on his arm, the one who had held the tiller and who, to wear the colours of the boat, had tucked a bunch of poppies behind her ear. Their entrance was greeted with shouts and applause, while he beamed, puffing out his chest and walking with a sailor's rolling gait, showing off the bruise from a blow on his cheek, luxuriating in the joy of being noticed. They were followed by the crew of their boat. A table was stormed and the row rose to awesome proportions.

'It appears,' Baugé explained, after listening to the conversations behind him, 'that the students recognized Hutin's woman, who used to live in the neighbourhood and now sings in a low dive in Montmartre. So they came to blows over her . . . Those students! They never pay for their women!'

'In any event,' said Pauline, starchily, 'she's jolly ugly, with her carroty hair . . . Honestly, I don't know where Monsieur Hutin picks them up, but each one is viler than the next.'

The colour had left Denise's face. She felt an icy chill come over her as though the blood had drained, drop by drop, from her heart. She had already felt a first shudder on the river bank, watching the speeding skiff; and now, she could no longer doubt it, the woman was with Hutin. With a lump in her throat and trembling hands, she stopped eating.

'What's wrong?' her friend asked.

'Nothing,' she stammered. 'It's a bit hot.'

But Hutin's table was next to theirs and when he had seen Baugé, whom he knew, he struck up a conversation in a high-pitched voice, so as to keep the attention of the room.

'I say,' he cried. 'Are you as clean-living as ever, in the *Bon Marché*?'

'Not as much as that,' the other man answered, going very red.

'Go on! They only take on virgins and they have a confessional constantly manned for any male assistants who look at them . . . A store where they make marriages[9] – no, thanks!'

There was a burst of laughter. Liénard, who was one of the crew, added:

'It's not like that at the *Louvre*. There, they've got a midwife on hand for the ladies' wear department. Honestly!'

Increased merriment. Even Pauline burst out laughing, she thought the midwife so funny. But Baugé felt aggrieved at the jokes about the purity of his firm's morals. All at once, he blurted out:

'You're a fine lot in *Au Bonheur des Dames*! Sacked for a wrong word and a boss who seems to be flirting with his lady customers!'

Hutin was no longer listening, having started a eulogy for *Place Clichy*. He knew one girl there who was so respectable that clients didn't dare ask her for help, for fear that she might be mortified. After that, he brought his plate over and told them that he had made one hundred and fifteen francs over the week – oh, it had been a stupendous week! Favier was left behind at fifty-two francs and the rest of the list was ditched entirely. You could see it, couldn't you? He was devouring the money and wouldn't go to bed before he had blown the hundred and fifteen francs. Then, as he was getting drunk, he laid into Robineau, that little runt from the second floor who pretended to be so superior that he did not like to be seen walking down the street with one of his sales staff.

'Shut up,' said Liénard. 'You're talking too much, my dear chap.'

The heat had increased and the candles were dripping on to the wine-stained tablecloths. Through the open windows, when the noise of the diners was suddenly stilled, came a distant, protracted voice, the voice of the river and its tall poplars as they lapsed into sleep in the tranquil night. Baugé had just asked for the bill, seeing that Denise was feeling no better, but had gone all white, her chin contorted by the effort of holding back her tears; but the waiter was nowhere to be seen and she had to put up again with Hutin's outbursts. Now, he said that he was smarter than Liénard, because while Liénard was merely consuming his father's money, he, Hutin, was consuming money which he had earned, the fruit of his intelligence. Finally, Baugé paid and the two women went out.

'There's one from the *Louvre*,' Pauline whispered in the first room, looking at a tall slender girl who was putting on her coat.

'You don't know her, you can't tell,' said the young man.

'That's what you think! Look how she's got up! Midwife's department, for sure. And if she's heard me, she must be pleased.'

They were outside. Denise heaved a sigh of relief. She thought she was going to die, in that stifling heat and all that shouting: she still explained her dizziness by lack of air. Now she could breathe again. Cool air filled the starry night and as the two young women were leaving the restaurant garden, a shy voice murmured through the darkness:

'Good evening, ladies.'

It was Deloche. They hadn't seen him at the back of the first room where he was dining alone, after walking here from Paris, for the sheer pleasure of it. When Denise, in her misery, recognized this friendly voice, she automatically gave in to the need for support.

'Monsieur Deloche, you must come back with us,' she said. 'Give me your arm.'

Pauline and Baugé were already walking on ahead. They were astonished. They would never have thought that it would happen like that, with that boy. However, since there was still an hour before they took the train, they walked to the end of the island, following the river-bank under the tall trees; and, from time to time, they would turn round and murmur:

'Where have they got to? Oh, there they are! It's funny, isn't it?'

At first, Denise and Deloche had remained silent. The din from the restaurant was dying away, acquiring the softness of music in the depths of night; and they were going forward into the chill of the trees, still burning hot from that furnace where the candles were going out one by one behind the leaves. Ahead of them, it was like a wall of darkness, a mass of shadows so dense that they could not even make out the pale line of the path. Despite this, they went forward slowly, but without fear. Then their eyes became accustomed to it and on the right they saw the trunks of the poplars like dark columns bearing the domes of their branches, shot through with stars, while the river, on the right, shone now and then through the dark like a tin mirror. The wind slackened and they could only hear the flowing of the river.

'I'm very pleased we met,' Deloche stammered at last, nerving himself to be the first to speak. 'You don't know how happy you've made me, by agreeing to walk with me.'

And, under cover of darkness, after several embarrassed words, he managed to tell her that he loved her. He had been wanting to write to her for a long time; and she might perhaps never have known, had it not been for the assistance of this lovely night, for this melodious water and these trees which shielded them with the curtain of their boughs. But she did not answer, still holding his arm as she walked with the same painful steps. He was trying to look at her face when he heard a gentle sob.

'Oh, good lord!' he said. 'You are crying, Mademoiselle, crying . . . Have I upset you?'

'No, no,' she murmured.

She tried to hold back her tears, but could not. Already, in the restaurant, she thought that her heart would burst; now, in this darkness, she gave way and was stifled by sobs at the thought that if Hutin had been in Deloche's place and was speaking tenderly to her in this way, she would be without the power to resist. Finally confessing this to herself filled her with confusion. Her cheeks burned with shame, as though under these trees she had fallen into the arms of that boy who had been showing off his women.

'I didn't mean to offend you,' Deloche repeated, almost starting to weep himself.

'No, listen to me,' she said, her voice still trembling. 'I am not at all angry with you. But please, I beg you, don't speak to me again as you have just done. What you ask is impossible. Oh, you are a nice boy and I would like to be your friend, but nothing more . . . Do you understand? Your friend . . .'

He shuddered. After going a few more steps in silence, he blurted out:

'So, you don't love me?'

And, when she avoided causing him further distress by a downright 'no', he continued in a gentle, pained voice:

'In any case, I was expecting it . . . I have never had any luck, I know that I cannot be happy. At home, I was beaten. In Paris, I've always been the scapegoat. You see, when you don't know how to steal other people's girlfriends and when you are not quick enough to earn as much money as they do, well, then you ought to lie down and die in a corner straightaway. Oh, don't you worry, I won't bother you any more. As for loving you, you can't stop me doing that, can you? I'll love you for free, like an animal. There we are! Everything is going wrong, that's my lot in life.'

He wept in his turn. She consoled him and, as they poured out their hearts to one another in friendship, they discovered that they were from the same part of the country: she from Valognes, he from Briquebec, thirteen kilometres away. It was a new bond between them. His father, a poverty-stricken little bailiff, with a morbidly jealous streak, used to hit him and call him a bastard, infuriated by his long, pale face and flaxen hair which, he said, did not belong in the family. They went on to speak of great meadows surrounded by hawthorn hedges, of covered paths vanishing under the elms and of roads with grassy lawns like alleys in a park. Around them as the darkness lightened, they could make out the rushes on the riverbank and the lacy patterns of the leaves, black against the shimmering stars; and a feeling of peace fell on them so that they forgot their woes, brought together by their misfortunes as good friends and colleagues.

'Well?' Pauline asked her eagerly, taking her aside as they came towards the station.

Denise understood what she meant from her smile and tone of affectionate curiosity. She blushed deeply as she replied:

'No, never, my dear! I told you, that's not what I want! He comes from back home. We were talking about Valognes.'

Pauline and Baugé were bewildered, having assumed something quite different and now not knowing what to think. Deloche left them at the Place de la Bastille; like all the probationers, he slept in the shop and had to be back there by eleven o'clock. Not wanting to go back with him, Denise, who had a theatre pass, agreed to go with Pauline to

Baugé's; in order to be closer to his mistress, he had taken a place in the Rue Saint-Roch. They took a cab and Denise was amazed when, on the way, she learned that her friend was going to spend the night with the young man. Nothing could be easier: you gave Madame Cabin five francs – all the young ladies took advantage of it. Baugé showed them his room, fitted out with old Empire-style furniture which his father had sent him. He got angry when Denise spoke of paying her share, but eventually accepted the fifteen francs sixty which she put on the dresser. But then he wanted to give her a cup of tea, struggled with a kettle on a spirit lamp, and had to go back downstairs to buy some sugar. It was striking midnight as he filled the cups.

'I must go,' Denise said again. But Pauline answered: 'Wait a bit . . . The theatres don't close this early.'

Denise felt awkward in this bachelor's room. She saw her friend stripped down to her petticoat and corset, and watched her getting the bed ready, airing it and fluffing up the pillows with her naked arms. She found it disturbing to have this homely preparation for a night of love going on in front of her and felt ashamed because it reawoke the memory of Hutin in her wounded heart. It did her no good, spending the day like this. At last, at a quarter past twelve, she left them. But she left in further embarrassment when, replying to her innocent 'good night', Pauline exclaimed without thinking:

'Thank you, it'll be a good one!'

The private door leading to Mouret's apartment and the other staff quarters was in the Rue Neuve-Saint-Augustin. Madame Cabin pulled the cord to open it and glanced up to see who was coming in. The hall was dimly lit by a night light. Denise found herself in its glow, anxious and hesitating because, coming round the corner of the street, she had seen the door close on the vague shadow of a man. It must be the director, coming back from an evening out, and the idea that he was there in the dark, waiting for her, made her feel one of those strange fears, with no rational basis, that he instilled in her even now. Someone was moving around on the first floor and boots were creaking. Hearing that, she lost her head and pushed open a door leading to the shop which was left open for the nightwatchman. She was in cotton prints.

'Oh, heavens! What can I do?' she stammered, quite overwhelmed.

She remembered that upstairs, there was another door which led to the rooms; the trouble was, one had to go through the whole shop. Even so, she preferred to make the journey, despite the darkness shrouding the galleries. There was no gaslight burning, only some oil lamps, far apart, fixed on the branches of the chandeliers; and these scattered lights, like yellow dots, their rays swallowed by the surrounding darkness, resembled the lanterns hanging in a coal mine. Great shadows loomed and it was hard to make out heaps of merchandise which assumed terrifying shapes – fallen columns, crouching beasts, thieves in ambush. The darkness was intensified by the heavy silence, broken by the distant sound of breathing. However, she started to find her way: linen, to her left, was a long pale streak, like the pallor of houses in a street under a summer sky. At first, she tried to cross directly through the hall, but ran up against heaps of calico and thought it safer to make her way past hosiery and then woollens. Here, she was startled by a sound of thunder – the sonorous snoring of Joseph, the porter, who slept behind mourning wear. She hurried into the hall, lit by a nebulous half-light from the glass ceiling; it seemed larger than usual, full of the nocturnal terrors of a church because of the stillness of its storage racks and the outlines of its huge rulers which looked like reversed crosses. Now she was fleeing. In haberdashery and in the glove department she again almost tripped over the duty porters, and only considered herself saved at last when she reached the staircase. But upstairs, arriving at the ladies' wear department, she was seized with terror when she saw the winking eye of a lantern walking along: it was two firemen doing their rounds, marking their progress on the dials of clocks. She stayed there for a minute trying to work out what it was, watching them as they moved from shawls to furnishings, then lingerie, terrified by their strange movement, the rasping keys and iron gratings which made a dreadful noise as they fell back. As they approached, she fled to the back of the lace department, but rushed out again at once when she heard a voice and ran to the connecting door. She had recognized Deloche, who slept in his department on a little iron bedstead which he set up himself every evening; and he was not yet asleep, but reliving the sweet moments of their evening, with wide-open eyes.

'What! Is that you, Mademoiselle?' said Mouret, whom Denise found in front of her on the staircase with a small pocket candle in his hand.

She stammered, trying to explain that she had just been looking for something in the department. But there was no annoyance at all in his look, at once paternal and curious.

'Do you have a theatre pass?'

'Yes, Monsieur.'

'And did you enjoy it? Which theatre did you go to?'

'I went out to the country, Monsieur.'

That made him laugh. Then, stressing the word, he asked her:

'Alone?'

'No, Monsieur, with a girl friend,' she said, her cheeks blushing purple, shamed by the thought that must have been in his head.

At this, he fell silent. But he was still looking at her, in her little black dress and her plain hat with only a single blue ribbon around it. Would this little savage grow up to be a pretty young woman? She smelled good from her outing in the fresh air, she was charming with her fine, startled hair over her forehead. And this man who, for six months, had been treating her like a child, sometimes giving her advice, yielding to the ideas of an experienced man, one who had a mischievous yearning to know how a woman might grow up and be corrupted in Paris, was laughing no longer, but felt an undefinable feeling of surprise and fear, mingled with tenderness. No doubt, it was some lover who had beautified her in this way. And at the thought, he felt as though a favourite bird had just drawn blood with its beak while he was playing with it.

'Good night, Monsieur,' Denise muttered and went on up without pausing further.

He did not reply, watching her as she went. Then he returned to his apartment.

CHAPTER 6

When the dead season of summer arrived, a wave of panic swept through *Au Bonheur des Dames.* It was the fear of dismissals, of the mass sackings that the management used to clear out the store when it was empty of customers in the hot days of July and August.

Every morning, when Mouret was doing his rounds with Bourdoncle, he would take the heads of department aside – the same whom he had been urging the previous winter to take on more staff than they needed, for fear that otherwise sales might suffer, at the risk of having to thin them out later on. Now it was a matter of reducing costs, putting a good one-third of the assistants on the street, the weaker being devoured by the stronger.

'Come now,' he said. 'You have people here who are not right for you. After all, we can't keep them here twiddling their thumbs.'

If the head of department hesitated, uncertain whom to sacrifice: 'You decide. Six salesmen should be enough for you. You can take more on in October, there are enough of them lounging around the streets!'

In any case, Bourdoncle took responsibility for the executions. His thin lips would utter a frightful: 'Go to the desk!', which descended like an axe. Anything would serve as an excuse for clearing the decks. He invented misdemeanours and seized on the slightest omission. 'You were sitting down, Monsieur: go to the desk!' 'Are you answering back? Go to the desk!' 'Your shoes are not polished. Go to the desk!' Even the bravest trembled at the sight of the slaughter that he left behind. Then, the guillotine was not working fast enough, so he thought up a trap that in a few days would effortlessly do away with the number of sales staff who had been condemned in advance. From eight o'clock onwards, he stood by the door with a watch in his hand; and after three minutes' grace, the pitiless: 'Go to the desk!' chopped off the breathless young things. It was a job smartly and cleanly done.

'You there! You've got a horrible face!' he said eventually to some poor devil whose crooked nose annoyed him. 'Go to the desk!'

Those who were spared got a fortnight's holiday, which was not paid; this was a more humane way of cutting costs. In any case, the assistants accepted the precariousness of their situation, driven by habit and necessity. Since arriving in Paris, they had moved around, starting their apprenticeship here, finishing it there, and were sacked or left of their own free will, quite suddenly, as it happened to suit. When the factory was not working, the workers did not get their daily bread; and it all happened as part of the unfeeling operation of the machine: a useless cog was calmly thrown aside, like an iron wheel towards which no one feels gratitude for services rendered. So much the worse for those who could not look after their interests!

Now, the departments spoke of nothing else. Every day, new stories did the rounds. Sacked assistants were named as one counts the dead at a time of plague. Shawls and woollens were especially hard hit: seven assistants vanished from there in one week. Then there was a drama in lingerie when a female customer complained of feeling ill, accusing the assistant who served her of eating garlic; and the girl was dismissed instantly, even though she was underfed and always hungry, and had been at the counter finishing some crusts of bread that she had saved up. At the slightest complaint from a customer, the management was pitiless: no excuse was accepted, the employee was always wrong and had to be thrown out like a defective instrument which impeded the efficient operation of the selling machine. His colleagues would hang their heads, not even trying to defend him. In the gust of panic, everyone feared for himself. One day when Mignot was taking out a parcel under his coat, in defiance of the rules, he was almost caught and for an instant thought he was out on the street; the notoriously lazy Liénard was only saved from expulsion because of his father's position in the drapery trade, one afternoon when Bourdoncle found him asleep on his feet between two piles of English velvet. But it was the Lhommes who were most worried, expecting their son Albert to be dismissed from one morning to the next: there was much dissatisfaction with the way he managed his cash desk, women would come and distract him, and twice Madame Aurélie had to plead for him with the management.

Denise, meanwhile, was so threatened by this clear-out that she lived in continual fear of disaster. Brave as she was, struggling with all the good cheer and common sense she could muster not to give in to nervous attacks, even so she was blinded by tears as soon as she shut the door of her room and despaired at the idea that she would be thrown on to the street, on bad terms with her uncle, not knowing where to go, without a penny saved and with the two children on her hands. Her feelings of the early weeks returned: she felt like a grain of millet beneath a crushing millstone; and she was totally hopeless when she considered how small she was in this huge machine which would grind her with calm indifference. She could have no illusion: if an assistant from ladies' wear was to be sacked, it would be her. No doubt the young ladies had worked on Madame Aurélie during the outing to Rambouillet, because since that time she had treated her sternly, with some resentment in her manner. In any case, they could not forgive her for having gone to Joinville, which was seen as a rebellion, a way of snubbing the whole department, appearing publicly outside with a girl from a rival section. Denise had never suffered so much at work and now she despaired of winning them over.

'Leave them!' said Pauline. 'They're show-offs and as stupid as a gaggle of geese!'

But it was precisely their young ladies' manners that intimidated Denise. Mixing daily with the customers, almost all the assistants took on airs and ended up in an indistinct social class, somewhere between the workers and the bourgeoisie; but beneath their skill in dressing, beneath the manners and ways of speaking they had acquired, there was often only a superficial learning, picked up through reading the popular newspapers, from speeches in the theatre and all the nonsense going the rounds on the streets of Paris.

'Do you know that Shockhead has a child?' Clara said one morning as she came into the department.

And when they expressed amazement:

'But I saw her yesterday evening, taking the kid out for a walk. She must have it in storage somewhere.'

A couple of days later, Marguerite had some more news when she came back from dinner:

'Well. I never. I've just seen Shockhead's lover. Would you believe it – he's a workman! Yes, a dirty little workman with yellow hair who was watching out for her through the windows.'

From then on, it was an established fact: Denise had a workman as her lover and was hiding a child somewhere in the neighbourhood. They plagued her with cruel, suggestive remarks. The first time that she understood, she went quite pale at the monstrosity of such assumptions. It was so frightful, she tried to explain, stammering out:

'But those are my brothers!'

'Oh, her brothers is it?' Clara said sarcastically.

Madame Aurélie had to intervene.

'Be quiet, ladies! You would do better to get on with changing these labels. Mademoiselle Baudu is quite free to misbehave outside. If only she would work when she's here!'

This tepid defence was a condemnation. The young woman, choking as though she had been accused of a crime, tried in vain to explain the facts. They laughed and shrugged their shoulders. The open wound on her heart remained. Deloche was so incensed when the rumour reached him that he spoke of boxing the ears of the young ladies in ladies' wear; only the fear that he might compromise Denise restrained him. Since their evening in Joinville, he had had a dog-like devotion for her, an almost religious affection that he expressed in looks of willing docility. No one must suspect these feelings, because they would both be teased about it, but this did not prevent him from dreaming about sudden acts of violence and avenging blows, if anyone should attack her in front of him.

Eventually, Denise stopped justifying herself. It was too hateful, no one would believe her. When one of her colleagues made some fresh allusion to the matter, she merely stared at her, sadly and calmly. In any case, she had other problems, material worries which were of greater concern to her. Jean was still being unreasonable, constantly bothering her with requests for money. Few weeks went by without her getting four pages from him with some story or other in it; and when the firm's postman gave her these letters, with their large, impassioned writing, she hurriedly put them in her pocket, because the assistants would make a show of laughing and chanting bawdy songs. Then, after making up some excuse to go and read the letters at the other end of the shop, she would be seized with terror: it seemed to her that poor Jean was done for. She was taken in by any tomfoolery, by extraordinary love stories which, in her ignorance in such matters, seemed to her even more hazardous than otherwise. He needed two francs to avoid the consequences of a woman's jealousy, and five francs, or six francs, to restore the honour of some poor girl whose father would otherwise kill her. She had confided in Robineau, who still behaved kindly towards her after their first meeting in Vinçard's, and he had got her some necktie sewing at five *sous* a dozen. At night, between nine o'clock and one, she could sew six dozen, which made one franc fifty, out of which she had to deduct a candle at four *sous*. But the remaining twenty-six *sous* supported Jean. She didn't complain about the lack of sleep and should have considered herself very happy, had not another catastrophe shattered her budget. At the end of the second fortnight, when she went to see the woman who supplied the ties, she found the door shut on her: bankruptcy, a business failure which took away her eighteen francs thirty centimes, a considerable sum which she had been absolutely counting on for the past week. This disaster threw all the misery at work into the shade.

'You're sad,' Pauline told her, when they met in the furnishings gallery. 'Tell me, do you need anything?'

But Denise already owed her friend twelve francs. Trying to smile, she answered:

'No, thanks. I didn't sleep well, that's all.'

It was 20 July, at the height of the panic over dismissals. Out of four hundred employees, Bourdoncle had already got rid of fifty and there were rumours of further sackings to come. However, she was not concerned about these looming threats, entirely taken up as she was with anxiety over another of Jean's affairs, this one more terrifying than all the rest. He needed fifteen francs that very day, which alone could save him from the vengeance of a deceived husband. The previous day, she had received a first letter, outlining the drama; then, in rapid succession, two others arrived, especially the last which she was just finishing when Pauline met her, in which Jean announced that he would be dead by evening if he did not have the fifteen francs. She was in torment. It was impossible to borrow it out of Pépé's rent, which she had paid two days earlier. Every misfortune was falling on her at once, because she had hoped to recover her eighteen francs thirty through Robineau, who might be able to find the woman who gave out the ties for knotting; but Robineau had got two weeks' holiday, so he had not returned the evening before, as expected.

Meanwhile, Pauline was still questioning her, in a friendly way. When the two of them got together like this at the back of some out-of-the-way department, they would chat for a few minutes, keeping a careful watch. Suddenly, the girl from lingerie made as though to leave: she had just seen the white tie of an inspector emerging from shawls.

'Oh, no! It's old Jouve!' she whispered, reassured. 'I don't know what's up with him, that old man, the way he laughs when he sees us together . . . In your shoes, I'd be worried: he's too nice to you. A sharp old dog, a real pest who thinks he's still talking to his troops.'

In fact, old Jouve was disliked by all the assistants, because he was so strict with them. More than half the dismissals were based on his reports. He had a great red nose like an ex-captain who had knocked around a good deal, and it only assumed a human appearance in departments staffed by women.

'What have I to worry about?' Denise asked.

'Why, he might expect some gratitude,' Pauline said with a laugh. 'Several of the young ladies butter him up.'

Jouve had moved away, pretending not to see them, and they heard him telling off a salesman in the lace department, who was guilty of watching a horse that had collapsed in the Rue Neuve-Saint-Augustin.

'By the way,' Pauline said, 'weren't you looking for Monsieur Robineau yesterday? He's back.'

Denise thought herself saved.

'Thank you. Then I'll go round and drop into silks. Too bad! They sent me upstairs to the workshop for a darning needle!'

They went their separate ways. Denise, looking busy, as though she were hurrying from one cash desk to the next, to correct a mistake, reached the stairs and went down to the hall. It was a quarter to ten and the bell had rung for the first table. The sunshine fell oppressively on the glass roof and despite its grey cloth blinds, the heat spread down through the still air. From time to time, a fresh gust rose from the floors, which some porters were sprinkling with a thin stream of water. There was a drowsiness, a summer siesta, in the empty spaces between the departments, like chapels where the shadows sleep after the last mass. Casual assistants stood around while a few rare customers walked along the galleries and crossed the hall with the weary steps of women tortured by the sun.

As Denise came down, Favier just happened to be measuring a light silk dress with pink dots for Madame Boutarel, who had arrived from the south the previous day. Since the beginning of the month, customers had been coming up from the country and one scarcely saw anything except dowdy women, yellow shawls, green skirts and the general jumble of the provinces. The assistants were so jaded that they no longer laughed. Favier went to haberdashery with Madame Boutarel and, when he got back, said to Hutin:

'Yesterday, it was all women from the Auvergne, today they're all Provençales. It's making my head ache.'

But Hutin leaped forward: it was his turn and he had spotted the 'pretty lady', as the department called that adorable blonde, while knowing nothing about her, even her name. They all smiled at her and not a week went by without her coming to *Au Bonheur des Dames*. This time she had with her a little boy of four or five. That got them talking.

'Is she married, then?' Favier asked, when Hutin came back from the cash desk where he had charged up thirty metres of duchess satin.

'Could be,' he replied. 'Though the kid proves nothing. It could belong to a friend. What is sure is that she's been crying. Oh, such a sad look! And red eyes!'

There was a silence while the two assistants stared into the far reaches of the shop. Then Favier said slowly:

'If she is married, perhaps her husband has been beating her.'

'Could be,' Hutin said again. 'Unless it's some lover who's stood her up.'

And, after a further silence, he added:

'As though I care!'

At that moment, Denise was crossing the silk department, slowing down and looking all round her, in search of Robineau. Not finding him, she went into the linen gallery, then walked past once more. The two assistants had noticed what she was up to.

'There's that skinny one again!' Hutin muttered.

'She's looking for Robineau,' said Favier. 'I don't know what they're cooking up together. Well, no hanky-panky, anyway; Robineau's too silly for that sort of thing. They say he's got her a little job, knotting neckties. Huh? What a business!'

Hutin decided to play a trick on Denise. When she walked past him, he stopped her and said:

'Are you looking for me?'

She blushed. Since the outing to Joinville, she had not dared to analyse her feelings, which were contradictory and confused. She kept on seeing him with the red-headed girl; and if she now trembled in his presence, it could be from embarrassment. Had she loved him? Did she still? She preferred not to stir up such things, which were painful for her.

'No, Monsieur,' she said awkwardly.

Hutin was amused by her unease.

'If you'd like us to serve him for you . . . Favier, could you give Mademoiselle a Robineau?'

She stared at him with that sad, calm look that was her reply to the hurtful remarks of the young ladies. Oh, he was unkind, adding his blows to the rest. And she felt a sort of grief, a last link shattered. Her face expressed such suffering that Favier, though not naturally soft-hearted, came to her rescue.

'Monsieur Robineau is in the stock room,' he said. 'He will no doubt come back for lunch. You can find him here this afternoon, if you need him.'

Denise thanked him and went back to ladies' wear, where Madame Aurélie was waiting for her, in a cold fury. What! She had been gone for half an hour! Where had she got to? Not in the work room, surely! The young woman hung her head, feeling that fate was piling misfortunes on her. It was all over, unless Robineau came back. However, she promised herself that she would go back down for him.

In silks, Robineau's return had sparked off a revolution. The department was hoping that he would not come back, fed up with the problems that people were continually making for him; and for a brief moment, indeed, still under pressure from Vinçard, who wanted to sell him his business, he nearly accepted the offer. Hutin's secret work, the mine that he had been laying for many long months under the feet of the under-buyer, was about to go off. While Robineau was on leave, when Hutin had taken over from him as first assistant, he had done all he could to harm him with the management and have himself put in his place, by a conspicuous eagerness to please: little irregularities were discovered and exposed, plans for improvement submitted, new designs that he had dreamed up. As a matter of fact, everyone in the department, from the new recruit aspiring to become a salesman, to the chief salesman coveting a managerial post, had only one obsession, which was to unseat the colleague above him in order to move up one step, and to devour him if he became an obstacle. And this clash of desires, with each one pushing against the next, was central to the smooth running of the machine which stimulated sales and lit a flame of success that amazed the whole of Paris. Behind Hutin was Favier, then behind Favier, the rest, all waiting in line. You could hear the jaws champing. Robineau was condemned and already everyone was taking away a bone. So when the under-buyer returned, there was a general murmur of discontent. There had to be an end to it: the attitude of the sales staff had seemed to him so threatening that the head of department, in order to allow the management to make up its mind, had just sent Robineau to the stock room.

'We'd rather all go, if they keep him,' Hutin announced.

This business annoyed Bouthemont, whose jolly manner was not suited to this kind of internal turbulence. It pained him to see only sullen faces on all sides; but he wanted to be fair.

'Come on, leave him alone, he's not doing anything to you.'

There was an outburst of protest:

'What! Not doing anything to us! He's impossible! Always on edge and so full of himself he's ready to walk right over you!'

This was the department's main complaint. Robineau, who had nerves like a woman, was intolerably stiff and touchy. They told dozens of stories about one little young man who had been made ill by it and lady customers he had humiliated with his cutting remarks.

'Well, gentlemen,' Bouthemont said, 'I can't take any action myself . . . I've informed the management and I'm just off to talk to them about it.'

The bell rang for the second dinner, a peal rising from the basement, faint and muffled in the still air of the shop. Hutin and Favier went down. Staff were arriving one by one, in no particular order, from every department, and hurrying down into the narrow entrance of the kitchen corridor, a damp passage where gaslights burned continually. The herd pushed its way in, without laughing or speaking, in the midst of a swelling clattering of dishes and a strong odour of food. Then, at the far end of the corridor, there was a sudden stop in front of a hatch. With piles of plates on each side, armed with forks and spoons which he dipped into copper pans, a cook was handing out the portions of food. And when he stepped aside, one could see the blazing kitchen behind his white-clad belly.

'Well, now,' said Hutin, consulting the menu, on a blackboard above the hatch. 'Beef with caper sauce or skate . . . They never have a roast in this dump! There's nothing to keep a body going in their boiled meat and fish!'

The fish was generally unpopular, because the pan stayed full. However, Favier did take the skate. Behind him, Hutin bent down and said:

'Beef in caper sauce.'

With a mechanical gesture, the cook stuck his fork in a piece of meat, then spooned some sauce over it. Hutin, stifled by the hot air from the hatch which hit him full in the face, had hardly taken his plate when behind him the words: 'beef in caper sauce . . . beef in caper sauce . . .', followed like a litany, while the cook ceaselessly forked up the pieces and bathed them in sauce, with the rapid, rhythmical movement of a well-regulated clock.

'This skate of theirs is cold,' Favier announced, not feeling any heat on his hand.

Now all of them were moving along, arms outstretched, holding their plates flat and anxious not to bump into one another. Ten steps further on was the bar, another hatch with a shining zinc counter on which the portions of wine were set out in rows – little bottles without corks, still damp from washing. So each of them, in his empty hand, took one of the bottles as he passed, then, well loaded and with a serious look, went to his table, taking care to keep everything balanced.

Hutin grumbled softly:

'What a performance, with all this in one's hands!'

The table that he shared with Favier was in the furthest dining room at the end of the corridor. Each of the rooms was like the next: they had once been cellars, four metres by five, which were then plastered over and done up as dining rooms. But the paintwork was peeling with the damp and the yellow walls were streaked with greenish patches, while the cellar windows, a narrow row of them which opened on the street at the level of the pavement, let in a ghostly light, constantly broken by the vague shadows of passers-by. Whether it was July or December, the heat here was stifling because of the hot steam carrying unpleasant smells from the nearby kitchen.

Meanwhile, Hutin was the first to go in. On the table, which was fixed to the wall at one end and covered with a waxed cloth, there were only glasses, forks and knives marking the places. Piles of spare plates stood at either end and down the middle of the table was a long loaf of bread, with a knife stuck handle-up in the middle. Hutin let go of his bottle, put down his plate and, after taking his napkin from the bottom of the rack, the only ornament on the walls, he sat down with a sigh.

'I'll say I'm hungry!' he muttered.

'That's always the way,' said Favier, sitting on his left. 'There's nothing to eat when you're starving.'

The table was filling up rapidly. It sat twenty-two. At first, there was only a loud clattering of forks, the ravenous greed of young men whose stomachs were hollow from working thirteen hours at a stretch. In the early days, the assistants had an hour for their meal and could go and have coffee outside, so they would wolf down their lunch in twenty minutes, hurrying to get out into the street. But this used to stir them up too much and they would come back distracted, with their thoughts on things other than selling; so the management decided that they could no longer go out, but that they could pay a three *sous* supplement for a cup of coffee, if they wanted one. Nowadays, as a result, they made the meal last, in no hurry to go back to their departments before time. Many of them, while swallowing great mouthfuls, read the newspaper which they folded and propped up against their bottles. Others, when the first pangs of hunger were satisfied, talked loudly, always returning to the inexhaustible subjects of bad food, what money they earned, what they had done the previous Sunday and what they would do the next.

'I say, what about your Robineau?' an assistant asked Hutin.

The silks' struggle against their under-buyer was the subject of talk in all departments. The matter was debated daily in the Café Saint-Roch until midnight. Hutin, struggling with his piece of beef, merely said:

'Well, he's back, Robineau.'

Then, suddenly losing his temper:

'Good heavens, this is donkey they've given me! It really is disgusting, I swear it is!'

'Don't you complain!' said Favier. 'I was foolish enough to take the skate. It's rotten.'

They were all talking at once and joking. In a corner of the table by the wall, Deloche ate in silence. He was cursed with a huge appetite which he could never satisfy and since he earned too little to pay for second helpings, he would cut off huge slices of bread for himself and devour the least appealing dishes with apparent enjoyment. So they all made fun of him, shouting:

'Favier, give Deloche your skate. That's how he likes it!'

'And your meat, Hutin. Deloche wants it for dessert.'

The poor lad shrugged his shoulders, not even bothering to reply. It was not his fault, if he was starving hungry. And, anyway, the others could say what they liked about the food, but they gobbled it up even so.

A slight whistling sound made them stop talking: Mouret and Bourdoncle had been spotted in the corridor. For some time now, there had been so many complaints from the employees that the management made a show of coming down to judge the quality of the food for itself. From the thirty *sous*[1] that they gave him, per head and per day, the chef had to pay for everything: food, coal, gas and staff; and they expressed naive astonishment when the result was not very good. That same morning, each department had delegated a salesman and Mignot and Liénard agreed to speak on behalf of their comrades. So, in the sudden silence, every ear was strained, listening to the voices coming from the next room, where Mouret and Bourdoncle had just entered. The latter declared that the beef was excellent and Mignot, gasping at this serene assertion, said: 'Chew it and see!', while Liénard, taking on the skate, said gently: 'But it stinks, Monsieur!' So Mouret gave them a cordial little address: he would do everything for the well-being of his employees, he was like a father to them, he would rather eat dry bread than think they were not properly fed.

'I promise to look into the matter,' he said, in conclusion, raising his voice so that he could be heard from one end of the corridor to the other.

The management investigation was over and the sound of forks resumed. Hutin muttered:

'Yes, count on it – and live on hot air! Oh, they're not sparing when it comes to fine words. If you want promises, here's plenty! Then they feed you old leather and kick you out of the door like a dog!'

The assistant who had previously questioned him repeated:

'So you were saying that your Robineau . . .?'

But his words were drowned in a clatter of dishes. The assistants changed their own plates and the piles at the two ends of the table went down. When a kitchen boy brought in some large tin dishes, Hutin shouted:

'Rice *au gratin*[2] – that tops it!'

'Here's two *sous*' worth of glue!' said Favier, serving himself.

Some of them liked it, others thought it too sticky. And the ones who were reading had nothing to say, engrossed in their newspaper's serialized novel and not knowing what they were eating. They were all wiping their foreheads. The narrow cellar was filled with reddish vapour and the shadows of people passing in the street, continuously, fell in black bands over the plain table cloth.

'Pass the bread to Deloche,' some joker shouted.

Each of them cut off his piece, then stuck the knife back in the loaf, up to the hilt; and the bread continued on its round.

'Who'll swap my rice for his dessert?' Hutin asked.

When he had done the deal with a thin little man, he also tried to sell his wine, but no one wanted that; they found it quite disgusting.

'I was telling you that Robineau is back,' he went on, against a background of laughter and overlapping conversations. 'Oh, it's a serious business . . . Just think: he's been debauching the sales girls. Yes, he was getting neckties for them.'

'Hush!' Favier whispered. 'Look, they're making up their minds about him.'

With a nod, he indicated Bouthemont who was walking along the corridor with Mouret and Bourdoncle on each side, all three of them deep in concentration, speaking emphatically, but in low voices. The dining room for the buyers and their assistants happened to be just opposite. When Bouthemont saw Mouret go by, he got up from the table, where he had finished eating, and was describing the problems in his department, and his own dilemma. The other two listened, still refusing to sacrifice Robineau, a first-class salesman, who dated back to the days of Madame Hédouin. But when he came to the story of the neckties, Bourdoncle got carried away. Was the man mad, acting as go-between to supply the salesgirls with extra work? The firm paid enough for these young ladies' time: if they were working for themselves overnight, they would work less during the day in the shop, that was obvious. So they were robbing them, risking their health – something that wasn't theirs to risk. The night was meant for sleep, they should all sleep, or they would be shown the door!

'Things are hotting up,' Hutin remarked.

Every time that the three men, in their slow walk, passed in front of the dining room, the assistants were looking out for them and commenting on their slightest gesture. They even forgot about the rice *au gratin*, in which a cashier had just found a trouser button.

'I heard the word *necktie*,' said Favier. 'And did you see Bourdoncle's nose suddenly go white?'

Meanwhile, Mouret was sharing his associate's indignation. The idea of a salesgirl being reduced to working at night seemed to him like an attack on the very principle of *Au Bonheur*. So who was this silly girl who could not manage on her commission from sales? But when Bouthemont named Denise, he softened, finding excuses for her. Oh, yes! That little girl: she was not yet very skilled and she had dependants, or so they told him. Bourdoncle interrupted to say that she should be sacked at once. They would never get anything out of such an ugly girl, as he had always said; and it was as though he was paying off a grudge. So Mouret, embarrassed, tried to make a joke of it. Good Lord! How strict the man was! Couldn't they forgive her this once? They'd call the guilty party in and give her a good scolding. In the end, Robineau was the one in the wrong, because he should have stopped her, being an old assistant who knew the ways of the firm.

'Well, well, now the boss is laughing.' Favier went on in astonishment, as the group once again passed in front of the door.

'By golly, if they insist on giving us their Robineau,' Hutin swore, 'we'll give them something to laugh about.'

Bourdoncle was looking straight at Mouret. Then he made a contemptuous gesture that meant he had finally understood and that it was crazy. Bouthemont was carrying on with his complaints: the sales staff were threatening to leave, and there were some excellent ones among them. But what appeared to have a greater effect on the two gentlemen was the rumour of a good relationship between Robineau and Gaujean: the latter, so it was said, was urging Robineau to set up his own business in the neighbourhood and offering him the most generous credit terms in order to make things awkward for *Au Bonheur des Dames*. There was a pause in the conversation. So! If this Robineau intended to make a fight of it . . . Mouret had become serious. He affected contempt and avoided taking a decision as if the matter was not important. They would see, they would speak to him. And straightaway he turned to joking with Bouthemont whose father, having arrived two days previously from his little shop in Montpellier, had almost suffocated with amazement and indignation on finding himself in the huge hall where his son presided. They were still laughing at the old gentleman, who had soon recovered his traditional southern self-assurance and started to run everything down, claiming that ladies' wear would end in the gutter.

'Here's Robineau now,' the head of department said softly. 'I sent him to the stock room to avoid an unpleasant confrontation . . . Excuse me for repeating this, but things have reached such a head that something must be done.'

As a matter of fact, Robineau, who was coming in, passed by the gentlemen and greeted them as he went to his table.

Mouret simply repeated: 'Very well, we'll see about it.'

They left. Hutin and Favier kept on waiting for them and when they did not reappear, sighed with relief. Was the management going to come down now at every meal and count each mouthful? It would be really nice, wouldn't it, if they couldn't even feel free while they were eating? The truth was that they had just seen Robineau coming back, and the boss's good humour made them uneasy about the outcome of the struggle they had undertaken. They lowered their voices, trying to think up new annoyances.

'I'm starving!' Hutin said aloud. 'You leave this table hungrier than when you sat down.'

Despite this he had eaten two portions of jam, his own and the one he had swapped for his rice. Suddenly, he shouted out:

'Damn it all, I'm getting another helping! Victor, give me a third jam!'

The waiter finished serving the dessert. After that, he brought the coffee and all those who wanted it gave him their three *sous* then and there. A few of the assistants had left and were strolling along the corridor, looking for dark corners where they could smoke a cigarette. The others slouched in front of the tables still laden with greasy dishes. They were rolling up crumbs of bread and going back over the same topics of conversation, surrounded by the smell of fat, though they were no longer aware of it, and by a heat like a Turkish bath, which reddened their ears. The walls were streaming and a slow asphyxiation drifted down from the mouldy vaults. With his back to the wall, Deloche, stuffed with bread, was digesting in silence and looking up at the window: his sport, every day after lunch, was to stare at the feet of the passers-by as they walked quickly along the street, cut off at the ankles, thick shoes, elegant boots and fine ladies' ankle boots, a constant coming and going of living feet, without heads or bodies. When it rained, it was very dirty.

'No! Not already!' Hutin exclaimed.

A bell was ringing at the end of the corridor and they had to clear the way for the third sitting. The kitchen boys arrived with buckets of warm water and large sponges, to wash the waxed cloths. Slowly, the rooms emptied, the assistants went back to their departments, dragging their feet on the stairs. In the kitchen, the cook had resumed his place behind the hatch, between his pans of skate, beef and sauce, armed with his forks and spoons, ready to start filling the plates again with his rhythmical movement like a well-regulated clock.

While Hutin and Favier were loitering behind the others, they saw Denise.

'Monsieur Robineau is back, Mademoiselle,' Hutin said, with exaggerated politeness.

'He's having lunch,' Favier added. 'But if it's very urgent, you may go in.'

Denise carried on down the stairs without answering or looking round. However, when she passed by the buyers' and under-buyers' dining room, she could not resist glancing inside. Robineau was there. She would try to speak to him during the afternoon; and she went on down the corridor until she reached her table, which was at the far end.

The women ate separately in two private rooms. Denise went into the first. This was also a former cellar, transformed into a refectory, but it had been done up more comfortably. The fifteen places at the oval table in the middle of the room were set further apart and the wine was in carafes. A dish of skate and a dish of beef in caper sauce was placed at either end. The young ladies were served by waiters in white aprons, which spared them the unpleasantness of having to take their portions themselves through the hatch. The management considered this more respectable.

'So did you go all the way round?' Pauline asked, already seated and cutting some bread.

'Yes,' Denise replied with a blush. 'I was looking after a customer.'

It was a lie. Clara nudged the girl next to her. What was up with Shockhead today? She was behaving quite strangely. She got letters from her lover, one after another; then she was running round the shop like a mad thing, claiming to have business in the workshop, but not even going there. Something was up, for sure. So Clara, while happily eating her skate – with the indifference of a girl who had once been fed on rancid pork – was talking about a dreadful murder that the papers were full of.

'Did you read about that man who chopped his mistress's head off with a razor?'

'Why!' exclaimed a little girl from lingerie with a sweet and delicate face. 'He found her with another woman. He did the right thing.'

But Pauline disagreed. What was this? Because you stopped loving a man, he was entitled to cut your throat? Oh, no! Not at all! And, breaking off, she turned to the kitchen boy:

'Pierre, I can't eat beef, you know . . . Ask them to make me a little extra, an omelette, huh? And, if possible, not over-cooked.'

While she was waiting, she took some chocolate pastilles out of her pocket, where she always kept some treat, and started to eat them with her bread.

'I mean to say, it's no joke having a man like that,' Clara went on. 'And some of them are so jealous! Only the other day, it was a workman who threw his wife down a well.'

She kept her eyes on Denise and thought she knew what was going on when she saw her go pale. Obviously, this coy little prude was afraid of getting her face slapped by her lover, whom she must be deceiving. It would be funny if he came right into the shop after her, as she seemed to be afraid he would. But the subject of conversation changed and one girl was describing how to get spots out of velvet. After that, they talked about a play at the Gaîté,[3] where some delightful little girls danced better than the grown-ups. Pauline, momentarily depressed by the sight of her omelette, which was overdone, cheered up on discovering that it did not taste too bad.

'Pass me the wine,' she said to Denise. 'You should order an omelette for yourself.'

'Oh, the beef's enough for me,' she answered, sticking to the food offered by the shop, however repulsive, in order to save money.

When the waiter brought the rice *au gratin*, the young ladies protested. They had left it, the week before, hoping not to see it again. Denise, whose mind was on other things – Clara's stories had made her anxious for Jean – was the only one to eat it, and they all watched her, with looks of disgust. There was an orgy of extras and they stuffed themselves with jam. Anyway, it was a matter of style: you ought to pay for your own food.

'You know the young gentlemen complained,' said the delicate girl from lingerie. 'And the management promised . . .'

She was interrupted by laughter and they turned to speaking about the management. All of them took coffee, except Denise, who could not digest it (or so she said). And they lingered in front of their cups, the girls from lingerie dressed simply in wool, like unassuming little bourgeoises, and the girls from ladies' wear in silk, napkins tucked under their chins to avoid stains, like real ladies coming down to take lunch in the scullery with their maids. They had opened the basement windows to change the stifling, foul-smelling air, but had to shut them immediately: the cab wheels seemed to be running right across the table.

'Hush!' Pauline whispered. 'Here's that old brute.'

It was Inspector Jouve. He would often wander around like this towards the end of the meal where the young ladies were. In any case, it was his job to supervise their dining rooms. With a smile on his face, he came in and walked round the table, sometimes even talking to them, asking whether they had enjoyed the meal. But, since they found him unsettling and annoying, they all hurried to get away. Even though the bell had not rung, Clara was the first to leave and others followed. Soon, only Denise was left with Pauline, who drank her coffee and finished her chocolate pastilles.

'I say!' she remarked as she got up. 'I'm going to send a waiter to fetch me some oranges. Are you coming?'

'In a while,' said Denise, nibbling at a crust of bread, determined to be the last to go, so that she could say something to Robineau as she went back.

However when she found herself alone with Jouve she felt a little bothered and finally left the table. But when he saw her heading for the door, he stood in her way.

'Mademoiselle Baudu . . .'

He was right in front of her, wearing a paternal smile. His large grey moustaches and close-cut hair gave him a very respectable military appearance; and he was thrusting out his chest, displaying his red ribbon.

'What is it, Monsieur Jouve?' she asked, reassured.

'I saw you again this morning talking upstairs behind the carpets. You know it's against the rules, and if I were to put in a report . . . Is she very fond of you, your friend Pauline?'

His moustaches twitched and a red glow suffused his huge nose, a gaunt, hooked nose suggesting bullish appetites.

'No? What is it about the pair of you that makes you so fond of each other?'

Denise could not understand, but felt uneasy again. He was getting too close to her, his face right next to hers.

'It is true, we were chatting, Monsieur Jouve,' she stammered. 'But there's no great harm in having a little chat . . . You're very good to me, thank you for that.'

He came closer still. Now she was really frightened: she remembered Pauline's words and stories she had heard about girls who had been terrorized by Old Jouve and had to purchase his goodwill. In the store, though, he was content with little intimacies, gently patting the cheeks of compliant young ladies with his puffy fingers, or taking their hands and keeping them in his, as though he had forgotten to let go. It all remained fatherly and the bull was only released outside when they agreed to take buttered bread in his house in the Rue des Moineaux.

'Stop it,' the young woman said softly, stepping back.

'Come now,' he said. 'You mustn't be so unfriendly to someone who always treats you well. Be a nice girl and come round this evening to have a slice of bread and a cup of tea. It would be a pleasure.'

Now she was struggling.

'No! No!'

The dining room was empty; the waiter had not returned. Jouve, listening for footsteps, looked quickly around and, very excited, not able to control himself, stopped being fatherly and tried to kiss her neck.

'Naughty girl, silly little . . . With hair like that, how can you be so silly? Come round this evening . . . It's just for a laugh . . .'

But she panicked, terrified by the approach of this burning face and the smell of his breath. Suddenly, she pushed him back, so hard that he staggered and nearly fell across one of the tables. Luckily, he landed against a chair, though the crash knocked over a carafe of wine, which spattered his white tie and soaked his red ribbon. He stayed there, without wiping it off, choking with rage at such rough treatment. Why! He was not expecting anything, he had not tried to force her, he was merely giving way to his good nature!

'Ah, Mademoiselle! You will regret this, I promise you.'

Denise had fled. As it happened, the bell was ringing and, still shaking, she was so upset that she forgot Robineau and went straight up to the department. After that she did not dare come back down. In the afternoon, since the sun was shining on the façade on the Place Gaillon, it was baking in the rooms of the mezzanine, in spite of the blinds. A few customers came and put the young ladies in a sweat without buying anything. The whole department was yawning, under Madame Aurélie's sleepy gaze. Finally, at around three o'clock, Denise noticed that the buyer was falling asleep, so she quietly slipped away and resumed her walk through the store, with her busy look. To pull the wool over any curious eyes that might be following her, she did not go straight down to silks; first of all, she pretended to have some business in lace and went up to Deloche to ask him something; then, on the ground floor, she went through cotton prints and into neckties where she stopped dead in surprise. Jean was standing in front of her.

'What! You, here?' she mumbled, going quite pale.

He had kept on his working clothes and was bareheaded, with his blond hair tousled and falling in curls over his girlish skin. Standing in front of a box of narrow black ties, he seemed to be deep in thought.

'What are you doing there?' she asked.

'Why, I was waiting for you,' he said. 'You won't let me come here, so I came in and said nothing to anyone. Oh, don't bother yourself. You can pretend not to know me, if you like.'

Sales assistants were already looking at them in astonishment. Jean lowered his voice.

'You know, she wanted to come with me. Yes, she is outside, on the square, by the fountain. Give us the fifteen francs quickly, or we're lost, as sure as the sun rises!'

At this, Denise became very agitated. People were giggling as they listened to this drama. As there was a stairway to the basement behind the tie department, she pushed her brother into it and hurried him down. When they got to the bottom, he went on with his story, embarrassed, looking for things to say and afraid that he would not be believed.

'The money is not for her; she is too distinguished . . . And her husband – well, he doesn't care a damn for fifteen francs! Even for a million, he wouldn't allow his wife . . . He's a glue manufacturer, did I tell you? Very respectable people . . . No, the money's for some swine, a friend of hers who saw us; and, you understand, if I don't give him fifteen francs, this evening . . .'

'Be quiet!' Denise muttered. 'In a moment. Keep on walking.'

They had come down as far as the despatch department. The dead season put this huge cellar to rest in the murky light from the basement windows. It was cold there and silent under the arched ceiling. Even so, a delivery boy was picking up the few packets for the Madeleine district from one of the boxes and, on the great sorting table, Campion, the head of despatch, was sitting, his legs hanging, eyes wide open.

Jean continued:

'The husband has this big knife . . .'

'Go on,' Denise said, still pushing him.

They followed one of the narrow corridors where the gaslights constantly burned. On either side of them in dark vaults, the reserve stock was piled up, making dark shadows behind the palisades. Finally, she stopped next to one of these wooden fences. Probably no one would come, but it was forbidden to be here and she felt a cold shudder.

'If the swine talks,' Jean went on, 'there's the husband with this big knife . . .'

'How do you expect me to find fifteen francs?' Denise cried in desperation. 'Can't you be sensible? Such odd things happen to you.'

He beat his chest. Among all his romantic inventions, he was not himself sure of the precise truth. He was simply dramatizing his lack of funds, but there was always some immediate need behind it.

'On all I hold dear, this time it's true . . . I was holding her like this and she was kissing me . . .'

Once again, she told him to be quiet, getting angry, tormented, driven to the limit.

'I don't want to know. Keep your misbehaviour to yourself. It's too sordid, do you hear me! And every week you torture me, I'm killing myself to keep you in money. Yes, I spend the night . . . Quite apart from the fact that you are taking the bread out of your brother's mouth.'

Jean was pale, gaping in astonishment. What! Sordid? He couldn't understand, when since they were children he had treated his sister as a friend, so it seemed quite natural to open his heart to her. But what most pained him was to learn that she was staying up at night. The idea that he was killing her and devouring Pépé's share upset him so much that he began to cry.

'You're right, I'm a scoundrel,' he cried. 'But it's not sordid – no, on the contrary! That's why one keeps doing it. You know, she's already twenty, this one, and thought she'd have a laugh because I'm only seventeen. My God! How I hate myself! I could slap my face!'

He had seized her hands and was kissing them, wetting them with his tears.

'Give me the fifteen francs, it will be the last time, I swear . . . But then, no, don't give me anything, I'd rather die! If I'm murdered by the husband, you'll be well rid of me.'

And, as she was crying too, he felt a pang of remorse.

'I say that, but I don't know. Perhaps he doesn't want to kill anyone. We'll manage, I promise, little sister. Farewell, then, I'm going.'

But the sound of footsteps at the end of the corridor startled them. She drew him back against the store room, in a dark corner. For a short time they could only hear the whistling of a gaslight near them; then the footsteps came nearer and, leaning out, she recognized Inspector Jouve, who had just started to march down the corridor. Had he come there by chance? Had some other supervisor, posted by the door, informed him? She was seized with such fear that she lost her head, pushed Jean out of the well of darkness where they were hiding and drove him ahead of her, stammering: 'Go away! Go away!'

The two of them broke into a run and could hear Inspector Jouve panting at their heels: he had also set off at the double. They went through the despatch department again and arrived at the foot of the glazed stairwell which opened on the Rue de la Michodière.

'Go away!' Denise repeated. 'Go away! If I can, I'll send you the fifteen francs anyway.'

Jean fled in a daze. The inspector, who came up gasping for breath, could only make out a corner of his white overall and the curls of his blond hair flying in the wind down the pavement. For a short while, he panted, recovering himself. He had a brand new white tie which he had got in the lingerie department; its knot was very wide and shone like snow.

'Well, here's a fine carry-on, Mademoiselle,' he said, with trembling lips. 'Yes, a fine carry-on, very fine indeed . . . If you expect that I'm going to put up with such a fine carry-on in the basement . . .'

He pursued her with the phrase as she made her way back to the shop, choking with emotion and unable to find a word to say in her own defence. Now she wished she hadn't run. Why not explain herself, show him her brother? People would be imagining dreadful things again: however much she swore, they wouldn't believe her. Once again, she forgot Robineau and went directly back to the department.

Without hesitation, Jouve went to the manager's office to make his report. But the porter told him that the director was with Monsieur Bourdoncle and Monsieur Robineau: the three of them had been talking for a quarter of an hour. Moreover, the door was ajar and he could hear Mouret pleasantly asking the clerk if he had had a good holiday. There was no question of him being dismissed; on the contrary, the conversation had turned to various steps that needed to be taken in the department.

'Do you want something, Monsieur Jouve?' Mouret asked. 'Come in.'

However, some instinct alerted the inspector. Bourdoncle had emerged and Jouve preferred to tell everything to him. Slowly, they walked through the shawls gallery, side by side, one leaning across and speaking in a very low voice, the other listening, without a muscle on his stern face revealing what he thought.

'Very well,' he said at length.

As they had just reached ladies' wear, he went in. Madame Aurélie happened to be telling Denise off. Where was she coming from now? Perhaps she wouldn't tell them this time that she had been up to the workshop. Really, they could not tolerate these constant disappearances any longer.

'Madame Aurélie!' Bourdoncle called.

He made up his mind to move decisively. He didn't want to consult Mouret, in case the director weakened. The buyer came over and once again the events were recounted in a low voice. The whole department waited, sensing some disaster. Finally, Madame Aurélie turned round with a solemn air.

'Mademoiselle Baudu . . .'

Her pasty emperor's mask had the inexorable immobility of omnipotence.

'Go to the desk!'

The dreadful sentence rang out loudly, in a department now empty of customers. Denise was standing upright and pale, not breathing. Then she stuttered out a few words:

'Me? Me? But why? What have I done?'

Bourdoncle answered coldly that she knew the answer and would do better not to demand an explanation; and he mentioned neckties, saying that it would be a fine thing if all the young ladies were to meet men in the basement.

'But he's my brother!' she shouted, with the pained anger of a raped virgin.

Marguerite and Clara started to laugh, while Madame Frédéric, usually so restrained, shook her head with an incredulous air. It was always her brother! It was really getting silly! So Denise looked at all of them: Bourdoncle, who had not wanted her from the very first; Jouve, who had stayed behind to give evidence and from whom she could expect no justice; then these girls whose hearts she had not won with nine months of cheerful courage, these girls who were in fact happy to see her leave. Why struggle? Why try to force herself on them when none of them liked her? And she went off without a further word, not even giving a last look at this room where she had struggled for so long.

As soon as she was on her own, however, by the balustrade above the hall, a sharper pain seized her heart. No one liked her and the sudden thought of Mouret deprived her of all resignation. No, she could not accept this dismissal. Perhaps he would believe that awful story about her meeting with a man in the basement. At this idea, a feeling of shame tormented her, an anguish greater than any she had ever experienced. She wanted to go to him and explain everything, just to let him know – because she did not mind leaving, as long as he knew the truth. And her old fear, that shudder which ran through her in his presence, suddenly burst out in a burning need to see him, and not to leave the store without swearing to him that she had not belonged to another man.

It was nearly five o'clock and the shop was coming back to life in the cooler air of the evening. She went quickly towards the director's office. But when she was in front of the door of his study, a despairing sadness swept over her once more. She felt tongue tied and the whole weight of the world pressed down on her. He would not believe her, he would laugh like the rest of them; and this fear made her feel weak. It was over. She would be better alone, vanished, dead. So, without even stopping to see Deloche or Pauline, she went directly to the desk.

'Mademoiselle,' the clerk said, 'you have twenty-two days, which makes eighteen francs seventy, to which must be added seven francs as a percentage and commission. That's correct, isn't it?'

'Yes, Monsieur, thank you.'

Denise was leaving with her money when she finally met Robineau. He had already heard about her dismissal and promised to find the woman who gave out the neckties for her. In a whisper, he consoled her, said how angry he was: what a life! Constantly at the mercy of some whim! To be thrown out from one minute to the next, without even being able to demand your salary for the whole month! Denise went upstairs to tell Madame Cabin that she would try to collect her trunk that evening. Five o'clock was striking as she found herself on the pavement on Place Gaillon, amid the cabs and the crowd.

That evening, when Robineau reached home, he received a letter from the management instructing him in four lines that, for reasons of internal administration, they would be obliged to dispense with his services. He had been with the firm for seven years, and that same afternoon, he had been talking to those same gentlemen. It was like a hammer blow. Hutin and Favier were chanting victory in silks as loudly as Marguerite and Clara were crowing in ladies' wear. Good riddance! A new broom sweeps clean! Only Deloche and Pauline, when they met in the chaos of the shop, expressed their sadness and missed Denise who was so sweet and so honest.

'Oh, if only she could succeed somewhere else,' the young man said. 'Then I'd like her to come back here and trample all over them, these mediocrities!'

Bourdoncle was the one who had to withstand the shock waves of Mouret's reaction in the matter. When the director learned of Denise's dismissal, he became very annoyed. He usually paid very little attention to staff, but this time he pretended to see it as an encroachment on his powers, an attempt to bypass his authority. Who was the boss around here? Did they think, by any chance, that they could give the orders? He needed to see everything, absolutely everything, and anyone who tried to resist would be broken like a straw. Then, when he had made his own inquiry into the affair, in a state of nervous anxiety that he was unable to conceal, he lost his temper again. The poor girl had not been lying: it really was her brother. Campion had recognized him plainly. So why dismiss her? He even spoke of taking her on again.

Meanwhile, Bourdoncle, with the strength of passive resistance, bent like a reed before the wind. He was studying Mouret. Finally, one day when he saw that his boss was calmer, he ventured to say, in a certain tone of voice:

'It's better for everyone that she's gone.'

Mouret was embarrassed and the colour rose to his cheeks.

'By jove,' he said, laughing, 'you may be right. Let's go and see what sales are like. Things are looking up, we made nearly a hundred thousand francs, yesterday.'

CHAPTER 7

For a moment, Denise stayed on the pavement, in the still scorching five o'clock sun, stunned. July was heating the water in the gutters and there were blinding reflections from the chalky summer light of the city. The catastrophe had been so sudden, they had expelled her so roughly, that she wondered where to go and what to do, while her hand mechanically turned over the twenty-five francs seventy centimes in her pocket.

A whole line of cabs prevented her from leaving the pavement beside *Au Bonheur des Dames*. When she was able to risk crossing between the wheels, she went over the Place Gaillon as though making for the Rue Louis-le-Grand; then she changed her mind and went down toward the Rue Saint-Roch. But she still had no plan in mind, because she stopped on the corner of the Rue Neuve-des-Petits-Champs and eventually took that street, after looking around her hesitantly. Reaching the Passage Choiseul, she turned into it and, without knowing how, came across the Rue Monsigny, then came back to the Rue Neuve-Saint-Augustin. Her head was buzzing and, seeing a porter, she remembered her trunk. But where could she have it taken, and why all this trouble, when only an hour earlier she still had a bed to sleep in that night?

Looking up at the houses, she started to study their windows. There were placards, one after another. She vaguely took them in, succumbing all the time to the inner turmoil that racked her. Was it possible? Alone from one minute to the next, lost in this huge, unfamiliar city! Yet she had to sleep and eat. One street followed another: Rue des Moulins, Rue Saint-Anne. She tramped through the whole district, going round in circles and always coming back to the one crossroads that she knew well. Suddenly, she stopped dead in amazement, She was once more in front of *Au Bonheur des Dames*; and, to escape this obsession, she started quickly down the Rue de la Michodière.

Thankfully, Baudu was not at his door and the *Vieil Elbeuf* seemed dead behind its black windows. She would never have dared to go to see her uncle, because he pretended not to know her nowadays and she did not want to become a burden to him in the misfortune that he had predicted for her. But on the far side of the street she saw a yellow placard: *Furnished Room to Let*. The house looked so poor, it was the first that had not scared her. Then she recognized it, with its two low storeys and its rust-coloured façade, squeezed between *Au Bonheur des Dames* and the former Hôtel Duvillard. At the door of the umbrella shop, old Bourras, with flowing hair and beard like a prophet, and spectacles on his nose, was examining the ivory on the knob of a walking-stick. As the tenant of the whole house, he sublet the two upper floors, furnished, in order to reduce his rent.

'Do you have a room, Monsieur?' Denise asked, on an impulse.

He looked at her with large eyes under his bushy eyebrows, surprised at seeing her. All the young ladies were known to him. And, observing her clean little dress and respectable appearance, answered:

'Wouldn't do for you.'

'How much is it?' Denise insisted.

'Fifteen francs a month.'

So she asked to have a look. In the narrow shop, since he was still staring at her with a look of astonishment, she told him about leaving the shop and not wanting to trouble her uncle. Eventually, the old man got a key from a board in the back of the shop, a dingy room where he did his cooking and slept; beyond it through a dusty window you could see the greenish light from an inner courtyard, barely two metres across.

'I'll go first, so you don't fall,' said Bourras in the damp alley beside the shop.

He stumbled against a step and went up, with further warnings. Look out! The banisters were up against the wall, there was a hole on this corner, sometimes the tenants left their dustbins here. In the total darkness, Denise could make nothing out, only feeling the cool of the old, damp plaster. However, on the first floor, a window opening on the yard allowed her to see dimly, as though at the bottom of a stagnant pool, the crooked stairway, the grimy walls and the peeling paintwork on the cracked doors.

'If only one of these two rooms was free,' Bourras said. 'You'd be fine there . . . But they are always occupied by ladies.'

On the second floor, the light increased, casting a raw pallor on the dilapidation of the place. A baker's boy lived in the first room; it was the other, at the back, that was empty. When Bourras opened it, he had to stay outside on the landing so that Denise could comfortably visit the room. The bed, behind the door, left just enough room for one person to get past. At the end there was a little walnut chest of drawers, a table in stained pine and two chairs. Lodgers who wanted to do some cooking had to kneel in front of the fireplace where there was a clay oven.

'God knows,' said the old man, 'it's not luxurious, but the window is pretty, you can see the people in the street.'

And, since Denise was looking in surprise at the corner of the ceiling, above the bed, where a lady on a fleeting visit had written her name, Ernestine, in the soot from a candle, he added genially:

'If we did repairs here, we'd never make ends meet . . . Anyway, that's all I've got.'

'I'll be fine,' the young woman said.

She paid a month in advance, asked for linen – a pair of sheets and two towels – and made her bed without delay, happy and relieved to know where she would be sleeping that night. An hour later, she sent a porter to fetch her case and settled in.

To begin with, she had two months of dreadful hardship. Since she could no longer pay Pépé's board and lodging, she had taken him in with her; he slept on an old wing chair which Bourras had lent them. She needed thirty *sous* precisely, per day, including rent, if she was prepared to live on dry bread for herself and give a little meat to the child. For the first fortnight, they got by: she had started with ten francs for housekeeping, then had the good luck to find the woman for the ties, who paid her the eighteen francs thirty. But after that, it was complete destitution, even though she applied to the stores, to the

Place Clichy, to the *Bon Marché*, to the *Louvre*. Everywhere, the dead season had put a halt to business; she was told to come back in the autumn; and more than five thousand sales staff, like herself, were out on the street, looking for work. So she tried to get odd jobs, but since she was not familiar with Paris, she did not know where to call and so accepted thankless tasks, sometimes without even getting her wages for them. Some evenings, she would let Pépé eat alone, a bowl of soup, telling him that she had had something outside. And she would go to bed, her head swimming, feeding only on the fever that burned her hands. When Jean came across her living in this poverty, he called himself a scoundrel, with such an agony of despair that she was forced to lie to him and still often found the means to give him a two-franc piece, to prove that she had some savings. She never wept in front of her children. On Sunday, when she could cook a piece of veal at the fire, kneeling in the fireplace, the narrow room echoed to their laughter – children without a care in life. Then, when Jean had gone back to his boss and Pépé was asleep, she spent a dreadful night, agonizing over the next day.

Other fears kept her awake. The two ladies on the first floor had visitors very late at night and sometimes a man would make a mistake, coming up and banging on her door. Bourras had calmly told her not to answer, so she put her head under the pillow, so as not to hear his curses. Then her neighbour, the baker, tried to annoy her: he didn't come home until morning and would wait for her when she went to fetch some water; he even made holes in the wall and spied on her while she was getting washed, so she was obliged to hang her clothes along the wall. But she suffered still more from men pestering her in the street and the continual obsession of passers-by. She could not go down to buy a candle, on these muddy pavements haunted by the debauchery of the old districts of Paris, without hearing heavy breathing behind her or crude remarks; and men would follow her right to the back of the dark alleyway, encouraged by the sordid appearance of the house. Why did she not have a lover? They were amazed, it seemed ridiculous, she was bound to succumb one day. She could not even understand it herself, with the threat of hunger and the desires stirred up in the overheated atmosphere around her.

One evening, Denise did not even have bread for Pépé's soup, when a gentleman with a decoration began to follow her. At the entrance to the alleyway, he started to get rough and, in a frenzy of disgust, she slammed the door in his face. Then, once she was upstairs, she sat down, her hands trembling. The child was asleep. What would she tell him, if he woke up and asked for something to eat? And yet, she only had to agree. Her poverty would be over, she would have money, dresses and a fine room. It was easy: they said that all women came to that eventually, because in Paris a woman could not live from her work alone. But something in her being revolted against it, without any indignation against other women, but simply rejecting what was demeaning and unreasonable. Her concept of life was logic, wisdom and courage.

Many times, Denise asked herself this question. She could hear an old ballad singing in her memory, about the sailor's betrothed who was preserved by her love from the perils of any assault on her virtue. In Valognes, she used to hum the sentimental refrain, looking down the empty street. So did she too have love in her heart to make her strong? She still thought about Hutin, with much uneasiness. Every day, she saw him go by under her window. Now that he was under-buyer, he walked alone, surrounded by the respect of mere sales assistants. He never looked up and she thought that what pained her was the young man's vanity, as she followed him with her eyes, not afraid of being noticed. But as soon as she saw Mouret, who also went by every evening, she started to tremble and hid away at once, her chest pounding. There was no reason why he should find out where she was living; and she was ashamed of the house and pained by what he might think of her, even though they might never meet again.

Moreover, Denise still lived within the orbit of *Au Bonheur des Dames*. A mere wall stood between her room and her former department: from early morning, she would start her working day again and hear the crowd building up with the increased volumes of sales. The slightest noise would shake the old shack stuck against the side of the colossus and she felt herself throb to this mighty pulse. And she could not avoid meeting people occasionally. Twice she had found herself confronted by Pauline, who offered her services, distraught at knowing how unhappy she was. She even had to lie, so as to avoid taking her friend to her room or accepting an invitation to visit her, on Sunday, at Baugé's. But she had a still harder time defending herself against the desperate affection of Deloche. He would wait for her, knew all about her worries and would hang around in doorways. One evening, he tried to lend her thirty francs – his brother's savings, he said, blushing deeply. Such chance meetings brought her back to the life of the store and concerned her with the lives of those who still worked there, as though she had never left.

No one came up to Denise's room. One afternoon, she was surprised to hear a knock on the door. It was Colomban. She stood up to greet him and he, stammering at first, very awkward, asked for her news and talked about the *Vieil Elbeuf*. Perhaps Uncle Baudu had sent him, thinking better of his severity (for he would still not even say hello to his niece, though he must be aware of the dire straits in which she found herself). But when she questioned the young man directly, he seemed still more embarrassed. No, no, it was not the boss who had sent him; and eventually he mentioned Clara: he just wanted to talk about Clara. Bit by bit, he became bolder, asking for advice, with the idea that Denise might be of some use to him with her former colleague. She tried in vain to discourage him, reproaching him for the suffering he was causing Geneviève for the sake of a heartless girl. He came back another time and got into the habit of coming to see her. This was enough for his shy love: he would constantly go over the same conversation, in spite of himself, trembling with joy at being with a woman who had been close to Clara. And Denise, as a result, lived still more in *Au Bonheur des Dames*.

It was in late September that the young woman experienced the direst poverty. Pépé had fallen ill, with a heavy, worrying cold. He should have had broth to feed him, but she didn't even have bread. One evening, in despair, she was sobbing, in one of those moods of utter depression that drive girls into the gutter or into the Seine, when old Bourras knocked gently on the door. He had with him a loaf of bread and a milk can full of soup.

'Here's something for the child,' he said in his brusque manner. 'Don't cry so loudly, it upsets my tenants.'

And when she tried to thank him, once more overcome by tears:

'Hush, hush, for goodness' sake! Come and talk to me tomorrow. I have work for you.'

Since the terrible blow that *Au Bonheur des Dames* had dealt him by setting up its umbrella and parasol department, Bourras no longer employed any assistants. He did everything himself, in order to keep down costs: cleaning, repairs and sewing. His customers, in any case, had diminished in number to the point where he sometimes did not have enough to occupy himself. So he had to invent work, the next day, when he settled Denise in a corner of the shop. But he couldn't let people die in his house.

'I'll give you two francs a day,' he said. 'When you find something better, take it.'

She was afraid of him and got through her work so quickly that he had trouble finding more for her to do. There were silk gores to sew and lace to mend. In the early days, she did not dare raise her head, uneasy at feeling him around her with his old lion's mane, his hooked nose and his piercing eyes under their stiff, bushy eyebrows. He had a harsh voice and wild gestures; mothers in the neighbourhood would scare their little children by threatening to send for him, as one might send for the police. Yet kids would never walk past his door without shouting some rude remark at him, which he did not even seem to hear. All his maniacal rage was directed against those wretches who dishonoured his trade with cheap, tawdry goods which even a dog, he said, would not want to use.

Denise shook when he thundered at her furiously:

'The craft is finished, do you hear! There's not even a proper handle any more. They make sticks – but handles! Finished! Find me a handle and I'll give you twenty francs.'

It was his pride as a craftsman: no maker in Paris could shape a handle like one of his, light and strong. Most of all, he would put charming inventiveness into carving the knob, always with a different theme: flowers, fruit, animals and heads, each executed in a free and lively way. All he needed was a penknife and you could see him for days, with his spectacles stuck on his nose, whittling a piece of box or ebony.

'A bunch of ignoramuses,' he said, 'who just stick silk on whalebone. They buy their handles wholesale, ready-made . . . And they sell it for what it's worth! The craft is finished!'

In the end, Denise lost her fear of him. He wanted Pépé to come down and play in the shop, because he loved children. When the boy was crawling on all fours, you couldn't move there, with her doing the mending in her corner and him sitting in front of the window, shaping the wood with his penknife. Now every day brought the same tasks and the same conversation. As he worked, he always came back to *Au Bonheur des Dames*, and never tired of explaining where he had got to in his awful struggle. He had been in the house since 1845 and had a lease of thirty years for a rent of eighteen hundred francs. Since he made a thousand francs by letting his four furnished rooms, he paid eight hundred francs for the shop. It was not a great deal, he had no expenses and could hold out for a long time yet. To listen to him, there was no doubt about his victory: he would devour the monster.

Suddenly, he broke off.

'Do they have dogs' heads like this, huh?'

And he blinked behind his spectacles, assessing the mastiff's head that he was carving, its lips drawn back and its teeth bared in a lifelike growl. Pépé, delighted with the dog, picked himself up and rested his two little arms on the old man's knees.

'As long as I can make ends meet, I don't care about the rest,' Bourras said, making a delicate adjustment to the tongue with the point of his knife. 'The rogues have killed off my profits; but even though I'm not making anything any longer, I'm not yet losing, or at least not much. And, as you see, I've decided to fight to the bitter end rather than give in.'

He brandished his knife, his grey hair swept upwards by the wind of his anger.

'And yet,' Denise suggested tentatively, without looking up from her needle, 'if they were to offer you a reasonable amount, it would be wiser to accept.'

At this, his savage obstinacy burst forth.

'Never! If my head was on the block, I'd still say no. Heavens above! I've still got ten years left on my lease and they won't have the house for ten years, even if I have to starve to death between four empty walls. Twice already they have tried to twist my arm. They offered me twelve thousand francs for my business and eighteen thousand for the years left on the lease, in all thirty thousand . . . But not for fifty thousand! I've got them, I want to see them lick my boots.'

'Thirty thousand francs is a fine sum,' Denise said. 'You could go and set up somewhere else. And suppose they were to buy the house?'

Bourras broke off for a moment to finish his mastiff's tongue, with a childlike smile vaguely hovering around his snowy face, the face of the Eternal Father. Then he started up again.

'The house? There's no risk of that! They were speaking of buying it last year, they were offering twenty thousand francs, twice what it's worth today. But the owner, an old fruit merchant, a rascal just like them, wanted to twist their arms. And, in any case, they were wary of me, knowing very well that I would be still less inclined to give way. No, no – here I am, here I stay! The Emperor with all his cannons will not drive me out.'

Denise did not dare say any more. She went on drawing her needle while the old man came out with a few more disjointed phrases, between nicks with his penknife: it was only just beginning, later they would see extraordinary things, he had ideas that would sweep their umbrella counter away; and behind his obstinacy was the rumbling of revolt of a small individual manufacturer against the invasion of cheap, mass-produced goods.

Meanwhile, Pépé had managed to climb up on Bourras' knees and was holding out an impatient hand towards the mastiff's head.

'Give me, Monsieur.'

'In a moment, little one,' the old man answered, his voice softening. 'He has no eyes, I have to make him some eyes now.'

As he was putting the last touches to an eye, he turned once more to Denise.

'Can you hear them? Are they still rumbling, next door? I swear, that's what exasperates me the most – having them constantly on my back, with their roar like a steam engine.'

His little table would tremble from it, he said. The whole shop was shaken and he spent his afternoons without a customer amid the shuddering from the crowd pressing into *Au Bonheur des Dames*. He constantly returned to the subject. Another good day, they were banging away behind the wall, silks must have made ten thousand francs; or else, he exulted: the wall had remained cold, a shower of rain had damped down their takings. And the least sound, the slightest murmur would give him material for endless comment.

'There! Someone's slipped. Oh, if they could only break their backs, the lot of them . . . That, dear, is some ladies having an argument. Good, good! . . . Huh! Do you hear the parcels going down to the basement? It's disgusting!'

Denise must not question his comments, or else he would bitterly remind her of the way she had been dismissed. Then she would have to tell him for the hundredth time about her experience in ladies' wear, how she had suffered at the start, the unhealthy little rooms, the poor food and the constant battle between the sales staff. And so the pair of them, from morning to evening, would speak of nothing except the shop, drinking it in at every moment in the very air that they breathed.

'Give me, Monsieur,' Pépé repeated eagerly, still holding out his hands.

The mastiff's head was finished. Bourras snatched it back, then held it out, playfully growling.

'Look out, he'll bite you . . . There, enjoy yourself and try not to break it, if you can.'

Then, returning to his obsession, he brandished his fist towards the wall.

'Even though you push until the house falls down, you won't have it – not if you invade the whole street.'

Denise now had bread every day. She was deeply grateful to the old merchant, appreciating what a good heart he had beneath his eccentric outbursts. However, the thing she wanted most was to find work somewhere else, because she could see that he was inventing odd jobs for her and realizing that he did not need anyone to work for him when his business was collapsing; it was out of pure charity that he employed her. Six months had passed and they had just slipped back into the winter lull. She despaired of finding anything before March; however, one January evening, Deloche, in a doorway where he had been waiting for her, gave her some advice. Why not go and inquire at Robineau's, where they might need someone?

In September, Robineau had decided to buy up Vinçard's business, even though he was afraid that he might be taking a risk with his wife's sixty thousand francs. He had paid forty thousand for the silk business and was setting himself up with the other twenty. It was not a lot, but he had Gaujean behind him, ready to support him with long-term credits. Since his falling out with *Au Bonheur des Dames*, Gaujean had dreamed of encouraging competition against the giant, and he felt sure of succeeding, if several specialized shops were to set up in the district, offering their customers a very varied choice of goods. Only the rich manufacturers in Lyon, like Dumonteil, could meet the demands of the large department stores; they were content to keep their looms busy with orders from them, looking for profits later by selling to smaller shops. But Dumonteil had solid financial backing, which Gaujean didn't. For a long time he had been a simple agent, only acquiring his own looms five or six years earlier, and he still gave employment to a lot of home workers, whom he supplied with the raw materials, then paid so much a metre. It was this system in fact that raised his costs and so prevented him from competing with Dumonteil to supply Paris-Bonheur. He resented this and saw Robineau as the instrument of a decisive battle against these novelty shops, which he accused of ruining French industry.[1]

When Denise arrived, she found Madame Robineau on her own. The daughter of an overseer of public works, knowing nothing about business, Madame Robineau retained the engaging naivety of a former pupil at a convent school in Blois. She was very dark-skinned and pretty with a gentle vivacity that made for great charm. Moreover, she adored her husband and this love was her life's blood. Denise was going to leave her name, but Robineau came back and took her on immediately; one of his salesgirls had in fact left only the day before to take a place at *Au Bonheur des Dames*.

'They're not leaving us a single good girl,' he said. 'But with you, at least, I'll be easy in my mind, because you're like me, you can't care for them much . . . Start tomorrow.'

That evening, Denise felt awkward about telling Bourras that she was leaving him. And, indeed, he called her ungrateful and flew into a rage. Then, when she tried to defend herself, with tears in her eyes, letting him know that she was not fooled by his charity, he also softened, stammering that he had a lot of work and that she was leaving him just when he was about to launch a new umbrella that he had invented.

'And what about Pépé?' he asked.

The child was Denise's great worry. She did not dare put him back with Madame Gras, but she couldn't leave him shut up alone in his room from morning to evening.

'Very well, I'll look after him,' the old man said. 'He'll be fine in my shop, the boy; we'll do some cooking together.'

And, when she refused, afraid that it would be a nuisance for him:

'Heaven's above, you don't trust me! I'm not going to eat the child!'

Denise was happier at Robineau's. He paid her very little, sixty francs a month and just her board, with no commission on sales, as in old-fashioned firms. But she was treated with plenty of kindness, especially by Madame Robineau, who was always smiling behind her counter. He, on the other hand, was nervous and worried, and occasionally snapped at her. After a month, Denise was part of the family, like the other sales assistant, a consumptive, uncommunicative little woman. There was no embarrassment in front of them: the Robineaus talked business over their meals in the back of the shop, which looked out on a large courtyard. It was there that one evening they decided to begin a campaign against *Au Bonheur des Dames.*

Gaujean had come to dinner. When the roast arrived, a simple joint of mutton, he broached the question in his bland Lyonnais voice, thickened by the Rhône mist.

'It's getting impossible,' he insisted. 'They turn up at Dumonteil's, don't they, get exclusive rights to a design, and carry off three hundred lengths then and there, demanding a reduction of fifty centimes a metre; and since they're paying cash, they profit by the eighteen per cent discount on top . . . Often, Dumonteil doesn't make twenty centimes. He works to keep his looms busy, because an idle loom is a dead one . . . So how do you expect us to keep up the struggle, with less equipment and most of all with our home-workers?'

Robineau, lost in thought, was forgetting his dinner.

'Three hundred lengths!' he murmured. 'It gives me the shivers when I take twelve – and then at ninety days. They can price it at one franc or two francs cheaper than we can. I calculate that there's a reduction of at least fifteen per cent on their list prices compared to ours . . . This is what's killing small businesses.'

He was going through a period of despondency. His wife was watching him with affectionate anxiety. She couldn't cope with business, her head aching with all those figures, and she didn't understand why anyone should be so worried about it, when it was so simple to laugh and love one another. Even so, it was enough for her that her husband wanted to win: she supported him ardently and would have died at her counter.

'But why don't all the manufacturers agree among themselves?' Robineau went on, raising his voice. 'They could lay down the law instead of bowing to it.'

Gaujean, who had asked for another slice of mutton, chewed it slowly.

'Ah! Why, indeed! As I told you, the looms must work. When you have factories here, there and everywhere, around Lyon, in the Gard, in the Isère, you can't let them lie idle a single day without huge losses . . . Then, people like us who sometimes use home-workers, and have ten or twelve looms, are more the masters of our own output, from the point of view of stock; while these big manufacturers are forced to have outlets all the time, turning over as much and as quickly as possible . . . That's why they're on their knees to the large stores. I know three or four who scrap over them and are prepared to lose money to get orders. They make it up with little firms like yours. Yes, they exist because of them and profit because of you. God only knows where the crisis will end!'

'It's outrageous!' Robineau exclaimed, finding relief in this cry of fury.

Denise listened in silence. In secret, she was on the side of the department stores, having an instinctive love of life and logic. They fell silent, eating some preserved green beans. And she eventually ventured to say cheerfully:

'The public isn't complaining, anyway!'

Madame Robineau could not repress a chuckle, which upset her husband and Gaujean. Naturally, the customers were pleased because, when it came down to it, they were the ones who benefited from a fall in price. The only trouble was that everybody had to make a living: where would they end up if, on the grounds of the general good, the consumer was fattened at the expense of the producer? A discussion started. Denise pretended that she was joking, while contributing some solid arguments: the middlemen were disappearing – factory representatives, salesmen, commission agents – which accounted for much of the lower price; moreover, the manufacturers could no longer even live without the large stores, because as soon as one of them lost their customers, bankruptcy was inevitable; finally, this was a natural evolution in trade, no one could stop things going where they had to go, when everybody was working at it, whether they wanted to or not.

'So, you're for those who put you out into the street, then?' Gaujean asked.

Denise blushed deeply. She was surprised herself at the vigour of her argument. What was in her heart for such a flame to flare up in her breast?

'Goodness me, no, I'm not!' she answered. 'Perhaps I was wrong, because you know far more about it than I do. But I said what I thought. At one time, prices were set by fifty firms, now they're made by four or five, which have brought them down because of the power of their capital and the strength of their customers. And so much better for the general public, that's all!'

Robineau did not lose his temper. He had taken on a serious expression and was looking at the tablecloth. He had often felt this breath of new business and the developments that the young woman spoke about; and, when he saw it clearly, he would sometimes wonder why he should struggle against a current that had such force and would carry everything before it. Madame Robineau, too, seeing her husband's thoughtful mood, looked approvingly at Denise, who had reverted to her modest silence.

'Come now,' Gaujean went on, to change the subject. 'All that is theory. Let's talk about our business.'

After the cheese, the maid had just served some different jams and pears. He helped himself to jam and ate it with a spoon, with the unselfconscious appetite of a man with a sweet tooth.

'Now, then, you have to beat off the challenge of their Paris-Bonheur, which was the basis of their success this year . . . I've arranged with several of my colleagues in Lyon to bring you an exceptional offer, a black silk, a faille that you can sell for five francs fifty . . . They're selling theirs at five francs sixty, aren't they? Well, this will be two *sous* less, which is enough: you'll sink them.'

The light had come back to Robineau's eyes. In his state of continual nervous torment, he often swung in this way from despair to hope.

'Do you have a sample?' he asked.

And, when Gaujean took a small square of silk out of his wallet, he reached a pitch of excitement, exclaiming:

'But it's finer than Paris-Bonheur! In any case, it's more striking, the weave is thicker . . . You're right, we must give it a try. Look, now! This time, I want them at my feet, or it's over with me!'

Madame Robineau, sharing his enthusiasm, declared that the silk was superb. Even Denise believed in their success. So the end of the dinner was very jolly. Voices were raised and it seemed that *Au Bonheur des Dames* was on its last legs. Gaujean, finishing off the pot of jam, described the enormous sacrifices that he and his colleagues would have to make if they were to provide such material cheaply; but they would ruin themselves, if need be: they had sworn to defeat the big stores. As coffee was being brought in, Vinçard arrived, which made them still merrier. He had been passing and came in to say hello to his successor.

'Splendid!' he exclaimed, feeling the silk. 'You'll sink them, I promise! By the way, you owe me a vote of thanks. I told you, didn't I: this business is a goldmine!'

He himself had just taken on a restaurant in Vincennes. This was an old dream which he had secretly harboured while he was struggling in the silk trade, terrified that he would not be able to sell his business before the crash and swearing to invest his meagre funds in something that would allow him to rob people at his ease. The idea of a restaurant had come to him after a cousin's wedding. Grub always sold, and they had just paid ten francs for some dishwater with noodles in it. When he saw the Robineaus, his joy at having saddled them with a rotten business that he had despaired of ever offloading put an even broader smile on his face with its round eyes and big, honest mouth, bursting with health.

'What about your aches and pains?' Madame Robineau asked considerately.

'What's that? My aches and pains?' he muttered in astonishment.

'Yes, you were a martyr to rheumatism when you were here.'

He remembered and blushed slightly.

'Oh, that. Yes, I still suffer from it, but you know, the country air . . . No matter, you got a good bargain. If it hadn't been for my rheumatism, I should have retired within ten years, on an income of ten thousand francs . . . on my honour!'

A fortnight later, the struggle began between Robineau and *Au Bonheur des Dames*. It was a famous battle: for a while, the whole Parisian market talked about it. Robineau, adopting his opponent's weapons, had advertised in the newspapers. In addition to that, he paid attention to his display, piling huge heaps of the celebrated silk in his window and proclaimed it on large boards from which the price of five francs fifty leapt out in giant figures. This was the figure that caused a stir with the ladies: two *sous* cheaper than in *Au Bonheur des Dames*, for a silk that seemed stronger. From the start, the customers flooded in: Madame Marty, claiming that she was saving money, bought a dress that she didn't need; Madame Bourdelais thought the material was lovely, but preferred to wait, no doubt guessing what would happen. And, sure enough, the following week Mouret went right ahead and brought Paris-Bonheur down by twenty centimes, to five francs forty. He had had a heated discussion with Bourdoncle and the managers, which ended with him convincing them that they had to accept the challenge, even if it meant losing on every sale: the twenty centimes were a simple loss, since they were already selling at cost price. It was a serious shock to Robineau, who didn't think that his rival would come down in price, because there was as yet no precedent for such suicidal competition and selling at a loss; and the stream of customers, following the lower price, had immediately turned towards the Rue

Neuve-Saint-Augustin, while the shop in the Rue Neuve-des-Petits-Champs emptied. Gaujean hurried up from Lyon and there were frantic discussions at the end of which they took a heroic decision: the silk would come down and be set at five francs thirty, a price below which no one in his right mind would go. The next day, Mouret flagged up his material at five francs twenty. After that, things went crazy: Robineau replied with five francs fifteen, Mouret dropped to five francs ten. Each of them was now battling *sou* by *sou*, losing considerable sums every time they made these gifts to the public. The customers laughed, delighted by the duel and excited by the mighty blows that the two firms were landing on one another, just to please them. Finally, Mouret dared fall to five francs. His staff were ashen-faced, stunned by this challenge to fate. Robineau, flattened, exhausted, also stopped at five francs, not daring to go any lower. They dug into their positions, face to face, with the wreck of their merchandise around them.

Honour was saved on both sides, but the situation was fatal for Robineau. *Au Bonheur des Dames* had advances and regular customers which allowed it to balance out its takings, while he was only supported by Gaujean and could not make up his losses on other goods, so he stayed flattened, sliding every day a little further down the slope towards bankruptcy. His boldness was killing him, in spite of the many customers who had flocked to him in the comings and goings of the battle. One of his secret agonies was to see these customers slowly drifting away, back to *Au Bonheur des Dames*, despite the money he had sacrificed and the efforts he had made to capture them.

One day, he even lost his temper. A customer, Madame de Boves, had come to look at coats at Robineau's, because he had added a ready-made clothing counter to the silks in which he specialized. She couldn't make up her mind and complained about the quality of the materials. Finally, she said:

'Their Paris-Bonheur is much stronger!'

Robineau merely informed her, with his best salesman's manner, that she was wrong, and was all the more respectful for fear of letting her see how furious he was.

'But just look at the silk in this cloak!' she went on. 'You'd swear it was a spider's web. Whatever you say, Monsieur, their silk for five francs is like leather beside this.'

He said nothing, the blood rising to his cheeks, his teeth clenched. As it happened he had had the clever idea of buying the silk for his ready-made clothes from his rival, so that Mouret and not he would lose money on the material. He simply cut off the selvage.

'Really? Do you think Paris-Bonheur is thicker?' he said softly.

'Oh, yes. A hundred times,' Madame de Boves replied. 'There's no comparison.'

He rebelled against this unfairness on the customer's part, disparaging the goods in spite of everything. And as she was still turning the cloak round with her contemptuous air, a small piece of the silver and blue selvage which the cutter had missed showed under the lining. At this, he was unable to contain himself any longer and confessed, not caring about the consequences.

'Well, Madame, this silk is Paris-Bonheur. I bought it myself, so there! Look at the selvage.'

Madame de Boves left in high dudgeon. Many of the ladies left him: the story had got about. And he, in the midst of this disaster, seized by the terror of the morrow, only worried about his wife, brought up in tranquil happiness and unable to live in poverty. What would become of her if a catastrophe threw them out on the street, with debts to pay? It was his fault, he should never have touched the sixty thousand francs. She had to console him. Wasn't the money his as much as hers? He loved her and that was all she asked; she gave him everything, her heart and her life. They could be heard kissing in the back of the shop. Little by little, the shop settled into its routine; every month, the losses grew, but at a slow rate, which put off the inevitable. A stubborn hope kept them on their feet and they were still declaring that *Au Bonheur des Dames* would soon be defeated.

'Huh!' he said, 'we're young, too. The future belongs to us.'

'And then, what does it matter – as long as you've done what you wanted,' she went on. 'As long as you're happy, I am, my dear heart.'

Denise was touched by their affection for one another. She was afraid, feeling that the collapse was unavoidable, but did not dare intervene. It was here that she finally understood the power of the new forms of retailing and felt an enthusiasm for this force that was transforming Paris. Her ideas were developing and a feminine grace had started to emerge from the wild child who stepped off the train from Valognes. Life was pleasant enough, though she was tired and had little money. After spending the whole day on her feet, she had to hurry home and take care of Pépé, whom Old Bourras, fortunately, insisted on feeding; but then there were further chores, a shirt to wash, a blouse to sew, quite apart from the child's noise, which made her head split. She never got to bed before midnight. Sunday was a day of hard toil: she cleaned the room and made herself tidy, so that she was often too busy to comb her hair before five o'clock. However, she did sensibly go out sometimes, taking the child for a long walk over to Neuilly; and their treat when they arrived was to drink a cup of milk in the yard of a dairyman who would let them sit down there. Jean scoffed at these outings; he would turn up occasionally on weekday evenings, then vanish, saying he had other visits to make. He no longer asked for money, but he had such a downcast look when he came that it worried his sister, who always had a five-franc piece put aside for him. This was her money for luxuries.

'Five francs!' Jean would burst out, every time. 'Crikey! You're too good to me . . . It just happens that the stationer's wife . . .'

'Hush!' said Denise. 'I don't want to know.'

But he thought that she was accusing him of boasting.

'I'm telling you, now, she's a stationer's wife . . . But, ah, what a splendid thing she is!'

Three months went by and spring returned. Denise refused an offer to go back to Joinville with Pauline and Baugé. She sometimes met them in the Rue Saint-Roch as she was leaving Robineau's. On one of these occasions, Pauline told her confidentially that she might perhaps marry her lover – if she was not sure, it was because they didn't at all like married sales staff at *Au Bonheur des Dames*. The idea of marriage surprised Denise and she did not venture to give her friend any advice. One day when Colomban had just stopped her near the fountain to talk about Clara, the girl herself just happened to cross the square, and Denise had to hurry away, because he was begging her to ask her former colleague if she would like to marry him. What was wrong with all of them? Why did they torment themselves in this way? She considered herself very happy not to be in love with anybody.

'Have you heard the news?' the umbrella merchant asked her one evening when she came home.

'No, Monsieur Bourras.'

'Well, the rascals have bought the Hôtel Duvillard. I'm surrounded!'

He was waving his great arms in a fit of rage that made his white mane of hair stand on end.

'You wouldn't believe what a piece of wheeling and dealing!' he went on. 'It appears that the building belonged to the Crédit Immobilier and their director, Baron Hartmann, has just made it over to that Mouret of ours . . . And now they've got me from the right, the left and behind – look: just like I'm holding the knob of this cane!'

It was true; they must have signed the contract on the previous day. Bourras' little house, squashed between *Au Bonheur des Dames* and the Hôtel Duvillard, hanging there like a swallow's nest in a crack in a wall, seemed liable to be crushed instantly as soon as the shop spread into the Hôtel Duvillard – and that day had come: the colossus was bypassing the puny obstacle, walling it in with its piles of merchandise, threatening to swamp it and absorb it by the sole force of its enormous suction; Bourras could feel its embrace squeezing his shop. He thought he could see it getting smaller and hear the dreadful mechanism roaring so loudly now that he was afraid of being swallowed up himself, of being sucked through to the other side with his walking sticks and his umbrellas . . .

'There! Can you hear them?' he cried. 'Wouldn't you say they're eating the walls! And in my cellar, in my attic, everywhere, there's that same noise of saw on plaster . . . No matter! They may flatten me like a sheet of paper. I'll stay even if they take my roof off and the rain pours in bucketfuls into my bed.'

This was when Mouret told them to make a new proposal to Bourras: they would increase the figure, buying his stock and his lease for fifty thousand francs. This made the old man doubly angry; he turned the offer down with an oath. Look how the scoundrels were robbing people, if they could pay fifty thousand francs for something that was not worth ten! He defended his shop like a respectable girl defending her virtue, in the name of honour and out of self-respect.

For a fortnight, Denise noticed that Bourras was preoccupied with something. He rushed around feverishly, measuring up the walls of his house and looking at it from the middle of the street, for all the world like an architect. Then, one morning, the workmen arrived. This was the decisive battle: he had had the daring notion of taking on *Au Bonheur des Dames* on its own ground, by making concessions to modern luxury. His customers, who criticized his gloomy shop, would surely come back when they saw it brand new and sparkling. First of all, they filled in the holes and whitewashed the outside walls. Then they repainted the woodwork on the shopfront in light green and even went to the extreme of splendour by gilding the signboard. Three thousand francs, which Bourras had kept aside as a last resort, were swallowed up. In fact, the neighbourhood was in turmoil: people came to look at him in the midst of this luxury, losing his head, not sure whether he was coming or going. He no longer seemed at home in these glittering surroundings, against these pastel colours, in his state of bewilderment, with his long beard and his hair. Now, passers-by were amazed when they stopped on the opposite pavement to see him waving his arms and carving his handles. And he was feverishly excited, afraid he might make something dirty, and sinking still further with this luxury business which he didn't understand at all.

Meanwhile, like Robineau, Bourras had begun his campaign against *Au Bonheur des Dames*. He had just launched his new invention, the rucked umbrella, which would later become popular. In any event, *Au Bonheur* immediately refined the invention, after which the struggle started over the price. He had one model at one franc ninety-five, in zanella[2] on a steel frame which, according to the label, would never wear out. But most of all he wanted to beat his rival with his handles, in bamboo, in dogwood, in olive wood, in myrtle and in rattan, every imaginable variety of handle. At *Au Bonheur*, they were less artistic, but paid attention to the material, advertising its alpaca and mohair, its serge and taffeta. And it carried the day. The old man said again that craftsmanship was done for and that he was reduced to carving handles for his own amusement, with no hope of selling them.

'It's my fault!' he exclaimed to Denise. 'Should I have stocked rubbish like that at one franc ninety-five? That's where new ideas get you. I wanted to follow the example of those robbers, so I deserve to starve for it!'

July was very hot. Denise really felt it in her narrow room, under the slate roof. So when she left the shop, she would fetch Pépé from Bourras and, instead of going upstairs straightaway, would take the air a little in the Tuileries Gardens, until they shut the gates. One evening, as she was walking towards the chestnut trees, she stopped dead in her tracks: she thought she recognized Hutin a few steps ahead, walking directly towards her. Then her heart started to beat violently. It was Mouret, who had taken dinner on the Left Bank and was hurriedly walking to Madame Desforges'. The young woman made a brusque movement to get out of his way and he looked up at her. Night was falling, yet he recognized her.

'It's you, Mademoiselle.'

She said nothing, overwhelmed at the fact he had deigned to stop. He smiled and hid his embarrassment beneath an amiably paternal manner.

'Are you still in Paris?'

'Yes, Monsieur,' she said at length.

She was slowly stepping backwards and trying to take her leave so that she could go on with her walk. But he himself retraced his steps, following her under the dark shadows of the great chestnuts. There was a chill in the air and children were playing in the distance, pushing hoops.

'This is your brother, isn't it?' he asked her, looking at Pépé.

The boy, quite unused to the presence of a gentleman and intimidated by it, was walking along gravely beside his sister, holding her hand.

'Yes, Monsieur,' she replied once more.

She blushed, remembering the dreadful things that Marguerite and Clara had said about her. Mouret apparently understood the cause of her blushing, because he added quickly:

'Let me say, Mademoiselle, that I owe you an apology . . . Yes, I only wish I could have told you sooner how much I regretted the mistake that was made. You were too hastily accused of misbehaving

. . . Well, what was done is done, but I would just like you to know that everyone in the store now knows about your sisterly feeling for your brothers . . .'

He went on, politely and with respect, an attitude to which the sales staff of *Au Bonheur des Dames* were not accustomed from him. Denise was more nervous than ever, but joy flooded her heart. So he knew that she had not given herself to anyone! The two of them remained silent and he stayed beside her, adjusting his pace to the small steps of the child; and the distant noises of Paris were fading away beneath the black shadows of the mighty trees.

'I have only one form of compensation to offer you, Mademoiselle,' he said after a while. 'Naturally, if you should wish to come back to us . . .'

She interrupted him, refusing with feverish haste.

'Monsieur, I cannot . . . Thank you, all the same, but I have found a place elsewhere.'

He knew that because someone had informed him a short time before that she was with Robineau. Calmly, charming her by the way he treated her as an equal, he talked about Robineau and paid tribute to him – a young man of great intelligence, if a little nervous. He would meet with disaster: Gaujean had burdened him with more than they could bear and both would come to grief. Denise, won over by his familiarity, began to open up and let him see that she was on the side of the big stores in the battle between them and the small businesses; she got quite excited, quoting examples, which showed that she was not only well-informed about the situation, but full of far-sighted, new ideas. He listened to her with surprise and delight, and turned round, trying to make out her features in the gathering dusk. She seemed no different, with her gentle face and simple dress; but a heady perfume rose from this modest self-effacement and he felt its power. The girl had no doubt matured in the atmosphere of Paris and was becoming a woman; and she unsettled him: sensible and reserved, yet with her lovely hair heavy with passionate yearnings.

'Since you're on our side,' he said with a laugh, 'why do you stay with our enemies? I mean . . . didn't someone tell me, too, that you were living with Bourras?'

'A fine old man,' she murmured.

'No, no! Come on! He's an old nutter, a madman who's going to force me to drive him out on the street when all I want is to get rid of him with a fortune! Anyway, it's not the place for you: his house has a bad reputation, he rents out to ladies . . .'

But he realized that he was embarrassing her and hastened to add: 'One can be respectable wherever one lives, and there is even greater merit in being so when you are not wealthy.'

They took a few more steps in silence. Pépé seemed to be listening with his attentive air of a precocious child. Sometimes, he looked up at his sister, astonished by her hot hand, which trembled slightly in his.

'I know!' Mouret said brightly. 'Would you like to be my ambassador? I was meaning to raise my offer again tomorrow and suggest the figure of eighty thousand francs to Bourras . . . You can be the first to inform him of it and tell him he's cutting his own throat. He may listen to you since you're his friend, and you would be doing him a real service.'

'I will!' Denise said, returning his smile. 'I'll take him the message, but I don't expect to succeed.'

Again, there was silence. Neither one of them had anything to say to the other. For a moment, he tried to talk about Uncle Baudu, then he had to leave the subject, seeing how uneasy she was about it. Meanwhile, they carried on walking side-by-side until finally, near the Rue de Rivoli, they came out into an alleyway where it was still light. Coming out from the darkness of the trees, it was like a sudden dawn. He realized that he could not keep her any longer.

'Good evening, Mademoiselle.'

'Good evening, Monsieur.'

But still he did not leave. Looking up, he had just glimpsed in front of him, at the corner of the Rue d'Alger, the lighted windows in the apartment of Madame Desforges, who was waiting for him. Then he looked back at Denise, seeing her clearly in the pale light of dusk: compared to Henriette she was a puny little thing; so why did she warm his heart in this way? It was a silly whim.

'This little boy is getting tired,' he went on, looking for something to say. 'Remember what I said, won't you: you're welcome to come back. You just have to knock on the door, I'll give you any compensation you could want . . . Good evening, Mademoiselle.'

'Good evening, Monsieur.'

After Mouret had left, Denise went back under the chestnuts, in the dark shadows. For a long time, she walked aimlessly between the huge tree trunks, her face burning and her head buzzing with a confusion of ideas. Pépé, still grasping her hand, had to stride along to keep up with her. She had forgotten him. Eventually, he said:

'You're going too fast, Sissy.'

So she sat down on a bench and, as he was tired, the child fell asleep across her knees. She held him, pressed against her virgin breast, staring into the shadows. An hour later, when she took him slowly back to the Rue de la Michodière, she was wearing her calm, sensible face.

'God in heaven!' Bourras shouted to her, as soon as he saw her in the distance. 'It's all over! That rascal Mouret has just bought my house.'

He was beside himself, thrashing around all alone in the middle of the shop, with such wild gestures that he risked smashing the windows.

'Oh, the bastard! The fruiterer wrote to me. And do you know how much he sold it for, my house? One hundred and fifty thousand francs, four times what it is worth! There's another fine thief, that one! Can you believe it: they put it down to the improvements I made. Yes, he made a big thing of the fact that the house had just been redecorated. Isn't it time they stopped making an idiot of me?'

It drove him mad to think that the money that he had paid out for paint and whitewash had benefited the fruiterer. Now Mouret had become his landlord: *he* was the one he would have to pay. From now on, he would be living in *his* house, one belonging to that hated rival. The very thought brought him to the pitch of fury.

'I knew I was hearing them making holes in the wall. Now they're here, it's as though they were eating off my plate.'

And, banging his fist down on the table, he shook the whole shop, making the umbrellas and the sunshades jump in their stands.

Stunned, Denise had not been able to get a word in. She stayed there quietly, waiting for the crisis to end, while Pépé, who was very tired, fell asleep on a chair. Finally, when Bourras calmed down a little, she decided to pass on Mouret's message. Of course, the old man was annoyed, but the very excess of his rage and the impasse he was in might make him accept on the spur of the moment.

'As it happens, I met someone,' she began. 'Yes, someone from *Au Bonheur*, who is very well informed. It appears that they are going to offer you eighty thousand francs tomorrow . . .'

He interrupted her with a dreadful roar:

'Eighty thousand francs! Eighty thousand francs! Not for a million, now!'

She tried to reason with him. But the shop door opened and she stepped back and went pale, struck dumb at seeing Uncle Baudu, with his yellow face and aged look. Bourras grasped his neighbour by the buttonholes in his coat and shouted in his face, without letting him say a word, aroused still further by his presence:

'Do you know what they have the gall to offer me? Eighty thousand francs! That's how low they've sunk, the bandits! They think I'm going to sell myself like a whore . . . Oh, they've bought the house and they think they have me now. Well, it's over; they won't get it! I might perhaps have given way to them, but since it's theirs, then let them try to take it from me!'

'So, is it true, then?' said Baudu, in his slow voice. 'I had heard the news, but I came round to find out.'

'Eighty thousand francs!' Bourras repeated. 'Why not a hundred thousand? The thing that makes me furious is all this money. Do they think they'll get me to do the dirty deed, with their money? They won't have it, by God's name! Never, never, do you hear?'

Denise broke her silence to say in her calm voice:

'They'll have it in nine years, when your lease runs out.'

And, despite her uncle being there, she urged the old man to accept. The struggle was becoming impossible, he was fighting against superior forces and he would be crazy to refuse the fortune that was being offered him. But he kept on saying no. In nine years, he hoped he would be dead and not have to see it happen.

'Do you hear, Monsieur Baudu?' he said. 'Your niece is on their side, they've given her the job of corrupting me. I swear to you, she is with those brigands.'

Up to this point, the uncle had not seemed to notice Denise. He looked up with the gruff, churlish movement that he used every time he saw her pass when he was standing by the door of his shop. But now, slowly, he turned round and looked at her. His thick lips were trembling.

'I know,' he said in a half-whisper.

He did not take his eyes off her. Denise, moved to tears, found him much changed by his sorrow, while he, feeling some vague remorse at not having helped her, may have been thinking of the poverty-striken life she had recently been leading. And then the sight of Pépé asleep on the chair, despite the loud voices, seemed to soften him.

'Denise,' he said simply, 'come round tomorrow with the boy and have some soup. My wife and Geneviève told me I should invite you, if we met.'

She blushed deeply and embraced him. As Baudu was leaving, Bourras, pleased by this reconciliation, shouted after him:

'Tell her off and put her right, there's some good in her . . . As for me, the house can fall down, they'll find me under the bricks.'

'Our houses are falling down already, neighbour,' said Baudu, glumly. 'We're all going to end up underneath them.'

CHAPTER 8

Meanwhile, the whole neighbourhood was talking about the great road that was to be opened from the new Opéra to the Bourse, to be called the Rue du Dix-Décembre.[1] The expropriation orders had gone out, and two teams of demolition workers were already knocking through the site from both ends, one taking down the old mansions of the Rue Louis-le-Grand, while the other broke up the flimsy walls of the old Vaudeville theatre. The pickaxes could be heard getting closer to each other, while the Rue de Choiseul and the Rue de la Michodière developed a fascination with their condemned houses. Within a fortnight the opening would cut a wide gash through them, full of din and sunshine.

But the district was even more stirred by the work at *Au Bonheur des Dames.* There was talk of considerable expansion, of a huge emporium with façades extending along the length of the three streets: the Rue de la Michodière, Rue Neuve-Saint-Augustin and Rue Monsigny. It was said that Mouret had made an agreement with Baron Hartmann, director of the Crédit Immobilier, that he could occupy the whole block, except the façade that was eventually to be built on the Rue du Dix-Décembre, where the Baron wanted to put up a rival for the Grand-Hôtel. All around, *Au Bonheur* was buying up leases, small shops were closing, tenants were moving house; and in the empty buildings, an army of workers was starting the alterations, in clouds of plaster. All alone, in the midst of these upheavals, Old Bourras' narrow hovel remained, motionless and untouched, obstinately clinging on between the high walls decked with builders.

In fact, the next day, when Denise went with Pépé to Uncle Baudu's, the street was blocked by a line of wagons that were unloading bricks in front of the old Hôtel Duvillard. Standing on the threshold of his shop, her uncle was staring at them with a melancholy air. The more *Au Bonheur des Dames* expanded, the more the *Vieil Elbeuf* seemed to shrink. To the young woman, the windows seemed blacker and more weighed down beneath the low mezzanine floor, which had round bay windows like a prison. The damp had further discoloured the old green sign and the whole façade, pallid and somehow shrunken, oozed misfortune.

'There you are,' said Baudu. 'Careful! They'd crush you if they could.'

In the shop, Denise felt the same heartache. The place seemed to her darker and to be lapsing more deeply into the somnolence of a ruin. There were wells of darkness in empty corners and dust was spreading over the counters and the boxes, while the bolts of cloth, which no one moved nowadays, gave off an odour of saltpetre in damp cellars. Madame Baudu and Geneviève stayed silent and motionless at the cash desk, as though in a quiet corner where no one would bother them. The mother was hemming napkins and the daughter, her hands resting on her knees, stared into the void ahead of her.

'Good evening, Aunt,' said Denise. 'I'm happy to see you again and if I have caused you any distress, please forgive me.'

Madame Baudu kissed her, deeply moved.

'My poor girl,' she answered. 'If I did not have so many other things to worry about, you would find me in better spirits.'

'Good evening, Cousin,' Denise went on, going to kiss Geneviève on the cheeks.

The other girl seemed to wake up with a start. She returned the kisses, unable to say a word. Then the two women picked up Pépé, who was holding his little arms out. And the reconciliation was complete.

'Well, it's six o'clock, let's sit down and eat,' said Baudu. 'Why didn't you bring Jean?'

'He should have been here,' Denise murmured in embarrassment. 'I saw him this morning and he gave me his solemn word . . . Oh, we mustn't wait for him. I expect his boss kept him behind . . .'

She guessed that he had become involved in one of his extraordinary affairs and wanted to excuse him in advance.

'So, let's sit down,' her uncle repeated.

Then, turning to the darkness at the back of the shop:

'Colomban, you can dine at the same time as us. No one will come.'

Denise had not noticed the assistant. Her aunt explained that they had had to dispense with the other salesman and the young lady. Business had got so bad that Colomban was enough; and even then, he spent hours with nothing to do, his head drooping as he lapsed towards sleep, with his eyes open.

The gas was burning in the dining room even though they were in the long days of summer. The cold, coming off the walls, struck Denise across the back and made her shiver a little as she went in. She recognized the round table, the places laid on the waxed cloth and the light coming from the fetid depths of the little courtyard. And, like the shop, these things seemed to her to have grown darker and to be weeping tears.

'Father,' said Geneviève, feeling embarrassed for Denise, 'would you like me to shut the window? It doesn't smell good.'

He was surprised, smelling nothing.

'Shut the window, if it amuses you,' he answered at length. 'But we shall be short of air.'

He was right: it was stifling. The dinner was a family affair and very simple. After the soup, and as soon as the maid served the boiled meat, the uncle inevitably turned to the people opposite. At first, he showed considerable tolerance, allowing his niece to have a different point of view.

'Heavens, you're quite free to support those great monster firms . . . Everyone is entitled to their own opinion, dear girl . . . If you're not even disgusted by the way they gave you the sack, then you must have some good reason for liking them, and I wouldn't hold it against you at all if you were to go back there . . . Isn't that right? No one here would hold it against her?'

'Oh, no,' Madame Baudu murmured.

Denise calmly set out her argument as she had done at Robineau's: the logical development of trade, the requirements of modern times, the size of these new establishments and finally the increasing benefits to the public. Baudu, wide-eyed and thick-lipped, listened with visible mental strain. Then, when she had finished, he shook his head:

'All that is a phantasmagoria. Trade is trade, you can't escape it . . . Oh, I admit they're successful, but that's all. I thought for a long time that they would come a cropper – yes, that's what I was expecting, so I waited for it to happen, do you remember? Well, no, it now seems that the thieves are the ones who make a fortune while honest people die in a cowshed . . . That's what it's come to, I have to bow before the facts. And I am bowing, my God! I'm bowing . . .'

Bit by bit he was seething with repressed anger. Suddenly, he waved his fork.

'But the *Vieil Elbeuf* will never concede! You heard what I said to Bourras: "Neighbour, you're giving in to charlatans: that painting and daubing of yours is a disgrace!"'

'Eat up,' Madame Baudu said, interrupting him, because she was concerned at seeing him getting worked up.

'No, wait. I want my niece to know where I stand. Listen to this, my girl: I'm like this jug, I don't move. They may succeed, then all the worse for them. I am taking my stand, that's all!'

The maid brought in a piece of roast veal and he cut it with trembling hands. He no longer had the same keen eye and mastery in measuring up the portions. An awareness of defeat deprived him of the self-assurance that he had once had, as a respected boss. Pépé thought that his uncle was getting cross and had to be calmed, by giving him some of the sweet course straightaway, some biscuits that were in front of his plate. At this, Baudu lowered his voice and tried to speak of something else. For a while, he chatted about the demolition work, and expressed approval for the Rue du Dix-Décembre, which would certainly increase business in the neighbourhood. But at this, once again, he returned to *Au Bonheur des Dames*. Everything brought him back to it: it was an unhealthy obsession. They were buried in plaster and had sold nothing since these carts full of building materials had been blocking the street. In any case, it would get to be so large it was ridiculous; customers would get lost in it, why not go to Les Halles?[2] And, try as he might, despite pleading looks from his wife, he went on from the building works to discuss the turnover of the shop. It was unbelievable, wasn't it? In less than four years, they had increased turnover by five times: at the last stocktaking, their annual receipts, which had stood at eight million, were now coming up to forty. In short, madness, something unprecedented, against which it was useless to struggle. They were constantly expanding: they now had a thousand employees and declared that there were twenty-eight departments. It was this number of twenty-eight departments, most of all, that drove him into a fury. Of course, they must have divided some of them into two, but others were completely new: for example, a furniture department and one for novelty goods. Could you imagine that? A novelty goods department! It just showed, these people had no pride, they would end up selling fish. Denise's uncle, while pretending to respect her ideas, eventually tried to persuade her.

'Honestly, you can't defend them. Can you imagine me adding a department for saucepans to my linen business? Huh? You'd tell me I was mad. At least admit you don't admire them.'

The young woman merely smiled, embarrassed, seeing the futility of arguing with him. He went on:

'Well, then, you're on their side. We won't say any more about it because there's no point in falling out again. That would be the end, if they came between my family and me! Go back there, if you want, but I forbid you to keep on bothering me with their nonsense!'

Silence reigned. His earlier aggression lapsed into this febrile resignation. As they were stifling in the narrow room, heated by the gas mantle, the maid had to reopen the window; and the damp, pestilential atmosphere of the yard blew across the table. Some sauté potatoes had appeared. They helped themselves slowly, without speaking.

'Well, now! Look at these two,' Baudu went on, pointing his knife towards Geneviève and Colomban. 'Ask them how they like that *Au Bonheur des Dames* of yours!'

Side by side, at the usual place where they had met twice a day for twelve years, Colomban and Geneviève were eating steadily. They had not uttered a word. Colomban, while exaggerating the stolid geniality of his expression, seemed behind his drooping lids to be hiding the inner fire that was consuming him, while Geneviève, her head bent still further by her heavy mass of hair, had given way to the secret suffering that was ravaging her.

'The last year has been a disaster,' Denise's uncle explained. 'We had to put off their marriage . . . No, do me a favour and just ask them what they think of your friends.'

To please him, Denise put the question to the young couple.

'I cannot like them, cousin,' Geneviève replied. 'But don't worry, not everyone hates them.'

And she looked at Colomban who was apparently absorbed in rolling some bread between his fingers. When he felt the young woman's eyes on him, he burst out:

'The filthy shop! Each one of them is a bigger rascal than the next! In short. It's like having the plague in the neighbourhood!'

'Listen to that! Listen to him!' Baudu shouted in delight. 'Here's one they won't ever get. You're the last, they won't make any more like you!'

But Geneviève kept on staring at Colomban with a stern and sorrowful face. Her look penetrated right into his heart and bothered him, so that he piled on the invective. Madame Baudu, sitting opposite them, was looking from one to the other, uneasily and in silence, as though guessing that some new misfortune was about to come from there. For some time, her daughter's sadness had frightened her; she felt the girl was dying.

'The shop is unattended,' she said at last, getting up from the table and wanting to put an end to the scene. 'Come on, Colomban, I thought I heard someone.'

They had finished, so they got up. Baudu and Colomban went to talk to a salesman who had come to take orders. Madame Baudu led Pépé away to show him some pictures. The maid had quickly cleared the table and Denise, lost in thought by the window, was taking an interest in the little yard when, turning round, she saw Geneviève, still at her place, staring at the waxed cloth which was still damp where the maid's sponge had wiped it.

'Are you unwell, cousin?' she asked.

The young woman said nothing, obstinately fixing her eyes on a tear in the cloth, as though entirely absorbed in her train of thought. Then she painfully raised her head and looked at the sympathetic face bending towards her own. Had the others gone? What was she doing on this chair? Suddenly, she was stifled by sobs and her head fell back on to the edge of the table. She was weeping, soaking her sleeve in her tears.

'Good heavens, what's wrong!' Denise exclaimed, astonished and dismayed. 'Shall I fetch someone?'

Geneviève had nervously clasped her arm, holding her back and stammering: 'No, no, stay here. Mamma mustn't know! With you I don't mind, but not the others, not the others! I can't help it, I swear. It's when I see myself all alone . . . Wait, I'm better now, I'm not crying.'

But the fit resumed, shaking her frail body with great shudders. It was as though the mass of her black hair was crushing the back of her neck; and as she rolled her troubled head from side to side on her folded arms, a pin came out of her hair and the hair poured across her back, swamping it in blackness. Meanwhile, Denise was trying to comfort her, without making a noise, for fear of attracting attention. She loosened her dress and was upset by the sight of her painful thinness: the poor girl had the hollow chest of a child, the nothingness of a virgin ravaged by anaemia. Denise took her hair in both hands – this magnificent hair that seemed to be draining the life out of her – and knotted it up firmly, to free her and give her room to breathe.

'Thank you, you're kind,' said Geneviève. 'Ah, I'm not fat, am I? I was better built, but it's all gone . . . Do up my dress or Mamma will see my shoulders. I hide them as much as I can. Oh, God! I'm not well, I'm not well at all!'

However, the crisis was over. She stayed, exhausted, on her chair, staring hard at her cousin. And, after a pause, she said:

'Tell me the truth, does he love her?'

Denise felt herself blushing. She fully realized that she was referring to Colomban and Clara, but she feigned surprise.

'Who do you mean, dear?'

Geneviève shook her head with an incredulous look.

'Don't lie, please. Do me the favour of letting me learn the truth, one way or another. Something tells me you must know. Yes, you were acquainted with that woman and I saw Colomban going after you and whispering to you. He was giving you some message for her, wasn't he? Oh, for pity's sake, tell me the truth. I swear it will do me good.'

Denise had never felt so uncomfortable. Faced with this child, reserved and silent, but guessing everything, she lowered her eyes. Yet she still found the strength to deceive her.

'But you are the one he loves!'

At this, Geneviève made a desperate gesture.

'Very well, you don't want to tell me. In any case, I don't mind, I have seen them. He is constantly going out on to the pavement to look at her. And she, up there, laughs like a halfwit. Of course, they meet somewhere outside.'

'Oh, no, I promise you that's not so!' Denise exclaimed, forgetting herself, carried away by the desire to reassure her at least on that point.

The young woman took a deep breath, and gave a weak smile. Then, in the weakened tones of a convalescent, she said:

'I'd like a glass of water . . . I'm sorry, I'm being a nuisance. It's there, on the buffet.'

And, when she had the jug, she emptied a large glass in a single gulp. Denise was afraid that she would do herself some harm, but Geneviève pushed her aside with her hand.

'No, no, leave me. I'm always thirsty . . . I get up in the night to have a drink.'

There was another pause. She continued quietly:

'If you only knew; for ten years I have been used to the idea of this marriage. When I was still wearing short dresses, Colomban was already mine . . . So I can't even remember how it happened. Living together all the time, staying shut up here next to each other with never anything to take our minds off each other, I must have started to think of him as my husband before the event. I didn't know if I loved him, I was his wife, that's all . . . And now he wants to go off with someone else! Oh, my God! My heart is breaking. Do you see? It's a kind of torment that I had never experienced. It catches me in the chest and in the head, then it spreads everywhere. It's killing me.'

Once again, tears were rising to her eyes. Denise, her own eyelids moistening in pity, asked her:

'Does my aunt suspect anything?'

'Yes, Mamma suspects, I think . . . As for Papa, he has too much on his mind, but he does not know the agony he is causing me by putting off the wedding . . . Mamma has often questioned me. She is worried when she sees me wasting away. Having never been very strong herself, she often tells me: "My poor girl, I didn't make you very sturdy." Then, children don't grow well in these shops. But she must be thinking that I really am getting too thin . . . Look at my arms: is that right?'

She had picked up the water jug again with a trembling hand. Her cousin tried to stop her from drinking.

'No, I'm so thirsty, leave me alone.'

They could hear Baudu's voice raised. So, yielding to an impulse of the heart, Denise knelt down and hugged Geneviève in her sisterly arms. She kissed her and swore that everything would be all right: that she would marry Colomban, get well and be happy. Then quickly she got up again. Her uncle was calling.

'Jean's here. Come on.'

It was, indeed, Jean – a Jean in a state of agitation, arriving for dinner. When they told him it was eight o'clock, his jaw dropped. It couldn't be: he'd just left his employer's. They teased him and said he must have come via the Bois de Vincennes. But as soon as he could he went up to his sister and whispered very softly to her:

'It's a little laundress who was taking back her washing. I've got a cab waiting outside. Give me five francs.'

He went out for a minute, then came back to have dinner, because Madame Baudu was absolutely insistent that he should not leave again without at least eating some soup. Geneviève had reappeared, with her usual silent, self-effacing manner. Colomban was half-dozing behind a counter. The evening went by, sadly and slowly, enlivened only by Uncle Baudu's footsteps as he paced back and forth from one end of the empty shop to the other. A single gas mantle was burning and the darkness fell from the low ceiling in great spadefuls, like black earth into a grave.

Months went by. Denise dropped in practically every day to cheer Geneviève up for a moment. But the depression was deepening around the Baudus. The building work across the road was a continual torment that intensified their misfortune. Even when they had a brief period of hope or some unexpected joy, the clatter of a wagon emptying out a load of bricks, the noise of a stone-cutter's saw or a simple shout from a builder was enough to spoil it in an instant. In fact, the whole neighbourhood was in turmoil: a sound of feverish activity emerged from behind the barrier of planks which extended along the three streets, getting in everyone's way. Even though the architect was using the existing buildings, he had opened them up on all sides in order to convert them; and, in the middle, in the space left by the courtyards, he was building a central gallery as large as a church, which was to have a main entrance opening on the Rue Neuve-Saint-Augustin, in the middle of the façade. At first, they had had a good deal of trouble constructing the basements, because they had come across seepage from the drains and 'made ground', brought in from elsewhere, which was full of human bones. After that, the sinking of the well had caused much concern in the nearby houses, a well a hundred metres deep, intended to produce five hundred litres of water a minute. Now the walls had risen as high as the first floor, and scaffolding, with wooden towers, enclosed the whole block; you could hear the constant creaking of winches hauling up cut stone blocks, the sudden unloading of metal flooring, and the clamour of this tribe of workers, accompanied by a sound of pickaxes and hammers. But what was most deafening of all was the shuddering of the machines: everything worked by steam and high-pitched whistles would split the air while, at the merest puff of wind, a cloud of plaster would lift off and settle on the surrounding roofs like a fall of snow. The Baudus were in despair as they watched this unrelenting dust get in everywhere, making its way through the most tightly closed wooden shutters, staining the linen in the shop and even insinuating itself into their bed. And the idea that they were breathing it in regardless and would eventually die of it made their lives a misery.

Moreover, the situation was going to get worse. In September, the architect, fearing that he might not be finished on time, decided to get them to work at nights. Powerful electric lights were set up[3] and from then on the noise never ended: one gang followed the next, the hammers hammered unceasingly, the machines whistled continually, and the level of clatter, never relenting, seemed actually to lift up the plaster and spread it around. Now the Baudus, driven to exasperation, even had to abandon sleep. They were shaken about in their alcove and the noises drifted into their nightmares whenever exhaustion overtook them. Then they would get up, barefoot, to soothe their fevered minds and, if they peeped out of the curtains, they were horrified by the vision of *Au Bonheur des Dames* blazing in the surrounding darkness, like a colossal smithy forging their ruin. In the middle of the half-constructed walls, pierced by empty bays, electric lamps cast wide blue beams of blinding light. Two o'clock in the morning struck, then three, then four. And in the tortured sleep of the neighbourhood, the building site, made larger by this lunar brightness, took on colossal and fantastic proportions, swarming with dark shadows, with clamorous workmen, their silhouettes gesticulating against the harsh whiteness of the new walls.

As Uncle Baudu had said, small businesses in the surrounding streets suffered another dreadful blow. Whenever *Au Bonheur des Dames* created a new department, more of the small shops around it collapsed. The disaster was widening and you could hear even the oldest establishments cracking. Mademoiselle Tatin, who had the lingerie shop in the Passage Choiseul, had just been declared bankrupt; Quinette, the glove-maker, would hardly last six months; the furriers Vanpouille were forced to sublet part of their shops; and though Bédoré and Sister, the hosiers in the Rue Gaillon, were still hanging on, it was clear that they were drawing on money that they had saved up in the past. And now, other ruins were piled on these long-predicted ones: the novelty goods department threatened a fancy goods dealer in the Rue Saint-Roch – Deslignières, a large, ruddy-faced man; while the furniture department was a blow to Piot & Rivoire, whose premises slumbered in the shadow of the Passage Sainte-Anne. People were afraid that the fancy goods dealer would have an apoplectic fit, because he was in a continual state of fury after seeing that *Au Bonheur* was offering purses at a thirty per cent discount. The furniture shop took it more calmly, pretending to laugh at these 'hand-me-downs' who thought they could sell tables and wardrobes; but customers were already leaving them and the new department promised to be a roaring success. It was all over: they had to resign themselves; and after these, others would be swept away, so there was no reason now why all the businesses should not be driven out one by one. One day, *Au Bonheur des Dames* would spread its roof across the whole neighbourhood.

Now, morning and evening, when the thousand employees came and left, they spread out in such a long queue across Place Gaillon that people stopped to look at them, just as they might watch a regiment marching past. The pavements were crowded with them for ten minutes and it struck the shop owners, standing at their doors, that they were not even sure how to provide for their one assistant. The last stocktaking at the department store, showing a turnover of forty million, had also shaken the neighbourhood to its foundations. The figure travelled from house to house, amid cries of surprise and anger: forty million! Could you imagine it! Of course, the net profits were at the most four per cent, with their huge overheads and their system of selling cheap. But a clear profit of sixteen hundred thousand francs was still a very decent amount: you could be happy with four per cent when you were dealing with such figures. They said that Mouret's original capital, the first five hundred thousand francs, increased each year by the total amount of profit – a capital sum that must now stand at four million – had crossed the counter ten times in goods. Robineau, when he made this calculation after the meal, when Denise was there, sat for a moment quite overcome, staring at his empty plate: she was right, it was this constant renewal of capital that gave the new trade its unbeatable strength. Only Bourras would not acknowledge the facts, refusing to understand, proud, but as thick as a post. A mass of thieves, that's all! Liars! Mountebanks who would be picked up from the gutter one fine morning!

Meanwhile the Baudus, though they wished to change nothing in the way the *Vieil Elbeuf* was run, were trying to remain competitive. Since the customers were not coming to them, they tried to reach the customers, through agents and salesmen. There was an agent at the time on the Place de Paris who had connections with all the big tailors and who would save little shops dealing in cloth and flannel when he agreed to represent them. Naturally, everyone wanted him and he was becoming quite a well-known figure; but Baudu, after trying to bargain with him, had the misfortune to see him come to an understanding with the Matignons in the Rue Croix-des-Petits-Champs. Two other agents robbed him, one after the other, and a third, an honest type, did nothing. It was slow death, without violent shocks, just a steady slowing down of business and customers lost one by one. The day came when the bills started to become a burden. Up to this point they had lived on their savings from better days, now they began getting into debt. In December, Baudu, horrified by the amount to pay in promissory notes, resigned himself to the cruellest sacrifice: he sold his country house in Rambouillet, a house that cost him a huge amount in constant repairs and where the tenants had not even paid the rent when he decided to part with it. Selling it killed the one dream of his life and his heart bled as for the loss of someone close to him. And he had to take seventy thousand francs for something that had cost him more than two hundred thousand. Even then, he was lucky to find the Lhommes, his neighbours, who finally agreed because they wanted to extend their land. The seventy thousand francs would keep the business going for some time longer. Despite all these defeats, they felt a renewed desire to struggle on: now perhaps, if they were careful, they might succeed.

On the Sunday when the Lhommes handed over the money, they accepted an invitation to dinner at the *Vieil Elbeuf*. Madame Aurélie was the first to arrive. They had to wait for the cashier, who came late, agitated by a whole afternoon of music. As for young Albert, though he had accepted the invitation, he failed to show up. In any event, it was a painful evening. The Baudus, living their stuffy, airless existence in their cramped dining room, felt uncomfortable in the cold wind that the Lhommes brought in, with their loose-knit family and their taste for the free life. Geneviève, upset by Madame Aurélie's imperious manner, did not open her mouth, while Colomban admired the woman: it gave him a thrill to think that she presided over Clara.

That night, before he joined his wife, who was already in bed, Baudu walked back and forth across the room for a long time. The weather was mild, a damp period of thaw. Outside, despite the shuttered windows and the drawn curtains, you could hear the machines growling as they worked away on the building site opposite.

'Do you know what I'm thinking, Élisabeth?' he said at length. 'I'm thinking that even though those Lhommes may be earning lots of money, I'd rather be in my shoes than in theirs . . . They're successful, I know that. Didn't the wife tell us that she's made nearly twenty thousand francs this year, which allowed her to take my poor little house from me? No matter! I may not have the house any longer, but at least I'm not out playing music in one place while you're off gadding about in another . . . No, believe me, they can't be happy.'

He was still suffering acutely from the great sacrifice he had made and felt a grudge against these people who had bought his dream. When he came close to the bed, he gestured, leaning close to his wife; then, going back to the window, he fell silent for a moment, listening to the noise of the building works. And he went back to his old accusations, to his desperate grievances against modern times: this was unprecedented, sales staff nowadays earned more than tradespeople, and cashiers were buying up the property of shop owners. This is why everything was falling apart, the family no longer existed, people lived in hotels, instead of eating their soup decently in their own homes. He ended by prophesying that young Albert would eventually consume the land at Rambouillet to pay for his actresses.

Madame Baudu listened, her head lying flat on the pillow and so pale that her face was the same colour as the linen.

At last, she said softly: 'They paid you.'

At that, Baudu fell silent. He walked along for a second or two, staring at the ground. Then he went on:

'They did pay me, that's true; and, after all, their money is as good as another's . . . It would be odd if we revived the shop with that money. Oh, if only I were not so old and tired!'

After this, there was a long pause. The draper's mind was full of vague plans. Suddenly, his wife began to speak, staring at the ceiling, without moving her head.

'Have you noticed your daughter, recently?'

'No,' he replied.

'Well, I'm a bit worried about her . . . She's getting paler and she seems to be in despair.'

He stood in front of her, quite surprised.

'Well, now! Why's that? If she's not well, she should tell us. We'll have to get the doctor in tomorrow.'

Madame Baudu still remained motionless. After a full minute, she merely said, in her thoughtful manner:

'I think we'll have to get this wedding to Colomban over and done with.'

He looked at her, then went on walking. He recalled certain things. Could it be that his daughter was falling ill because of his assistant? Did she love him so much that she couldn't wait? Here was another misfortune! This was most disturbing, especially since he himself had definite ideas on the marriage. He would never have chosen to conclude it in present circumstances. Yet anxiety softened his heart.

'Fine,' he said at last. 'I'll speak to Colomban.'

And, without saying any more, he went on with his walk. Soon, his wife's eyes closed and she lay asleep, quite white, like a dead person. He was still walking up and down. Before going to bed, he opened the curtains and had a look: on the far side of the street, the gaping windows of the old Hôtel Duvillard opened gaps into the building site where the workers could be seen hurrying about in the blaze of the electric lights.

The following morning, Baudu led Colomban to the back of a narrow storeroom on the mezzanine floor. He had decided the night before what he was going to say.

'My boy,' he began. 'You know I have sold my property in Rambouillet. This will give us one more chance. But, most of all, I want to have a little chat with you.'

The young man, who seemed to be dreading this interview, waited with an awkward look. His small eyes were blinking in his broad face and his mouth was hanging open, a sign with him of some deep inner turmoil.

'Listen carefully,' the draper went on. 'When Old Hauchecorne handed the *Vieil Elbeuf* on to me, the firm was prosperous; he himself had taken it over from Old Finet, in good condition. You know how I feel: I should consider I was doing something disgraceful if I were to hand this family heirloom over to my children in a worse state than I found it, which is why I have always put off your marriage to Geneviève . . . Yes, I was stubborn, I hoped to restore our old fortunes, I wanted to put the books in front of you and say: "Look! The year I came here, we sold this many pieces of cloth and this year, the year I am leaving, we've sold ten thousand or twenty thousand more . . ." In a word, you see, that's a promise I made to myself, from a very natural desire to prove that the firm has not lost while in my hands. Otherwise, I should feel I was robbing you.'

He was choking with emotion. Blowing his nose to recover, he asked: 'Why don't you say something?'

But Colomban had nothing to say. He shook his head and waited, more and more troubled, thinking he could guess where the boss was leading – to a speedy marriage. How could he refuse? He would never have the strength. But what of that other girl, the one he dreamed about at night, his flesh consumed with such desire that he would throw himself naked on to the floor, afraid that he might die of it!

'Now here,' Baudu went on, 'we have the money that may save us. The situation is getting worse day by day, but perhaps if we make one last, supreme effort . . . In any case, I wanted to warn you. We are going to gamble everything on one last throw. If we are beaten, well, then it will be the end of us. The only thing is, my poor boy, that because of it we shall have to put off your wedding again, because I don't want to hurl the two of you all alone into the fight. That would be a coward's way, wouldn't it?'

Colomban, much relieved, had sat down on some pieces of flannelette. His legs were still trembling. He was afraid that he might show how happy he was, so he had his head lowered and was tapping his fingers on his knees.

'Why don't you say something?' Baudu repeated.

No, he was saying nothing, he could find nothing to say. So the draper continued slowly:

'I was sure that it would upset you . . . You must be brave. Pull yourself together, don't stay like that . . . Most of all, I want you to understand my position. Could I hang such a millstone round your neck? Instead of leaving you a good business, I might be leaving you a bankruptcy. No, that's the kind of thing only a scoundrel would do. Of course, all I want is your happiness, but no one will ever make me act against my conscience.'[4]

He continued talking in this way for a long time, struggling in the midst of contradictory statements, being a man who would have preferred to be understood without being forced to spell everything out. Since he had promised his daughter together with the shop, strict honesty obliged him to hand both over in good condition, without blemishes or debts. The trouble was, he was weary and the burden was getting too heavy for him: there was a pleading tone in his hesitant voice. The words stumbled even more as he tried to get them out and he was hoping for Colomban to explode with some urgent plea from the heart, but nothing came.

'I know,' he murmured, 'that old people don't have the same enthusiasm . . . With the young, things flare up afresh. They have eager passions, that's natural . . . But no, no, on my word of honour, I can't do it! If I were to give in to you now, you would reproach me for it later.'

He fell silent, shivering. And as the young man stayed with his head lowered, he asked him for the third time, after a painful silence:

'Why don't you say something?'

At last, without looking up, Colomban replied:

'There is nothing to be said . . . You are the master, you are wiser than all of us. Since you demand it, we shall wait and try to be sensible.'

It was all over. Baudu still hoped that he would throw himself into his arms and cry: 'Father, you rest, we shall take over the fight, give us the shop as it is, so that we can perform a miracle and save it!' Then he looked at him and felt ashamed, secretly accusing himself of wanting to trick the children. The shopkeeper's old fanatical decency and honesty revived in him: it was this cautious lad who was right, because there was no sentiment in business, only figures.

'Kiss me, my boy,' he said in conclusion. 'That's settled, we shan't talk about the wedding again for a year. First of all, we must think about business.'

That evening, in their room, when Madame Baudu was questioning her husband about the outcome of the talk, he had recovered his optimistic determination to fight the battle himself, in person, to the end. He was full of praise for Colomban: a reliable lad, who knew what he thought and one brought up according to the best principles – for example, not the person to have a joke with his customers, like those coxcombs at *Au Bonheur*. No, he was honest, he was family and he didn't gamble on sales as though he was gambling on the Stock Exchange.

'So when's the wedding?' Madame Baudu asked.

'Later,' he answered. 'When I'm in a position to keep my promises.'

Without a gesture, she said simply:

'It will kill our daughter.'

Baudu, boiling with anger, had to restrain himself. He was the one who would be killed, if people kept upsetting him like this all the time! Was it his fault? He loved his daughter and talked about giving his blood for her, but despite that he could not arrange for the business to prosper when it didn't want to prosper. Geneviève would have to be a bit reasonable and wait for the figures to improve. What the devil! Colomban would wait, no one was going to steal him from her!

'It's incredible!' he said over and over. 'Such a well brought-up girl.'

Madame Baudu said nothing. Of course, she had guessed Geneviève's jealous torments, but she did not dare confide in her husband. A peculiar kind of female modesty had always kept her from talking to him about certain intimate subjects. When she didn't answer, he redirected his anger against the people opposite, shaking his fists towards the building site where, that evening, they were hammering in iron girders with great blows.

Denise was going to return to *Au Bonheur des Dames*. She had realized that the Robineaus, though they were forced to cut down on staff, did not know how to dismiss her. If they were to survive any longer, they had to do everything by themselves. Gaujean, obstinate in his bitterness, was extending their credit and even promised to find money for them, but they were starting to feel scared; they wanted to try frugality and good housekeeping. For the past fortnight, Denise had felt that they were uneasy when she was there, so she had to be the first to speak and tell them that she had a position somewhere else. It was a relief, Madame Robineau was very touched and hugged her, swearing that she would always miss her. But when, in answer to their question, the young woman said she was going back to Mouret's, the colour drained from Robineau's face.

'You're right!' he cried emphatically.

It was less easy announcing the news to Old Bourras. Yet Denise had to give him notice and hated to do it, because she felt deeply grateful to him. As it happened, Bourras was beside himself with anger, being right in the midst of the din caused by the nearby building site. Wagons full of building materials barred the way to his shop, pickaxes were hammering on his walls, and everything in the place – umbrellas and walking sticks – jumped up and down to the beat of the hammers. You felt that the hovel, obstinately staying put in the midst of this demolition, would burst asunder. But the worst thing was that the architect, wanting to join the existing departments in the shop with the new departments being created in the old Hôtel Duvillard, had decided to construct a tunnel under the little house that lay between them. This house did belong to the firm of Mouret & Co. and since the lease stated that the tenant should agree to permit any repairs, one morning some workmen turned up. At this, Bourras almost had apoplexy. Wasn't it enough to stifle him from all sides – right, left and centre? Now they had to grab him by the feet and eat away the ground beneath him! So he drove off the builders and had recourse to the law. Repair work, yes – but this was improvements! The neighbourhood thought he would win his case, though they guaranteed nothing. In any event, the proceedings looked as though they would last a long time and people were fascinated by this endless duel.

On the day when Denise finally plucked up enough courage to give him notice, Bourras had just returned from seeing his lawyer.

'Would you believe it!' he exclaimed. 'Now they're saying that the house is unstable and trying to prove that the foundations have to be remade. Confound it! They've worn it out from shaking it with their infernal machines. It's not surprising if it's falling down.'

Then, when the young woman had announced her decision to leave and go back to *Au Bonheur des Dames*, with a salary of a thousand francs, he was so stricken by it that he merely raised his old, trembling hand to heaven. Overcome with emotion, he fell back into a chair.

'You! You!' he stammered. 'Well, then, I'm the only one left. There's no one except me!'

After a pause, he asked:

'And what about the child?'

'He'll go back to Madame Gras,' Denise replied. 'She was very fond of him.'

There was another silence. She would have preferred to see him furious, swearing and hammering with his fist; this old man, crushed and choked with emotion, pained her. But gradually he pulled himself together and started to shout again.

'A thousand francs, you couldn't refuse that. You'll all go. So off with you, leave me alone. Yes, alone, do you hear! There's one person who will never bow his head. And tell them that I will win my lawsuit, even if I have to sell the shirt off my back for it!'

Denise was not due to leave Robineau until the end of the month. She had seen Mouret again and everything was settled. One evening, she was about to go up to her room when Deloche, who had been waiting for her in a doorway, stopped her. He was delighted, he had just learned the great news and the whole shop was talking about it, or so he said. And he joyfully told her all the gossip in the various departments.

'You know, the ladies in ladies' wear are making a big thing of it!'

Then he abruptly changed tack:

'By the way, do you remember Clara Prunaire? Well, it seems that the boss has . . . Well, you see what I mean?'

He was blushing, while she, going quite pale, exclaimed:

'Monsieur Mouret!'

'An odd choice, don't you think?' he went on. 'A woman who looks like a horse . . . At least, the little laundress whom he had a couple of times last year was quite sweet. Anyway, that's his business.'

When Denise got into her room, she felt faint. She must have walked up the stairs too fast. Leaning against the window, the image of Valognes suddenly came into her mind – the empty street with moss-covered cobbles that she used to see from her window as a child; and she was seized with a need to return there, to take refuge in the peace and oblivion of the provinces. Paris got on her nerves, she hated *Au Bonheur des Dames* and didn't know why she had agreed to return there. Undoubtedly, she would suffer again in that place; she was already suffering from some vague feeling of malaise, after what Deloche had told her. And, for no reason, a fit of weeping caused her to leave the window. She cried for a long time and found the strength to go on.

At lunchtime the next day, as Robineau had sent her out on an errand and she was going past the *Vieil Elbeuf*, she pushed open the door, seeing that Colomban was alone in the shop. The Baudus were having lunch and you could hear the sound of forks from the little dining room.

'Come in,' said the assistant. 'They're eating.'

She motioned for him to be quiet and pulled him into a corner, then, lowering her voice, said:

'You're the one I want to talk to. Don't you have a heart? Can't you see that Geneviève loves you and that this is killing her?'

She was shaking all over, seized again by her fever of the previous day. As for Colomban, startled, astonished by this sudden assault, he could find nothing in reply.

'Listen,' she continued. 'Geneviève knows that you're in love with someone else. She told me so, sobbing like a lost soul. Oh, poor child, she's so desperately thin. If you could only see her little arms, it would make you weep. I mean, you can't let her die like that!'

At last he spoke, completely shattered.

'But she's not ill, you're exaggerating . . . I don't see it . . . And then, it's her father who's putting off the wedding . . .'

Denise bluntly told him he was lying. She realized that the slightest resistance from the young man would have changed the uncle's mind. But Colomban's surprise was genuine: he really had not observed Geneviève's slow decline. The revelation was very unpleasant for him: while he was unaware of it, there was nothing too much with which to reproach himself.

'And who for?' Denise went on. 'For a nothing! Don't you know anything about the woman you love? I didn't want to upset you, until now, so I've often avoided answering your constant questions. Well, I'll tell you: she goes with everybody, she doesn't care a bit for you, you'll never have her – or else, you'll have her as the others do, once, in passing.'

He listened, white as a sheet and, at each sentence she flung at him between clenched teeth, his lips trembled a little. Seized with a desire to hurt him, she gave way to a fury of which she had been unaware.

'In fact, if you want to know,' she said in one final outburst, 'she's with Monsieur Mouret!'

Her voice was choking and she went even paler than he had. The two of them looked at one another.

Then he stammered:

'I love her.'

At this, Denise felt ashamed. Why was she talking in such a way to this boy, what reason did she have to get so upset about it? She said nothing, but the simple words that he had spoken echoed in her heart with the sound of a distant bell, deafening her: 'I love her, I love her'. And it grew in intensity. He was right, he could not marry someone else.

Turning round, she saw Geneviève in the dining-room door.

'Be quiet!' she said quickly.

But it was too late: Geneviève must have heard. Her face was drained of blood. And, at that very moment, a customer opened the door, Madame Bourdelais, one of the last to remain faithful to the *Vieil Elbeuf*, where she found the goods reliable – though Madame de Boves had long since followed the fashion and gone over to *Au Bonheur*, and even Madame Marty no longer came, entirely captivated by the seductive qualities of the displays across the road. So Geneviève was obliged to go forward and say, in a toneless voice:

'What can I do for Madame?'

Madame Bourdelais wanted to see some flannel. Colomban brought some out of a box and Geneviève showed it; the two of them, their hands cold, found themselves together behind the counter. Meanwhile, Baudu was the last to emerge from the little dining room, after his wife, who had gone to sit on the bench behind the cash desk. At first he took no part in the sale, standing and looking at Madame Bourdelais, after he had smiled at Denise.

'That's not pretty enough,' Madame Bourdelais said. 'Show me something stronger.'

Colomban brought down another length of cloth. There was a silence while she examined it.

'How much is this?'

'Six francs, Madame,' Geneviève replied.

The customer drew herself up abruptly.

'Six francs! But they have the same thing opposite for five.'

A slight grimace flitted across Baudu's face. He could not resist joining in, very politely. Madame must be mistaken, this item should have been put on at six francs fifty and it was impossible for them to sell it for five francs. It must assuredly be some other item.

'No, no,' she repeated, with the stubbornness of a bourgeoise who liked to think she knew all about it. 'The material is the same. Theirs may even be a little thicker.'

Eventually, the discussion got quite heated. Baudu, his face bilious, was making an effort to keep a smile on it. His bitterness against *Au Bonheur des Dames* was rising in his throat.

'Really,' Madame Bourdelais said at length. 'You must treat me better than this or else I'll go across the road, like everyone else.'

At that, he lost his head and, shaking with repressed anger, shouted:

'Well, then, go across the road!'

Immediately, she got up, very insulted, and went out, without turning round, remarking:

'That's what I shall do, Monsieur.'

They were dumbstruck, all taken aback by the boss's violence. He himself was left startled and trembling at the idea of what he had just said. The remark had burst out without him intending it, the explosion of a long build-up of bitterness. And now the Baudus, without moving, their hands hanging at their sides, watched Madame Bourdelais crossing the street. She seemed to be taking their prosperity with her. When, with calm steps, she passed through the high door of *Au Bonheur des Dames*, when they saw her back swallowed up by the crowd, they had the feeling that something was being torn out of them.

'There's another one they have taken from us!' the draper muttered.

Then, turning to Denise and knowing about her new job, he added:

'And, they've taken you back . . . Well, I don't hold it against you. Since they have the money, they are the stronger.'

Denise, still hoping that Geneviève had not heard Colomban, whispered in her ear:

'He loves you, cheer up.'

But the other girl answered very softly, but in a voice of utter despair:

'Why are you lying to me? Look – he can't restrain himself, he's looking up there . . . I know that they have stolen him from me, as they steal everything.'

She sat down on the bench behind the cash desk, close to her mother. The latter must have realized what had happened to her daughter, because her pained eyes looked from her to Colomban and then back to *Au Bonheur*. It was true, they were stealing everything: the father's prosperity, the mother's dying child and, from the girl, the husband she had been waiting for over the past ten years. Seeing this doomed family, Denise, her heart filled with compassion, felt afraid for a moment that she was doing wrong. Wasn't she about to put her shoulder to the wheel that was crushing these poor folk? But it was as though she was being driven by some force and she did not feel that she was doing wrong.

'Puh!' said Baudu, to keep his spirits up. 'It won't kill us. One customer lost, two gained. Do you hear me, Denise? I've seventy thousand francs here that will cause Mouret some sleepless nights . . . Come on the rest of you! Don't look so glum!'

He couldn't cheer them up and himself fell back into pale-faced anxiety. All of them kept looking at the monster, drawn to it, possessed by it, gorging on their misfortune. The building work was coming to an end and the façade had been cleared of scaffolding, revealing a whole section of the vast edifice with its broad, clear windows opening in its white walls. At that moment, there were eight carriages lined up along the pavement, now that the road was open again for traffic, and boys were loading them one after another in front of the despatch office. Under the sunshine, a ray of which was glancing along the street, the green panels with their yellow and red trimmings shone like mirrors and sent blinding reflections to the depths of *Au Vieil Elbeuf*. Smart-looking coachmen, dressed in black, held the horses on tight reins – splendid teams, shaking their silver bits. And whenever a carriage was full, there was a deep rumbling sound on the paved street which shook the little shops near by.

Confronted with this triumphal procession which they had to endure twice a day, every day, the Baudus' heart broke at last. The father's resolve weakened as he wondered where this continual flow of goods could be going, while the mother, made sick by the distress of her daughter, looked on without seeing, her eyes filled with heavy tears.

CHAPTER 9

One Monday, 14 March, *Au Bonheur des Dames* launched its new shop with a great display of summer fashions, which was to last three days. Outside, a bitter wind was blowing and the passers-by, surprised by this return of winter, hurried along, buttoning their coats. However, the neighbouring shops were bubbling with emotion and you could see the pale faces of the small tradesmen pressed against their windows as they counted the first carriages to stop at the grand new entrance in the Rue Neuve-Saint-Augustin. This doorway, as high and deep as a church porch, surmounted by a sculptural group – Industry and Commerce linking hands amid a host of symbolic figures and designs – was shielded by a vast canopy, freshly gilded so that it seemed to light up the pavement with a burst of sunlight. The frontage of the building extended to left and right, its whitewash still glaringly new, turning round into the Rue Monsigny and the Rue de la Michodière and occupying the whole block except for the island by the Rue du Dix-Décembre where the offices of the Crédit Immobilier were to go up. All along this development, which was like a barracks, the shopkeepers could look up and see the goods piled behind the plate-glass windows which, from the ground to the second floor, opened the store up to daylight. And this huge cube, this colossal emporium blocked out their view of the sky, as though contributing to the cold that made them shiver in the depths of their icy little shops.

Meanwhile, Mouret was there from six o'clock, giving his final orders. In the centre, along the axis from the grand entrance, a broad gallery ran from one end to the other, flanked to left and right by two narrower ones, the Monsigny Gallery and the Michodière Gallery. The courtyards had been glazed in and transformed into halls, and iron staircases went up from the ground floor with iron bridges thrown across from one end to the other, on both floors. The architect, who happened to be an intelligent one, a young man enchanted with the new age,[1] had used stone only for the basements and the pillars at the corners, otherwise constructing the whole framework of iron, with columns supporting the assemblage of beams and joists. The counter-arches of the floors and the internal dividing walls were of brick. Space had been gained everywhere, air and light entered freely, and the public wandered around at ease beneath the bold vaults of the widely spaced trusses. It was a cathedral of modern trade, light yet solid, designed for a congregation of lady customers. Downstairs, in the central gallery, after the special offers at the door, there were ties, gloves and silks; the Monsigny Gallery was occupied by white linens and printed cottons, the Michodière Gallery by haberdashery, hosiery, cloth and woollens. Then, on the first floor, came ladies' wear, lingerie, shawls, lace and other new departments, while bedding, carpets, soft furnishings and all such bulky items which were hard to move had been relegated to the second floor. At the moment, there were in all thirty-nine departments and eighteen hundred employees, of whom two hundred were women. A whole world was burgeoning there, in the echoing life beneath the high metal naves.

Mouret's sole passion was the conquest of woman. He wanted to make her queen in his house and he had built this temple so that he could have her at his mercy. His whole tactic was to intoxicate her with attentive gallantry, to trade on her needs and to exploit her feverish desires. So, day and night, he racked his brain, searching for new ideas. He had already had two lifts put in, padded with velvet, to spare delicate ladies the effort of climbing the stairs. In addition to that, he had just opened a buffet, where biscuits and syrups were served free, and a reading room, a monumental gallery, over-extravagantly decorated, in which he was even venturing to hold exhibitions of painting. But his most subtle idea, directed at women without any idle vanity, was to reach the mother through the child. He used every strength and exploited every feeling, setting up departments for little boys and girls and stopping the mothers as they walked by, to offer their babies pictures and balloons. These free balloons were a stroke of genius, red balloons, handed out to every female customer, made of fine rubber and bearing the name of the shop in large letters. Floating through the air, held on the end of a string, they carried a living advertisement along the streets!

His great strength, above all, was advertising. Mouret might spend three hundred thousand francs a year on catalogues, newspaper advertisements and posters. To launch his new summer fashions, he had distributed two hundred thousand catalogues, fifty thousand of them abroad, translated into every language. Nowadays he had them illustrated with prints and even accompanied by samples, stuck on to the pages. It was a burst of publicity, with *Au Bonheur des Dames* coming before the eyes of the whole world, spread across walls, newspapers and even curtains in the theatre.

It was his contention that a woman was powerless against advertising, that in the end she must inevitably be drawn towards the source of the noise. Moreover, he would set still more clever traps for her, and show the skill of an analyst of human nature in his dissection of her. Thus, he had discovered that she could not resist a low price and would buy something that she did not need, if she thought she was getting a bargain; he based his system of price reduction on this observation, progressively cutting the price of unsold items and preferring to sell them at a loss, to remain faithful to the principle of rapid turnover of goods. Then he went deeper into a woman's heart and had recently dreamed up 'returns', a masterpiece of jesuitical seduction. 'Take it, take it, Madame, you can always return it to us if you no longer like it.' And the woman, who had been holding out, was given this ultimate excuse, the opportunity to repent of her folly. She took the item, with a clear conscience. Now, returns and price reductions were part of the standard workings of modern trade.

But where Mouret showed himself to be an unparalleled master was in the internal layout of the shops. He made an absolute rule that no corner of *Au Bonheur des Dames* should remain empty; everywhere, he demanded noise, people, life . . . because life, he said, attracts life, breeds and multiplies. All sorts of practical consequences derived from this rule. First of all, there must be a crush at the entrance; from the street, it should look like a riot; and he achieved this crush by putting cut-price articles at the door, boxes and baskets overflowing with cheap goods, so that the common people would pile up, blocking the passage, giving the impression that the shops were bursting with customers, even though quite often they were only half full. After that, along the galleries, he knew the art of disguising lines that were not going fast, for example shawls in summer and cotton prints in winter: he would place them between the busy departments and drown them in noise. So far, he was the only person to think of putting carpets and furniture up on the second floor, these being departments where there were fewer customers; on the ground floor, they would have formed cold, empty spaces. If he had known how, he would have made the street run through his shop.

Just now, Mouret was suffering from a crisis of inspiration. On Saturday evening, while taking a final look over preparations for the great Monday sale, which had been preoccupying them for a month, he suddenly realized that the classification of departments that he had chosen to use was clumsy. Yet it was an absolutely logical classification, with materials on one side and ready-made garments on the other, an intelligent arrangement that should allow the customers to find their own way around. This was an arrangement that he had dreamed up, long ago, in the confusion of Madame Hédouin's narrow shop; and now, on the day when the dream was becoming reality, he felt unsure about it. Abruptly, he exclaimed that they would have to 'break it all up' for him. They had forty-eight hours; a whole section of the shop would have to be moved. The staff, startled, bewildered, rushing around, had to spend the two nights and the whole of Sunday in the midst of the most dreadful chaos. Even on Monday morning, an hour before opening time, the goods were still not in place. The boss was definitely going mad, no one could understand it, and there was general consternation.

'Come on! Hurry up!' Mouret shouted, with the quiet assurance of genius. 'Here are some more costumes that I want taken upstairs . . . And is the Japanese display set up on the main landing? . . . One final effort, my lads, and you'll soon see how much we sell!'

Bourdoncle, too, had been there since first light. He was no better able than anyone else to understand and his eyes followed Mouret around with anxious looks. He did not dare ask him any questions, knowing what kind of answer he would get, in such moments of crisis. Yet, finally, he nerved himself to it, and asked softly:

'Was it really necessary to turn everything upside down like this on the day before the sale started?'

At first, Mouret shrugged his shoulders, without answering. Then, as the other man ventured to pursue the subject, he burst out.

'So that the customers could all crowd into the same corner, I suppose? A brilliant mathematician's idea I had there! I'd never have got over it! Don't you see: I was putting all the crowd in one place. A woman would come in, go straight to the place she wanted, go on from skirts to dresses, then from dresses to coats, and then off home, without even getting lost a little! Not a single one would even have seen the store!'

'Ah,' said Bourdoncle. 'But now that you've scrambled it all up and put everything all over the place, the staff will be wearing themselves out taking the customers from one department to another.'

Mouret shrugged his shoulders in contempt.

'Do I care! They're young, it will build them up. And all the better if they walk around. It will seem as though there are more of them, they will add to the crowd. Let there be a crush, so much the better.'

He laughed and, lowering his voice, condescended to explain his thinking:

'Listen, Bourdoncle, and watch what happens. First of all, the constant toing and froing of customers spreads them around, multiplies them and makes them lose their heads. Secondly, since they have to be taken from one end of the store to the other, for example if they want the lining after buying the dress, these journeyings in every direction make the store seem three times as large to them. And thirdly, they are obliged to go through departments where they would not otherwise have set foot, where there are temptations to catch them as they go by, and they succumb. Fourthly . . .'

Bourdoncle was laughing with him. So Mouret, delighted, stopped to shout at the boys:

'Very good, lads! Now, sweep it a bit and see how beautiful it will be!'

But, turning round, he noticed Denise. He and Bourdoncle were in front of the ladies' wear department which he had chosen to split, sending dresses and costumes up to the second floor, at the other end of the store. Denise, the first to come down, was staring in amazement, bewildered by the new arrangement.

'What's happening?' she asked. 'Are we moving?'

Her surprise seemed to amuse Mouret, who loved these dramatic gestures. Denise had been back in *Au Bonheur* since the beginning of February and had been happily surprised to find the staff polite and almost respectful. Madame Aurélie behaved with particular consideration, Marguerite and Clara seemed resigned, and even Old Jouve bowed and scraped, with an embarrassed look, as though trying to make up for the unfortunate memory of what had happened. It was enough for Mouret to say the word and everyone was whispering, their eyes following her. In the midst of all this friendliness, the only things that hurt her were the peculiar sadness of Deloche and Pauline's inexplicable smiles.

Meanwhile, Mouret was still regarding her with his air of delight.

'So what are you looking for, Mademoiselle?' he asked at length.

Denise had not noticed him. She blushed slightly. Since she had come back, he had been showing small signs of interest in her which she found very touching. Pauline (though she couldn't think why) had given her a detailed account of the affair between the boss and Clara: where he saw her, how much he paid her. She frequently returned to the subject and even added that he had another mistress, that Madame Desforges, as everyone in the shop knew. These stories upset Denise and when confronted by him she experienced the old fear, an uneasiness in which her gratitude had to struggle against anger.

'It's all this upheaval,' she murmured.

At this, Mouret came closer so that he could say more quietly:

'This evening, after the sales, come up to my office. I want to talk to you.'

This disturbed her. She bowed her head, but said nothing. In any case, she was going into the department and the other girls were arriving. But Bourdoncle had heard what Mouret said and looked at him with a smile. He even dared say, when they were alone:

'That one again! Take care or it may start to get serious!'

Mouret hotly refuted the suggestion, hiding his feelings behind an air of superior nonchalance.

'Forget it! It's a joke! The woman who nets me has yet to be born, dear chap!'

And, as the shops were now opening at last, he hurried off to give a last look at the various departments. Bourdoncle shook his head. That Denise, sweet and simple as she was, was starting to worry him. He had won the first round by roughly dismissing her. But now she was back and he considered her a serious enemy, saying nothing to her face, but awaiting events.

He caught up with Mouret, who was downstairs in the Saint-Augustin Hall opposite the entrance, shouting:

'Is someone trying to make a fool of me? I said to put the blue parasols around the edge. Take it all down, and quickly!'

He refused to listen to any explanation and a team of boys had to rearrange the parasols. When he saw customers coming, he even had the doors closed for a moment, saying that he would not open as long as the blue parasols were in the centre. It ruined his composition. The top window-dressers, Hutin, Mignot and a few others, came to take a look, and rolled their eyes, but they pretended not to understand, belonging to a different school of display.

Finally, the doors were reopened and the crowd poured in. In the very first hour, before the shops were full, there was such a crush under the porch that they had to call for the constables so that people could keep moving along the pavement. Mouret had judged correctly: all the housewives, a massed troop of petty bourgeoises and women in bonnets,[2] launched themselves on the bargains, seconds and remnants, which were displayed right on the street. Hands were constantly reaching up to feel the lengths of cloth hanging at the entrance: a calico for seven *sous*, a wool and cotton *grisaille* for nine *sous*, and most of all an Orleans[3] at thirty-eight centimes which was devastating the poorer purses. There was much shoving and furious pushing around bins and baskets in which piles of cut-price items – lace for ten centimes, ribbons for five *sous*, garters for three, gloves, skirts, ties, socks and cotton stockings – crumbled and vanished as though eaten up by the hungry crowd. Despite the cold weather, there were not enough assistants selling in the open air on the street to meet demand. A fat woman started to scream. Two little girls were nearly suffocated.

The crush grew throughout the morning. Around one o'clock, queues formed and the street was blocked, as in a riot. Just then, as Madame de Boves and her daughter Blanche were standing on the opposite pavement, unable to make up their minds, they were approached by Madame Marty, who also had her daughter, Valentine, with her.

'Well then?' said Madame de Boves. 'What a crowd! It's murder in there. I shouldn't have come out. I was in bed, but I got up to get a bit of fresh air.'

'The same with me,' said her friend. 'I promised my husband I'd go and see his sister in Montmartre. Then, on the way, I remembered that I needed a piece of braid. I might as well buy it here as anywhere else, don't you think? Oh, It won't cost me a *sou*! In any case, I don't want anything.'

But their eyes were fixed on the door and they were caught up and carried away by the gust of the crowd.

'No, no, I'm not going in,' Madame de Boves muttered. 'I'm afraid. Come on Blanche, let's go, we'll be crushed.'

But her voice was growing weaker and gradually she gave in to the desire to follow everyone inside, her fears dissolving in the irresistible attraction of the crush. Madame Marty, too, had ceased to resist. She kept saying:

'Hold my dress, Valentine. Well, I never! I've never seen such a thing! What can it be like inside!'

These ladies, carried forward by the current, were by now unable to turn back. Just as a river draws towards it all the wandering streams in a valley, so it seemed that the flow of customers, pouring through the hallway, was swallowing up the passers-by in the street, drawing people in from the four corners of Paris. They moved forward only slowly, pressed so close that they could hardly draw breath, supported by shoulders and bellies which felt soft and warm; and their satisfied desire was gratified by this tedious approach which stimulated their curiosity. It was a jumble of ladies dressed in silk, petty bourgeoises in cheap dresses, bareheaded girls, all lifted and intoxicated by the same passion. A few men, swamped by the swelling bosoms, were looking anxiously around them. A nursemaid, right in the thick of it, lifted her baby above her head while it laughed happily. And just one scrawny woman was losing her temper, pouring out a string of abuse, accusing the lady next to her of elbowing her.

'I really think they'll have the skirt off me,' Madame de Boves kept saying.

Silent, her face still pink from the fresh air, Madame Marty stood on tiptoe to see forward over the heads of the others to where the shops opened out. The pupils of her grey eyes were as small as those of a cat emerging into the light and she had the rested and bright look of someone waking up.

'Ah, at last!' she said with a sigh.

The ladies had just broken through. They were in the Saint-Augustin Hall, and greatly surprised to find it almost empty. But a sense of well-being swept over them, it felt as though they were entering springtime after the winter of the street. Outside, the cold winds that carry March showers were blowing, while here in the galleries of *Au Bonheur des Dames*, the fine weather warmed them with light materials, the flowery shine of pastel shades and the rural delights of summer fashions and parasols.

'Look at that!' Madame de Boves exclaimed, stopping in her tracks and staring upwards.

It was the display of parasols – all open, curved like shields, they covered the hall from the glazed bay of the ceiling to the varnished oak on the cornice. They were festooned around the arcades of the upper storeys, they fell in garlands along the columns, they marched in serried ranks along the balustrades and even on the banisters of the staircases, and everywhere, symmetrically arranged, splashing the walls with red, green and yellow, they were like great Venetian lanterns, lit up for some enormous carnival. At the corners there were complicated designs, stars made of parasols at thirty-nine *sous*, their light colours, pale blue, creamy white or soft pink, shining with the soft glow of a night-light, while above them vast Japanese shades, across which golden cranes flew in a purple sky, blazed with a fiery incandescence.

Madame Marty hunted for a word to express her delight and found nothing better than:

'It's magical!'

Then, trying to decide where she was: 'Come now, the braid is in haberdashery . . . I'll buy my braid, then go.'

'I'll come with you,' said Madame de Boves. 'That's right, Blanche, isn't it? We'll just walk through the shop, that's all.'

But, as soon as they came through the door, the ladies were lost. They turned left and, since haberdashery had been moved, they found themselves right among the ruches and collarettes, then costume jewellery. It was very hot in the covered galleries, like a greenhouse, damp and confined, heavy with the vapid smell of materials which deadened the tramping of the crowd. So they came back to the door, where a stream of people was starting to make its exit, an endless line of women and children with a cloud of red balloons floating above them. Forty thousand balloons were prepared and there were boys specially employed to hand them out. As one watched the customers leave, it was like a flight of huge soap bubbles through the air on the end of invisible wires reflecting the fire of the parasols. The whole shop was lit up.

'It's a world in itself,' Madame de Boves announced. 'You can't tell where you are.'

However, the ladies could not stay in the whirlpool around the door, pushed by those entering and leaving. Fortunately, Inspector Jouve came to their aid. He was standing under the porch, serious, alert, watching each woman as she went past. Particularly responsible for shop security, he kept a watch for thieves and would follow pregnant women when a glint in their eyes made him suspicious.

'Haberdashery, ladies?' he said politely. 'To the left, look, over there, behind hosiery.'

Madame de Boves thanked him. But Madame Marty had turned round and seen that her daughter, Valentine, was no longer beside her. She was getting alarmed when she caught sight of her, already a long way off, at the end of the Saint-Augustin Hall, completely absorbed by a hawker's stand with piles of women's cravats for nineteen *sous*. Mouret used this method of direct selling, with salesmen touting goods, catching the customer and taking her money – because he used every form of advertising and laughed at the reticence of some of his rivals who thought that the merchandise should speak for itself. Special salesmen, idle, quick-talking Parisians, disposed of large amounts of small, cheap items in this way.

'Oh, mother,' Valentine murmured. 'Look at those cravats. They've got a bird embroidered in the corner.'

The salesman was offering the item, swearing that it was all silk, that the manufacturer had gone bankrupt and that they would never again find such a bargain.

'Nineteen *sous*! Is it possible?' Madame Marty said, as captivated as her daughter. 'Well! I can easily take two, it won't ruin us.'

Madame de Boves was scornful. She hated direct selling: she would run away when some salesman called to her. Madame Marty was surprised: she didn't understand this nervous aversion to sales talk, because she was just the opposite, one of those women happy to be assaulted and to succumb to the caress of a public offer, with the pleasure of handling everything and wasting her time in pointless chatter.

'Now,' she said, 'let's quickly go and get my braid. I don't even want to see anything else.'

However, as they were passing through scarves and gloves, she gave way once more. There, in the diffused light, was a display in which bright, jolly colours created the most enchanting effect. The counters were arranged symmetrically to transform the area into a French formal garden, radiant with every gentle shade of flower. On the bare wood of the counter, emptying out of boxes or from over-filled shelves, a harvest of headscarves exhibited the bright red of geraniums, the milky white of petunias, the golden yellow of chrysanthemums and the sky blue of verbenas. Higher up, on brass stems, another burst of flowers was wreathed – fichus tossed up, ribbons unfolding, a whole brilliant sash stretching up, curling around the columns and multiplied in the mirrors. But what astonished the crowd was in the glove department, the Swiss chalet made entirely of gloves, Mignot's masterpiece which had taken two days' work. First of all, there were black gloves to form the ground floor, then came straw-coloured gloves, grey-green gloves and deep red gloves, spread across the display, forming the window frames, suggesting balconies and standing in for tiles.

'How can I help Madame?' asked Mignot, when he saw Madame Marty standing in front of the chalet. 'These are Swedish gloves, top quality, at one franc seventy-five.'

He was persistent, calling out to customers from the back of his counter as they walked past and importuning them with politeness. As she shook her head, he went on:

'Tyrolean gloves at one franc twenty-five, Turin gloves, for children, embroidered gloves in every colour . . .'

'No, thank you, I don't need anything,' Madame Marty declared.

But he felt that her voice was softening and launched a more brutal attack, thrusting the embroidered gloves in front of her. Her resolve weakened and she bought a pair. Then, as Madame de Boves looked at her smiling, she blushed.

'There! What a child I am! If I don't hurry up and buy my braid, I'm lost.'

Unfortunately, there was such a crowd in haberdashery that she couldn't find anyone to serve her. The two of them had been waiting for ten minutes and were becoming impatient when they met Madame Bourdelais and her three children, which took their minds off it. Madame Bourdelais explained, in her unhurried, practical woman's manner, that she wanted to show all this to the children. Madeleine was ten, Edmond eight and Lucien four, and they were laughing with delight. This was an inexpensive treat which they had been promised long ago.

'I'm going to buy a red parasol, they're so amusing,' exclaimed Madame Marty suddenly, who was tapping her feet, impatient at staying here with nothing to do.

She chose one for fourteen francs fifty. Madame Bourdelais, after watching her with a disapproving look, said cheerfully:

'You're quite wrong to be in such a hurry. In a month's time you could have had that for ten francs. They won't catch me!'

She explained a whole theory of good housewifery. Since shops were lowering their prices, one only had to wait. She didn't want to be exploited by them, she was the one who took advantage of their real bargains. She even made it a grudge contest, boasting that she had never left them a *sou* of profit.

'Now, then,' she said at last. 'I promised to show my little brood the pictures upstairs in the lounge. Come with me, you've got time.'

So the braid was forgotten and Madame Marty gave in at once, while Madame de Boves refused, preferring to go all round the ground floor first. In any case, the ladies hoped to meet again on the top floor. Madame Bourdelais was looking around for a staircase when she saw one of the lifts and pushed the children into it to make the outing complete. Madame Marty and Valentine also got into the narrow lift where everyone was tightly packed, but the mirrors, the velvet-covered seats and the moulded bronze doors kept them so occupied that they reached the first floor without feeling the machine slide gently upwards. And there was another treat for them in the lace gallery. As they were going past the buffet, Madame Bourdelais did not forget to fill her little family with syrups. It was a square room with a wide marble counter. At each end, a trickle of water flowed from silver-coloured fountains and behind them the bottles were lined up on narrow shelves. Three waiters were endlessly filling and wiping glasses. To control the thirsty customers, they had to form them into a queue with the help of a velvet-covered barrier, like the ones they use outside theatres. Some people, losing all conscience at the sight of these free treats, had made themselves ill with them.

'Well, now, where are they?' Madame Bourdelais shouted, when she emerged from the crush after wiping the children with her handkerchief.

But she saw Madame Marty and Valentine at the far end of another gallery, a long way off, both of them sinking beneath a heap of petticoats and still buying. It was finished; mother and daughter vanished, carried away by their spending fever.

When she finally reached the reading and writing room, Madame Bourdelais settled Madeleine, Edmond and Lucien in front of the large table, then went to fetch some albums of photographs for them from a bookshelf. The vaulted ceiling of the long room was heavy with gilding, enormous fireplaces faced one another at either end, second-rate paintings in very ornate frames covered the walls and between the columns, in front of each of the arched bays that opened on the shop there were tall green plants in majolica pots. A large number of silent customers were standing around the table which was covered in newspapers and magazines, with a supply of writing paper and ink pots. Some ladies were taking off their gloves and writing letters on paper with the letterhead of the shop which they crossed out with a stroke of the pen. A few men, leaning back in their armchairs, were reading the newspapers, but a lot of people just sat around doing nothing: husbands waiting for their wives who had been let loose in the store, discreet young ladies expecting the arrival of a lover, or aged relatives left behind as though in a cloakroom, to be retrieved on departure. And all these people, slouching in their chairs, glanced occasionally along the open bays into the depths of the galleries and the halls from where a distant rumbling rose up, amid the tiny sounds of scratching pens and rustling papers.

'What! Are you here?' said Madame Bourdelais. 'I didn't recognize you.'

Near some children, a woman was vanishing between the pages of a magazine. It was Madame Guibal. She seemed annoyed at the meeting. But she pulled herself together at once and said that she had come up here to sit down for a while, to escape the crush of the throng. And when Madame Bourdelais asked if she had come to buy anything, she replied languidly, letting her lids droop over the harsh egoism in her eyes:

'Oh, no . . . On the contrary, I'm bringing something back. Yes, some door-hangings I'm not pleased with. But there's such a crowd that I'm waiting to get into the department.'

She went on talking, saying how convenient it was, this system of returns. Before that, she never used to buy anything, but now she did sometimes let herself be tempted, though she brought back four things out of five. She was starting to become known at all the different counters for the peculiar deals which she struck, in a state of constant dissatisfaction, bringing the goods back one by one after retaining them for several days. Yet even as she spoke, she kept her eye on the doors to the reading room and seemed relieved when Madame Bourdelais went back to her children in order to explain the photogaphs to them.

Almost at the same moment, Monsieur de Boves and Paul de Vallagnosc came in. The Count, who was pretending to show the new shops to the young man, exchanged a brief look with her, after which she went back to her reading, as though noticing nothing.

'Hello, Paul!' said a voice behind these gentlemen.

It was Mouret, doing his rounds of the various departments. Handshakes were exchanged and he immediately asked:

'Did Madame de Boves do us the honour of coming?'

'Dear me, no!' the Count replied. 'And she was very sorry not to. She is unwell – oh, it's nothing too serious!'

Then, suddenly, he pretended to notice Madame Guibal. He hurried off and went up to her, bareheaded, while the other two merely nodded from a distance. She, too, feigned surprise. Paul gave a smile: now he understood – and he quietly told Mouret how he had met the Count in the Rue Richelieu. The Count had tried to escape, then decided to take him along to *Au Bonheur des Dames*, on the excuse that you absolutely had to see it. For a year, the lady had taken what money and pleasure she could from the Count, never writing to him, but giving him assignations in public places – churches, museums, shops – so that they could make an arrangement.

'I do believe that they change their hotel room at every meeting,' the young man said softly. 'Last month he was on a tour of inspection. He wrote to his wife every other day, from Blois, Libourne, Tarbes . . . yet I'm quite sure I saw him going into a respectable boarding-house in Batignolles . . . Just look at him! Isn't he handsome, standing in front of her as proper and upright as the state official he is! That's the old France for you, dear fellow, the old France!'

'What about your marriage?' Mouret asked.

Paul, not taking his eyes off the Count, said that they were still waiting for his aunt to die. Then, with a triumphal air:

'There! D'you see that? He bent down and slipped her an address. And now she's accepting it – with her most virtuous expression. Terrible woman, that delicate redhead with her air of insouciance . . . I say, there are some fine goings-on in your place.'

'Ah,' Mouret said with a smile. 'These ladies are in their own place here, not mine.'

After that, he joked about it. Love, like swallows, brought luck to a house. Of course, he knew all about the girls who hung around the departments and the ladies who just happened to meet a friend there; but, even if they didn't buy, they made it look busy, they warmed up the shops. Even as he spoke, he took his old school mate and stood him on the threshold of the reading room, opposite the great central gallery, its string of halls opening out below. Behind them, the reading room maintained its calm, with little sounds of nervous pens and folding papers. An old gentleman had fallen asleep over *Le Moniteur*[4] and Monsieur de Boves was studying the paintings with the obvious intention of losing his future son-in-law in the crowd. Alone in the midst of this calm, Madame Bourdelais was entertaining her children, very loudly, as though the place belonged to her.

'You see, they are at home,' Mouret repeated, waving his arms across the crush of women bursting out of every department.

At that moment, Madame Desforges, who had almost had her coat pulled off in the crowd, finally got in and was crossing the first hall. Then, once she got to the main gallery, she looked up. It was like the concourse of a railway station, surrounded by the balustrades of the two upper storeys, cut by suspended stairways and crisscrossed with bridges. The iron stairways, in double spirals, formed daring curves with many landings. The iron bridges hung high up in straight lines across the void.[5] And all this cast iron beneath the white light of the glass roof composed an airy architecture of complicated lacework which let the daylight through – a modern version of a dream palace, a Tower of Babel with storey piled on storey and rooms expanding, opening on vistas of other storeys and other rooms reaching to infinity. Moreover, iron reigned on all sides, the young architect having had the honesty and courage not to disguise it beneath a coat of whitewash or to imitate stone and wood. Downstairs, so as not to detract from the goods, the décor was sober, with large expanses of the same, neutral colour. Then, as the metal framework rose upwards, so the capitals of the columns grew richer, the rivets formed rosettes, the brackets and the corbels were laden with moulded sculptures. Finally, at the top, the painting shone out green and red, in the midst of a profusion of gold: streams of gold, harvests of gold, even on the windows where the panes were enamelled and encrusted with gold. Beneath the covered galleries, the visible bricks on the vaults were also enamelled with bright colours. Mosaic and faience were incorporated in the décor, brightening up the borders and adding a fresh note to moderate the severity of the whole; while the staircases with their banisters of red velvet were decked out with a strip of moulded, polished iron, shining like the steel on a breastplate.

Although she was already acquainted with the new building, Madame Desforges had stopped, struck by the bustling life that seethed that day beneath the huge vault. On the ground floor, around her, the crowd continued to flow in the same double current from the entrance or towards the exit, and this was perceptible as far as the silk department – a very mixed crowd, though in the afternoon there were more ladies among the petty bourgeoises and the housewives, many women in mourning, with their large veils, and errant wet nurses protecting their charges with their broad elbows. And this sea, these many-coloured hats, these bare heads, blonde or black, flowed from one end of the gallery to the other, blurred and drab amid the sharp, vibrant colours of the materials. Madame Desforges could see nothing but huge placards everywhere with enormous figures on them, standing out as garish stains against the bright Indian prints, the lustrous silks and the dark woollens. Piles of ribbons gashed across heads, a wall of flannel spread out like a promontory and everywhere the mirrors extended the shops, reflecting displays with fragments of the public, faces reversed, portions of shoulders and arms, while to the left and to the right the side galleries opened up vistas, snowy depths of white linens or the speckled pits of hosiery, far-away, vanishing, lit by the rays of light shining through some glazed bay, where the crowd was no more than a dust of humanity. Then, when Madame Desforges looked up, she could see along the stairways and on the suspended bridges, around the banisters on every floor, a continuous, humming, upward flow, a whole tribe suspended in the air, travelling past the spaces in this enormous metal frame and silhouetted black against the diffuse glow from the windows. Huge gilded chandeliers hung from the ceiling, the banisters were bedecked with carpets, embroidered silks and gold-encrusted materials which hung across them in shining banners, while from one end to the other there were flights of lace, tremblings of muslin, silken trophies and apotheoses of half-naked models; and above all this confusion, right at the top, the bedding department appeared to be suspended, displaying little beds with mattresses and draped with white curtains, a dormitory of boarding-school girls asleep amid the trampling of the customers, which grew rarer as one rose, department by department, towards the top of the building.

'Would Madame like some cheap garters?' a salesman asked Madame Desforges, when he saw her standing still. 'All silk, twenty-nine *sous*.'

She did not deign to answer. Around her, salesmen were barking their wares with ever greater ardour. But she wanted to find her way. Albert Lhomme's cash desk was on her left. He knew her by sight and allowed himself a friendly smile, quite unflustered in the midst of the heaps of receipts all round him, while Joseph behind him was struggling with the box of string, unable to keep up with wrapping the parcels. At this, she knew where she was: silks must be in front of her. But it took her ten minutes to reach them, the crowd was swelling so rapidly. The red balloons were multiplying in the air on the end of their invisible threads, gathering in clouds of purple, gently drifting towards the doors and continually pouring out into Paris; and she had to duck her head under the flying balloons when they were held by very young children, with the threads wound round their little hands.

'Well, now, Madame! So you took the risk!' Bouthemont said cheerfully as soon as he saw Madame Desforges.

Nowadays the head of department, who had been introduced to her by Mouret himself, sometimes went to her house to take tea. She found him common, but very pleasant, with a strong, sanguine temperament which both surprised and entertained her. Two days earlier, as it happens, he had quite blatantly told her about Mouret's affair with Clara, not for any particular purpose, but just because he was a rough lad who enjoyed a laugh. Gnawed by jealousy, but hiding her pain beneath an air of contempt, she had come to try and find out about this girl, a young lady from ladies' wear, that was all he had told her, without giving her a name.

'Would you like something from us?' he went on.

'Yes, of course, or I should not have come. Do you have some foulard for a morning gown?'

Smitten by a desire to see the young lady, she was hoping to get her name out of him. He immediately called Favier and went on talking to her while waiting for the salesman to finish serving a customer – as it happens, the 'pretty lady', that beautiful blonde that they sometimes talked about in the department, without knowing anything about her, even her name. This time, the pretty lady was in deep mourning. Whom had she lost: her husband or her father? Surely not her father, or she would have seemed more sad. So what did they think? She was not a kept woman, she had had a real husband. Unless, of course, she was mourning her mother. For a few minutes, despite the press of work, the department speculated.

'Hurry up, this is intolerable!' Hutin shouted to Favier, who had just led his customer to a cash desk. 'When that lady is here, you drag it out for ever. She doesn't give a fig for you!'

'And I give still less for her,' the salesman replied, angered by this.

But Hutin threatened to mention him to the management if he didn't show more respect for the customers. He had become intolerable, strict and cantankerous, since the department had united to get him Robineau's job. He was even so unbearable, after the promises of good fellowship that he had formerly made to his colleagues, that nowadays they secretly supported Favier against him.

'Come on, don't answer back,' Hutin snapped. 'Monsieur Bouthemont wants you to get him some foulard, the lightest designs.'

In the middle of the department, a display of summer silks lit the hall with a burst of sunrise, like a star rising amid the most delicate shades of light: pale pink, soft yellow and limpid blue – Iris's drifting veil in all its glory. There were foulards as soft as clouds, surahs lighter than the down floating from trees and moiré Peking silks as supple as the skin of a Chinese virgin. There were pongees from Japan, tussores and corahs from India,[6] not to mention our own light silks in stripes, checks and flower patterns, every design imaginable, conjuring up ladies in furbelows walking beneath the great trees of some park on a May morning.

'I'll take this one, the Louis XIV, with the bunches of roses,' Madame Desforges said eventually.

And while Favier was measuring it out, she made one last attempt to get something out of Bouthemont, who had stayed with her.

'I'm going up to ladies' wear to look at some travelling coats. Is she a blonde, the young lady in your story?'

The head of department was starting to feel uneasy at the way she kept pressing him and merely smiled. Then, at that moment, Denise walked by. She had just handed over Madame Boutarel to Liénard in merinos (this was the provincial lady who came up to Paris twice a year to scatter all the money she had saved on her housekeeping around the departments of *Au Bonheur des Dames*). Since Favier was already bringing Madame Desforges' foulard, Hutin stopped him, just to get on his nerves.

'No need, Mademoiselle will be good enough to conduct Madame.'

Denise was disturbed, but quite happy to take the material and the invoice. She could not meet the young man face to face without a sense of shame, as though he reminded her of some old indiscretion; but she had only sinned in her dreams.

'Tell me,' Madame Desforges whispered to Bouthemont, 'could it be this awkward little girl? Has he taken her back, then? She must be the heroine of the affair!'

'Perhaps,' said the head of department, still smiling and now determined not to tell her the truth.

So Madame Desforges, preceded by Denise, slowly climbed the stairs. She had to stop every three seconds to avoid being swept down by people coming in the other direction. In the living vibration of the whole building, the iron stringboards shuddered underfoot as though responding to the breath of the crowd. On every step, a tailor's dummy was solidly attached, motionlessly exhibiting an article of clothing: suits, jackets, dressing-gowns . . . And they looked like two ranks of soldiers for some triumphal parade, each with a little wooden peg like the handle of a dagger sticking out of the red flannelette, which seemed to bleed from a freshly cut neck.

Madame Desforges was just reaching the first floor when she was stopped in her tracks by a stronger wave than the rest. Now, below her, she had the departments on the ground floor, all that spreading crowd of customers which she had just gone through. This was a new sight, an ocean of heads in miniature, hiding the women's blouses and teeming like an ants' nest. The white placards were now only thin lines, the piles of ribbons were flattened and the promontory of flannel reached across the gallery like a narrow wall, while the carpets and embroideries that bedecked the banisters hung at her feet like banners for a procession fixed to the rood screen in a church. In the distance she could see corners of side galleries, as one might make out the corners of neighbouring streets with black specks of passers-by from a church steeple. But what most surprised her – her eyes tired and blinded by the burst of mingled colours – was that when she closed her eyes she could sense the crowd more, with its dull sound like a rising tide and the body heat it gave off. A fine dust rose from the floors, heavy with the smell of woman, the smell of her linen and the nape of her neck, her skirts and her hair, a penetrating, all-embracing odour which was like the incense of this temple dedicated to the cult of women's bodies.

Meanwhile, Mouret was still standing in front of the reading room with Vallagnosc and breathing in this scent, intoxicated by it, repeating:

'They are at home. I know some who spend the whole day here, eating cakes and writing letters. All that's left is for me to put them to bed.'

This joke made Paul smile, though, in the boredom induced by his pessimism, he still thought the swirling of this human flood ridiculous – for bits of cloth. When he came to say hello to his former schoolmate, he would go away almost irritated at seeing him so vibrant with life in the midst of his tribe of coquettes. Surely one of them, empty of head and heart, would teach him how stupid and pointless life was? As it happened, that day Octave did seem to be losing some of his admirable poise. He who usually breathed fire into his customers with the quiet skill and ease of a man operating a machine, seemed to be caught up himself in the gust of passion raging through the shops. Since seeing Denise and Madame Desforges going up the great staircase, he had been speaking more loudly and gesticulating involuntarily; and, while making sure not to turn his head round towards them, he showed signs of nervous excitement the closer they came: his face blushed and his eyes had something of the enraptured bewilderment that would start to flicker in the eyes of the lady purchasers after a while.

'You must get frightfully robbed,' said Vallagnosc who considered that there was something criminal in the appearance of the crowd.

Mouret flung his arms wide.

'My dear chap, you can't begin to imagine.'

After which, nervously, delighted to have something to talk about, he produced endless details, recounted particular events and classified them.[7] First of all, there were women who were professional thieves, but they did the least harm, because the police knew all of them. After that, there were kleptomaniacs who suffered from a perversion of desire, a new kind of neurosis that a nerve doctor had distinguished, perceiving in it the extreme result of the temptation exercised by department stores. Finally, there were pregnant women who specialized in particular items; for example, in the house of one, the police commissioner had found two hundred and forty-eight pairs of pink gloves, stolen from every store in Paris.

'The women here have such odd eyes,' Vallagnosc muttered. 'I was watching them with their greedy, shame-faced look of mad creatures. A fine way to teach people honesty!'

'Puh!' Mouret answered. 'Even though we try to make them feel at home, we can't let them carry off the merchandise under their coats. And some very distinguished people. Last week, we had the sister of a pharmacist and the wife of a high court judge. We try to come to some arrangement.'

He paused to point out Inspector Jouve, who was at that very moment following a pregnant woman downstairs on the ribbon counter. This woman, whose huge belly was taking a lot of pushing from the throng, was accompanied by a friend, no doubt there to ward off any too violent shocks. Every time the pregnant woman stopped at a display, Jouve kept his eyes on her, while the other woman beside her was freely rummaging in the bottom of the boxes.

'Oh, he'll catch her,' said Mouret. 'He's up to all their tricks.'

But his voice was shaking and his laugh forced. Denise and Henriette, on whom he had kept constant watch, finally passed behind him, having had a lot of trouble breaking free of the crush. So he turned round, gave his customer the discreet nod of a friend who does not want to compromise a woman by stopping her in public. Henriette, however, being on the alert, clearly saw the look with which he had first given Denise. This girl must definitely be the rival whom she had been curious to see.

In ladies' wear, the sales staff were losing their heads. Two of the young ladies were ill and Madame Frédéric, the under-buyer, had calmly given in her notice the previous day, passing by the cash desk to settle her account and dropping *Au Bonheur des Dames* from one minute to the next, as the shop itself dropped its employees. Since the morning, even in the fever of the sale, no one had talked about anything except this affair. Clara, who was kept in the department on the whim of Mouret, thought it was 'terrific'. Marguerite told them how exasperated Bourdoncle was, while Madame Aurélie was vexed, saying that Madame Frédéric could at least have told her about it; no one had ever seen such dissimulation. Though Madame Frédéric had never confided in anyone, they suspected her of having left the clothing business altogether to marry the owner of a public baths near Les Halles.

'Does Madame want a travelling coat?' Denise asked Madame Desforges, after offering her a chair.

'Yes,' the other woman replied sharply, having made up her mind to be rude.

The new arrangement of the department was richly severe: tall wardrobes of carved oak, windows as wide as the wall panels and a red carpet that stifled the continual sound of the customers' footsteps. While Denise was looking for some travelling coats, Madame Desforges glanced round and caught sight of herself in a mirror. She paused to take stock. Was she getting old, then, that a man should be unfaithful to her with the first girl who came along? The mirror reflected the whole bustling department, but she could only see her own pale face, not hearing Clara, behind her, telling Marguerite about one of Madame Frédéric's little secrets, the way that every morning and evening she would go all the way round through the Passage Choiseul, to give the impression that she lived on the Left Bank.

'Here are our latest models,' said Denise. 'We have them in various colours.'

She spread out four or five coats. Madame Desforges looked at them scornfully, becoming more critical with each one. Why have these gathers which made the coat look skimpy? And this one, with its square shoulders, looked as if it had been carved out with an axe. Even when one was travelling, one didn't want to look like a sentry box.

'Show me something else, Mademoiselle.'

Denise unfolded the clothes and folded them up again without a sign of irritation. This patient serenity made Madame Desforges fume even more. Her eyes constantly went back to the mirror opposite her. Now she was looking at herself in it beside Denise and making comparisons. Could anyone possibly prefer that insignificant creature? Now she remembered: the creature was the one whom she had seen some time ago looking so stupid as she started work, as clumsy as a goose girl straight up from her village. She certainly held herself better nowadays, all prim and proper in her silk dress. But how mean she was, how ordinary!

'I'll show Madame some other models,' Denise said quietly.

When she came back, the scene began again. Now the cloth was worthless and too heavy. Madame Desforges turned round and raised her voice, trying to get Madame Aurélie's attention in the hope of having her scold the young woman. But since Denise's return, she had gradually won the department over. Now she was on home ground and the buyer even attributed to her those rare qualities of the true sales assistant: gentle determination and smiling assurance. So Madame Aurélie just shrugged her shoulders a little and took care not to interfere.

'Would Madame be good enough to suggest what kind of coat she wants?' Denise asked again, with that polite insistence of hers that nothing would discourage.

'But you don't have anything!' Madame Desforges exclaimed.

She stopped, surprised at feeling a hand on her shoulder. It was Madame Marty, whose spending fever was taking her from one shop to another. Her purchases had grown to such an extent since the kerchiefs, the embroidered gloves and the red parasol that the last salesman had just decided to put the parcel on a chair rather than break his arms with it, and he was walking in front of her pulling the chair piled with skirts, towels, curtains, a lamp and three doormats.

'What's this?' she said. 'Are you buying a travelling coat?'

'Good heavens, no! They're frightful!' Madame Desforges replied.

But Madame Marty had come across a striped coat that she thought was not bad. Her daughter Valentine was already looking at it. So Denise, to dispose of the item (which was one of last year's models), called Marguerite over and she, on a wink from her colleague, presented it as an exceptional bargain. After she had sworn that the price had been lowered twice – taking it from one hundred and fifty to one hundred and thirty, and now to one hundred and ten – Madame Marty succumbed to the temptation of getting something cheap. She bought it; and the salesman who had been accompanying her left the chair and the bundle of invoices attached to the goods.

Meanwhile, behind the ladies, in the midst of the hustle and bustle of the sale, the departmental gossip about Madame Frédéric went on.

'Really? Did she have someone?' a little assistant, new to the department, was saying.

'The man with the baths, silly!' Clara answered. 'You need to be careful with those quiet widows.'

Then, while Marguerite was writing the bill for the coat, Madame Marty turned round and, giving a hardly perceptible wink in the direction of Clara, whispered very softly to Madame Desforges:

'You know, that's Monsieur Mouret's current fling.'

The other woman looked at Clara in surprise, then back at Denise, and said:

'No, not that big girl, the little one!'

And, as Madame Marty was not really sure of her facts, Madame Desforges added, more loudly, with a lady's contempt for a chambermaid:

'Perhaps it's the big one and the little one – and any other ones who care to!'

Denise had heard. She turned her wide, pure eyes on this lady whom she didn't know, yet who was hurting her in this way. Of course, this must be the one they had told her about, the woman that the boss saw outside. In the look that passed between them, Denise exhibited such sad dignity and such frank innocence, that it embarrassed Henriette.

'Since you have nothing possible to show me,' she said brusquely, 'take me to dresses and suits.'

'Good idea!' said Madame Marty. 'I'll come too. I wanted to find a suit for Valentine.'

Marguerite took the chair by its back and dragged it along, tipped up on its back legs, which this kind of transportation eventually wore down. Denise only carried the few metres of foulard that Madame Desforges had bought. It was quite a journey, now that dresses and suits were on the second floor at the far end of the shop.

So the great trek began along the crowded galleries. At the head went Marguerite, dragging the chair like a little carriage and slowly opening up a path. From lingerie onwards, Madame Desforges started to complain: how ridiculous they were, these bazaars where you had to walk two leagues to find anything at all! Madame Marty also said she was dead with exhaustion, but took no less profound a pleasure in this tiredness, the slow extinguishing of all her strength in the midst of this inexhaustible display of merchandise. Mouret's stroke of genius had her utterly in its grip. As they went along, she stopped at every department. She made a first halt at wedding dresses and linen, tempted by some blouses which Pauline sold her – and Marguerite was rid of the chair, because Pauline had to take it. Madame Desforges could have carried on walking, the quicker to free Denise, but she seemed happy at feeling her there, behind her, patient and motionless, while she also stopped, to give advice to her friend. At baby clothes, the ladies exclaimed in delight, but bought nothing. Then Madame Marty started to succumb once more, falling successively to a black satin corset, some fur sleeves (reduced, because of the season), and some Russian lace which was used in those days to trim the table linen. All these things piled up on the chair, the packets mounted higher and higher, making the wood creak, and successive sales assistants harnessed themselves to it with increasing difficulty as it grew heavier and heavier.

'This way, Madame,' said Denise after each stop, without a murmur of complaint.

'This is ridiculous!' Madame Desforges exclaimed. 'We'll never get there. Why not put dresses and suits close to ladies' wear? What chaos!'

Madame Marty, whose pupils were dilating, intoxicated by this parade of riches dancing before her eyes, kept saying beneath her breath:

'Good Lord! What will my husband say? You're right, there's no order in this shop. You lose your way, you do foolish things . . .'

The chair had difficulty crossing the great central landing because Mouret had just filled that up with a mass of novelty goods: cups on gilded zinc stands, shoddy boxes, cases and liqueur cabinets. In his opinion, people were moving around too freely here and he wanted them to stifle in the crowd. Over there, he had allowed one of his salesmen to exhibit curios from China and Japan on a little table – a few cheap trinkets that the customers were fighting over. It was an unexpected success and he was already thinking of expanding this stall. While two boys were carrying the chair up to the second floor, Madame Marty bought six ivory buttons, some silk mice and a cloisonné matchbox.

On the second floor, the trek resumed. Denise, who had been ferrying customers around like this since the morning, was dropping with tiredness, but she remained polite, with her gentle good manners. She had to wait for the ladies again in soft furnishings where a delicious cretonne had caught the eye of Madame Marty. Then, in furniture she was attracted by a worktable. With trembling hands, she laughed and begged Madame Desforges to stop her spending any more, when a meeting with Madame Guibal gave her an excuse. It happened in carpets, where Madame Guibal had at last arrived to return a whole batch of oriental door-curtains which she had bought five full days ago. She was standing talking in front of the salesman, a sturdy lad with arms like a wrestler who from morning to night carried around weights heavy enough to flatten an ox. Naturally, he was disturbed by this 'return' which deprived him of so much per cent, so he was trying to make the customer feel uneasy, suggesting some unsavoury event, probably a ball given with the curtains which had been taken from *Au Bonheur des Dames*, then sent back to avoid having to hire them from a dealer. He realized that some thrifty high-class ladies did this kind of thing. Madame must have a reason for sending them back and if it was the designs or the colours that Madame didn't like, he would show her something else; they had a very complete range. In answer to all these insinuations, Madame Guibal calmly replied, with regal confidence, that the curtains were not to her taste, without deigning to offer any further explanation. She refused to look at any others and he had to give in, because sales staff were under orders to take goods back, even if they could see that they had been used.

While the three ladies were going away together and Madame Marty came back regretfully to the worktable, which she did not need at all, Madame Guibal calmly told her:

'Well, then, you can take it back. Didn't you see? It's as easy as that. Why not let them take it round to your house? You put it in your drawing room, you look at it and then, when you're bored with it, send it back.'

'Now there's a good idea!' Madame Marty exclaimed. 'If my husband gets too angry, I'll give everything back to them.'

She had found the great excuse and went on buying, not even bothering to count – with a secret need to keep everything, because she wasn't the kind of woman who returned goods.

They did finally get to dresses and suits. But as Denise was about to hand Madame Desforges' foulard over to some sales girls, the lady seemed to change her mind and said that she would definitely take one of the travelling coats, the light grey one; so Denise had to wait obligingly to take her back to ladies' wear. The young woman could feel that these whims of an imperious customer reflected the desire to treat her as a servant, but she had sworn to carry out her duties and kept calm despite the thumping of her heart and her outraged pride. Madame Desforges bought nothing in dresses and suits.

'Oh, Mamma,' Valentine said. 'Suppose they had that little suit in my size . . .'

Very softly, Madame Guibal explained her tactics to Madame Marty. When she liked a dress in a shop, she had it sent round, copied the pattern, then sent it back. So Madame Marty bought the suit for her daughter, whispering:

'What a good idea! You're very practical, I must say, dear lady.'

The chair had had to be left behind. It had remained stranded in the furniture department, next to the work table. The weight was becoming such that the back legs were likely to break, so it was agreed that all the purchases should be brought together at one desk, then taken down to the despatch room.

So the ladies, still led by Denise, began to wander. They appeared again in all departments. They were everywhere on the stairways and along the galleries, stopping at any moment when they met someone they knew. In this way, near the reading room, they came across Madame Bourdelais and her three children. The latter were all carrying parcels: Madeleine had a dress for herself under her arms, Edmond was carrying a collection of little shoes and the youngest, Lucien, was wearing a brand new képi on his head.

'You, too!' said Madame Desforges to her old school friend, with a laugh.

'Don't talk to me about it!' Madame Bourdelais exclaimed. 'I'm furious. Now they're catching you through these little children! You know I don't buy luxuries for myself, but how can you resist the little dears who want everything? I just came to give them a walk and now I'm taking the whole shop away with me!'

Mouret, who was still there with Vallagnosc and Monsieur de Boves, was listening to her with a smile. She saw him and complained merrily, with underneath a touch of real irritation, about these traps for maternal kindness. She was indignant at the idea that she had just succumbed to the fevers of advertising, while he, still smiling, bowed, savouring his triumph. Monsieur de Boves had manoeuvred himself to get closer to Madame Guibal, eventually following her while trying once again to lose Vallagnosc; but the latter, exhausted by the throng, hurried over to join the Count. Denise had stopped once again to wait for the ladies; her back was turned and even Mouret pretended not to see her. At this, Madame Desforges, who had the acute instincts of a jealous woman, was in no further doubt. As he complimented her, taking a few steps in her direction, as a gracious host, she was thinking, wondering how she could pin him down for his treachery.

Meanwhile, Monsieur de Boves and Vallagnosc, walking ahead of Madame Guibal, were arriving at the lace department. Situated near ladies' wear, this was a luxurious room, where the showcases had drawers of carved oak that would fold back. Spirals of white lace wound around the columns, which were covered in red velvet, and festoons of guipure lace hung from one end of the room to the other, while on the counters were cascades of large cards completely enveloped in Valenciennes, Mechlin and needlepoint. At the back, two ladies were sitting in front of a measuring board covered in mauve silk across which Deloche was throwing lengths of Chantilly while they watched, silently, unable to make up their minds.

'Well I never!' said Vallagnosc, in great surprise. 'You told me Madame de Boves was unwell, but here she is, on her feet over there, with Mademoiselle Blanche.'

The Count started involuntarily, while giving a sidelong glance towards Madame Guibal.

'My word, it's true!' he said.

It was very hot in the lace room. The customers, with pale faces and shining eyes, were stifling. It was as though all the seductive powers of the store had been leading up to this supreme temptation: in this remote alcove was the Fall, this was the corner of perdition in which even the strongest would succumb. Their hands buried themselves in the overflowing lengths of lace and came away trembling like a drunkard's.

'I think these ladies are ruining you,' Vallagnosc went on, entertained by this chance meeting.

Monsieur de Boves gave the gesture of a husband all the more certain of his wife's good sense since he did not give her a penny. She, after going through every department with her daughter and not buying anything, had come to land in lace, consumed by unsatisfied desire. Exhausted as she was, she still managed to keep upright in front of a counter. She was rummaging around in the heap, her hands becoming weak and with warm flushes rising to her shoulders. Then suddenly, while her daughter's head was turned and the salesgirl was walking away, she tried to slip a piece of Alençon under her coat. But she was shaking and dropped the lace, hearing Vallagnosc saying in an amused voice:

'We've caught you, Madame.'

For a few moments, she went quite pale and was struck dumb. Then she explained that she was feeling much better and wanted to get some air. And finally, noticing that her husband was with Madame Guibal, she recovered completely and looked at them in such a supercilious way that Madame Guibal felt obliged to say:

'I was with Madame Desforges when these gentlemen ran into us.'

Just then, the other ladies were arriving. Mouret had been accompanying them and kept them a minute longer to show them Inspector Jouve, who was still pursuing the pregnant woman and her friend. It was very odd, you couldn't imagine how many shoplifters were arrested in the lace department. Madame de Boves, as she listened to him, saw herself between two gendarmes, forty-five years old, well-dressed, with a prominent husband; but she felt no pang of conscience, merely thinking that she should have slipped the lace into her sleeve. Jouve, meanwhile, had just decided to arrest the pregnant woman, deciding that he would never catch her in the act and, in any case, suspecting her of filling her pockets with such sleight of the hand that he was deceived by it. But when he took her to one side and searched her, he was embarrassed to find nothing on her, not a kerchief, not a button. The friend had vanished. Suddenly, he understood: the pregnant woman was only there to distract him, it was the friend who was shoplifting.

The ladies were amused by the tale. Mouret, slightly put out, merely said:

'Old Jouve has been tricked this time, but he'll have his revenge.'

'Oh, I doubt if he's up to it,' Vallagnosc remarked. 'In any case, why do you display so many goods? It serves you right if people steal from you. You shouldn't offer such temptation to poor, defenceless women.'

This was the last word, which rang like the sharp note of the day, in the rising fever of the shops. The ladies separated and went through the cluttered departments one last time. It was four o'clock and the rays of the setting sun were shining obliquely through the wide bays of the façade, casting a sideways light on the windows of the halls; and, in this fiery red glow, thick clouds of dust, stirred since morning by the tramping of the crowd, rose like a golden mist. A sheet of fire spread through the great central gallery, outlining the staircases, the hanging bridges and all the tracery of floating iron against a backcloth of flame. The mosaics and faience of the friezes glistened, the greens and reds of the paintwork glowed in the reflection from the copious amounts of gold. It was like a living heap of embers in which the displays, the palaces of gloves and kerchiefs, the garlands of ribbons and lace, the tall stacks of woollens and calico and the mottled beds blossoming with light silks and calicos, now seemed to be burning away. Mirrors shone. The display of parasols, like round shields, gave off glints like gleaming metal. In the distance, beyond some spreading shadows, were far-away departments, giving flashes of light and swarming with legions made white by the sun.

In this final hour, in the midst of this overheated air, women ruled. They had taken the shops by storm and were encamped as in conquered territory, like an invading horde settled in, surrounded by the ravaged merchandise. The sales staff, deafened, broken, were merely their things, to be disposed of with sovereign tyranny. Fat ladies were jostling everybody. The slimmest stood their ground and became arrogant. All of them, heads held high, gesturing curtly, felt fully at home, with no consideration for one another, exploiting the place to the uttermost, carrying off the very dust from the walls. Madame Bourdelais, anxious to recoup her losses, had taken her three children back to the buffet where the customers were now pushing and shoving in a fury of eagerness, even the mothers gorging themselves on Malaga. Since the opening, they had consumed eighty litres of syrup and seventy bottles of wine. After buying her travelling coat, Madame Desforges had got them to give her some free pictures at the cash desk and was leaving, trying to think how she could get Denise to her house and humiliate her in Mouret's presence, to watch their reaction and have definite proof. Finally, as Monsieur de Boves managed to vanish into the crowd and disappear with Madame Guibal, Madame de Boves, followed by Blanche and Vallagnosc, felt inspired to ask for a red balloon, even though she had bought nothing. It was always like that, she refused to go away empty-handed – and in this way she could make friends with her concierge's little girl. At the counter where the balloons were given out, they were starting on the fortieth thousand – forty thousand red balloons launched in the hot air of the shop and a whole cloud of red balloons even now sailing from one end of Paris to the other carrying the name of *Au Bonheur des Dames* into the heavens!

The clocks rang five. Of all the ladies, only Madame Marty remained with her daughter in the final paroxysm of the sale. Dead tired, she could not drag herself away, drawn by such a powerful force that she kept coming back, pointlessly, dragging her unsatisfied curiosity from one department to the next. This was the time when the mob, stirred up by advertising, finally lost its head. The sixty thousand francs of paid advertisements in the newspapers, the ten thousand posters put up on the walls, the two hundred thousand catalogues distributed, having emptied their purses, now left their nerves in the aftershock of their intoxication; and they were stunned by all Mouret's gimmicks: bargains, returns and a constant succession of flattering attentions. Madame Marty hovered around the tables where the salesmen were still hoarsely crying their wares, amid the sound of money tumbling into the cash desks and parcels tumbling down to the basement. Once more, she walked through the ground floor, linens, silks, gloves, woollens; then she went back up, abandoning herself to the metallic vibration of the hanging staircases and the flying bridges, returning to ladies' wear, lingerie and lace; and continuing even up to the second floor, with bedding and furniture; and all around the assistants, Hutin and Favier, Mignot and Liénard, Deloche, Pauline, Denise, their legs giving way beneath them, were making one final effort, snatching victories from the customers' final burst of passion. Since the morning, that passion had been growing, little by little, like the intoxication that exuded from the materials as they were handled. The crowd blazed beneath the fiery light of the five-o'clock sun. Now Madame Marty had the excited, nervous face of a child who has drunk wine unmixed with water. She had come in with clear eyes and a fresh complexion from the chill of the street, but they had gradually been seared by the spectacle of all this luxury and the harsh colours, the continual pounding of which had stirred her passion. When she left at last, after saying that she would pay on delivery, terrified by the amount of her bill, she had the drawn features and wide eyes of a sick woman. She had to fight to escape from the relentless crush around the door: they were slaughtering each other there in the fight for bargains. Then, on the pavement, where she had been reunited with her lost daughter, she shuddered in the cold air and remained bewildered, a victim of the unsettling neurosis of a great store.

That evening, as Denise was coming back from dinner, a boy called her:

'Mademoiselle, they're asking for you in the director's office.'

She had forgotten Mouret's order that morning that she should go by his study after the sale. He was on his feet waiting for her. As she went in, she did not push the door back into place, but left it open.

'We are pleased with you, Mademoiselle,' he said. 'And we would like to express our satisfaction in some way. You know the disgraceful manner in which Madame Frédéric left us. From tomorrow you will replace her as under-buyer.'

Denise listened, frozen with surprise. In a trembling voice, she muttered:

'But, Monsieur, there are salesgirls with much greater seniority in the department.'

'Well, what does that matter?' he asked. 'You are the most able and the most serious. I chose you because you are the natural choice. Aren't you pleased?'

At this, she blushed. Inside her was a feeling of happiness and a delicious confusion in which her earlier alarm vanished. So why had she thought first of all of what people would assume when they heard about this unexpected favour? And she remained uncertain, despite the gratitude welling up in her. He meanwhile smiled at her in her plain silk dress, with no ornament except the regal luxury of her blonde hair. She had become more refined, her skin whiter, her manner more considerate and serious. The puny insignificance of earlier times was giving way to a subtly penetrating charm.

'You're very kind, Monsieur,' she stammered. 'I don't know how to tell you . . .'

But she stopped dead. Lhomme was standing in the doorway. In his good hand, he carried a great leather wallet and his crippled arm was pressing a huge portfolio against his chest, while behind him his son Albert was staggering under an enormous weight of bags.

'Five hundred and eighty-seven thousand, two hundred and ten francs, thirty centimes!' the cashier cried, his soft, worn face seeming to light up as though with a burst of sunlight, reflected off such a sum.

This was the day's takings, the highest that *Au Bonheur des Dames* had ever made. Far off, in the depths of the shop through which Lhomme had just slowly proceeded, with the heavy tread of an over-laden ox, could be heard the hubbub, the stirrings of surprise and joy left behind by this vast sum of money as it passed.

'But that's magnificent!' Mouret said in delight. 'My good Lhomme, put it down, have a rest, you're exhausted. I shall have this money taken to the central counting-house. Yes, yes, put it all on my desk. I want to see the pile.'

He was as merry as a child. The cashier and his son unloaded their burden. The wallet gave out a clear golden sound, two of the bags burst open, letting out streams of silver and copper and corners of banknotes were emerging from the portfolio. A whole end of the great desk was covered with it, like the collapse of a fortune that had been collected in ten hours.

After Lhomme and Albert had left, wiping the sweat from their faces, Mouret stayed motionless for a moment, lost in thought, staring at the money. Then, looking up, he noticed Denise, who had stepped back. At this he started to smile again and forced her to come forward, eventually saying that he would give her what she could pick up with one hand – and there was an amorous game behind the joke.

'Go on! In the wallet, I bet you'll get less than a thousand francs, your hand is so small!'

But she shrank back again. Did he love her then? Suddenly, she understood, she felt the rising flame of desire with which he had enveloped her since she had come back into ladies' wear. What threw her into even greater consternation was that she could feel her heart beating furiously. Why was he teasing her with all this money, when she was overflowing with gratitude and he could have conquered her with one friendly word? He was coming closer, still joking, when, to his great annoyance, Bourdoncle appeared, on the excuse of letting him know the number of entries, the enormous figure of seventy thousand customers who had come to *Au Bonheur* that day. And she quickly left, after thanking him once again.

CHAPTER 10

On the first Sunday in August, they were doing the stocktaking, which had to be finished that evening.[1] From morning, as on any weekday, all the staff were at their places and the work began, with the doors closed and not a customer in the store.

Denise had not come down at eight o'clock with the other sales staff. Since the Thursday she had kept to her room because of a twisted ankle which she had got going up to the workshops, but she was now much better. However, since Madame Aurélie was spoiling her, she took her time, putting her shoes on with difficulty, determined to make her appearance on the floor. Nowadays, the young ladies' rooms occupied the fifth floor of the new buildings on the Rue Monsigny: there were sixty of them, on either side of a corridor, and they were more comfortable, though still furnished with the same iron bedstead, large wardrobe and little walnut dressing table. This meant that in their private lives the sales girls paid more attention to cleanliness and to their looks, developing a taste for expensive soaps and fine linen as part of a natural upward progress towards the bourgeoisie as their situation improved[2] – though one could still hear outbursts of swearing and slamming doors in the morning rush from what was much like a lodging house. In any case, as an under-buyer, Denise had one of the largest rooms, her two dormer windows overlooking the street. Now well-off, she could afford luxuries: a red eiderdown with a lace cover, a little rug in front of the wardrobe and two blue glass vases on the dressing-table with some fading roses.

When she had got her shoes on, she tried to walk around the room. She had to lean on to the furniture because she was still limping. But the ankle would warm up. Even so, she had been right to refuse an invitation to have dinner at Uncle Baudu's that evening and to ask her aunt to take Pépé out: she had put him back to board with Madame Gras. Jean, who had come to see her the day before, was also having dinner at their uncle's. She was still trying to walk gently around, promising herself that she would go to bed early to give her leg some rest, when the supervisor, Madame Cabin, knocked on her door and gave her a letter, with a mysterious look.

Shutting the door and amazed at the knowing smile the woman had given her, Denise opened the letter. She lowered herself into a chair: the letter was from Mouret, who said he was pleased at her recovery and invited her to come down that evening and have dinner with him, since she could not go out. There was nothing objectionable about the tone of the letter, at once familiar and fatherly, but it was impossible for her not to understand what it implied – everyone in *Au Bonheur des Dames* knew the real meaning of these invitations; they were legendary. Clara had had her dinner, so had others, all the girls who caught the boss's eye. And, as the wits among the employees used to say, after dinner came the dessert. The blood gradually spread across the young woman's white cheeks.

So, letting the letter slip between her knees, her heart thumping, Denise remained staring at the blinding light of one of the windows. There was a confession that she had been forced to make to herself, in this very room, on sleepless nights: if she still trembled when he went past, she knew now that it was not for fear, and the unease that she had once felt, her earlier anxiety, could only be the frightened ignorance of love, the first stirring of affection in her timid naivety. She did not reason about it, she felt simply that she had always loved him, since that first moment when she had shivered and stammered in front of him. She had loved him when she feared him as a pitiless master, she had loved him when her bewildered heart had dreamed of Hutin, thoughtlessly yielding to a need for tenderness. She might even have given herself to another, but she had never loved anyone but this man who could terrify her with a single look. And all the past returned, unfolding in the brightness of the window: the deprivations of her early days, that sweet walk beneath the dark foliage of the Tuileries Gardens, and finally his desire which she had felt brushing against her since she returned. The letter had fallen to the ground, but Denise was still looking at the window, dazzled by the full sunlight.

Suddenly, there was a knock on the door and she hurriedly picked up the letter and slipped it into her pocket. It was Pauline, who had managed to escape from her department on some excuse or other and had come for a chat.

'Are you better, dear? We never see each other any more.'

However, since it was forbidden to go back to the rooms in the day, and especially to shut oneself in with another person, Denise took her to the end of the corridor where there was a common room, a friendly gesture from the director to the young ladies, who could converse there or work, until eleven o'clock and bedtime. The room, white and gold, had the bare ordinariness of a hotel drawing room; it contained a piano, a table in the middle, armchairs and sofas under white dust covers. Moreover, after a few evenings together in the first flush of novelty, the sales girls could no longer meet there without immediately starting an argument. They had to learn to live together: there was a lack of harmony in this little phalansterian city. Meanwhile, little went on there in the evenings except that Miss Powell, under-buyer in corsets, would drum out some Chopin on the piano, her much-envied talent finally driving the others away.

'You see, my foot's better,' said Denise. 'I was on my way down.'

'What's this?' her friend exclaimed. 'What enthusiasm! Now if I had an excuse, I'd stay here and spoil myself a bit.'

The two of them were sitting on a sofa. Pauline's attitude had changed since her friend had become under-buyer in ladies' wear. There was now a hint of respect behind her good-natured friendliness, a note of surprise at the idea that the self-effacing little salesgirl of the old days was on her way to the top. Even so, Denise was very fond of her and would confide in no one else in the constant hustle and bustle of the two hundred women that the shop now employed.

'What's the matter?' Pauline asked briskly, when she saw the other girl looking nervous.

'Nothing,' Denise assured her, with an embarrassed smile.

'Yes, there is. Something's up. Don't you trust me any more? You always used to tell me your troubles.'

Nothing would calm the beating of Denise's heart and the feeling in her throat, so she gave in. She held the letter out to her friend, stammering:

'Here! He's just written to me.'

In private, they had never yet spoken openly about Mouret. But even this silence was like an admission of what was secretly on their minds. Pauline knew everything. After reading the letter, she hugged Denise and took her round the waist, murmuring softly:

'My dear, let me be frank, I thought it had already happened. Don't get upset: I promise, the whole shop must think the same as I do. For heaven's sake! He appointed you under-buyer so quickly, and then he's always after you, it's blindingly obvious!'

She gave Denise a big kiss on the cheek, then asked her:

'You will go this evening, won't you?'

Denise looked at her without answering, then, quite suddenly, burst into tears, her head on her friend's shoulder. Pauline was very surprised.

'Come on, calm down. There's nothing to get so upset about.'

'No, no,' Denise stammered. 'Please leave me. If only you knew how unhappy I am! Since getting that letter, I haven't known what's happening to me. Just let me cry, it will make me feel better.'

Pauline felt very sympathetic, but still didn't understand. To start with, he wasn't seeing Clara any more. They did say that he visited some lady outside, but there was no proof of it. And then, she explained that one couldn't be jealous of a man in his position. He had too much money. After all, he was the boss.

Denise listened and, if she had not already known she was in love, she would have been unable to doubt it when she felt how the name of Clara and the mention of Madame Desforges struck at her heart. She could hear Clara's unpleasant voice and see Madame Desforges leading her round the shop, with the contempt of a rich lady.

'So would you go, if it was you?' she asked.

Pauline, without pausing for thought, exclaimed:

'Of course I would, what else could you do?'

Then, on reflection, she added:

'I mean, once. Not now, because now I'm getting married to Baugé, and it wouldn't be right, would it?'

Baugé, who had left the *Bon Marché* a short time earlier to join *Au Bonheur des Dames*, was going to marry her around the middle of the month. Bourdoncle didn't like married couples, but they had permission and even hoped they might get a fortnight's leave.

'You see!' Denise declared. 'When a man loves you, he marries you. Baugé's marrying you.'

Pauline had a good laugh.

'But darling, it's not the same thing, is it? Baugé is marrying me because he's Baugé. He's my equal, so it follows. While, as for Monsieur Mouret! Do you think Monsieur Mouret can marry his salesgirls?'

'No! No! No!' the other girl exclaimed, appalled at the absurdity of the question. 'And that's why he shouldn't have written to me.'

This argument completely astonished Pauline. Her heavy face, with its gentle little eyes, took on a look of maternal pity. Then she got up, opened the piano lid and softly played 'Le Roi Dagobert'[3] with one finger, no doubt to cheer things up. In the bare common room, its white covers seeming to intensify the emptiness, one could hear the street noises, the distant lament of a woman selling green peas and calling her wares. Denise had slumped to the bottom of the sofa, her head against the wooden back, shaking with a further outburst of sobs which she was smothering in her handkerchief.

'Again!' said Pauline, turning round. 'You really aren't being sensible about this. Why did you bring me here? We'd have done better to stay in your room.'

She knelt down in front of her and started to lecture her again. How many others would love to be in her place! In any case, if she didn't like the thing, there was a simple answer: she just had to say no, without getting so worked up about it. But she should think carefully before risking her job by a refusal which was impossible to explain, since she was not committed elsewhere. After all, was it so dreadful? And the sermon was concluding with some jolly, whispered jokes, when they heard a noise in the corridor.

Pauline ran to the door to take a look.

'Hush, it's Madame Aurélie!' she said quietly. 'I'm off. And you – wipe your eyes. You needn't let everyone know.'

When Denise was alone she stood up and smothered her tears. Then, with still trembling hands, afraid at being discovered like this, she closed the piano lid, which her friend had left open. She could hear Madame Aurélie knocking at her door, so she left the common room.

'What! You're up!' the buyer said. 'That's very silly of you, child. I was just coming up to see how you were and to tell you that we didn't need you downstairs.'

Denise assured her that she was better and that it would do her good to keep busy and take her mind off things.

'I won't get tired, Madame. You can put me on a chair and I'll do some paperwork.'

The two of them went down. Madame Aurélie was very considerate and insisted that Denise lean on her shoulder. She must have noticed the young woman's red eyes, because she kept giving her sidelong glances. She must have known a lot of things.

It was an unexpected victory: Denise had conquered the department. Where she had formerly struggled for ten months, suffering the torments of a skivvy and a scapegoat, without exhausting the ill will of her colleagues, she had now managed to impose herself on them in just a few weeks, so that they were docile and respectful. She had been greatly helped in this thankless task of winning over their hearts by the sudden liking that Madame Aurélie had taken to her. People whispered that the buyer was Mouret's confidante, that she performed some delicate services for him and that if she had so warmly taken the young woman under her protection, it must be because she had been recommended to her in some particular way. But Denise had also turned on all her charm to disarm her enemies – and the job was all the harder since they had to forgive her her appointment as under-buyer. The young ladies called it unfair and accused her of getting the job 'over dessert' with the boss; they even added some quite foul details. But despite their opposition, the title of under-buyer had an effect on them and Denise acquired an authority that astonished and won over the most hostile among them. She soon found herself the object of flattery, from the newest arrivals; her sweetness and modesty did the rest. Marguerite came round and only Clara continued to show her ill will, still daring to call her by the old insult of 'shockhead', which no one found amusing nowadays. For the brief period in which she had caught Mouret's fancy, she took advantage of it to slacken on her work, being a lazy, vain gossiper. Then, as he quickly tired of her, she did not even bother to make any recriminations, being incapable of jealousy in the amorous merry-go-round of her existence and satisfied merely to enjoy the benefit of the tolerance shown to her idleness. However, she did consider that Denise had robbed her of the succession to Madame Frédéric. She would never have accepted it, because of the amount of stress involved, but she was irritated by the lack of courtesy, because she had the same right to the job as Denise, and even a prior right.

'Look at that! They've got the new mother up from her bed,' she muttered when she saw Madame Aurélie supporting Denise on her arm.

Marguerite shrugged her shoulders and said:

'Do you think it's funny?'

The clocks were striking nine. Outside a warm blue sky had started to heat up the streets, cabs were driving towards the railway stations and the people of the town dressed in their Sunday best were making their way in long lines towards the woods in the suburbs. Inside the shop, which was drenched in sunlight through the great open bay windows, the imprisoned employees had just started the stocktaking. The handles had been taken off the doors, and people would stop on the pavement staring through the windows, astonished to find the place shut when they could see such frantic activity inside. From one end of the galleries to the other, from the top of each floor to the bottom, the staff hurried and bustled; arms were raised, parcels flew over heads; and all this in the midst of a storm of shouts and figures tossed back and forth, in mounting confusion, like waves breaking in a deafening din. Each of the thirty-nine departments was doing its work separately, paying no heed to its neighbours. In any case, they had hardly started on the shelves and there were still only a few lengths of cloth on the floor. The machine had to warm up if they were to finish that same evening.

'Why have you come down?' Marguerite asked gently, talking to Denise. 'You'll do yourself an injury and we've got everyone we need.'

'That's what I told her,' said Madame Aurélie. 'But she still wanted to give us a hand.'

All the young ladies crowded around Denise. Work stopped. They complimented her and listened to how she got her sprain, interrupting her with exclamations. Finally, Madame Aurélie made her sit down at a table and it was agreed that she would simply write down the items as they were called out. Anyway, on stocktaking Sunday any employee capable of holding a pen was enlisted: inspectors, cashiers, clerks, even the shop boys; then the different departments would share out these temporary assistants, to get the job done quickly. So Denise found herself between the cashier Lhomme and the porter Joseph, both of whom were leaning over large sheets of paper.

'Five top coats, linen, fur-trimmed, size three, at two hundred and forty!' Marguerite called out. 'Four of the same, size one, at two hundred and twenty!'

Work resumed. Behind Marguerite, three assistants were emptying the cupboards, sorting the items and giving them to her in bundles. When she had called them out, she threw them on the tables where they piled up bit by bit in huge heaps. Lhomme wrote them down, Joseph drew up another list against which to check Lhomme's. Meanwhile, Madame Aurélie herself, helped by three other sales assistants, was counting the silk garments on her side, while Denise wrote them on the list. Clara's job was to look after the piles, putting them to one side and heaping them up along the tables so that they took as little room as possible; but she was not much good at it and the heaps of clothes were already collapsing.

'I say,' she asked a little assistant who had joined them that winter. 'Are you getting a rise? You know they're going to put the under-buyer on two thousand francs, which will give her nearly seven thousand, with her commission.'

The little assistant, without pausing in the action of passing over some cloaks, said that if they didn't give her eight hundred francs, she'd give them her notice. Wages went up on the day after the stocktaking, which was also the time when the turnover of the year was established and the heads of department took their percentage on the increase in this figure over that of the previous year. So despite all the din and bustle, there was a passionate exchange of gossip. Between calling out the items, they talked only about money. The rumour was that Madame Aurélie would make over twenty-five thousand francs, and a figure of that magnitude caused a great deal of excitement among the young ladies. Marguerite, the best sales assistant after Denise, had made four thousand five hundred francs – fifteen hundred francs of fixed salary and around three thousand francs in commission. As for Clara, she could not reach as high as two thousand five hundred in all.

'I don't give a damn for their increases,' she went on, still talking to the little salesgirl. 'If Papa was dead, believe me, I'd tell them all where to get off . . . But one thing that does annoy me are the seven thousand francs that slip of a woman is earning. Don't you think, huh?'

Madame Aurélie savagely interrupted this conversation. She turned round, with her supercilious air:

'Won't you be quiet, ladies! Upon my word, I can't hear myself think!'

Then she carried on shouting: 'Seven mantles, old style, Sicilian, size one, at one hundred and thirty! Three pelisses, surah, size two, at a hundred and fifty! Are you with me, Mademoiselle Baudu?'

'Yes, Madame.'

So Clara had to look after the armfuls of clothes piling up on the tables. She pushed them to one side and gained some room. But she soon had to leave them again to talk to a sales assistant who was looking for her. It was Mignot, from gloves, who had escaped from his department. He whispered a request for twenty francs. He already owed her thirty, which he had borrowed the day after a horse race when he had lost his week's wages on a bet. This time, he had squandered the commission he had got the previous day and did not even have ten *sous* left for Sunday. Clara had ten francs on her, which she lent with fairly good grace. Then they chatted, talking about an outing which six of them had made to a restaurant in Bougival, where the women had paid their share: this was better, everyone was easy. Then Mignot, hoping to get his full ten francs, went to whisper something to Lhomme, who stopped writing and seemed very disturbed. But he did not dare refuse and was looking for a ten-franc piece in his wallet, when Madame Aurélie, surprised at no longer hearing Marguerite, who had had to stop what she was doing, noticed Mignot and understood what was going on. She barked at him to get back to his own department and stop bothering her girls. The truth is that she was worried about this young man, a great friend of her son Albert, who was always mixed up with him in various disreputable pranks which she was afraid would get him into trouble one day. So when Mignot had got his ten francs and vanished, she couldn't refrain from telling her husband:

'Honestly! How can you let yourself be gulled like that?'

'But, dearest, I really couldn't refuse the young man . . .'

She interrupted him with a shrug of her powerful shoulders. Then, as the girls were secretly enjoying this family row, she went on severely:

'Come, now, Mademoiselle Vadon, don't go to sleep.'

'Twenty top coats, double cashmere, size four, at eighteen francs fifty!' Marguerite replied, in her sing-song voice.

Lhomme, head down, was back at his writing. His salary had been raised bit by bit to nine thousand francs, and he remained deferential towards Madame Aurélie, who was still contributing nearly three times as much to the family budget.

For a while, the work went ahead. The figures flew around, the bundles of clothes rained down heavily on the tables. But Clara had found another amusement: she was teasing Joseph, the porter, about a crush he was supposed to have on a young lady in samples. This woman, already twenty-eight, thin and pale, was a protégée of Madame Desforges, who asked Mouret to take her on as a sales assistant, telling him a touching story: she was an orphan, the last of the Fontenailles,[4] an old aristocratic family from Poitou, who had come up to Paris with a drunken father and remained decent despite their circumstances, but she had unfortunately not received enough education to make a living as a governess or by giving piano lessons. Mouret usually lost his temper when people recommended girls in reduced circumstances to him: as far as he was concerned, there were no more helpless, unbearable and insincere creatures than those; and, in any case, you couldn't be a sales assistant just by wanting to, it was a complex, skilled job that had to be learned. Despite this, he did take Madame Desforges' protégée, but put her in the samples department, as he had already (just to please some friends) found places for two countesses and a baroness in the publicity service, where they wrote out labels and envelopes.

Mademoiselle de Fontenailles earned three francs a day, which barely allowed her to live, in a little room on the Rue d'Argenteuil. It was because he saw her sad and poorly dressed that Joseph, who had a soft heart beneath his unbending, uncommunicative old soldier's exterior, was eventually touched by her. He would not admit it, but he blushed when the young ladies in ladies' wear teased him about it – because samples were in a room near their department and they had observed him constantly prowling around the door.

'Joseph's mind is wandering,' Clara muttered. 'His head keeps turning towards lingerie.'

Mademoiselle de Fontenailles had been requisitioned and was helping with the stocktaking on the trousseau counter. In fact, the porter did keep on glancing towards that counter, so the sales assistants started to laugh. This embarrassed him and he got back to his papers, while Marguerite, to stifle a rising tide of merriment, shouted even louder:

'Fourteen jackets, English cloth, size two, at fifteen francs!'

Madame Aurélie's voice was drowned as she tried to call out some cloaks, so very indignantly, with majestic slowness, she said:

'A little less loud, Mademoiselle. We are not in a market. And you are all very silly, to let yourself be amused by this childish nonsense when time is so short.'

Sure enough, as Clara was not keeping watch on the parcels, there was a disaster. Some coats collapsed and all the piles on the table went with them, falling on top of each other. The carpet was covered with them.

'There you are! What did I tell you?' the buyer yelled, quite beyond herself. 'Pay some attention to what you're doing, Mademoiselle Prunaire. This is really too much!'

However, a shudder went round: Mouret and Bourdoncle, who were doing their inspection, had just come into view. The calls resumed and the pens scratched away, while Clara hastily started to pick up the clothes she had dropped. The boss did not interfere with the work. He stayed for a few minutes, smiling, but saying nothing; only his lips gave a slightly feverish tremor, in his happy and victorious stocktaking face. When he saw Denise, he had to restrain himself from making a gesture of astonishment: had she got up then? His eyes met those of

Madame Aurélie; then after hesitating for a moment, he went off towards trousseaux.

Meanwhile, Denise had been alerted by the slight murmur and looked up. After recognizing Mouret, she simply bent over her sheets again. All the time she had been writing mechanically in response to the regular roll-call of goods, she had been feeling a sense of inner calm. She had always given way like that to the first onrush of emotion: tears choked her and her torment was doubled by what she felt; then her good sense would return and she found a fine, calm courage, a sweet and inexorable strength of will. Now, with her eyes clear and her complexion pale, she was entirely absorbed in her work, without a tremble, determined to crush her heart and act only according to her will.

The clocks struck ten and the level of noise from the stocktaking rose, in the hustle and bustle of the departments. And under the constant shouts coming from every direction, the same piece of news was whispered from one to another with astonishing rapidity: every sales assistant now knew that Mouret had written that morning to invite Denise to dinner. The indiscretion was Pauline's. As she was coming down, still shaken, she had met Deloche in lace and, without noticing that Liénard was talking to the young man, she had got it off her chest.

'My dear, it's happened . . . She's just got a letter. He's invited her for this evening.'

Deloche went pale. He knew what she was talking about, because he often questioned Pauline and they talked every day about their shared friend, how Mouret liked her and how one of those famous invitations would settle the whole matter. As it happened, she told him off for secretly loving Denise, who would never give him anything, and she shrugged her shoulders when he applauded her for resisting the boss.

'Her foot's better, so she's coming down,' Pauline went on. 'Don't pull that long face. What's happening is a piece of luck for her.'

And she hurried back to her department.

'Ah, I see!' muttered Liénard, who had overheard this. 'It's the young lady with the twisted ankle. Well, you were quite right not to wait too long to defend her in the café yesterday evening!'

He went off in his turn and by the time he got back to woollens, he had already told the story to four or five salesmen. And from there, in less than ten minutes, it did the round of the whole shop.

Liénard's last remark recalled something that had taken place the evening before at the Café Saint-Roch. Nowadays, Deloche and he were inseparable. The other man had taken over Hutin's room at the Hôtel de Smyrne, when Hutin was appointed under-buyer and had rented a little three-room apartment. So the two assistants came together in the morning to *Au Bonheur*, and waited for each other in the evening so that they could leave together. Their rooms were adjacent and overlooked the same dark courtyard, a narrow, foul-smelling pit. They got on well though they were not at all alike, one thoughtlessly squandering the money he drew from his father, the other penniless and tormented by ideas of saving – because they had one thing in common, their incompetence as salesmen, which left them vegetating in their departments, never getting a rise. Outside the shop, they lived chiefly in the Café Saint-Roch. This café, empty during the day, filled up around half past eight with a flood of sales staff, emptied on to the street through the high door on the Place Gaillon. From this time on, there was a deafening noise of dominoes, laughter and shrieking voices, all in the midst of a thick cloud of pipe smoke. Beer and coffee flowed. In the left-hand corner, Liénard asked for expensive drinks, while Deloche made do with his single glass of beer, which he took four hours to drink. It was here that he heard Favier, at a nearby table, saying the foulest things about Denise: how she had 'hooked' the boss by raising her skirts when she went up a staircase in front of him. Deloche had restrained himself from hitting him. Then, as Favier went on, saying that the girl came down every night to meet her lover, Deloche went mad with anger, calling him a liar.

'What a foul swine! He's lying, do you hear! Lying!'

And, trembling with emotion, he bared his heart, stammering out:

'I know her, I know all about it . . . She's only ever felt anything for one man, yes, for Monsieur Hutin, and even then he didn't realize it, he can't even boast of having touched her with the tips of his fingers.'

An account of this row, twisted and exaggerated, was already delighting the whole shop, when the story of Mouret's letter went round. As it happened, the first person to whom Liénard told the news was a salesman in silk. In the silk department, stocktaking was well underway. Favier and two other employees were standing on stepladders, emptying the boxes and, as they did so, passing the lengths of material to Hutin. He was standing in the middle of a table, shouting out the figures after looking at the labels; then he threw the items down on to the floor, where the clutter was rising like an autumn tide. Other members of staff were writing and Albert Lhomme was helping these gentlemen, his face blotchy after a sleepless night in a low dive in La Chapelle. A flood of sunshine was pouring down from the glass roof of the hall, through which one could see the radiant blue of the sky.

'Won't someone draw the blinds!' Bouthemont shouted, only worried about supervising the work. 'This sunshine is unbearable!'

Favier, who was on tiptoe reaching for a length of silk, muttered quietly:

'How can they shut people inside in this magnificent weather! No chance of it raining on stocktaking day! And they keep you under lock and key like galley slaves, when all Paris is out and about.'

He handed the piece to Hutin. The length in metres was marked on the label and every time a sale was made, reduced by the appropriate amount, which made the work a lot simpler. The under-buyer shouted:

'Fancy silk, small squares, twenty-one metres, at six francs fifty.'

And the silk went to increase the pile on the ground. Then he continued a conversation he had already started, asking Favier:

'So he wanted a fight, did he?'

'Yes, indeed. There I was quietly drinking my beer. He was wasting his time, wasn't he, contradicting me, when the girl's just had a letter from the boss inviting her to dinner. Everyone's talking about it.'

'What! Hasn't it already happened, then?'

Favier handed him another piece.

'That's right! I'd have sworn it. I thought they were an old couple already.'

'Ditto, twenty-five metres!' Hutin yelled.

There was a dull thud as the cloth fell, as he added quietly:

'You know she used to live it up when she was in that old fool Bourras' house.'

By now, the whole department was enjoying the gossip, though without interrupting the work. The young woman's name was whispered, backs were heaving and noses sniffed the juicy story. Even Bouthemont, who relished a naughty piece of gossip, could not refrain from a joke in such bad taste that he burst out laughing at it himself. Albert woke up and swore he had seen the under-buyer in ladies' wear between two soldiers at Le Gros-Caillou. Mignot was just coming down with the twenty francs he had borrowed, so he stopped and slipped ten francs into Albert's hand, making an appointment for that evening for a little party they had planned, but postponed through lack of funds, which was now possible, despite the scanty amount they had in hand. But handsome Mignot, when he heard about the letter, made a remark of such crudity that Bouthemont felt obliged to say something:

'Now that's enough, gentlemen. It's none of our business. Come on, come on, Monsieur Hutin.'

'Fancy silk, small squares, thirty-two metres at six francs fifty!' Hutin shouted.

The pens worked away again, the parcels fell regularly and the pool of cloth rose constantly as though the water of a river was draining into it. The calling of fancy silks never ended. Favier, in an undertone, pointed out that the results of the stocktaking would be fine: the management would be pleased, that fathead Bouthemont might be the best buyer in Paris, but you couldn't imagine such a clod when it came to selling. Hutin smiled, delighted, agreeing with a friendly look; because, having himself previously introduced Bouthemont to *Au Bonheur des Dames*, to get Robineau out, he was now undermining Bouthemont's position in the hope of taking it for himself. The war was the same as before, waged with perfidious insinuations whispered in the bosses' ears and excessive enthusiasm to get himself noticed, a real campaign conducted with sly affability. Meanwhile Favier, whom Hutin treated with new condescension, was furtively observing him, cold and thin, with a bilious face, as though counting the mouthfuls in this stocky little fellow and waiting for his workmate to eat up Bouthemont before eating him up in his turn. He was hoping to have the under-buyer's job, if the other man became head of department. Then, they'd see. And the pair of them, caught up in the fever which spread from one end of the shop to the other, chatted about probable pay rises, while still continuing to call the stock of fancy silks: they guessed that Bouthemont would reach his thirty thousand francs that year; Hutin would pass ten thousand; and Favier estimated his fixed salary and commission at five thousand, five hundred. Every season the turnover of the department grew, the sales staff rose in rank and doubled in salary, like officers on campaign.

'Now, now! Aren't they finished, those little silks?' Bouthemont asked abruptly and with irritation. 'And what a dreadful spring it's been, raining all the time. People are only buying black silks.'

His large, jovial face clouded. He was watching the pile rising on the ground, while Hutin – in a sonorous voice, with a note of triumph – shouted louder than ever:

'Fancy silk, small squares, twenty-eight metres, at six francs fifty!'

There was a whole box of it left. Favier, his arms aching, was slowing down. But as he was handing the last pieces to Hutin, he whispered:

'I say, I was forgetting: did anyone ever tell you that the under-buyer in ladies' wear used to have a crush on you?'

The young man seemed very surprised.

'What! What do you mean?'

'Yes, it was that great booby Deloche who whispered it to us ... And I remember, at one time how she used to make eyes at you.'

Since being appointed under-buyer himself, Hutin had given up singers from low dives and would be seen out with schoolteachers. Underneath, he was very flattered, but he replied contemptuously:

'I like them with more flesh on, dear boy; and then I don't go with just anyone, as the boss does.'

He broke off to shout:

'White matt silk, thirty-five metres, at eight francs seventy-five!'

'Ah, at last,' Bouthemont muttered with relief.

But a bell was ringing for the second lunch sitting, which was Favier's. He got down off the stepladder and another assistant took his place. He had to step over the flood of pieces of cloth which had risen still higher on the floors. Now, in every department, similar tumbled heaps littered the ground. Bit by bit the boxes, the shelves and the cupboards were emptying, while the goods flowed out from every direction, under people's feet and between the tables in a continual tide. From linens, you could hear the heavy falls of piles of calico; in haberdashery, there was a faint clicking of boxes; and distant rumbles came from the furniture department. All voices joined in the chorus together, sharp, high voices, deep, bass voices, while figures sang through the air and a crackling din rose up through the vast nave, the noise of forests in January when the wind whistles in the branches.

Favier finally managed to get out and took the staircase up to the dining rooms. When the shop was enlarged, they had been moved up to the fourth floor in the new building. As he hurried, he caught up with Deloche and Liénard who had started before him, so he dropped back to walk with Mignot, who was following behind.

'Damn!' he said in the kitchen corridor, when he saw the blackboard where the menu was written. 'You can see it's stocktaking time. A real treat! Chicken or minced lamb, and artichokes in oil. Their lamb won't have many takers!'

Mignot chuckled and said:

'So there's a run on chicken, is there?'

Meanwhile, Deloche and Liénard had taken their dinners and gone. Then, leaning over the counter, Favier said loudly:

'Chicken.'

But he had to wait because one of the boys who was cutting the bird had just nicked his finger and this had caused a commotion. He stayed opposite the opening, looking into the kitchen, a huge place with equipment to match, with its central stove above which, by a system of chains and pulleys, two rails fixed on the ceiling brought over the colossal saucepans which four men could not have lifted. Cooks, all white in the deep red of the cast-iron stove, standing on iron ladders and supplied with large ladles for skimming, were keeping an eye on the evening's stew. Then, next to the wall, were grills large enough to grill martyrs, pots that would fricassé a sheep, a monumental plate-warmer and a marble basin filled by a continuous stream of water. In addition to this, on the left, you could see a washroom, some stone sinks as big as swimming pools, while on the other side, on the right, there was a larder where you could half see red sides of meat hanging on steel hooks. A machine for peeling potatoes was working with the tic-tac of a mill. Two small carts, full of cleaned salad, were going past, pulled by kitchen hands, who were going to put them to keep cool under a fountain.

'Chicken,' Favier repeated, impatiently.

Then, turning round, he added in a lower voice:

'One of them has cut himself. It's disgusting, he's bleeding into the food.'

Mignot wanted to take a look. The queue of shop assistants was lengthening, with laughs and elbowings. Now the two young men, their heads at the window, were starting to pass remarks about this phalansterian kitchen, where the least utensil, even skewers and basting spoons, became gigantic. They had to serve two thousand lunches and two thousand dinners, quite apart from the fact that the number of staff was increasing every week. It was a huge pit which in a single day swallowed up sixteen hectolitres of potatoes, one hundred and twenty pounds of butter and six hundred kilograms of meat. At every meal, three barrels had to be tapped: nearly seven hundred litres of wine were served at the bar.

'Ah, at last!' Favier muttered when the server reappeared, spearing a thigh for him out of a large dish.

'Chicken,' Mignot said behind him.

The pair of them, carrying their plates, went into the refectory after taking their share of wine from the bar, while behind their back the word 'chicken' sounded endlessly, at regular intervals, and the server's fork speared the portions, with a quick, rhythmical little noise.

Now the assistants' dining room was huge, easily accommodating the five hundred places for each of the three sessions. The places were set on long mahogany tables, aligned in parallel across the room. At either end, similar tables were reserved for inspectors and heads of department. In the middle there was a counter for extras. The gallery was lit by large windows to right and left which gave a bright white light, and the ceiling, though it was four metres high, seemed low, brought down by the excessive expansion of the room's other dimensions. The only ornaments on the walls, which were painted in light yellow gloss, were the boxes for napkins. Beyond this first dining room was another for the porters and coachmen, where meals were served at any time, as needed.

'What, Mignot! Have you got a leg, too?' said Favier, when he had sat down at one of the tables, opposite his friend.

Others were settling in around them. There was no tablecloth and the plates gave a cracked sound as they landed on the wooden board; and in this corner everyone was exclaiming at the prodigious number of chicken legs.

'More chickens that are all legs!' Mignot said.

Those who had bits of the carcass were annoyed. However, the food had greatly improved since the refurbishment. Mouret no longer dealt with a contractor for a fixed amount; he also managed the kitchen himself and had made it an organized service, like any other department, with a head, deputy head and inspector. It cost more, but he got better work from a better-fed staff – a form of practical humanitarianism that had long troubled Bourdoncle.

'Come now, mine is tender even so,' Mignot continued. 'Pass the bread, please!'

The large loaf was doing the rounds, and after cutting himself a slice, the last person stuck the knife back in the crust. Latecomers were hurrying in and savage appetites, doubled by the hard work of the morning, panted along the long tables from one end of the dining room to the other. There was a louder and louder clicking of forks, the *gluck-gluck* of bottles being emptied, the chink of glasses slammed down and the grinding sound of five hundred solid jaws energetically chewing. The occasional word was smothered in full mouths.

Meanwhile, Deloche, who was sitting between Baugé and Liénard, found himself almost opposite Favier, only a few places away. Each had cast a look of resentment at the other and their neighbours were whispering, having heard about their row the evening before. Then they laughed at Deloche's bad luck: always hungry, he always by some cruel twist of fate got the worst portion of anyone at his table. Today, he had sat down with a chicken neck and a scrap of the carcass. He let them tease him and stayed silent, eating large mouthfuls of bread and dissecting the neck with the infinite skill of a young man who knew how to respect meat.

'Why don't you complain?' Baugé asked.

He shrugged his shoulders. What was the use? It never came to anything. When he complained, things just got worse.

'You know the cotton-reelers have their own club now,' Mignot said suddenly. 'Just so: the Bobbin Club. It meets at a wine merchant's in the Rue Saint-Honoré where they hire a room on Saturdays.'

He was talking about the salesmen in haberdashery. At this, the whole table cheered up. Between two mouthfuls, in half-smothered voices, everyone made some remark, adding some detail; only the persistent readers stayed silent, absorbed, their noses stuck in a newspaper. There was general agreement: every year, shop workers were going up in status. Half of them, nowadays, spoke German or English. The smart thing was no longer to kick up a rumpus at Bullier,[5] or tour the café-concerts to whistle at the singer if she was ugly. No, twenty or so of them would get together and form a club.

'Do they have a piano like the drapers?' Liénard asked.

'Does the Bobbin Club have a piano? I should say it does!' said Mignot. 'They play, they sing. There is even one of them, little Bavoux, who recites poetry.'

The merriment increased and they made fun of little Bavoux, but behind the laughter there was a lot of respect. Then they started talking about a Vaudeville play in which a haberdasher was the villain; several of them were cross about this, while others were anxious about how long they would be kept that evening, because they had to go out to receptions, in decent families. And, from every side of the huge room, there were similar conversations, in the midst of the rising clatter of crockery. To get rid of the smell of food and the hot mist rising from five hundred plates, they had opened the windows, while the lowered blinds were burning from the heavy August sun. Hot blasts came from the street and golden reflections coloured the ceiling, bathing the sweating diners in a reddish light.

'It's not right to shut us up on a Sunday in such weather,' Favier said again. This remark brought the young gentlemen to the stocktaking. It had been a splendid year. So they came back to salaries and increases, the everlasting subject, the one fascinating question that excited them all. It was always the same on days when they had chicken: there was over-excitement, and eventually the noise became unbearable. When the waiters brought the artichokes with oil, you could no longer hear yourself speak. The duty inspector had been told to be lenient.

'By the way,' said Favier. 'Do you know the latest?'

But his voice was drowned. Mignot asked:

'Who doesn't like artichokes? I'll swop my dessert for an artichoke.'

No one answered. Everybody liked artichokes. This lunch would be remembered as a good one, because they had seen that there were peaches for dessert.

'He's invited her to dinner, dear chap,' Favier said to the person on his right, finishing his story. 'What! Didn't you know?'

The whole table knew, but they had grown tired of talking about it since that morning. And jokes, always the same ones, went from one to another. Deloche shuddered and eventually began to stare at Favier, who kept repeating:

'If he hasn't had her already, he's going to . . . And he won't be the first comer, oh no! He won't be the first.'

Now he, too, was looking at Deloche and added in a provocative manner:

'Those who like bones can have her for five francs.'

Suddenly Favier's head went down. Deloche, completely carried away, had just thrown his last glass of wine in his face, stammering:

'Here, you filthy liar! I should have given you a wash yesterday.'

There was an uproar. A few drops had spattered Favier's neighbours, while only his hair was slightly damp. The wine had been thrown too violently and landed on the far side of the table. But people were getting angry. Was he sleeping with her, to defend her like that? What an animal! He deserved a good slap round the face, to teach him how to behave. Then the voices were lowered because someone warned that the inspector was coming; there was no need to involve the management. Favier just said:

'If he'd got me, then there'd have been trouble.'

After which it all ended in derision. Deloche was still trembling; and when, wanting a drink to hide his embarrassment, he grasped his glass with a shaking hand, they burst out laughing. He put the glass down awkwardly and started to suck the leaves of an artichoke that he had already eaten.

'Give the carafe to Deloche,' said Mignot calmly. 'He's thirsty.'

More laughter. The young gentlemen took clean plates from the piles set out at intervals along the table, while the waiters were bringing round the dessert, peaches in baskets. And they all held their sides when Mignot added:

'Every man to his taste. Deloche likes his peaches in wine.'

Deloche did not budge. His head lowered and as if deaf, he appeared not to hear the jokes and felt desperate regret for what he had just done. They were right: what entitled him to defend her? They were going to think all sorts of dreadful things; he would have fought against himself for having compromised her in such a way, while trying to clear her name. Just his luck. He would do better to die at once, because he couldn't even give way to a good impulse without doing something stupid. Tears rose to his eyes. Wasn't it his fault, too, if the whole shop was talking about the letter the boss had written her? He could hear them sniggering and making crude remarks about that invitation, which only Liénard had heard about; and he accused himself: he should not have let Pauline talk about it in front of Liénard; he felt responsible for the indiscretion.

'Why did you tell people that?' he asked, in a pained voice. 'It was very wrong.'

'Me!' Liénard answered. 'But I only told one or two people, swearing them to secrecy. Does anyone know how things get around?'

When Deloche made up his mind to drink a glass of water, the whole table burst out laughing again. The assistants were finishing their meals, sitting back in their chairs, waiting for the bell to ring and shouting at one another across the room in a relaxed, well-fed way. Few extras had been asked for at the central table, especially since on that day it was the management who paid for coffee. The cups steamed, sweating faces shone in the light haze, floating like the blue vapours of cigarette smoke. At the windows, the blinds hung motionless without flapping. One of them was pulled up and a flood of sunlight flowed across the room, setting the ceiling ablaze with light. The hubbub of voices echoed from the walls so loudly that the bell was not heard at first except by the tables next to the door. They got up and the rout of their departure filled the corridors for a long time.

Deloche hung back to avoid the witticisms which were still being hurled at him. Even Baugé left before him, and Baugé was usually last to leave, making a detour to meet Pauline just as she was going to the ladies' dining room: this was an arrangement they had and the only chance they had to see one another for a minute during the working day. But on this occasion, just as they were ardently kissing one another in a corner, Denise, who was also on her way up to have lunch, surprised them. She had been walking slowly because of her foot.

'Oh, darling!' Pauline stammered, blushing deeply. 'You won't tell, will you?'

Baugé, with his heavy limbs and giant's build, was also shaking like a child. He muttered:

'They could easily sack us. Even though we're engaged, they don't expect you to kiss, the brutes.'

Denise was quite disturbed and pretended not to have seen them. Baugé was just hurrying off when Deloche, who had taken longer than anyone, appeared in his turn. He wanted to say he was sorry and stammered out a few phrases that Denise at first failed to grasp. Then, when he started to reproach Pauline for having spoken in front of Liénard, and Pauline was obviously embarrassed, Denise at last had the explanation of all the whispers behind her back that morning. It was the story of the letter doing the rounds. She shuddered again as she had when she first read the letter and felt all these men were undressing her.

'I didn't know,' Pauline repeated. 'In any case, there's nothing wicked about it. Let them talk, I swear they're jealous!'

'I don't hold it against you, dear,' Denise said eventually, in her sensible way. 'You only told the truth. I did receive a letter and it's up to me to reply.'

Deloche went off in an unhappy state, for it seemed clear to him that Denise accepted the situation and would keep the appointment that evening. When the two girls had had lunch, in a small dining room next to the big one, where the women were served in more comfortable surroundings, Pauline had to help Denise on her way down, because her foot was getting tired.

Downstairs, as the afternoon warmed up, the stocktaking went on more loudly than ever. It was time to put their backs into it – that moment when, faced with the meagre progress of the morning, a supreme effort had to be made to finish by evening. Voices were raised still higher and you could see nothing except waving arms, constantly emptying shelves and the throwing of goods, until you could no longer walk because the tide of piles and bundles on the floors had reached as high as the counters. A sea of heads, waving fists and flying limbs seemed to extend the full length of the shop until it became a distant confusion like a riot. This was the last feverish shudder of the machine before it burst; while outside, the occasional passer-by, pale with the stifling boredom of Sunday, still went past the great windows around the closed shop. On the pavement of the Rue Neuve-Saint-Augustin, three tall, sluttish girls without hats were standing, rudely pressing their faces to the windows, trying to see what on earth was cooking up inside.

When Denise got back to ladies' wear, Madame Aurélie let Marguerite finish calling the clothes. All that remained was to do some checking and for this, needing silence, she retired to the sample room, taking the young woman with her.

'Come with me, we'll collate the lists, then you can add up.'

She tried leaving the door open so that she could keep an eye on the young ladies, but the noise came in and she couldn't hear herself speak even at the back. It was a huge square room with nothing in it except chairs and three long tables. In a corner were large mechanical knives for cutting up samples. Whole lengths of cloth came through here: in a year, they would send out more than sixty thousand francs' worth of material, cut down into strips. From morning to evening the knives cut up silk, wool and linen, with the sound of a scythe. After that, the sample books had to be made up and stuck or sewn together. There was also a little printing press between the two windows, for the labels.

'Keep it down!' Madame Aurélie shouted from time to time, unable to hear Denise reading the items.

When the first lists had been compared, she left the young woman at one of the tables, absorbed in adding up the figures. Then, almost immediately, she was back with Mademoiselle de Fontenailles, who had been passed on to her by trousseaux, because they no longer needed her. She would do some adding as well, so they would save time. But the appearance of the 'Marquise' (as Clara unkindly called her) had stirred up the department: they started to laugh and to tease Joseph, and vicious words came through the door.

'Don't move back, you're not at all in my way,' Denise said, feeling very sorry for her. 'Here! We can both use my inkwell, one is enough.'

Mademoiselle de Fontenailles was so stupefied by her ill-treatment that she could not even find a word of thanks. She probably drank: she was thin and there were livid patches on her skin, only her slender white hands still indicating the distinction of her ancestry.

Meanwhile, the laughter suddenly faded and all that could be heard was the regular rumbling of the work in hand. Mouret was once more making a tour of the departments. Then he stopped, looking for Denise and was surprised at not seeing her. He motioned to Madame Aurélie to come over and they went off to one side for a moment, talking quietly. He must have been questioning her. She nodded towards the sample room, then appeared to be giving him an account of something. No doubt she was reporting that the young woman had been crying that morning.

'Excellent!' Mouret said, coming closer. 'Show me the lists.'

'Over here, Monsieur,' the buyer answered. 'We escaped from the noise.'

He followed her into the next room. Clara was not fooled by all this: she said quietly that they might as well go and fetch a bed straight away. But Marguerite started throwing the clothes to her more quickly to keep her occupied and to shut her mouth. Wasn't the under-buyer a good workmate? It was nobody's business what she got up to. The department was starting to take her side, the assistants were getting more excited all the time, while Lhomme and Joseph spread their backs, as though walling themselves in silence. And Inspector Jouve, who had seen Madame Aurélie's manoeuvre from afar, directed his steps towards the door of the sample room, walking with the steady pace of a sentry keeping guard over the affairs of his superior.

'Give Monsieur the lists,' the buyer said as she came in.

Denise handed them over and remained looking up. She had jumped slightly, but then controlled herself and was keeping very calm, though her cheeks were pale. For a moment, Mouret appeared to be absorbed in the lists of goods, not looking at the young woman. There was silence. Then, Madame Aurélie, who had gone over to Mademoiselle de Fontenailles, who had not even turned round, seemed displeased with her adding up and said under her breath:

'Go and help them in parcels. You're not used to figures.'

She got up and went back to the department, where she was greeted with whispers. Joseph, under the mocking scrutiny of the young ladies, was writing unevenly, while Clara, though delighted to have some unexpected help, hated all women in the shop and shoved her around. How ridiculous it was to give in to the love of an ordinary worker, when you were a marchioness! What's more, she envied her that love.

'Good! Very good!' Mouret repeated, still pretending to read.

Meanwhile, Madame Aurélie did not know how to leave in her turn, in a decent way. She wandered around, checking the mechanical knives, furious that her husband was not inventing some reason to call her over; but he was no use when it came to serious matters: he would die of thirst beside a pond. It was Marguerite who had the common sense to ask her to help with something.

'Coming,' the buyer replied.

And, now that she could do so with dignity, with an excuse for the young ladies who were watching her closely, she finally left Mouret and Denise alone, after getting them in the room together. She went out with such a majestic step and air of nobility that the sales assistants did not even dare to smile.

Mouret had slowly put down the lists on the table. He was looking at the young woman, who had remained seated, pen in hand. She did not look away, but more of the colour had drained from her face.

'You'll come, this evening?' he asked, in a low voice.

'No, Monsieur,' she replied. 'I cannot. My brothers are due to go to my uncle's and I promised to dine with them.'

'But what about your foot! It's too hard for you to walk.'

'Oh, I can manage to go that far, I'm feeling much better since this morning.'

He, too, had gone pale, confronted with this calm refusal. A nervous tic made his lips twitch. But he contained himself and resumed the manner of a concerned employer, simply interested in one of his young ladies:

'Come now . . . What if I were to beg you. You know how highly I think of you.'

Denise kept her attitude of respect.

'I am very touched, Monsieur, by your kindness towards me and I thank you for your invitation. But, I repeat, it is impossible. My brothers are expecting me this evening.'

She stubbornly refused to understand his meaning. The door was still open and she could very well feel the whole shop urging her on. Pauline had amicably called her a great booby, but the others would laugh at her, if she refused the invitation. Madame Aurélie, who had gone off, Marguerite, whose voice she could hear rising, Lhomme's back, which she could see, motionless and discreet – all of them wanted her to fall, all of them were throwing her to the master. And the distant rumble of the stocktaking, those millions of goods being shouted out here, there and everywhere and being turned over by the armful, were like a hot wind which blew passion towards her.

There was a silence. From time to time, the noise drowned out Mouret's words, accompanying them with the tremendous din of a king's fortune, won in battle.

'So, when will you come?' he asked once more. 'Tomorrow?'

Denise was disturbed by this simple question. For a moment, she lost her calm and stammered out:

'I don't know . . . I can't . . .'

He smiled and tried to take her hand, which she pulled back.

'What are you afraid of?'

But she was already raising her head and looking directly at him, and she said, smiling in her sweet, honest way:

'I'm not afraid of anything, Monsieur. One just does what one wants to do, isn't that so? I don't want to, that's all!'

As she finished speaking, she was surprised to hear a creaking sound. She turned round and saw the door slowly shutting. It was Inspector Jouve who had taken it upon himself to pull it to: the doors were part of his responsibility and none of them should remain open. Then he went gravely back to his post. No one seemed to notice this door, which had been so simply closed. Only Clara whispered some obscenity in the ear of Mademoiselle de Fontenailles, whose face was dead and absolutely white.

Denise, meanwhile, had got up. Mouret said to her in a low, trembling voice:

'Listen . . . I love you. You've known it for a long time, so don't play the cruel game of feigning ignorance with me. But you needn't be afraid. Twenty times, I have wanted to call you into my study. We should have been alone, I had merely to bolt the door. But I preferred not to . . . You see, I'm talking to you here, where anyone can enter. I love you, Denise.'

She was standing, white-faced, listening and still looking directly at him.

'Tell me, why do you refuse? Is there nothing you need? Your brothers must cost you a lot of money. What ever you may ask, whatever you may demand of me . . .'

She stopped him with a word:

'Thank you, I'm already earning more than I need.'

'But I am offering you freedom, a life of pleasure and luxury. I would set you up in your own place, I would ensure you a small fortune.'

'No, thank you. I should be bored doing nothing. I have been earning my living since I was ten years old.'

He made a frantic gesture. She was the first who had not given in. He had had only to stoop to pick up the others; all of them had been awaiting his will like the submissive servants they were. Now this one was saying no, without even giving a reasonable excuse. His desire, which had been held in for so long, was flaring, exasperated by her resistance. Perhaps he was not offering enough; so he doubled the offer, pressing her harder still.

'No, no, thank you,' she answered each time, without faltering.

Finally, he could not restrain this cry from the heart:

'Can't you see how I am suffering! Yes, it's ridiculous, but I'm suffering like a child.'

Tears welled up in his eyes. Once again, there was silence. They could still hear the soft rumbling of the stocktaking beyond the closed door. It was like a fading sound of triumph, the accompaniment becoming more unobtrusive for the master's defeat.

'Yet, if I wanted to!' he said in a passionate voice, grasping her hands.

She let him hold them, her eyes paled and all her strength drained away. The warm hands of this man filled her with heat and a delicious sense of languor. Oh, God! How she loved him! How sweet it would be to hang her arms around his neck and rest her head on his chest!

'I want you, I want you!' he repeated, wildly. 'I will expect you this evening, or else I shall be obliged to. . .'

He was becoming violent. She gave a little cry, the pain that she felt in her wrists giving her back her strength. With a movement, she freed herself and then, standing bolt upright, seeming all the taller because of her weakness, she said:

'No, leave me . . . I am not a Clara, to be dropped the next day. And, in any case, Monsieur, you love someone, yes, that lady who comes here . . . Stay with her. I cannot share.'

Surprise left him motionless. What was she saying, then? What did she want? Never had the girls he picked up in the shop been bothered about being loved. He should have laughed at her, but this attitude of affection and pride completed the bewilderment in his heart.

'Monsieur,' she continued. 'Open this door. It is not proper for us to be like this together.'

Mouret obeyed and, with pounding temples, not knowing how to disguise his feelings, he called back Madame Aurélie, got angry about the stock of cloaks and said they would have to lower the price and go on lowering it until not one was left. This was the rule of the firm: they swept everything away every year and would sell at a loss of sixty per cent rather than keep an old model or shop-soiled length of cloth. As it happened, Bourdoncle had come looking for the director and had been waiting for some time in front of the door that Jouve had closed, Jouve having whispered a word in his ear, with a serious look. He was losing patience, though not enough to dare interrupt the tête-à-tête. Was it possible? On a day like this, with that wretched little creature? When the door did finally open, Bourdoncle started talking about fancy silks, of which they were going to have a huge stock. It was a relief for Mouret, who could shout to his heart's content. What was Bouthemont thinking about? He walked away, saying that he couldn't understand how a buyer could be so untalented and stupid as to get in greater supplies than there was demand.

'What's got into him?' Madame Aurélie muttered, quite upset by these reproaches.

The young ladies looked at each other in surprise. By six o'clock the stocktaking was finished. The sun was still shining, a yellow summer sun, its golden rays slanting through the windows of the halls. In the heavy air of the streets, weary families were already returning from the suburbs, carrying bunches of flowers and dragging children behind them. One by one the departments fell silent. All one could hear from the ends of the galleries were the late calls of some assistants emptying a last shelf. Then the voices too fell silent and all that was left of the noise of the day was a great shudder rising above the tremendous rout of goods. Now the boxes, the shelves, the wardrobes and the cupboards were empty. Not a metre of cloth, not a single object had remained in place. The huge shop displayed only the skeleton of its fittings, the containers absolutely clean as they had been on the day they were put in. This nudity was the visible proof of the total and precise account of the stocktaking, while on the ground were piled sixteen million francs' worth of goods, a rising sea that had eventually submerged the tables and the counters. The assistants, swimming around in it up to their shoulders, had started to replace every item. They hoped to finish around ten o'clock.

As Madame Aurélie, who was in the first sitting for dinner, was coming down from the dining room, she brought the total turnover for the year, a figure immediately reached by adding the totals from the various departments. The amount was eighty million, ten million more than the previous year; there had been no real fall except in fancy silks.

'If Monsieur Mouret is not happy, I really don't know what he wants,' said the buyer. 'Look, he's over there, at the top of the great staircase, looking furious.'

The young ladies went to have a look. He was standing alone, grim-faced, above the millions scattered at his feet.

At that moment, Denise came up to her. 'Madame,' she said, 'would you be kind enough to let me go now? I'm not of any more use, because of my foot and as I have to go to dinner at my uncle's, with my brothers . . .'

Amazement. So she hadn't given way? Madame Aurélie hesitated and seemed about to forbid her to go out, her voice snappy and displeased, while Clara was shrugging her shoulders, quite incredulous: come on! It was quite simple: he didn't want her any more! When Pauline learned what had come of it, she was next to layettes, with Deloche. The young man's sudden joy made her angry: she was really doing herself some good, wasn't she? Perhaps he was pleased that his friend was silly enough to lose herself a fortune. And Bourdoncle, who did not dare disturb Mouret in his savage isolation, was walking along amid the noise, himself depressed and full of concern.

Meanwhile, Denise was coming down. As she reached the bottom of the little staircase on the left, slowly, holding on to the banister, she came across a group of sniggering salesmen. Her name was mentioned and she felt that they were still talking about her adventure. They had not noticed her.

'Come on! What a show!' Favier was saying. 'She's a real little slut. I even know someone she tried to take by force.'

He was looking at Hutin who, to preserve his dignity, was standing apart and not taking part in the jokes. But he was so flattered by the envious looks the others were giving him, that he deigned to mutter:

'You don't know how she bothers me, that girl!'

Denise, stricken to the heart, gripped the rail. They must have seen her, because they all went off, laughing. He was right, she blamed herself for her ignorance in the past, when she had thought about him. But what a coward he was and how she despised him now! She was deeply disturbed: how strange it was that a moment ago she had the strength to reject a man whom she adored, while she had once felt so weak in front of this miserable boy, whose love she had only dreamed of? Her common sense and her courage failed her in these contradictions of her being, which she could no longer understand. She hurried across the hall. Then some instinct made her raise her head, just as an inspector was opening the door, which had been closed since the morning. And she saw Mouret. He was still at the top of the staircase, on the large central landing, overlooking the gallery. But he had forgotten the stocktaking, he could not see his empire, these shops bursting with wealth. Everything had vanished: the resounding victories of yesterday, tomorrow's colossal fortune. With desperate eyes, he followed Denise and when she had gone through the door, nothing was left, the building became black.

CHAPTER 11

That day, Bouthemont was the first to arrive at Madame Desforges' for four o'clock tea. Alone once more in her large Louis XIV drawing room, with its cheerful, light-coloured brass fittings and brocaded silk hangings, she got up impatiently, saying:

'Well?'

'Well,' the young man replied, 'when I told him that I would surely visit and pay my respects to you, he formally promised to come.'

'Did you let him know that I was expecting the Baron today?'

'Of course, that's what seemed to make his mind up.'

They were speaking of Mouret. The previous year, he had taken a sudden liking to Bouthemont, to the extent of sharing his leisure time with him; he had even introduced him to Henriette, glad to have an obliging confidant who would help to put a little fun into a relationship that was starting to bore him. So it was that the buyer from silks had eventually become the confidant of both his boss and the pretty widow: he ran little errands for them, talked about one with the other and sometimes helped them to patch up quarrels. In her fits of jealousy, Henriette went so far as to adopt a tone of intimacy which surprised and embarrassed him, because she lost the circumspection of a woman of the world whose greatest art was saving appearances.

She burst out: 'You should have brought him. I would have been sure then.'

'Heavens!' he said, with a good-natured laugh. 'It's not my fault if he keeps on giving me the slip, nowadays. Oh, he likes me well enough, though. Without him, I'd be in trouble there.'

As it happens, his position in *Au Bonheur des Dames* had been under threat since the last stocktaking. Even though he had claimed it was all to do with the rainy weather, he was not forgiven for overstocking considerably on fancy silks; and, since Hutin was exploiting this mistake and undermining his position with the management in a new wave of furious cunning, Bouthemont could feel the ground giving way beneath his feet. Mouret had condemned him, now doubtless getting bored with a witness who was making it hard for him to break off his affair and who enjoyed a familiarity from which he, Mouret, had nothing to gain. But with his usual tactics, he was hiding behind Bourdoncle: it was Bourdoncle and the other directors who demanded Bouthemont's dismissal at every board meeting, he said, while he held out against them, forcefully defending his friend, at the risk of serious problems for himself.

'In any case, I shall wait,' Madame Desforges continued. 'You know that girl is due here at five o'clock. I want to see them together. I must know the truth about them.'

She went back over the plan which she had dreamed up in her excitement, repeating that she had asked Madame Aurélie to send her Denise, to look at a coat which did not fit. When she had the girl in her room, she would easily find some excuse for calling Mouret in and would then act accordingly.

Bouthemont, sitting opposite her, examined her with his fine, laughing eyes, trying to make them look serious. This jolly lad with his inky black beard, a loud-mouthed merrymaker whose face was coloured by his hot Gascon blood, was thinking that society ladies were not much, really, and liable to let out a fine flood when they dared to tell you their secrets. One thing was sure: his friends' mistresses, who were shop girls, would never give so much away.

'Come, come,' he finally ventured to say. 'What difference does it make to you, when I swear that there is absolutely nothing between them?'

'Precisely!' she cried out. 'That one, he loves. I don't care about the others, those casual encounters, the fancies of a day.'

She spoke of Clara with contempt. They had told her that, after Denise refused him, Mouret had turned to this tall redhead, with a head like a horse, no doubt quite deliberately, because he kept her in the department, showing her off and showering her with presents. In any event, over the past three months or so, he had been living for pleasure alone, throwing his money around with such prodigality that people had started to talk. He had bought a house for a second-rate actress and at the same time was being devoured by two or three women of loose morals who seemed to be trying to outdo each other in silly, expensive whims.

'It's that creature's fault,' Henriette said. 'I can tell that he's ruining himself with other women because she has rejected him. In any case, what do I care for his money! I should have preferred him poor. You know how much I love him, now that you are our friend.'

She stopped, with a lump in her throat, about to burst into tears; then, in a gesture of abandonment, held her two hands out to him. It was true, she adored Mouret for his youth and his success: no man had ever possessed her so entirely, so thrilled her flesh and her self-esteem. But, at the idea of losing him, she could also hear the knell of her fortieth year and wondered with terror how she would replace this great love.

'Oh, I'll have my revenge on him,' she murmured. 'I'll have my revenge, if he misbehaves.'

Bouthemont had not let go of her hands. She was still beautiful. The only trouble was, she would be an awkward mistress and he did not much like that kind. Yet it deserved thinking about; the problems might be worth risking.

'Why don't you set yourself up on your own account?' she said suddenly, dropping his hands.

He was not sure how to respond. Then he said:

'But it would take a lot of capital . . . Last year, I did turn this idea over in my head. I'm quite certain that there are enough customers in Paris for one or two more department stores. The only thing is, you would have to choose your area. The *Bon Marché* has the Left Bank, the *Louvre* has the centre, and in *Au Bonheur*, we have sewn up the rich districts in the west. What's left is the north, where you could set up in competition with *Place Clichy*. And I'd found a terrific site, just by the Opéra . . .'

'Well then?'

He laughed loudly.

'Well, can you believe it? I was silly enough to talk about it to my father. Yes, I was such an idiot, I asked him to look for investors in Toulouse.'

And he merrily went on to describe how angry the old man had been, in his little shop in the provinces, railing against the big stores in Paris. Old Bouthemont, who couldn't bear to think of his son earning thirty thousand francs, replied that he would give his money and that of his friends to charity before offering a centime to one of those department stores that were the brothels of trade.

'In any case,' the young man concluded, 'you would need millions.'

'Suppose we could find millions?' Madame Desforges said simply.

He looked at her, suddenly becoming serious. Was this just the remark of a jealous woman? But she did not give him time to question her, adding: 'Well, you know how much interest I take in you. We'll speak about it later.'

The bell in the antechamber had sounded. She got up and he, with an instinctive movement, pushed his chair back, as though they already risked being caught out together. There was silence in the salon with its merry hangings and with such a profusion of green plants that there seemed to be a small wood growing between the windows. Standing up and turning her ear towards the door, she waited.

'It's him,' she said softly.

The servant announced:

'Monsieur Mouret, Monsieur de Vallagnosc.'

She could not restrain a movement of anger. Why had he not come on his own? He must have gone to look for his friend, afraid that he would be left alone in tête-à-tête with her. Then she smiled, and held out her hand to the two men.

'What a rare visitor you are becoming . . . That applies to you too, Monsieur Vallagnosc.'

One thing that she could not bear was the fact that she was putting on weight, and she would force herself into dresses of black silks, to hide her increasing embonpoint. Yet her pretty head, with its dark hair, was still pleasant and delicate. Mouret could still say to her in a familiar tone, after looking her over in a glance:

'Why, there's no point asking you how you are. You're as fresh as a rose.'

'Oh, I'm only too well,' she said. 'In any case, I could have died without you knowing anything about it.'

She was looking at him, too, and thought him nervous and tired, with heavy eyes and a dull complexion.

'What's more,' she continued, in a voice that she tried to make lightly mocking, 'I can't return the compliment. You don't look well this evening.'

'Work!' said Vallagnosc.

Mouret made some vague gesture without replying. He had just seen Bouthemont and was nodding to him amiably. When they were really close, he used to take the buyer out of the department himself at the height of the afternoon rush so that they could go round and see Henriette. But times had changed. He half whispered:

'You left early . . . You know, your absence was noticed and they're pretty furious over there.'

He was talking about Bourdoncle and the other board members as though he were not their manager.

'Oh!' Bouthemont muttered anxiously.

'Yes. I want a word with you. Wait for me and we'll leave together.'

Meanwhile, Henriette had sat down again and, while listening to Vallagnosc, who was telling her that Madame de Boves would probably be coming, she kept her eyes on Mouret. He had fallen silent again and was looking at the furniture or examining the ceiling. Then, when she started to complain with a laugh about the fact that she only had men at her four-o'clock tea, he forgot himself to the extent of remarking:

'I thought Baron Hartmann would be here.'

Henriette went pale. Of course, she knew that he came to visit her only in order to meet the Baron, but he might have refrained from thrusting his indifference in her face. At that very moment, the door opened and the servant stood behind it. When she questioned him with a nod, he leaned over and said very quietly to her:

'It's about that coat. Madame asked me to tell her . . . The young lady is here.'

At this, she raised her voice, so that she could be heard. All the pain of her jealousy could be felt in the words: 'Let her wait!' – spoken with dry contempt.

'Should I show her into Madame's dressing room?'

'No, no, leave her in the antechamber.'

And, when the servant had left, she calmly resumed her conversation with Vallagnosc. Mouret, who had lapsed back into weariness and boredom, had heard without understanding, only half paying attention. Bouthemont, concerned by the matter, was deep in thought. But almost immediately, the door reopened and two ladies were introduced.

'Just think,' said Madame Marty. 'I was getting out of my carriage when I saw Madame de Boves approaching through the arcade.'

'Yes,' the latter added, by way of explanation. 'It's fine and since my doctor is always telling me to walk . . .'

Then, after a general round of handshakes, she asked Henriette:

'Are you getting a new chambermaid, then?'

'No,' the other woman asked in astonishment. 'Why?'

'I've just seen a young girl in the antechamber . . .'

Henriette interrupted her with a laugh.

'Isn't that right? All these shop girls look like chambermaids. Yes, it's some young lady who has come to alter a coat.'

Mouret stared at her, feeling a faint suspicion in his mind as she continued, with forced merriment, describing how she had bought the article at *Au Bonheur des Dames* the previous week.

'What this?' said Madame Marty. 'Doesn't Sauveur dress you any more?'

'Yes, dear, she does, but I wanted to experiment. And I'd been rather pleased with something else I bought, a travelling coat. But this time, it was quite another story. Whatever you say, they don't dress you well in that shop of yours. Oh, I don't bother, I can say these things in front of Monsieur Mouret! You never will dress a really distinguished woman.'

Mouret did not try to defend his store, still looking at her and reassuring himself: she wouldn't dare. It was Bouthemont who had to speak up for *Au Bonheur des Dames*.

'If all the society ladies who dress with us were to boast about it,' he responded cheerfully, 'you would be quite amazed at our customers. Order a made-to-measure piece from us and it will be just as good as anything from Sauveur, at half the price. But there you have it: it's because it's cheaper that it's not so good.'

'So doesn't the coat fit?' Madame de Boves went on. 'Now I recognize the young lady. It's quite dark in your antechamber.'

'Yes,' Madame Marty agreed. 'I was wondering where I'd seen that figure. Well, off you go my sweet, don't worry about us.'

Henriette gave a gesture of contemptuous indifference.

'Oh, any time. There's no hurry.'

The ladies continued their debate on department store clothes. Then Madame de Boves spoke about her husband who, according to her, had just gone off on a tour of inspection to visit the stud farm at Saint-Lô, while Henriette was telling them that old Madame Guibal had been called to Franche-Comté because one of her aunts was ill. In addition to that, she was not expecting Madame Bourdelais that evening, because at the end of every month she shut herself up with a seamstress to go through all the family's linen. Meanwhile, Madame Marty seemed to have some deep-seated anxiety. Monsieur Marty's post at the Lycée Bonaparte was threatened, after the poor man had given some lessons in various seedy institutions where you could buy a *baccalauréat*; he was coining money as fast as he could, feverishly, to satisfy the spending mania that was ruining his household. Seeing him weep one evening, thinking he was to be dismissed, she had the idea of asking her friend Henriette to approach a director in the Ministry of Education whom she knew. Henriette eventually calmed her with a word. Moreover, Monsieur Marty was going to come himself to learn his fate and offer his thanks.

'You seem indisposed, Monsieur Mouret,' Madame de Boves remarked.

'Work!' Vallagnosc repeated, with ironic imperturbability.

Mouret had jumped up, like a man upset at having forgotten himself in that way. He took his usual place at the centre of the circle of the ladies and recovered all his charm. He was concerned about the new winter lines and talked about a large consignment of lace; and Madame de Boves questioned him about the price of Alençon lace, because she might be buying some. Now she was reduced to saving the thirty *sous* she spent on her carriage fare and went home ill after looking in all the shop windows. Wrapped in a coat that was already two years old, she dreamed of trying all the expensive materials she saw on her regal shoulders; but then it was as though someone had torn them from her very flesh, when she woke up in her patched dresses, with no hope of ever satisfying her passion.

'Monsieur le Baron Hartmann,' the servant announced.

Henriette noticed the happy handshake that Mouret gave this new arrival. The Baron greeted the ladies and gave the young man the penetrating look that sometimes lit up his fat Alsatian face.

'Still talking about cloth!' he said, smiling.

Then, as a regular visitor to the house, he allowed himself to ask:

'That's a very charming young lady in the antechamber. Who is it?'

'Oh, no one,' Madame Desforges replied, in a nasty voice. 'A shop girl who is waiting.'

But the door remained half-open and the servant brought in the tea. He went out, came back again and put down the china service on the little table, followed by plates and biscuits. A bright light, softened by the green plants, lit up the copper fittings in the huge drawing room and bathed the silken surface of the furniture in cheerful softness. And every time the door opened, you could see a dark corner of the antechamber, lit only by its ground glass windows. There in the darkness a vague shape could be seen, motionless and patient. Denise was standing. There was a leather-covered bench, but pride forbade her to sit on it. She realized that she was being insulted. She had been there for the last half hour, without a gesture or a word. The ladies and the Baron had stared at her as they went past, and now the voices from the drawing rooms reached her in faint snatches. All this pleasant luxury assaulted her with its indifference; yet still she did not move. Suddenly, through the doorway, she recognized Mouret. He, too, had just sensed her presence.

'Is that one of your sales girls?' asked Baron Hartmann.

Mouret succeeded in hiding his emotions, but his voice trembled, none the less.

'It seems so, but I do not know which one.'

'It's the little blonde from ladies' wear,' Madame Marty hastened to inform him. 'The under-buyer, I think.'

Henriette looked at him in her turn.

All he said was: 'Oh!'

He tried to talk about the celebration of the King of Prussia's visit,[1] which had started the previous day. But the Baron mischievously returned to the subject of shopgirls in large stores, pretending that he wanted to learn about the subject and asking questions: where did they usually come from, were they as loose-living as rumour had it? A long discussion followed.

'Really?' he said repeatedly. 'Do you really think they behave themselves?'

Mouret defended their honour with such conviction that it made Vallagnosc laugh. Then Bouthemont interrupted, to spare his boss further embarrassment. Of course, there were all kinds among them, some sluts and some fine young women. What's more, their moral standards were improving. At one time, it was practically only the worst element in the trade that ended up in drapery, poor girls from obscure backgrounds; but now, there were families in the Rue de Sèvres who were actually bringing their kids up to work in the *Bon Marché*. In short, if they wanted to behave, they could, because unlike the working girls on the streets of Paris they did not have to feed and house themselves: they had their meals and a bed, so their lives were assured, hard though they were. The worst thing was their vague, indeterminate situation, between shop girls and ladies. Thrown into all that luxury, without any basic education, they formed a nameless class apart: this was the source of their misfortunes and their vices.

'I must say, I don't know of a more unpleasant group of creatures,' said Madame de Boves. 'There are times when you want to give them a good slap.'

Whereupon the ladies vented their spleen. They tore each other to pieces behind the counters, one woman devouring another, in a bitter rivalry of money and beauty. There was this surly jealousy of the salesgirls towards well-dressed customers, the ladies whose manners they tried to copy and a still greater jealousy of badly dressed, petty bourgeois customers against the salesgirls, with their silk dresses, whom they expected to humble themselves like servants for a purchase of ten *sous*.

'Let it rest!' said Henriette. 'They're all up for sale, the wretches, like their merchandise!'

Mouret forced a smile. The Baron was looking at him, impressed by his ability to control himself; so he changed the subject, speaking once more about the welcome for the King of Prussia: it would be magnificent and all branches of trade in Paris would profit. Henriette said nothing, seemingly deep in thought, but in fact torn between the desire to make Denise wait still longer in the antechamber and the fear that Mouret, now he was aware of her being there, would leave. So eventually she left her chair and said: 'Would you excuse me?'

'Of course, my dear!' Madame Marty exclaimed. 'Look! I'll do the honours.'

She got up, took the tea pot and filled the cups. Henriette had turned towards Baron Hartmann.

'Will you stay for a few minutes more?'

'Yes, I want to talk to Monsieur Mouret. We'll invade your little drawing room.'

At that, she left and her black silk dress brushed against the door with a sound like the slithering of a viper in the undergrowth.

At once, the Baron manoeuvred it so that he could take Mouret out, leaving the ladies to Bouthemont and Vallagnosc. They started to talk in low voices standing by the window in the adjoining room. This was an entirely new business affair. Mouret still dreamed of carrying out his old plan to take over the whole segment from the Rue Monsigny to the Rue de la Michodière and the Rue Neuve-Saint-Augustin to the Rue du Dix-Décembre for *Au Bonheur des Dames*. In the vast block of houses, there was still a huge frontage on the last-named street that he did not own; this was enough to spoil his success. He was tormented by the need to round off his conquest and to raise a monumental façade there like an apotheosis. As long as the main entrance was in the Rue Neuve-Saint-Augustin, that dark street belonging to Old Paris, his work was incomplete, and lacked logic. He wanted to proclaim it before the New Paris on one of those young avenues[2] down which the great throng of this century's end passed by in the full light of day. He could see it establishing itself as the dominant, giant palace of trade, casting a greater shadow over the city than the old Louvre. Up to now, however, he had come up against the obstinacy of the Crédit Immobilier, which would not alter its original plan of putting up a rival to the Grand-Hôtel along that façade. The plans were ready and they were only waiting for the Rue du Dix-Décembre to be cleared to start on the foundations. At last, in one final effort, Mouret had almost persuaded Baron Hartmann.

'Well,' the Baron began. 'We had a board meeting yesterday and I came here with the idea that I might meet you, so that I could keep you up-to-date. They're still holding out.'

The young man could not repress a gesture of irritation.

'It's unreasonable. What do they say?'

'Good heavens, they're saying what I told you myself and am still somewhat inclined to think . . . Your façade is a mere ornament, the new building would only increase the area of your shops by one-tenth and it means putting very large amounts of money into mere advertising.'

At this, Mouret burst out:

'Advertising! Advertising! In any case, this advertising would be in stone and would bury the lot of us. Don't you realize that it would multiply our takings by ten! We'd make up the money in two years. What does it matter if it's what you call wasted land, if this land brings in a huge rate of interest! You'll see the crowd when our customers are no longer blocking the Rue Neuve-Saint-Augustin, but can freely pass along a wide street down which six carriages could easily travel abreast.'

'I agree,' the Baron said, with a laugh. 'But you're a poet in your way, as I've told you before. The board considers that it would be risky to expand your business any further. They want to be cautious on your behalf.'

'What! Cautious! I don't understand. The figures are there: don't they show the constant rise in our sales? First of all, with a capital of five hundred thousand francs, I had a turnover of two million. That capital was turned over four times. Then it became four million, was used ten times and produced forty million francs in turnover. Finally, after successive increases, I have just established through my last stocktaking that the turnover has now reached a total of eighty million, which means that the capital, which has hardly increased, since it stands at only six million, has gone across our counters in merchandise more than a dozen times.'

He was raising his voice and tapping the fingers of his right hand on the palm of the left, beating in the millions as though cracking nuts. The Baron interrupted.

'I know, I know. But surely you don't expect to keep on increasing in that way?'

'Why not?' Mouret asked, naively. 'There's no reason why it should stop. The capital can be turned over fifteen times, as I've long been saying. In some departments, it will be turned over twenty-five or thirty times. Then . . . well, then we'll find a way to put it to further use still.'

'So eventually you'll drink up all the money in Paris, like a glass of water?'

'I expect we will. Doesn't Paris belong to women and don't women belong to us?'

The Baron put both hands on his shoulders and looked at him with a paternal air.

'Now, now! You're a good lad and I like you . . . Impossible to resist you. We'll discuss the idea seriously and I hope I can persuade them. So far, we have had nothing but praise for you. The dividends are astonishing the Exchange. You must be doing the right thing and it would be better to put more money into your concern than to get into competition with the Grand-Hôtel, which might be risky.'

Mouret's excitement died down and he thanked the Baron, but without his usual burst of enthusiasm. And the Baron saw his eyes turn towards the door of the next room, full of the dull anxiety that he was trying to hide. Meanwhile, Vallagnosc had come up, realizing that they were no longer talking business. He stood near them, listening to the Baron who was murmuring in the blasé tone of an old Lothario:

'By the way, I think they're having their revenge.'

'Who do you mean?' Mouret asked, in embarrassment.

'Why, those women . . . they're tired of belonging to you, so you belong to them, my dear fellow. Tit for tat!'

He was joking, knowing about the young man's notorious love affairs. The house he had bought for the actress, and the huge sums expended on women whom Mouret had picked up in private dining rooms amused him as though they excused the follies that he had once committed himself. His old experience rejoiced in them.

'Really, I don't understand,' said Mouret.

'Now, now, you understand perfectly well. They always have the last word. So I was thinking: it's not possible, he's boasting, he can't be that clever! And here you are! Take everything from a woman, exploit her like a coal mine, because afterwards she'll be the one who exploits you and makes you cough up! Be careful, because she'll get more blood and money out of you than you ever did out of her.'

He was laughing even more and Vallagnosc, beside him, was chuckling, without saying a word.

'Good Lord, you have to try everything once,' Mouret confessed in the end, pretending that he too was amused. 'Money is idiotic if you don't use it.'

'There I agree with you,' said the Baron. 'Enjoy yourself, dear chap. I'm not going to sermonize you or worry about the large investment we have in you. You have to sow your wild oats, it gives you a clearer head later on . . . And then, it's not unpleasant to ruin oneself, if one is the sort of man who can rebuild a fortune. But while money is nothing, there are other kinds of suffering . . .'

He paused, his laughter becoming sad, old sorrows echoing in the irony of his scepticism. He had followed the duel between Henriette and Mouret with the curiosity of someone who was still deeply interested in struggles of the heart when they involved others, and he could feel that the crisis point had arrived; he guessed what was going on, knowing the story of that Denise whom he had glimpsed in the antechamber.

'Oh, where suffering is concerned, that's not my speciality,' Mouret said with bravado. 'It's already enough to have to pay.'

The Baron looked at him for a few seconds in silence. Without wanting to press the point, he slowly added:

'Don't make yourself out to be worse than you are. You would lose more than your money. You'd pay with your flesh, my friend.'

He paused to ask: 'Isn't that right, Monsieur de Vallagnosc; it happens?' – on a lighter tone again.

'So they say, Monsieur le Baron,' Vallagnosc replied simply.

At that moment, the door of the room opened and Mouret, who was about to reply, gave a little jump. The three men turned round. It was Madame Desforges, looking very light-hearted, putting just her head round the door and calling in a hurried voice: 'Monsieur Mouret! Monsieur Mouret!'

Then, when she saw the others:

'Oh, gentlemen, if you would be so kind, I'm going to take Monsieur Mouret away from you for a minute. He's sold me a dreadful coat, so it's the least he can do to give me his advice. This girl is an idiot who has no idea about the matter . . . Come on, I'm waiting.'

He paused, struggling against himself and shrinking from the scene that he knew was coming. But he had to obey. The Baron said, in a tone that was at once paternal and mocking:

'Go on, go on, dear boy, Madame needs you.'

So Mouret followed her. The door shut behind him and he thought he heard Vallagnosc give a snigger that was stifled by the hangings. In any case, his strength was exhausted. Since Henriette had left the salon, and he knew that Denise was at the back of the apartment, in her jealous hands, he had been feeling increasing anxiety, a nervous torment that made him keep his ears pricked, as if shuddering at a distant sound of weeping. What could this creature be thinking up to torture him? All his love, a love that still surprised him, went to the young woman, as well as his support and consolation. Never before had he loved in this way, with this powerful charm in the midst of suffering. His attachments, those of a busy man, and even Henriette, so clever, so pretty, whom it had flattered him to possess, were only a pleasant pastime, or sometimes a calculating one, in which he looked for nothing but profit and pleasure. He used to leave his mistresses' bedrooms calmly and go home to sleep, enjoying his bachelor's freedom, with not a regret or a worry in his heart. Nowadays, on the other hand, his heart would beat in anguish, his life belonged to another and he no longer found the oblivion of sleep in his great lonely bed. Denise was always with him. Even now, there was no one but her and he felt that he would rather be here to protect her, even as he followed the other one, dreading some unpleasant scene.

First of all they crossed the silent, empty bedroom. Then Madame

Desforges, pushing open a door, went into the study with Mouret behind her. It was a rather large room, hung with red silk and furnished with a marble dressing-table and a three-piece wardrobe with tall mirrors. As the window overlooked the courtyard, it was already dark, and two gaslights had been lit, their brackets, nickel-plated, extending to the right and left of the wardrobe.

'Now then,' said Henriette. 'Perhaps it will work better this time.'

Mouret had come into the room to see Denise standing in the middle of the bright gaslight. She was very pale, modestly squeezed into a waisted cashmere jacket and a black hat, and holding over one arm the coat from *Au Bonheur*. When she saw the young man, her hands shook a little.

'I'd like this gentleman to tell me what he thinks,' Henriette said. 'Help me, Mademoiselle.'

Denise went over and had to try the coat on her again. At the first fitting she had put pins in the shoulders, which were wrong. Henriette turned round, examining herself in front of the wardrobe.

'Will it do? Tell me honestly.'

'Truly, Madame, I have to say it's not right,' said Mouret, wanting to shorten the proceedings. 'But there's no problem, the young lady will take your measurements and we'll make you another.'

'No, I want this one, I need it at once,' she snapped back. 'The trouble is, it needs to be let out round the bust and it's too loose here, between the shoulders.'

Then, in her dry voice, she went on:

'You won't put it right just by looking at me, Mademoiselle! Examine it, find the answer, that's your job.'

Denise, without opening her mouth, started to pin the coat up again. It took a long time: she had to go from one shoulder to the next and even, at one moment, she had to bend down, almost to her knees, to pull the front of the coat down. Standing above her, submitting to her attentions, Madame Desforges wore the hard face of a mistress who is difficult to please. Happy at being able to subject the girl to this servant's work, she snapped out orders, watching Mouret's face for the least reaction.

'Put a pin there. No, no, not there, here, near the sleeve. Don't you understand anything? That's quite wrong, it's starting to go loose again. Careful, you're pricking me!'

Twice more, Mouret tried in vain to interrupt and put an end to this scene. His heart was beating faster, with the humiliation of his love; and he loved Denise all the more, touched with affection by her noble silence. Though the young woman's hands still shook a little, at being treated in this way in front of him, she accepted the requirements of her job with the proud resignation of a spirited girl. When Madame Desforges realized that they would not give themselves away, she looked for some other expedient and decided to be good to Mouret, showing him off as her lover. So, when the pins ran out:

'My dear, will you look in the ivory box on the dressing-table . . . Oh, no! Is it empty? Be a sweet and look on the mantelpiece in the bedroom, you know, by the mirror . . .'

She was making him at home, establishing him as a man who had slept there and who knew where the brushes and combs were kept. When he brought her back a handful of pins, she took them one by one, obliging him to stay standing next to her, looking at him and talking softly:

'I'm not a hunchback, am I? Give me your hand and feel the shoulders, just to see. Am I like that?'

Denise slowly looked up, paler than ever, and silently went back to pinning up the coat. Mouret could see only her heavy mass of blonde hair, twisted on the delicate nape of her neck, but the shudder that went through her seemed to tell him of the unhappiness and shame on her face. Now she would reject him, she would send him back to this woman who did not even conceal their affair from strangers. He felt his fists clench: he wanted to hit Henriette. How could he make her be quiet? How could he tell Denise that he adored her, that only she existed for him now, and that he would sacrifice all his old ephemeral attachments for her? A prostitute would not have behaved with the suggestive familiarity that this bourgeoise was adopting. He took away his hand and repeated:

'You are wrong to insist, Madame, since I myself agree that this garment is not right for you.'

One of the gas mantles was hissing and, in the humid, stifling air of the room, this hot breath was all one could hear. The mirrors on the wardrobe reflected bright patches of light on the red silk hangings, across which flickered the shadows of the two women. A flask of verbena, which someone had forgotten to close, gave off the vague, vanishing smell of fading flowers.

'There, Madame, that's all I can do,' Denise said at last, getting to her feet.

She felt exhausted. Twice she had stuck the pins into her hands, as though blinded, with a mist in front of her eyes. Was he part of this? Had he made her come, in revenge for her refusal, to show her that other women loved him? The thought made her blood run cold: she could never remember having needed so much courage, even at the worst times in her life, when she had been starving. It was nothing for her to be humiliated in that way, but to see him almost in another woman's arms, as if she were not even there!

Henriette was examining herself in the mirror. Once again, she erupted in cruel words.

'This is a joke, Mademoiselle. It fits less well than before. See how tight it is across the bust. I look like a wet nurse.'

At that, Denise, driven to the limit, made an unfortunate remark.

'Madame is a little plump. We can't make Madame's figure less plump.'

'Plump, plump!' said Henriette, also going pale. 'Now you're becoming insolent, young lady. Really! I advise you not to pass judgement on others.'

The pair of them, face to face and trembling, stared at one another. They were no longer lady and shop girl, merely women, as though made equal by their rivalry. One had violently torn off the coat and thrown it on a chair, while the other flung the last pins remaining in her hand on to the dressing-table without looking where they were going.

'What amazes me,' said Henriette, 'is that Monsieur Mouret will stand for such insolence. I did think, Monsieur, that you were more choosy with your staff.'

Denise had recovered her plucky calm, and replied gently:

'If Monsieur Mouret keeps me on, it is because he has nothing to reproach me with . . . I am ready to apologize to you, if he asks me to.'

Mouret was listening, mesmerized by this quarrel, unable to find the words to end it. He detested these rows between women, which harshly affronted his constant need for harmony and good manners. Henriette wanted to make him say something to condemn the girl and, since he remained silent, still wavering, she struck him with one last insult.

'Very well, Monsieur, if I have to endure the insults of your mistresses in my own home . . .! Some creature you picked up in the gutter . . .'

Two large tears sprang to Denise's eyes. For a long time, she had been holding them back, but her whole being flinched before this insult. When he saw her crying, in silent, desperate dignity, without striking back, Mouret waited no longer, his heart going out to her in a great wave of tenderness. He took her hands and stammered:

'Quickly, my child, go, go away and forget this house.'

Henriette, dumb with amazement, choked with anger, stared at them.

'One moment,' he said, folding the coat up himself. 'Take this garment with you. Madame can buy another one somewhere else. And don't cry, I beg you. You know how highly I esteem you.'

He accompanied her to the door and shut it behind her. She had not said a word, but a pink flush had risen to her cheeks and her eyes filled with fresh tears, tears of delicious sweetness.

Henriette was suffocating; she had taken out her handkerchief and was pressing it to her lips. This was the very opposite of what she had intended: she had fallen into her own trap and was now devastated at having pushed things too far because of the torments of her jealousy. To be abandoned for such a creature! To be despised in her presence! She felt it as more a blow to her pride than to her love.

'So, that's the girl you love?' she managed to say, when they were alone.

Mouret did not answer at once. He walked from the window to the door, trying to repress the violence of his feelings. Finally, he stopped and, very politely, in a voice that he wanted to sound cold, he said simply:

'Yes, Madame.'

The gas mantle was still hissing, in the stifling air of the room. Now there were no more dancing shadows across the reflections from the mirrors and the room seemed bare, as if it had returned to a mood of deep sadness. Henriette suddenly flung herself into a chair, twisting a handkerchief in her feverish hands and repeating through her sobs:

'My God, how miserable I am!'

He looked at her for a few seconds without moving. Then, quite calmly, he left. She wept alone in the silence among the pins scattered across the dressing-table and the floor.

When Mouret got back to the small drawing room, only Vallagnosc was still there, the Baron having gone to rejoin the ladies. Since his mind was still in some turmoil, he sat down at the back of the room on a sofa and his friend, seeing that he was not himself, kindly came and stood in front of him, to shield him from curious stares. At first, they looked at one another, without a word. Then Vallagnosc, who seemed inwardly to be enjoying Mouret's distress, eventually asked in his ironic tone:

'Are you having a good time?'

Mouret seemed not to understand at first, but when he recalled their previous conversations on the emptiness, the stupidity and the pointless pain of existence, he replied:

'Of course, I've never lived so intensely. Oh, my friend, don't mock, the shortest hours are those when one is tortured to death!'

He lowered his voice and went on merrily, behind the tears he had not properly wiped away:

'You know it all, don't you? The pair of them have just torn my heart to shreds. But, you know, it's good, the wounds that they leave are good, almost as good as a caress . . . I'm broken, I can't go on, but it doesn't matter, you can't believe how much I love life. Oh, I'll have her in the end, that child who rejects me!'

Vallagnosc said simply:

'And then?'

'Then? Why, I'll have her! Isn't that enough? I suppose you think you're strong because you refuse to be a fool and to suffer! You're just gullible, nothing more! Why don't you try wanting one, then possessing her at last! It compensates in a minute for all your suffering.'

But Vallagnosc was pretending to be even more pessimistic than he was. What was the point in working so hard, since money couldn't buy everything. Had it been him, he would have shut up shop and taken a nice rest as soon as he realized that with all those millions one couldn't even buy the woman one wanted! As he listened, Mouret became solemn, then started again emphatically, believing in the omnipotence of his own will:

'I want her, I'll have her! And if she does escape me, just you see what a place I'll build to recover from her. Oh, it'll be magnificent, it really will! You don't understand what I'm talking about, old chap. If you did, you would realize that action is its own reward. Doing, creating, struggling against harsh realities and either defeating them or being defeated – all of human joy and health are there!'

'It's just another way to drug oneself,' the other man murmured.

'Well, I'd rather be drugged . . . One way or the other, you have to die and I'd rather die of passion than of boredom!'

They were both laughing now, because this reminded them of their old arguments at school. Vallagnosc, in a languid voice, chose to point out the banality of everything, exhibiting a kind of bravado in his belief in the stagnation and emptiness of his life. Yes, the next day he would be bored at the Ministry as he had been the day before; in three years, he had had an increase of six hundred francs. He was now earning three thousand six hundred, not even enough to smoke a decent cigar; it was getting increasingly unsuitable and if he didn't kill himself, it was through simple laziness: he couldn't be bothered. Mouret brought up the subject of his marriage to Mademoiselle de Boves and he replied that, though the aunt obstinately refused to die, the match was to be concluded; at least, he thought so; the parents were agreed but he pretended not to have any will power in the matter. Why want or not want, when it never turned out as you hoped? For example, look at his father-in-law, who had expected Madame Guibal to be an indolent blonde, good for an hour's amusement, and whom the lady was now whipping along like an old horse being driven to death. While people thought he was busy inspecting the stud at Saint-Lô, in fact she was polishing him off in a little house he had rented for her in Versailles.

'He's happier than you are,' said Mouret.

'Oh, yes, that's for sure!' Vallagnosc declared. 'It could be that misbehaving is the only way to have fun.'

Mouret had recovered. He was thinking of getting away, but he didn't want his departure to look like flight. So, determined to take a cup of tea, he went back into the large drawing room with his friend, both of them joking and laughing. Baron Hartmann asked if the coat fitted at last, and without flinching, Mouret said that he had given up on it. There was a gasp. While Madame Marty hastened to pour out his tea, Madame de Boves accused shops of always making clothes too tight. In the end, he managed to sit down beside Bouthemont, who had not moved. Attention turned away from them and, in answer to Bouthemont's anxious questions, eager to learn his fate, Mouret did not wait to get into the street before informing him that the gentlemen on the board had decided to relinquish his services. Between each sentence, he drank a sip of tea, while insisting on his own distress. Oh, there had been an argument from which he was only just recovering, because he had left the room in a fury. But what could one do? He could not break off relations with the gentlemen over a simple matter of staff. Bouthemont, who had gone very pale, even had to thank him.

'This must be a dreadful coat,' Madame Marty observed. 'Henriette is still at it.'

As it happened, her prolonged absence was starting to embarrass everyone. But at that moment, Madame Desforges reappeared.

'Have you given up, too?' Madame de Boves asked merrily.

'What do you mean?'

'Because Monsieur Mouret told us that you couldn't fit into it.'

Henriette showed the greatest possible surprise.

'Monsieur Mouret was joking. The coat will do very well.'

She was smiling and seemed very calm. She must have bathed her eyelids, because they were fresh, with no redness. Even though her whole being was shuddering and bleeding still, she found the will to hide her torment behind the mask of her charming social persona. She offered Vallagnosc a sandwich with her usual laugh. Only the Baron, who knew her well, noticed the slight contraction of her lips and the dark fire that smouldered despite her in the depth of her eyes, and guessed what had just occurred.

'Good heavens, everyone to her taste!' said Madame de Boves, also accepting a sandwich. 'I know women who wouldn't buy a ribbon anywhere but in the *Louvre*. Others swear by the *Bon Marché* . . . It must be a matter of temperament.'

'The *Bon Marché* is so provincial,' said Madame Marty. 'And people jostle you so much in the *Louvre*.' The ladies had started on department stores again. Mouret had to give his opinion, so he came back to the middle of the circle, and pretended to be fair. The *Bon Marché* was an excellent firm. Solid, respectable; but the *Louvre* certainly had a more fashionable clientele.

'But I suppose you prefer *Au Bonheur des Dames*,' the Baron said with a smile.

'Yes,' Mouret said calmly. 'We like our customers.'

All the ladies agreed. That was it: it was like going on a spree at *Au Bonheur*, they felt constantly caressed by flattery, an enveloping adoration that entrapped the most upright among them. The shop's huge success came from this amorous seduction.

'By the way,' said Henriette, who was trying to appear as though she had nothing on her mind, 'what are you doing with my protégée, Monsieur Mouret? You know: Mademoiselle de Fontenailles.'

And, turning to Madame Marty, she added:

'A marchioness, my dear, a poor girl in dire straits.'

'And she's earning three francs a day sewing sample books,' said Mouret. 'I think I'm going to marry her off to one of my assistants.'

'Oh, what a dreadful thing!' Madame de Boves exclaimed.

He looked at her and said quite calmly:

'Why is that, Madame? Isn't it better for her to marry a fine, hard-working lad than to risk being picked up by some good-for-nothings on a street corner?'

Vallagnosc tried to interrupt with a joke.

'Don't encourage him, Madame, or you'll have him telling us that all the noble families in France should start selling cloth by the yard.'

'At least it would be a respectable fate for many of them,' said Mouret.

Eventually they did laugh, because the paradox seemed so ridiculous. He went on praising what he called the 'aristocracy of labour'. A slight blush had appeared on the cheeks of Madame de Boves, who was infuriated by the expedients to which her need reduced her, while Madame Marty, on the other hand, applauded, feeling full of remorse when she thought of her poor husband. Just at that moment, the servant introduced the teacher, who had come to look for her. He was more dried and desiccated than ever by hard work, in his threadbare, shiny top coat. After he had thanked Madame Desforges for mentioning him at the Ministry, he cast towards Mouret the terrified look of a man meeting the disease that will kill him. And he was amazed when the other man spoke to him.

'It's true, isn't it, Monsieur, that work leads to everything?'

'Work and savings,' he replied; and a faint shudder ran through him. 'Don't forget savings, Monsieur.'

Meanwhile, Bouthemont had remained motionless in his chair, Mouret's words still ringing in his ears. He got up at last and went over to whisper to Henriette:

'You know, he's just given me the sack. Oh, very kindly! But the devil knows, he'll regret it! I've just thought of a name, *Aux Quatre Saisons*, and I'll set up near the Opéra.'

She looked at him and her eyes darkened.

'Leave it to me. I'm with you. Wait.'

She led Baron Hartmann into the bay of a window. Without any preliminaries, she recommended Bouthemont, explaining that he was a young man who would revolutionize Paris in his turn when he could set himself up. When she mentioned backing for this new protégé, the Baron, though nothing surprised him any more, could not repress a gesture of alarm. This was the fourth young man of genius that she had entrusted to him and he was starting to feel ridiculous. But he did not refuse outright, because he found the idea of starting up a competitor to *Au Bonheur des Dames* quite pleasing. In banking, he had already hit on the notion of setting up competitors in this way, to discourage others. And, then, the adventure amused him. He promised to look into it.

'We must talk this evening,' Henriette whispered, coming back to

Bouthemont. 'Around nine o'clock, without fail . . . The Baron is ours.'

At that moment, the huge rooms filled with voices. Mouret who was still standing at the centre, surrounded by the ladies, had recovered his old charm. He was laughing and arguing that he did not overcharge for his clothes, but could show them the figures that would prove he was saving them thirty per cent. Baron Hartmann was watching him, seized again by the fraternal admiration of an old wencher. So! The duel was over, Henriette was floored and she was certainly not destined to be the one in Mouret's future. He had a mental image of the modest profile of the young woman he had seen as he came through the antechamber. There she was, patient, alone, and formidable in her gentle sweetness.

CHAPTER 12

It was on 26 September that they started work on the new façade of *Au Bonheur des Dames.* As he had promised, Baron Hartmann had got the project through at the last general meeting of the Crédit Immobilier. Finally, Mouret was close to realizing his dream: this façade that would extend along the Rue du Dix-Décembre was like the expansion of his fortune itself. He wanted to celebrate the laying of the first stone. He held a ceremony, gave presents to his sales staff and in the evening fed them on game and champagne. They observed his joyful mood on the site and the victorious gesture with which he sealed the stone with a tap of the trowel. For some weeks he had been uneasy, troubled by some nervous torment which he was not always able to conceal. This triumph brought a respite and a distraction from his pain. Throughout the afternoon, he seemed to have recovered the good spirits of a healthy man. But by dinner time, when he walked through the dining room to drink a glass of champagne with his employees, he once more seemed feverish, his smile forced and his features betraying the unadmitted pain that was eating him up. It was a relapse.

The following day in ladies' wear, Clara Prunaire tried to be unpleasant to Denise. She had noticed Colomban's bemused love for her, and thought she could make fun of the Baudus. While Marguerite was sharpening her pencil and waiting for customers, she said loudly to her:

'You know my lover opposite? I'm starting to feel sorry for him in that dark old shop where no one ever goes.'

'He's not so badly off,' Marguerite replied. 'He's going to marry the boss's daughter.'

'Well, I never!' Clara exclaimed. 'It would be fun, then, to snatch him. I'll do it, honest I will!'

She went on, pleased to sense Denise's indignation. Denise could forgive her anything, but at the idea of her cousin Geneviève dying, finished off by this cruelty, she was beside herself with anger. At that moment, a customer arrived and as Madame Aurélie had just gone down to the basement, she took on the management of the counter and called Clara over.

'Mademoiselle Prunaire, you would do better to look after this lady than to chatter.'

'I wasn't chattering.'

'Be quiet, would you. Look after this lady at once.'

Clara submissively resigned herself. When Denise laid down the law, without raising her voice, not one of them resisted. Her very gentleness had endowed her with absolute authority. For a moment, she walked around silently among the young ladies, who were looking serious again. Marguerite had gone back to sharpening the lead of her pencil, which kept breaking. She was the only one who still supported the under-buyer in her resistance to Mouret, shaking her head and not confessing to the child she had had by accident but announcing that if one suspected how much trouble could arise from doing something foolish, one would choose to behave.

'Are you losing your temper?' said a voice behind Denise.

Pauline was walking through the department and had witnessed the scene. She was smiling and spoke in a low voice.

'I must,' Denise answered, also in a whisper. 'I can't keep order among my charges otherwise.'

The other girl shrugged her shoulders.

'Forget it, you could be queen of us all, if you wanted.'

She still could not understand her friend's refusal. She had married Baugé at the end of August – a really stupid move, as she used to say cheerfully. Now the fearsome Bourdoncle treated her as a bungler, who was no good for trade any more. She was afraid that one fine day they would pack the two of them off to love each other somewhere else, because the gentlemen in the management had decreed that love was detestable and fatal for sales. It had reached the point that when she met Baugé in the store she would pretend not to know him. She had just had a scare because Old Jouve almost caught her talking to her husband behind a pile of towels.

'Look! He's followed me,' she said, after giving Denise a lively account of this adventure. 'Can you see him sniffing after me with that great nose of his!'

Jouve was indeed just coming out of the lace department, in a neat white tie, eyes peeled for any misdemeanour. But when he saw Denise, he straightened up and went by with a friendly nod.

'Saved!' Pauline muttered. 'You made him change his mind about that all right, dear. By the way, if something unpleasant did happen, you'd speak up for me, wouldn't you? Come, now, no need to look all wide-eyed innocence. Everyone knows that a word from you could turn the whole place upside down.'

She hurried back to her department. Denise was blushing, troubled by these well-meaning allusions. What's more, it was true. She had a vague notion of her power from the flattery around her. When Madame Aurélie came back and found the department quiet and active under the watchful eye of her deputy, she gave her a friendly smile. She was even cooling towards Mouret, to show more and more amiability towards someone who might, one fine morning, covet her own job as buyer. Denise's reign had begun.

Only Bourdoncle was adamant. First of all, the silent war that he continued to wage against the young woman was based on a natural antipathy. He hated her for her sweetness and charm. Then he opposed her as a fatal influence that would endanger the firm, should Mouret ever succumb. The boss's commercial intelligence, he thought, must collapse in the midst of this inappropriate tenderness: what they had gained through women would be lost through this one woman. They all left him cold, he treated them all with the contempt of a man without passion whose vocation was to live off them, and whose last illusions had gone when he saw them naked and exposed for what they were, in the base dealings of his trade. Instead of being intoxicated by the scent of seventy thousand customers, it gave him dreadful headaches and he would beat his mistresses as soon as he returned home. What most disturbed him about this little salesgirl who had gradually become so powerful, was that he could not believe she was disinterested and honest in her refusal. As far as he was concerned, she was playing a part, and the most subtle of parts, because if she had succumbed on the first day, Mouret would no doubt have forgotten her by the next; while, by denying herself to him, she had aroused his desires and was driving him mad, making him capable of any idiocy. A debauched woman, a knowing whore would not have acted any differently from this innocent girl. So Bourdoncle could not see her, with her bright eyes, her sweet face and her whole straightforward attitude, without now being seized by real fear, as though he had before him a disguised cannibal, the dark enigma of womanhood, death wearing the shape of a virgin. How could he defeat the tactics of this false innocent? All he wanted was to learn her wiles so that he could expose them in the plain light of day. She was bound to make some mistake, he would catch her with one of her lovers and she would be dismissed again, so that the store could once more function like a fine and well-made machine.

'Keep a look out, Monsieur Jouve,' Bourdoncle kept telling the inspector. 'I'll reward you personally.'

But Jouve's heart was not in the work because he had experience of women and thought he might take the side of this child, who could be the sovereign mistress tomorrow. Though he no longer dared touch her, he still found her devilishly pretty. In the old days, his colonel had killed himself for just such a lass, with an unexceptional face, delicate and modest, but able to captivate a man's heart with a single look.

'I'm keeping my eyes open all the time,' he said. 'But I swear to you, I can't find anything.'

However, the stories went about, a string of dreadful gossip, behind the flattery and the respect that Denise felt all round her. At the moment, every one was saying that Hutin had once been her lover; they couldn't swear that the affair was still going on, just that they suspected them of seeing one another from time to time. And Deloche too was sleeping with her, they were constantly meeting in dark corners and talking for hours. It was really disgraceful!

'So, is there nothing about the chief assistant in silks and nothing about the young man in lace?' Bourdoncle kept asking.

'No, Monsieur, nothing so far,' said Inspector Jouve.

Deloche was the one with whom Bourdoncle had the most hope of catching Denise out. One morning, he had seen them himself laughing together in the basement. Meanwhile, he treated the young woman as an equal adversary, because he no longer despised her, but thought her strong enough even to sink him, for all his ten years' service, if he lost the match. He would always end by saying: 'I suggest you look particularly at the young man in lace, they're always together. If you catch them, call me, I'll take care of the rest.'

Mouret, meanwhile, was in anguish. Was it possible for this child to torment him so? He could still see her first arriving at *Au Bonheur des Dames* with her heavy shoes, her thin black dress and her unkempt look. She stammered, everyone used to make fun of her and even he had found her ugly to begin with. Ugly! Now she could overcome him with a look, she was bathed in radiance whenever he looked at her! Then there had been the time when she was at the bottom of the pile, rejected, teased and treated by him like some curious animal. For months he had tried to see how such a young woman would develop and had been amused by the experiment, not realizing that his heart was at stake. Bit by bit, she had grown in stature and become a force to reckon with. Perhaps he had loved her from the first minute, even at the time when he thought he felt only pity. Yet he had not been captivated by her until their walk under the chestnuts in the Tuileries Gardens. His life had begun then, hearing the laughter of a group of little girls and the distant tinkling of a fountain, while she was walking beside him in the warm dusk, saying nothing. Since then, he knew nothing, his fever had risen constantly and all his flesh and his being had been hers. Was it possible, a girl like that? Now when she appeared, the rustling of her dress seemed so powerful that he reeled from it.

He had resisted for a long time and sometimes still rebelled, wanting to free himself from this ridiculous obsession. What was it in her that could entrap him in this way? Had he not seen her without shoes on her feet? Hadn't he taken her on almost out of charity? If she had at least been one of those magnificent creatures that turn every head –

but this scrap of a girl, this nothing! The truth was, she had one of those docile faces about which you couldn't say anything in particular. She probably wasn't very bright either, because he remembered her bad start on the sales floor. Then, after each of his rages, there was a revived rush of passion in him, like a sacred terror at having insulted his idol. She possessed everything that he found good in a woman: courage, gaiety, simplicity; and from her sweetness and softness rose a charm with the penetrating subtlety of a scent. You could not avoid seeing her and being near her as with any other woman, then soon the charm would work with a slow and invincible power – and if she deigned to smile, you were hers for ever. At that moment everything in her white face would smile: her blue eyes, her cheeks, her dimpled chin; and her heavy blonde hair would seem to light up as well, with a regal, conquering beauty. He would admit defeat: she was as intelligent as she was beautiful, her intelligence coming from the best of her being. Some education may have rubbed off on the other salesgirls in his shop, giving them that brittle varnish of women who have risen above their class, but she had no pretentious manners, retaining the charm and savour of her origins. The most far-reaching business ideas, born of practical experience, sprouted behind that narrow forehead, its clean lines revealing her will power and love of order. And he would have clasped his two hands together to beg her pardon for having blasphemed, in his moments of rebellion.

So why did she refuse him with such obstinacy? He had begged her twenty times, increasing his offers, offering money, lots of money. Then he decided that she must be ambitious, so he promised to appoint her buyer as soon as a department had a vacancy. But she refused, and went on refusing! It was incredible to him, a struggle in which his desire was reaching fever pitch. The situation seemed impossible: this child would eventually give in, because he had always considered a woman's virtue as something relative. He could see no other goals because everything was vanishing into this need to have her in his apartment at last, to sit her on his knees and kiss her lips; and before this vision he felt the blood pound in his veins and was left trembling, overwhelmed by his powerlessness.

From now on, his days drifted past in the same painful obsession.

The image of Denise got up with him in the morning. He had dreamed about her in the night and she followed him to the large desk in his study where he signed bills and money orders from nine to ten, a task that he carried out mechanically without her presence ever leaving him, still saying no in her calm manner. Then at ten o'clock, the board meeting, more like a cabinet meeting, a gathering of the twelve investors in the business, which he had to preside over. They talked about matters of internal organization, they considered purchases and decided on displays; and she was there still, he could hear her soft voice in the midst of the figures and could see her clear smile in the most complicated financial situations. After the meeting she accompanied him on his daily inspection of the departments, came back with him in the afternoon to the director's study, and stayed near his chair from two to four while he welcomed a host of visitors, manufacturers from all over France, major industrialists, bankers and inventors – a constant coming and going of wealth and intellect, a crazy dance of millions of francs, brief discussions in which the most costly ventures on the Paris market were mulled over. If he should forget her for an instant while deciding about the success or failure of a firm, he would find her standing there, with a tug on his heartstrings; his voice would fade and he would wonder what was the use of all this money being stirred around, since she did not want him. Finally, when five o'clock struck, he had to sign the post and the mechanical movements of his hand began again, even as she rose above him, dominating him more than ever, taking him over entirely to keep him for herself through the solitary and passionate hours of the night. Then, the next day, the same round began again, days that were so active and full of immense labour . . . yet the slender shadow of a child was enough to devastate them with anguish.

But it was most of all during his daily inspection of the shop that he felt his unhappiness. To have built this huge contraption, to reign over such a world and to be in such torment, because a mere slip of a girl doesn't want you! He despised himself, borne down by the fever and the shame of his sickness. Some days, he would feel disgusted by his power and experience only nausea from one end of the store to the other. At other times, he wanted to extend his empire and make it so great that she might perhaps give in, out of admiration and awe.

First of all, down in the basement, he would stop by the chute. It was still in the Rue Neuve-Saint-Augustin, but they had had to widen it, so that it was now a river bed over which the continual stream of goods flowed with the mighty rush of a torrent. There were deliveries from all round the world, rows of lorries from all the railway stations, and a ceaseless unloading, a flood of boxes and bales pouring under the ground, swallowed up by this insatiable building. He watched the cascade falling into his place and considered that he was one of the masters of the public wealth, that he held the fate of French manufacturing in his hands, and that he could not buy a kiss from one of his salesgirls.

Then he went into the reception, which now occupied the part of the basement running along the Rue Monsigny. Twenty tables were lined up there, in the pale light from the basement windows, and a whole army of clerks was hurrying around, emptying the boxes, checking the goods and marking them up; and you could still hear the endless rumbling of the chute next door, drowning the sound of voices. Heads of departments would stop him, there were problems to solve, orders to confirm. The basement was filling up with the soft glow of satin, the whiteness of sheets, in a mighty unpacking where furs mixed with lace and novelty goods with oriental drapes. He would slowly walk among these disordered riches, piled up in their raw state. Upstairs, they would light up on the displays, release a surge of money across the counters, carried off as soon as they arrived by the raging current of sales that swept through the store. Mouret would consider how he had offered the girl silks, velvet. Anything that she wanted, by the handful, in these huge piles, and that she had refused with a little shake of her blonde head.

After that, he would go to the other end of the basement, to make his habitual inspection of the despatch department. Endless corridors stretched out, lit by gaslight, and to right and left the storerooms, behind their wooden pickets, were like subterranean shops, a whole market quarter, with haberdashery, lingerie, gloves and knick-knacks sleeping in the dark. Further on was one of the three heaters, and further still, a fire warden's post guarding the main gas metre, enclosed in its metal cage. In despatches, he would find the sorting tables already piled high with parcels, packets and boxes, constantly brought down in baskets, while Campion, the head of department, would tell him how the work was progressing. Meanwhile, the twenty men under Campion's orders would be sorting the parcels into compartments, each of which bore the name of a quarter of Paris; from here, the boys would take them up to the vans lined up along the pavement. There were cries, names of streets called out, instructions shouted, all the din and hurry of a steamship about to raise anchor. For a moment he would stay motionless, watching this discharging of the goods which he had just seen the shop swallowing up at the other end of the basement: the vast current would end here, emerging at this point into the street, after depositing gold in the tills. His eyes glazed over. This colossal despatching had no importance any longer, he had only the sense of journeying, the idea of departing for distant lands and leaving everything, if she insisted on saying no.

So he went back up and continued his inspection, talking and getting more excited, unable to take his mind off her. On the second floor, he visited the mail order department, seeking a quarrel and silently infuriated by the perfect operation of this machine that he himself had set in motion. This department was one that increased daily in importance; it now needed two hundred employees, some of them opening, sorting and reading the letters which arrived from the provinces and abroad, while others were putting the goods that the letter-writers requested into pigeonholes. The number of letters was increasing so fast that they no longer kept count of them; instead they would weigh them, up to a hundred pounds a day. Feverishly he would march through the three rooms occupied by the department, interrogating Levasseur, the manager, on the weight of the mail: eighty pounds, sometimes ninety, and on Mondays a hundred. The figure kept rising and he should have been delighted. But he was left shuddering at the noise that the nearby team of packers was making nailing down cases. He trudged round the shop in vain: his obsession was fixed in his head and as he watched his power unfold, the operation of the mechanism and the army of staff displayed before him, he felt only the more strongly the insult of his powerlessness. Orders were coming in from all over Europe, it took a special van from the post office to bring all the mail, and she said no, she still said no.

He would go down and visit the central counting-house, where four cashiers kept the two giant safes through which, in the previous year, eighty-eight million francs had passed. He glanced at the office for checking invoices, which employed twenty-five men, selected from among the most serious members of staff. He went into the clearing-house, a service employing thirty-five young men, apprentice accountants who had to check the debit notes and calculate the percentages for the sales staff. He went back to the counting-house, got annoyed at the sight of the safes and walked around among these millions, driven mad by the senselessness of it all. She said no, still no.

Still no, in every department, in the sales counters, in the halls, everywhere in the shop! He went from silks to drapery, from linens to lace, climbing up from one floor to another, stopping on the suspended walkways, carrying out his inspection in obsessive, painful detail. The firm had grown too large, he had added this department, and then this one, he ruled over this new domain, his empire was spreading to this industry, his latest conquest; and it was no, still no, despite everything. Now his staff could populate a small town: he had fifteen hundred sales assistants, and a thousand other employees of every kind, including forty inspectors and seventy cashiers; the kitchens alone employed thirty-two men; there were ten people in advertising, three hundred and fifty porters in livery, twenty-four permanent fire wardens. In the stables – regal stables, in the Rue Monsigny, opposite the shops – there were one hundred and forty-five horses, a wealth of carriage teams that were already famous. The first four carriages that had upset the local shopkeepers when the store still only occupied the corner of Place Gaillon, had gradually risen to no less than sixty-two: small handcarts, one-horse carriages, and heavy two-horse carriages. They were constantly going backwards and forwards across Paris, driven in a dignified manner by coachmen in black and bearing the gold and purple insignia of *Au Bonheur des Dames*. They even went beyond the city limits and into the suburbs: you could meet them in the sunken lanes of Bicêtre, along the banks of the Marne and even in the shady roads of the Saint-Germain forest; sometimes, at the end of a silent, sunlit avenue in the middle of nowhere, you would see one appear and go past at a trot with its magnificent animals, exhibiting the garish advertising on its varnished side-panels to the mysterious peace of nature. He dreamed of sending them further still, to the nearby *départements*, and would have liked to hear them trotting along all the roads in France from one frontier to another. But he did not even go down to visit his horses, whom he loved. What was the point in this conquest of the world, since it was no, always no?

Now in the evening when he reached Lhomme's desk, he still looked out of habit at the takings, written on a card that the cashier stuck on an iron spike beside him. The figure seldom fell below a hundred thousand francs and sometimes rose to eight or nine hundred thousand on days of special events; and this figure no longer sounded in his ear like a clarion call; he regretted looking at it, taking away only bitterness, hatred and contempt for money.

But Mouret's sufferings were to increase. He became jealous. One morning, in the boardroom, before the meeting, Bourdoncle dared to suggest to him that the little girl in ladies' wear was laughing at him.

'How do you mean?' he asked, going very pale.

'Oh, yes! She actually has lovers here.'

Mouret forced a smile.

'I don't think about her any more, my good fellow. You can tell me . . . So who are these lovers?'

'Hutin, they tell me, and another salesman in lace, Deloche, that tall dunce of a lad. I'm not swearing to it, I haven't seen them. But they say it stands out a mile.'

There was a silence. Mouret pretended to be sorting some papers on his desk to hide the trembling of his hands. At length, without looking up, he said:

'We'll need proof; try to get me proof . . . Oh, as far as I'm concerned, as I said, I couldn't care less, because she has started to get on my nerves. But we can't stand for such things going on in the store.'

Bourdoncle replied simply:

'Don't worry, you'll have proof one of these days. I'm keeping an eye open.'

So Mouret finally lost all peace of mind. He did not dare to return to this conversation, but lived in constant expectation of a catastrophe that would break his heart. His agony made him fearful and the whole shop shook with fear. He scorned to hide behind Bourdoncle and carried out the executions himself, out of some bitter, nervous urge, feeling relief at the abuse of his power, that power which could do nothing for the satisfaction of his one, sole desire. Each of his inspections became a massacre and the staff did not see him appear nowadays without a shudder of panic going from one counter to the next. As it happened, they were just reaching the dead season of winter and he was clearing out the departments, piling up his victims, pushing all of them into the street. His first thought was to expel Hutin and Deloche; then he realized that if he did not keep them, he would never know anything. So the others paid for them, no one felt safe. In the evening, when he was alone, his eyes filled with tears.

One day, more than the rest, terror reigned. An inspector thought he saw Mignot in gloves stealing. There were always odd-looking girls lurking around by his counter and one of them had just been arrested, her hips laden and her bust stuffed with sixty pairs of gloves. After that, they organized a watch and the inspector caught Mignot in the act, helping a tall blonde in her tricks, a former sales assistant from the *Louvre* who had ended walking the street. The operation was simple: he pretended to be trying gloves on her, waited until she had taken her fill, then took her to the cash desk where she paid for one pair. That day, Mouret was there. Usually, he would rather not get mixed up in this sort of scandal, which quite often happened – because, despite the operation of the well-tuned machine, a great deal of anarchy reigned in some departments of *Au Bonheur des Dames* and not a week went by without a member of staff being sacked for stealing. Even the management preferred to hush these thefts up as much as possible, considering it unnecessary to bring in the police and expose one of the fatal drawbacks of large stores. However, that day, Mouret needed to lose his temper and he set about handsome Mignot, who was shaking with fear, his face ashen and contorted.

'I ought to call for a constable,' he yelled, in the midst of the other sales assistants. 'But tell me, who is this woman? I swear, I'll send for the police commissioner if you don't tell me the truth!'

They had taken the woman away and two salesgirls were undressing her. Mignot stammered:

'Monsieur, I've never seen her before . . . She is the one who came . . .'

'Don't lie to me!' Mouret interrupted, louder than ever. 'And there's no one here who warned us! You're all in it, I swear you are! This is highway robbery, we're being stripped, pillaged and sacked! It's reached the point where you can't trust anyone to leave the store without searching their pockets!'

There were murmurs around. The three or four customers who were buying gloves were astonished and alarmed by it all.

'Be quiet!' Mouret shouted again. 'Or else I'll clear the shop!'

Bourdoncle had run across, concerned at the prospect of a scene. He whispered a few words in Mouret's ear: the matter was becoming more and more serious, and he persuaded him to take Mignot into the inspectors' office, a room on the ground floor near the Gaillon entrance. The woman was there, calmly putting her corset back on. She had just named Albert Lhomme. Mignot, questioned again, lost his head and started to sob: it wasn't his fault, it was Albert who would send him his mistresses; at first he would just help them a bit, letting them take advantage of bargains; then, when they eventually started stealing, he was already too deeply compromised to inform the gentlemen upstairs. And the latter learned about a whole series of extraordinary thefts: goods taken by girls who would go off and fasten them under their skirts in the luxurious lavatories near the buffet, among the green plants; purchases that a salesman would 'forget' to call out at a cash desk when he took a customer there, then sharing the price with the cashier; right down to fake 'returned goods', items which they would say had been brought back so that they could pocket the fictitiously reimbursed money; and not counting the classic theft, packets taken out at night under an overcoat, rolled around the waist or even hanging down the legs. In the past fourteen months, thanks to Mignot and, no doubt, other sales assistants whom they refused to name, Albert's cash desk had thus seen all sorts of unsavoury dealings and flagrant misdemeanours, involving amounts of money that would never be known for certain.

Meanwhile, the news had spread round every department. Those with uneasy consciences trembled, while those more certain of their own honesty still dreaded a general sweep of the broom. Albert had been seen vanishing into the inspectors' office. Then Lhomme went in, gasping for breath, his face flushed and his neck already knotted with apoplexy. After that, Madame Aurélie herself was called and she, holding her head high in the face of the insult, had the fat, puffy, pallid features of a wax mask. The inquiry lasted a long time and no one knew the precise details. They said that the buyer in ladies' wear had given her son a clout that would knock his head backwards and that the father, that decent old chap, was weeping, while the boss, quite unlike his usual, charming self, was swearing like a fishwife and was determined to hand the guilty parties over to the courts. But in the end they hushed it up. Only Mignot was sacked at once. Albert did not disappear until two days later; no doubt his mother had pleaded for the family not to be dishonoured by immediate expulsion. But the terror haunted the place for several days more, because after this scene, Mouret had taken to walking from one end of the shop to the other, with a fearful look, hacking down anyone who even dared to look up at him.

'You, Monsieur! What are you doing there, counting flies? Go to the cash desk!'

Finally, the day came when the storm broke even over the head of Hutin. Favier, who had been appointed under-buyer, was eating away at the buyer in order to dislodge him. It was his usual tactic of sly reports to the management and taking advantage of opportunities to catch the head of department making mistakes. So one morning as Mouret was walking through silks, he stopped, surprised at seeing Favier changing the labels on a sale of black velvet.

'Why are you lowering the prices?' he asked. 'Who told you to do that?'

The under-buyer, who had been making a lot of fuss about this job, as though trying to attract the boss's attention as he went past, realizing what would happen, replied with an air of false astonishment:

'But, it was Monsieur Hutin, Monsieur.'

'Monsieur Hutin! So where is this Monsieur Hutin?'

When the buyer had come up from reception, where an assistant went to fetch him, there was a heated debate. What! Was he putting prices down on his own initiative! But he seemed quite astonished himself, since he had only mentioned the reduction to Favier without giving any definite instruction. So the latter took on the pained expression of an employee who finds himself obliged to contradict his superior – though of course he was happy to take the blame if it was a question of getting him out of a tight spot. Suddenly, things got worse.

'Do you understand, Monsieur Hutin!' Mouret shouted. 'I've never put up with people doing such things of their own accord. Only the management decides the price of goods.'

He went on, in a harsh voice, making some cruel remarks, much to the surprise of the assistants, because normally such discussions took place in private and in any case this was something that could indeed be the result of a misunderstanding. They could feel that he had something like a secret grudge. So he had finally caught him out, that Hutin who was assumed to be Denise's lover! He could relieve himself a bit, by forcing the man to acknowledge that he was the master! And he blew the event up, eventually insinuating that the lowering of the price might disguise some dishonest intention.

'Monsieur,' Hutin kept saying. 'I meant to suggest this reduction to you. It's necessary, as you know, because this velvet isn't selling.'

Mouret cut him short with one last wounding remark.

'Very well, Monsieur. We'll look into the matter. But don't do it again, if you want to keep working here.'

He turned his back on them. Hutin, dazed and furious, could find no one but Favier to express his feelings to and swore to him that he would throw his resignation in that creature's face. Then he stopped talking about resignation and simply went over all the worst accusations of the sales assistants against the management. Favier, his eyes bright, defended himself with a great show of sympathy. He had to answer, didn't he? And then, how could anyone expect such a fuss over nothing? What was the matter with the boss lately to make him such a pain in the neck?

'Oh, everyone knows what's the matter with him,' said Hutin. 'Is it my fault if that tart in ladies' wear is driving him up the wall! Yes, yes, old chap, that's what's behind it all. He knows that I've slept with her and doesn't like the idea. Or else, she's trying to get me thrown out, because I embarrass her. I tell you this: she'll know all about it, if I get my hands on her.'

Two days later, Hutin had gone in person upstairs to the dressmakers' workshop under the roof to instruct one of the girls, when he got a bit of a shock at seeing Denise and Deloche leaning on a window sill at one end of a corridor and so engrossed in some private conversation that they did not even turn round. He had just got the idea of surprising them when he noticed that Deloche was weeping. On the way down, he met Bourdoncle and Jouve on the stairs and told them some story about a fire extinguisher with its door apparently missing: this would ensure that they went up and came across the pair. Bourdoncle was the first to find them. He stopped in his tracks and told Jouve to go and look for the director, while he stayed there. Jouve had to obey, but was very upset at having to become involved in such a business.

This was an obscure corner of the vast world inhabited by the people of *Au Bonheur des Dames*. You reached it by a maze of stairways and corridors. The workshops occupied the attic space, a succession of low, mansarded rooms, lit by broad bays set in the zinc roof and furnished solely with long tables and big iron stoves. Here, there were lines of seamstresses, lacemakers, upholsterers and dressmakers, who lived in winter and summer in stifling heat, surrounded by the smell peculiar to their craft; and you had to walk the whole length of the aisle, turn left after the dressmakers and go up five steps before coming to this out-of-the-way bit of corridor. The occasional customer brought here by a salesman for an order, would pant for breath, exhausted and fearful, with the sensation that she had been going round in circles for hours and was a hundred miles from the pavement.

Denise had already found Deloche waiting for her several times. As the under-buyer, she was in charge of relations between the department and the workshop, where they only made models and did repairs; at any time, she might come up with an order. He would wait for this, invent some excuse and set off after her, then pretend to be surprised when he met her at the door of the dressmakers' shop. Eventually, she would laugh about it, as though these meetings were agreed. The corridor ran alongside the reservoir, a huge metal cube containing sixty thousand litres of water; there was another, of equal capacity, on the roof, which you could get to up an iron ladder. For a moment, Deloche would talk, leaning one shoulder against the reservoir and as ever resting his large frame, which was bent with tiredness. There were singing sounds of water, mysterious sounds which resonated musically through the sheet metal. Despite the deep silence, Denise would turn around anxiously, thinking she had seen a shadow pass over the bare walls, which were painted a light yellow. But soon they were drawn to the window; they would lean on the sill, absorbed in their laughter and chatting endlessly about memories of their childhood home. Below them, they could see the vast glazed roof of the central gallery, a lake of glass enclosed by distant rooftops as though between rocky shores. And beyond that they could only see the sky, an expanse of sky which cast the reflection of its passing clouds and the soft blue of its firmament on the sleeping water of the window panes.

That day, Deloche happened to be talking about Valognes.

'I was six years old and my mother would take me in a cart to the town market. It's at least thirteen kilometres you know; we had to leave Briquebec at five o'clock . . . It's lovely, where we live. Do you know it?'

'Yes, I do,' Denise answered slowly, staring into the distance. 'I went there once, but I was quite small. Roads, with grass on either side, isn't that right? And, here and there, sheep in pairs, pulling on the ropes that tethered them.'

There was a silence, then she carried on, with a faint smile:

'Now, we have straight roads for miles and miles, between shady trees. We have pastures surrounded by hedges that are higher than I am, with horses and cows in them . . . We have a little stream and the water is very cold, under the bushes, in a place I know well.'

'Just like us, just like us!' Deloche cried in delight. 'There's nothing but grass and everyone fences in his piece with hawthorns and elm trees and they're at home and it's all green – ah, a green that you don't find in Paris! Oh, heavens, how I used to play in the sunken lane, on the left, coming down from the mill!'

Their voices faded away and they stayed staring on the sunlit lake of the glass roof, lost in thought. They saw a mirage rising out of this dazzling expanse of water, pastures stretching to infinity, the Cotentin moistened by the breath of the ocean and bathed in a luminous mist that melted the horizon to a delicate watercolour grey. Down below, beneath the huge iron frame, in the silk hall, there was the rumbling of sales, the shuddering of the machine at work. The whole house vibrated with the trampling of the crowd, the haste of the assistants and the life of the thirty thousand people pressed against one another down there. And they, carried away by their dreams, sensing that deep, dull sound that made the roofs tremble, thought they were hearing the sea wind blowing over the grass and shaking the great trees.

'My God, Mademoiselle Denise!' Deloche stammered. 'Why are you so unkind to me? I love you so much!'

There were tears in his eyes and when she tried to stop him with a gesture, he went on earnestly:

'No, no, let me say this once more. We would get on so well together. You always have something to talk about when you come from the same part of the world.'

He was choking and she at last managed to say gently:

'You're not being sensible, you promised me that you wouldn't talk about this. It's impossible. I feel a lot of affection for you because you're a really decent boy, but I want to stay free.'

'Yes, yes, I know,' he said, in a hoarse voice. 'You don't love me. Oh, you can say it! And I understand, there's nothing lovable about me. Why, there's only been one good moment in my life, that evening when I met you in Joinville, do you remember? For an instant under the trees, when it was so dark, I thought your arm was trembling and I was silly enough to think . . .'

Once again, she cut him short. Her sharp ears had just heard Bourdoncle's and Jouve's steps at the end of the corridor.

'Listen, there's someone walking.'

'No,' he said, stopping her from leaving the window. 'It's in the tank: there are always extraordinary noises coming out of it, you'd think there was a crowd of people inside.'

He went on shyly with his loving complaints, but she was not listening any more, but daydreaming at this soft talk of love and looking across the roofs of *Au Bonheur des Dames*. To left and right of the glass-roofed gallery, other galleries and halls shone in the sun, between gables with windows symmetrically aligned like the wings of an army barracks. Metal frames, ladders and bridges rose up, standing out in lacy patterns against the blue of the sky, while the chimney from the kitchens gave out a thick factory smoke and the square water tank, held up by cast-iron pillars, took on the peculiar look of some barbarous structure, raised up to this height by the pride of some man. In the distance, Paris rumbled.

When Denise came back from these spaces and from this extension of the store in which her thoughts wandered as though in some lonely place, she noticed that Deloche had taken hold of her hand. His face looked so devastated that she did not pull it back.

'Forgive me,' he murmured. 'It's over now. I should be too unhappy if you were to punish me by taking away your friendship. I swear to you that I wanted to talk about other things. I had told myself that I would understand the situation and behave sensibly.'

His tears were flowing again and he tried to stop his voice trembling.

'Because, at last, I know my fate in life. My luck is not going to change now. Beaten there, beaten in Paris, beaten everywhere. I have been here for four years and I'm still the last in the department. So I wanted to tell you not to feel sorry because of me. I shan't trouble you. Try to be happy, love someone else . . . Yes, I should be glad. If you are happy, I am. It will be a happiness for me.'

He could not go on. As if to seal his promise, he had put his lips on the young woman's hand, kissing it with the humble kiss of a slave. She was very touched and said simply, with a tender affection that moderated the pity in the words: 'My poor boy!'

But they shuddered and turned round. Mouret was standing there.

For the past ten minutes, Jouve had been looking through the shop for the director. He was on the site of the new façade in the Rue du Dix-Décembre. Every day he spent long hours here, trying to interest himself in the work which he had dreamed of for so long. This was his refuge against all torments, amid the builders who were setting up the corners in shaped stone and the metal workers putting down the girders for the framework of the building. Already the façade had emerged from the ground, with an outline of the huge porch, the bays on the first floor and a sketchy outline of a palace. He climbed the ladders, discussed the ornamentation (which had to be quite new) with the architect, stepped over ironwork and bricks and went down into the cellars; and the panting of the steam engine, the tick-tack of the winches, the banging of hammers and the din made by this tribe of workmen in this great cage surrounded by a fence of echoing planks, managed to dull his senses for a moment. He emerged white with plaster and black with iron filings, his feet spattered by water from the taps, so little cured of his sickness that the pain would return and beat his heart with louder and louder blows as the clatter of the building site faded behind him. On this particular day, something had cheered him up: he was excited by looking in a sketchbook at the drawings of the mosaics and enamelled terracotta designs that were to decorate the frieze, when Jouve came to fetch him, breathless and very annoyed at having to dirty his topcoat among all these materials. To begin with, he shouted that whatever it was could wait; then, at a quiet word from the inspector, he followed him, trembling, entirely caught up in his obsession again. Nothing existed, the façade had crumbled before being put up; what use was this supreme triumph of his pride, if the sole name of a woman, whispered softly, could torment him so!

Upstairs, Bourdoncle and Jouve thought it wise to disappear. Deloche had fled. Only Denise stayed face to face with Mouret, paler than usual, but looking him frankly in the eye.

'Mademoiselle, please follow me,' he said in a hard voice.

She followed him and they went down two floors, passing through furniture and carpets, without a word. When he was in front of his office, he opened the door wide.

'Go in, Mademoiselle.'

He closed the door behind them and walked over to his desk. The director's new office was more luxurious than the old one, the rep had been replaced by a hanging of green velvet, an ivory-encrusted bookcase occupied a whole side, but there was nothing on the other walls except the portrait of Madame Hédouin, a young woman with a handsome, calm face, smiling in her gilt frame.

'Mademoiselle,' he said at last, trying to maintain an attitude of cold severity. 'There are things that we cannot tolerate. Proper behaviour is essential . . .'

He paused, looking for the right words, so as not to give way to the anger that was rising inside him. What! That was the boy she loved, that miserable salesman, the laughing-stock of his department! She preferred the meanest and most clumsy lad of all to him, the master! He had seen them, he had seen her letting him hold her hand and the boy covering it with kisses.

'I've been very kind to you, Mademoiselle,' he said, making a further effort. 'I did not expect that this would be my reward.'

Denise's eyes, as soon as she came in, had been drawn to the portrait of Madame Hédouin and, upset as she was, she was still preoccupied by it. Whenever she went into the director's office, her eyes met those of this painted lady. She was somewhat intimidated by her, yet she felt that she was very kind. This time, she seemed to find her somehow protective.

'Indeed, Monsieur,' she said softly. 'I was wrong to stop and talk, and I apologize for that mistake. The young man comes from the same part of the country as I do.'

'I'll dismiss him!' Mouret yelled, putting all his pain into this furious cry.

And, giving way to his feelings and forgetting that he was a director telling off a salesgirl who had broken the rules, he launched into a violent tirade. Was she not ashamed? A young girl like herself, succumbing to such a creature! Then he started to make dreadful accusations, suggesting that she had been with Hutin and others as well, in such a rush of words that she could not even protest. But he was going to make a clean sweep, he would kick out the lot of them. Instead of the severe reprimand that he had decided to give her, as he walked behind Jouve, he was behaving with jealous fury.

'Yes, your lovers! They told me and I was stupid enough not to believe them. I was the only one! The only one!'

Denise gasped for breath, horrified, as she listened to these frightful reproaches. At first she did not understand. My God! Did he think she was a fallen woman? At one particularly harsh word, she started to walk towards the door, saying nothing. And when he made a gesture to stop her, she said: 'No, Monsieur. I am leaving. If you believe what you are saying, I do not want to remain a second longer in this house.'

He dashed in front of the door.

'At least, defend yourself! Say something!'

She stood there, bolt upright, in icy silence. For a long time he plied her with questions, growing increasingly anxious; and once again the silent dignity of this virgin was like the cunning ruse of a woman who knew just how to manipulate a man's passion. She could not have played a part that would throw him at her feet, more than ever torn by doubt, more than ever anxious to be convinced.

'Come, now, you say he is from your part of the world. Perhaps that is where you met. Swear to me that nothing has passed between you.'

Then, since she persisted in her silence and still wanted to open the door and leave, he finally lost his head, in a supreme outburst of misery.

'My God! I love you, I love you. Why do you enjoy tormenting me so? Surely you can see that nothing more exists, that the people I am talking about only affect me because of you and that from now on you are the only person who matters to me in the world . . . I thought you were jealous, so I sacrificed my own enjoyment. They told you that I had mistresses; well, I have none any longer, I hardly go out. Were not you the one that I preferred, at that lady's house? Did I not break with her in order to be yours alone? I am still waiting for a word of thanks or a sign of gratitude . . . And if you are afraid that I will go back to her, put your mind at rest: she is taking her revenge by helping one of my former assistants to found a rival firm. So, must I fall to my knees before I can touch your heart?'

This was the point he had reached. He, who would not stand for any misconduct by his salesgirls, who threw them out at the slightest whim, was now reduced to begging one of them not to leave and not to abandon him in his misery. He barred the door against her and was prepared to forgive her, to look the other way, if she would deign to lie. And what he had said was true: he was starting to feel disgust at the women he picked up backstage in little theatres or late-night restaurants; he was not seeing Clara any more, he had not set foot again in Madame Desforges', where Bouthemont now reigned, awaiting the opening of the new shop, *Les Quatre Saisons*; the papers were already full of advertisements for it.

'Tell me, do I have to go down on my knees?' he repeated, his voice choked as he forced back his tears.

She restrained him with her hand, unable to conceal her own emotions and deeply touched by this suffering passion.

'You are wrong to upset yourself, Monsieur,' she finally answered. 'I swear that those dreadful stories are all lies. That poor boy just now is as innocent as I am.'

She said this with her usual frank expression and her clear eyes looking directly ahead.

'Very well, I believe you,' he murmured. 'I shall not dismiss any of your colleagues, since you have taken all of them under your protection. But then why do you reject me, if you are not in love with anyone?'

The young woman was suddenly overtaken by a sense of embarrassment, of troubled modesty.

'You do love someone, don't you?' he went on in a trembling voice. 'Oh, you can tell me, I have no right to dictate your feelings. You love someone.'

She blushed deeply, her heart on her lips, feeling that it would be impossible to lie when this feeling betrayed her, this horror of lying that showed the truth on her face.

'Yes,' she eventually confessed weakly. 'Please, Monsieur, I beg you, let me be, you are distressing me.'

Now, in her turn, she was suffering. Was it not already enough to have to defend herself against him? Did she also have to defend herself against herself, against the gusts of tenderness that constantly threatened to sap her courage? When he spoke in that way and she saw him so moved, so devastated, she could not think any longer why she refused him; and it was only later, in the very depths of her nature as a wholesome young woman, that she found the pride and good sense that kept her upright, with her virgin's determination. It was not so that she could keep to some notion of virtue that she remained obstinate, but by an instinct for her own happiness and to satisfy her need for a calm life. She would have fallen into the man's arms, abandoning her flesh, seduced in her heart, had she not felt a sense of outrage, almost of repulsion at the ultimate gift of her being, casting herself into the unknown. A lover made her afraid with that panic fear that makes a female pale at the approach of the male.

Meanwhile, Mouret had made a gesture of dismal discouragement. He could not undertand. He turned back to his desk and was leafing through papers that he let fall at once, saying:

'I am not keeping you, Mademoiselle. I cannot keep you here against your will.'

'But I don't wish to go,' she replied, smiling. 'If you believe me to be of good conduct, I shall stay. One should always believe women to be respectable, Monsieur. I can assure you, there are many who are.'

Denise's eyes had involuntarily lifted towards the portrait of Madame Hédouin, that lovely and intelligent woman whose blood, they said, brought luck to the firm. Mouret followed her gaze and he shuddered, for it seemed to him that he had heard his dead wife speak the words: it was a remark of hers that he recognized. It was like a resurrection; he saw in Denise the good sense and balanced judgement of the woman he had lost, right down to the soft voice and the dislike of empty words. It touched him and he felt even sadder than before.

'You know that I am yours,' he murmured in conclusion. 'Do what you will with me.'

So she went on merrily: 'That's right, Monsieur. A woman's opinion, however humble she may be, is always worth listening to, when she is at all intelligent. I shall do nothing with you except to make you a decent man, if you put yourself in my hands.'

She was joking, with that simple air of her that was so charming. He gave a weak smile in return and accompanied her to the door, like a lady.

The following day, Denise was appointed buyer. The management had split the department of dresses and suits, creating a children's clothes department especially for her, which was set up close to ladies' wear. Since her son had been dismissed, Madame Aurélie was quaking, because she felt that the gentlemen were cooling towards her and she could see the young woman's power increasing day by day. Were they going to sacrifice her to Denise, on some excuse or other? Her puffy, Roman emperor's face seemed to have grown leaner with the shame that now stained the dynasty of the Lhommes; and she made a point of going home every night on her husband's arm, the couple having been brought together by misfortune and realizing that the trouble lay in the irregularity of their home life; while the poor man, more deeply affected than she was and morbidly anxious that he too would be suspected of theft, would count the takings twice over, noisily, performing miracles with his bad arm. So when Madame Aurélie saw Denise going to be buyer in children's wear, she felt such joy that she became more affectionate towards her. It was really good that she had not taken her place; and she overwhelmed her with friendship, treated her from now on as an equal and often went to chat with her in the next department, in a grand way, like a queen mother paying a visit to a young queen.

Moreover, Denise was now at the top. Her appointment as buyer had overcome the last resistance among those around her. Though they still chattered, because of the itching of the tongue that ravages any meeting of men and women, they would bow very low, to the ground. Marguerite, who had become under-buyer in ladies' wear, was full of praise. Even Clara, with an unadmitted feeling of respect for this good luck which she could not achieve, had accepted defeat. But her victory was still more complete over the gentlemen: over Jouve, who did not talk to her nowadays unless he was bent double; over Hutin, anxious as he felt his job crumbling under his feet; and, finally, over Bourdoncle, who was reduced to impotence. When he had seen her emerging from the director's office, smiling, with her usual calm air, and the next day the director demanded that the board create this new department, he too had accepted the inevitable, defeated by the sacred terror of womankind. He had always given way like this to Mouret's charm, acknowledging him as his master, despite his strokes of genius and his ridiculous passions. This time, the woman had proved the stronger and he was expecting to be carried off by the disaster.

Meanwhile, Denise remained calm and charming in her triumph. She was touched by the signs of consideration and wanted to see them as expressing sympathy for the hardship of her early days and for the final success of her enduring courage. So she greeted the slightest expression of friendship with laughter and joy, which made her really loved by some people because she was so kind and welcoming, always ready to give her heart. She only felt an invincible repulsion for Clara, having learned that the girl had amused herself – as she said when joking about the idea – by taking Colomban to her room one evening, so that the salesman, carried away by his passion now that it was satisfied, was sleeping away from home, while poor Geneviève was dying. At *Au Bonheur des Dames* they talked about it and considered the whole thing quite a joke.

But this sorrow, the only one that she had outside, did not spoil Denise's even temper. Most of all, you had to see her in her department, surrounded by her tribe of children of all ages. She loved children, so she could not have been better placed. Sometimes, there would be fifty or so girls and the same number of boys, a whole rowdy school full, let loose with their burgeoning desire for allurement. Their mothers would lose their heads. But Denise, conciliating, smiling, got the whole lot of them to sit down on rows of chairs. And when there was a little pink girl in the group whose face she liked she would serve her herself, bringing the dress, trying it on the chubby shoulders, with the gentle consideration of a big sister. Light bursts of laughter would ring out and little cries of joy explode, amid the scolding voices. Sometimes a girl of nine or ten, already quite grown up, with a cloth jacket round her shoulders, would look at the effect in the mirror, turning this way and that, her face concentrating and her eyes shining with the need to please. The wrappings would clutter up the counters, dresses in pink or blue Indian cloth for children from one to five, sailor suits in light woollen material, pleated skirts and blouses with decorations in percale, Louis XV costumes, cloaks, jackets, a clutter of small clothes, childishly stiff and charming, rather like the wardrobe of a group of large dolls which had been removed from the cupboards and ransacked. Denise always had some sweets at the bottom of her pockets to soothe a little child weeping desperately at not being allowed to take away some red breeches; and she lived there among the little ones, as though in her own family, rejuvenated by this innocence and freshness constantly flowing past her skirts.

Nowadays, she would have long friendly conversations with Mouret. When she had to go to the management to take orders or to tell him something, he would keep her back chatting; he liked to listen to her. This was what, with a laugh, she would call 'making a decent man out of him'. All sorts of plans were developing in her sensible, shrewd Norman head, ideas about the new commerce which she had already dared to mention at Robineau's and some of which she had expressed on that fine evening when they walked in the Tuileries. She was unable to look after something, to see a business working, without having an urge to put some order in it, to improve the mechanism. So, since she first joined *Au Bonheur des Dames*, she had been worried chiefly by the precarious situation of the employees; she hated sudden dismissals, finding them awkward and unfair, and damaging to everyone, the firm as much as the staff. She still remembered the hardships of her early days and she was moved to pity every time she met some newcomer in the shop with aching feet and eyes swollen with tears, dragging her misery along with her under her silk dress, in the midst of the older girls' embittered persecution. This dog's life made the best of them bad and the sad procession began: all of them eaten up by the job before the age of forty, disappearing into the unknown, several of them dying, consumptive or anaemic, killed by exhaustion or the bad air, some ending on the streets, the luckiest married and buried in some little shop in the provinces. Was it human, was it right, this appalling consumption of flesh by the department stores every year? She pleaded the case of the cogs in the machine, not for sentimental reasons, but with arguments that rested on the interest of the owners. When you want a reliable machine, you use good iron; if the iron cracks or is broken, work stops and you have all the repeated expense of starting up again and a waste of energy. Sometimes, she would get excited, seeing the huge, ideal store, the phalanstery of trade, in which everyone would have a precise share of the profits according to his or her deserts, as well as security for the future, ensured by a contract. At this, Mouret would cheer up, despite his depression. He accused her of socialism, and embarrassed her by showing how hard it would be to put into practice; because she was speaking from the simplicity of her soul and she would roundly put her trust in the future when she saw some dangerous pitfall lurking in her idealistic plans. Yet he was shaken and seduced by this young voice, still trembling from the sufferings it had endured, and expressing such conviction when it suggested reforms that could strengthen the firm. He would listen to her, and tease her; but the situation of the sales staff was gradually improving, mass dismissals were being replaced by a system of leave given in the low season, and they were going to set up a mutual assurance society which would guarantee the workers against unemployment and give them a retirement pension. It was to be the seed of the vast trade unions of the twentieth century.[1]

Moreover, Denise did not confine herself to dressing the wounds from which she herself had bled; her sensitive, feminine ideas, tentatively suggested to Mouret, enchanted the customers. She also delighted Lhomme by supporting a project which he had long cherished, which was to set up an orchestra, all of whose members would be chosen from among the staff. Three months later, Lhomme had a hundred and twenty musicians under his baton and the dream of his life was accomplished. A huge festival was organized in the shop, with a concert and a ball, to exhibit the music of *Au Bonheur* to its customers and to the world. The newspapers wrote about it. Even Bourdoncle, dismayed by these innovations, had to admit that the publicity was huge. After that, they set up a games room for the staff, with two billiard tables and tables for trictrac[2] and chess. Evening classes were held in the shop, in English and German, as well as in grammar, arithmetic and geography; there were even lessons in riding and fencing. A library was set up with ten thousand volumes available to borrowers. They also had a resident doctor who gave free consultations; and there were baths, buffets and a hairdresser's. All life was there, everything was to be had without leaving the building: study, food, bed and clothing. *Au Bonheur des Dames* was sufficient to its own pleasures and its own needs in the midst of the great city, full of the racket made by this city of work which was thriving on the dungheap of old streets, open at last to the full light of day.

So there was a change in people's opinion of Denise. Even as Bourdoncle, defeated, kept desperately repeating to his cronies that he would have done a good deal to put her in Mouret's bed himself, it was generally acknowledged that she had not given in and that her omnipotence resulted from her refusal. From then on, she became popular. The kindnesses that people owed her were not overlooked and she was admired for her strength of will. Here, at least, was someone who had the boss by the throat and was avenging them all because she knew how to get more out of him than promises! She had come at last, the one who got a bit of respect for poor folk! When she walked through the shop, with her fine, obstinate head and her gentle, yet invincible look, the assistants smiled at her, they were proud of her, they would have liked to show her off to the crowd. Denise was happy to be carried along on this growing tide of sympathy. My God, was it possible? She saw herself arriving in her miserable skirt, overawed and lost in the midst of the workings of this fearsome machine; and for a long time she had the feeling that she was nothing, barely a grain of corn beneath the millwheels that grind a world; and now, she was the very soul of this world, she was all that mattered in it, she could with a word drive the colossus forward or slow it down, leaving it harmless at her little feet. Yet she had not wanted any of this, she had simply arrived, with no designs on anything, but with the sole charm of her sweet nature. At times, her dominion caused her an anxious feeling of surprise: why did they all obey her? She was not pretty, she was not cruel. Then she smiled, easy in her mind, with only goodness and good sense in her, and that love of truth and logic that were all her strength.

Once in favour, one of Denise's greatest joys was to be able to help Pauline, who was pregnant and very worried because two assistants in the past fortnight had had to leave in the seventh month of their pregnancy. The management would not stand for such accidents, maternity was forbidden, on the grounds that it was inconvenient and indecent; at a pinch, marriage might be permitted, but children were forbidden. Of course, Pauline had a husband in the shop, but she was mistrustful even so and it did not make things any less impossible for her in the department. In order to delay her dismissal, should it come, she tightened her clothes until she could hardly breathe, determined to hide it as long as she could. In fact, one of the two salesgirls who had been dismissed had just given birth to a stillborn child, after torturing her waist in that way; they were not even sure that the girl herself could be saved. Meanwhile, Bourdoncle watched Pauline's complexion grow dull and noticed a painful stiffness in the way she walked. One morning he was near her in trousseaux when a boy from the shop, taking a parcel, knocked into her so roughly that she put both hands on her belly and let out a cry. At once, Bourdoncle led her off, got her to confess and raised the question of her dismissal with the board, on the grounds that she needed fresh country air: the story of the blow would come out and the effect on the public would be disastrous were she to have a miscarriage like the one that occurred the previous year in babywear. Mouret, who was not at the meeting, could only give his opinion that evening. But Denise had had time to intervene and he silenced Bourdoncle on the grounds of the firm's own interests. Did they want a riot among mothers by upsetting any lady customers who had recently given birth? It was decreed, in the most grandiloquent terms, that any married assistant who became pregnant would be entrusted to a special midwife as soon as her presence on the floor might become an outrage to morality.

The next day, when Denise went up to see Pauline, who had had to go to the sick bay after the blow she had received, she embraced her friend eagerly on both cheeks.

'How good you are! If it had not been for you, they would have kicked me out . . . And don't worry, the doctor says it's nothing.'

Baugé was there, on the other side of the bed, having escaped from his department. He too stammered out his thanks, embarrassed in front of Denise, whom he now treated as someone who had made it into a superior class. Oh, if ever he heard any other dirty rumours about her, he'd soon shut those jealous people's mouths! But Pauline sent him away, with a friendly shrug of the shoulders.

'My poor darling, you talk such rubbish! Off you go and let us have a chat.'

The sick bay was a long, well-lit room, with a row of twelve beds behind white curtains. This is where they cared for live-in assistants, when they did not prefer to go back to their families. On this day, however, Pauline was alone here, near one of the large windows overlooking the Rue Neuve-Saint-Augustin. So they began to exchange confidences and whisper affectionately, in the midst of this pure white linen, in this drowsy air, scented with a vague smell of lavender.

'So does he really do whatever you want? What a hard one you are to put him in such agony! Come on, tell me all about it, since I dare to raise the subject. Do you hate him?'

She was holding Denise's hand, with Denise sitting beside the bed and leaning on the bolster; and, at this unexpectedly direct question, she was suddenly overcome, her cheeks blushing red, and gave way to her feelings. The secret came out, as she hid her head in the pillow, murmuring:

'I love him!'

Pauline was astonished.

'What! You love him! But then it's quite simple. Say yes.'

Denise, her face still hidden, shook her head violently. She said no precisely because she loved him, without trying to explain it. She agreed, it was ridiculous, but that's how she felt and she could not be different. Her friend's surprise increased and at length she asked:

'You mean all this is to get him to marry you?'

Denise sat up with a jolt. She was horrified.

'Marry me? Him? Oh, no, no, I swear I've never wanted any such thing! No, such an idea never entered my head – and you know how much I detest a lie!'

'Maybe, dearest,' Pauline said gently. 'But if you had wanted to get married, you wouldn't have gone about it any differently. It has to finish somewhere and all that's left is marriage, since you don't want the other thing . . . Listen, I must warn you that everyone has the same idea: yes, they're all convinced that you're holding out on him so that you can get him in front of the Mayor. Good Lord, what an odd woman you are!'

And she had to console Denise whose head had fallen back on to the bolster where she was sobbing and saying that she would have to go, since people were constantly attributing all sorts of things to her that never even entered her head. Of course, when a man loved a woman, he should marry her. But she was not asking for anything or plotting anything. All she wanted was to be left alone to live with her joys and sorrows like anyone else. She would leave.

At the same moment, downstairs, Mouret was walking through the shop. He had tried to forget everything by visiting the building site again. Months had gone by and the façade was raising its monumental shape behind the huge cloak of planks that hid it from passers-by. A whole army of decorators had started work, craftsmen in marble, porcelain and mosaic. The central group, above the door, was being gilded while on the pediment they were already fixing the pedestals that were to receive the statues representing the manufacturing towns of France. From morning to evening all along the Rue du Dix-Décembre, recently opened, there was a crowd of onlookers, chins in the air, seeing nothing, but entranced by the wonders of this façade which (they told each other) would revolutionize Paris when it was inaugurated. And it was on this site, a hive of activity, among the artists who were completing the realization of the dream, started by the builders, that Mouret had just felt more bitterly than ever the emptiness of his wealth. The thought of Denise had suddenly put a lump in his throat, that thought which constantly shot through him like a flame or like the pangs of some incurable disease. He had fled, not finding a word of satisfaction, fearing to show his tears and leaving behind him a sense of disgust in his triumph. This façade, which was finally standing, seemed small to him, like one of those walls of sand that children build, and they could have extended it from one end of the city to the next and raised it as high as the stars, without it being able to replace the void in his heart, that only the 'yes' of a child could fill.

When Mouret got back to his office, he was choking with repressed sobs. What did she want, then? He no longer dared to offer her money, but the vague idea of marriage appeared, despite his reluctance as a young widower. So in the irritation of his powerlessness, the tears ran. He was unhappy.

CHAPTER 13

One morning in November, Denise was giving the first instructions to her department when the Baudus' maid came to say that Mademoiselle Geneviève had had a very bad night and that she wanted to see her cousin at once. The young woman had been getting weaker day by day, and had been forced to take to her bed the day before last.

'Tell her that I shall be down at once,' Denise replied, very anxious.

The blow that had finished Geneviève had been the sudden disappearance of Colomban. At first, after being teased by Clara, he had spent the night with her; then giving up to the madness of desire that can overtake a furtive, chaste young man, having become the slave of this woman, he did not return one Monday morning but simply wrote his employer a letter of farewell, in the careful language of a man about to commit suicide. Perhaps, behind his infatuation, you might also find the calculating cunning of someone delighted to escape from a disastrous marriage, because the draper's shop was as sick as his future wife and it was a good time to break off through some act of folly. And everyone spoke of him as a fatal victim of love.

When Denise reached the *Vieil Elbeuf*, Madame Baudu was alone there. She was motionless behind the cash desk, her little white face, ravaged by anaemia, guarding the silence and emptiness of the shop. There was no more assistant. The maid gave a flick of the duster to the shelves – and there was even talk of replacing her by a cleaner. A black chill fell from the ceiling; hours passed without a single customer coming to disturb this gloom and the goods, which were never moved, were increasingly affected by the saltpetre in the walls.

'What's wrong?' Denise asked anxiously. 'Is Geneviève in danger?'

Madame Baudu did not answer at once. Her eyes filled with tears. Then she stammered:

'I don't know, they don't tell me anything . . . Oh, it's over, it's all over!'

Her tearful eyes looked around the dark shop as though she could feel her daughter and the business departing together. The seventy thousand francs from the sale of the house in Rambouillet had vanished in less than two years into the gulf of competition. The draper had made considerable sacrifices in the struggle against *Au Bonheur des Dames*, which now had men's clothes, hunting velvet and liveries. In the end he was totally crushed by his rival's flannelette and flannels, a variety so great that it had never been seen on the market before. Little by little, the debt had grown. Finally, as a last resort, he had decided to mortgage the ancient building on the Rue de la Michodière where Old Finet, the ancestor, had founded the firm; and now it was only a matter of days before it all crumbled: the very ceilings would collapse and vanish into dust, like some barbaric, worm-eaten structure carried away on the wind.

'Father is upstairs,' Madame Baudu continued, in her broken voice. 'We spend two hours each there. Someone has to keep guard here, oh, just as a precaution, because in fact . . .'

She finished the sentence with a gesture. They would have put up the shutters, had it not been for their enduring pride as tradespeople which made them want to look their neighbours in the face.

'I'll go up then, Aunt,' said Denise, getting a lump in her throat at the sight of this resigned despair which even the lengths of material exuded.

'Yes, go up, go quickly, my dear. She's expecting you, she's been asking for you all night. There's something she wants to tell you.'

But at that moment Baudu came downstairs. His bile gave a greenish tinge to his yellow features and his eyes were bloodshot. He was still walking softly as he had when leaving the bedroom and said quietly, as though he could be heard from upstairs: 'She's sleeping.'

Exhausted, he slumped down on a chair. Mechanically, he wiped his forehead, as breathless as a man who has just finished some hard physical labour. There was a silence, then at length he said to Denise:

'You'll see her in a while. When she's asleep, she seems to be better.'

There was a further silence. The father and mother, face to face, looked at one another. Then, in a half-whisper, he went over his miseries again, not naming anyone or addressing anyone in particular.

'I swear to you, I should never have believed it. He was the last person . . . I'd brought him up like my son. If someone had come to me and said: "They'll take him away from you too, you'll see him tumble," I would have said: "In that case, the Good Lord is dead!" But he did it, he fell for them! Oh, the wretch, he who knew so much about real business, who had learned all my ideas! And for a monkey, for one of those puppets who parade themselves in the windows of bawdy houses! No, do you see, it's against all reason!'

He shook his head, his eyes looking down, staring vaguely across the damp stone floor, worn by generations of customers.

'Do you know what?' he went on, speaking in a lower voice. 'Well, there are times when I feel I am myself most to blame for our misfortune. Yes, it's my fault, if our poor daughter is up there, consumed with fever. Perhaps I should have married them at once without giving in to my demon of pride, my stubborn determination not to hand over the firm in a less prosperous state. Now she would have the one she loves and perhaps their youth would achieve the miracle here that was beyond me. But I am an old fool, I understood nothing, I didn't think that you could fall ill from such a cause. It's true! That boy was amazing: he had a gift for selling, as well as honesty, simple manners and discipline in everything; in short, he was my pupil.'

He looked up, still defending his ideas even in the assistant who had betrayed him. Denise could not bear to hear him accuse himself and she told him everything, carried away by her pity at seeing him so humble, his eyes full of tears, when he had once reigned here as the gruff, absolute master.

'Uncle, please don't find excuses for him. He never loved Geneviève and he would have left earlier if you had tried to bring the marriage forward. I spoke to him about it myself. He knew perfectly well that my poor cousin was suffering because of him, yet as you see that did not prevent him from leaving. Ask my aunt.'

Without making a sound, Madame Baudu nodded in confirmation.

At this, the draper became paler still, while his eyes were further clouded by tears. He stammered:

'It must be something in the blood. His father died last summer from too much philandering.'

Mechanically he ran his eyes round the dark corners of the room, going from the bare counters to the full shelves, then came back to his wife who was still sitting upright at the cash desk, waiting vainly for their vanished customers.

'So it's the end,' he went on. 'They have killed our business and now one of their hussies is killing our daughter.'

No one said a word. Occasionally, in the still air beneath the stifling low ceiling, the stone floor resonated with the sound of passing carriages like the drums in a funeral cortège. And, in the midst of this melancholy sadness – the dying of the old businesses – they heard a dull banging from somewhere in the house. It was Geneviève who had just woken up and was beating with the stick they had left her.

'Quickly,' said Baudu, jumping up. 'Try to laugh: she mustn't know.'

He went up the stairs, urgently rubbing the signs of weeping from his eyes. As soon as he opened the door on the first floor they could hear a weak voice, a desperate voice, pleading:

'Oh, I don't want to be alone. Don't leave me alone. Oh, I'm so afraid of being alone!'

Then, when she saw Denise, Geneviève grew calmer and gave a smile of pleasure.

'So you've come! It's been such a long wait for you since yesterday. I was starting to think you had abandoned me as well.'

It was pitiful. The young woman's room overlooked the courtyard, a little room, palely lit. To begin with, her parents had brought the patient to their own room, above the street, but the sight of *Au Bonheur des Dames* opposite was so upsetting for her that they had to take her back. Now she was lying flat, such a slight figure beneath the blankets that one could no longer sense the shape or the existence of a body. Her thin arms, burning with a consumptive fever, moved constantly and uncontrollably, as though searching for something, while her black hair, heavy with passion, seemed to have grown thicker, as though with a voracious life of its own, devouring her poor face which displayed the final death throes of a family in decline, driven into the shadows in this vault of old Parisian trade.

Meanwhile, Denise was watching her, her heart breaking with compassion. She said nothing, for fear that she would burst into tears. Finally, she murmured softly:

'I came at once. Is there anything I can do for you? You were asking for me. Do you want me to stay?'

Geneviève kept her eyes fixed on her, breathing rapidly, with her hands still moving across the folds on the blanket.

'No, thank you. I don't need anything. I just wanted to kiss you.'

Her pupils were swollen with tears. At this Denise quickly bent over and kissed her cheeks, shuddering as she felt these burning, hollow cheeks against her lips. But the sick girl had grasped her, holding her in a desperate embrace. Then she looked across at her father.

'Do you want me to stay?' Denise said again. 'Is there anything you have to do?'

'No, no.'

Geneviève kept on looking towards her father, who remained there, with a haggard look, unable to speak. Eventually, he understood and left without a word. They heard his heavy footsteps on the stairs.

'Tell me, is he with that woman?' the patient asked immediately, grasping her cousin's hand and making her sit down on the edge of the bed. 'Yes, I wanted to see you because you are the only one who can tell me. They are living together, aren't they?'

Denise, taken aback by these questions, had to stammer out the truth and the rumours going around the shop: that Clara, bored with this lad who had landed on her, had already turned him out; and Colomban, devastated, followed her everywhere like a beaten dog, trying from time to time to get her to meet him. They said that he was going to find a position at the *Louvre*.

'If you love him so much, he might still come back to you,' she went on, to appease the dying girl with this last hope. 'Get well soon and he will admit he has done wrong and marry you.'

Geneviève interrupted her. She had listened with all her strength and a silent passion that raised her up in the bed, but now she fell back.

'No, don't say that. I know that it's all over. I don't say anything, because I hear Papa crying and I don't want to make Mamma more ill. But I am going, and I asked to see you tonight because I was afraid of not lasting till tomorrow. Oh, God! To think that he is not even happy!'

When Denise protested, assuring her that her state was not so serious, she interrupted her again and suddenly threw back the blanket with the chaste gesture of a virgin who, in her death, has nothing left to hide. Bare to the waist, she said quietly:

'Just look at me: is that not the end?'

Trembling, Denise got up from the bed, as though afraid that she might destroy this pitiful nakedness with a breath. It was the end of the flesh, the body of a betrothed woman exhausted by waiting and returned to the emaciation of a young child. Geneviève slowly covered herself, saying:

'You see, I am not a woman any longer. It would be wrong to want him still.'

Both of them fell silent, looking at one another again, but finding no words. It was Geneviève who spoke next:

'Go on now, don't stay here, with all you have to do. And thank you: I was tormented by the need to know. Now I am satisfied. If you see him again, tell him that I forgive him. Farewell, my dear Denise. Give me a good kiss; it will be the last.'

The young woman kissed her, protesting: 'No, no, don't torment yourself, you need care, that's all.'

But the sick girl shook her head obstinately and smiled: she was sure. As her cousin finally turned to leave, she said:

'One moment. Knock with the stick, so that Papa will come. I'm so afraid of being alone.'

Then, when Baudu was there, in the dismal little room where he spent hours sitting, she put on a smiling face and called out to Denise:

'Don't come tomorrow, there's no point. But I'll expect you on Sunday and you can spend the afternoon with me.'

The next morning at six, as day was breaking, Geneviève died, after four hours of dreadful agony. The funeral fell on a Saturday, on a grey day under an ashen sky which weighed on the shivering city. Hung with white cloth, the *Vieil Elbeuf* was a white patch shining on the street, and the candles, burning in the gloom, looked like stars shining faintly through the dim light of dusk. Crowns of pearls and a large bouquet of white roses lay across the coffin, a little girl's narrow coffin, set down in the dark alleyway beside the house and so low on the pavement and close to the gutter that passing carriages had already spattered the drapery. The whole of this old neighbourhood exuded damp and a smell of mouldy cellars, with the constant bustle of people on the muddy pavement.

Denise arrived at nine o'clock to be with her aunt. But as the procession was about to leave, her eyes burning with tears, but no longer crying, she begged Denise to go with the body and keep an eye on her uncle, because the family were worried to see him silent, despairing and driven almost out of his mind with grief. Downstairs, Denise found the street full of people. The small businesses of the neighbourhood wanted to offer the Baudus a mark of their sympathy and their eagerness to do so was also like a demonstration against *Au Bonheur des Dames*, which was accused of responsibility for Geneviève's long agony. All the monster's victims were there: Bédoré and Sister, the hosiers of the Rue Gaillon; Vanpouille Brothers, the furriers; Deslignières, the fancy goods merchant; and Piot & Rivoire, the furniture sellers. Even Mademoiselle Tatin, who sold linen, and Quinette, who sold gloves, both long since driven out by bankruptcy, had felt duty-bound to come, the first from Batignolles, the other from the Bastille, where they had had to go to work for other people. The hearse had been accidentally delayed and while they waited, all these mourners, trampling the mud, cast looks of hatred towards *Au Bonheur des Dames*, whose clear windows and merry, shining displays seemed an insult in the face of the *Vieil Elbeuf*, which saddened the far side of the street with its grief. The heads of a few curious assistants appeared behind the glass, but the colossus remained as indifferent as a steam engine at full speed, careless of those it might run down on its way.

Denise looked around for her brother Jean. Eventually she saw him in front of Bourras' shop and went over to suggest that he kept close to their uncle, so that he could support him if he had difficulty walking. For the past few weeks, Jean had been serious, as though he had some anxiety on his mind. That day, squeezed into a black frock coat, now a fully grown man, earning twenty francs a day, he seemed so dignified and sad that his sister was intrigued by it, because she had not suspected him of being so fond of their cousin. She had left Pépé with Madame Gras, to spare him any unnecessary distress, promising that she would fetch him in the afternoon so that he could give their uncle and aunt a kiss.

Meanwhile, the hearse was still not coming and Denise was watching the candles burning, very moved by it all, when she jumped at the sound of a familiar voice behind her. It was Bourras. He had waved to a chestnut seller who had a stall opposite in a narrow space beside a wine merchant's and was saying:

'Hey, Vigouroux, would you do me a favour? As you see, I'm shutting up shop. If anybody comes, tell them to drop by later. But don't worry, no one will come . . .'

Then he stayed waiting with the rest of them on the edge of the pavement. Embarrassed, Denise had looked up at the shop. Now he was letting it go: all you could see in the window were a few pitiful, straggling umbrellas, full of holes, and canes blackened by the gaslight. All the improvements he had made – the soft green paintwork, the mirrors, the gilded sign – were already showing cracks and dirt, with the rapid, woeful deterioration of false luxury, painted over ruins. Yet, even though the old cracks were reappearing and the damp patches had spread under the gilt, the house was still there, obstinately clinging to the side of *Au Bonheur des Dames*, like a disfiguring wart which, though it was chapped and rotting, would not fall off.

'Oh, the swine!' Bourras grumbled. 'They don't even want us to take her away!'

The hearse, which was at last arriving, had collided with a carriage from *Au Bonheur*: it was driving off with its varnished panels shining like stars through the mist, carried by the fast trot of two magnificent horses. The old merchant cast a sidelong glance at Denise which shone out from beneath his bushy eyebrows.

Slowly, the cortège set off, splashing through the puddles, in the silence created by the sudden halt of horse-drawn cabs and omnibuses. When the coffin, hung with white, crossed the Place Gaillon, the sombre stares of the mourners once more turned to the windows of the department store, where only two salesgirls had come to watch, glad of the diversion. Baudu was walking with heavy, mechanical steps behind the hearse; he had shaken his head when Jean, walking close to him, offered an arm. Then, after the long line of people, came three funeral carriages. As they were cutting across the Rue Neuve-des-Petits-Champs, Robineau ran up to join the procession, looking aged and very pale.

A large number of women were waiting at Saint-Roch, the small tradespeople of the neighbourhood who had been afraid they would overcrowd the bereaved house. The occasion was turning into a riot, and when after the service the procession set off once more, all the men followed again, even though it was a long walk from the Rue Saint-Honoré to the Montmartre cemetery. They had to go back up the Rue Saint-Roch and pass for a second time in front of *Au Bonheur des Dames*. It was like an obsession, the meagre body of this young woman being carried around the store, like the first victim to fall in a time of revolution. At the door, red flannel cloths were flapping in the wind like flags and a display of carpets burst out in a blood-red flowering of huge roses and blossoming peonies.

Meanwhile, Denise had got into one of the carriages, racked by such burning doubts and with such sadness oppressing her that she no longer had the strength to walk. As it happened, they paused in the Rue du Dix-Décembre, by the scaffolding of the new façade which was still obstructing the traffic. She noticed old Bourras lagging behind, dragging his leg, right under the wheels of the carriage of which she was the only occupant. He would never get to the cemetery. He looked up and saw her, then got in.

'It's my confounded knees,' he grumbled. 'Don't shrink back! You're not the one we hate!'

She felt his friendship and his fury, as in the old days. He muttered away, saying that old rogue Baudu was made of stern stuff, to keep going after such a series of body blows. The procession had started to move forward again slowly and if she leaned out she could indeed see her uncle insisting on marching behind the hearse with his heavy steps, which seemed to be beating time for the dull, painful movement of the cortège. So she sat back in her corner and listened to the old umbrella merchant talking endlessly, to the long melancholy swaying of the carriage.

'Shouldn't the police clear the public highway? It's been more than eighteen months that they have been blocking it with their façade – and another man was killed there a few days ago. No matter! Now, when they next want to expand, they'll have to put bridges over the streets. They say that there are two thousand seven hundred of you employed there and that the turnover will reach a hundred million this year. A hundred million! Good Lord, a hundred million!'

Denise had no answer. The procession had just started down the Rue de la Chaussée-d'Antin, where it was held up by traffic. Bourras went on talking, his eyes blank, as though he were now dreaming out loud. He could still not understand the triumph of *Au Bonheur des Dames*, but he had to admit that the old sort of trade was finished.

'Poor Robineau has had it, he looks like a drowning man. And the Bédorés and the Vanpouilles are going down – like me, their legs won't hold them. Deslignières will die of apoplexy, Piot & Rivoire have had jaundice. Oh, we're a pretty sight; a fine cortège of carcasses we make for the dear child! It must be odd, for people watching this line of bankrupts going past. And it seems that the clear-out is continuing. The scoundrels are opening departments for flowers, for fashions, for perfumes, for shoes, and who knows what else? Groguet, the perfumer on the Rue de Grammont, might as well shut up shop and I don't give ten francs for Naud, the cobbler on the Rue d'Antin. The plague has spread as far as the Rue Sainte-Anne where within two years we'll see the last of Lacassagne, who does feathers and flowers, and Madame Chadeuil, even though her hats are famous. Then there'll be others, and others still! All the businesses in the neighbourhood will go the same way. When drapers start selling soap and clogs, they might easily get a yearning to sell fried potatoes. My, oh, my! The world is going mad!'

The hearse was now crossing the Place de la Trinité; and, from her corner of the dark carriage, where Denise was listening to the unbroken lament of the old merchant, rocked by the funereal pace of the procession, as they came out of the Rue de la Chaussée-d'Antin, she could see the body already on its way up the slope of the Rue Blanche. Behind her uncle, marching on with the blind, silent steps of a stunned bull, she felt she could hear the tramp of a herd on its way to the slaughterhouse, the rout of the shopkeepers of a whole neighbourhood, their small businesses plodding towards their ruin with the damp sound of worn shoes slapping the black Parisian mud. Meanwhile, Bourras went on speaking in a lower voice that seemed to have been slowed down by the sharp rise of the Rue Blanche.

'As for me, I'm done for. But I'm hanging on still and I won't let him go. He lost his appeal again. Oh, it cost me a pretty packet, nearly two years of trials, plus the solicitors and the barristers! No matter: he won't go under my shop: the judges have decided that such works could not properly be called repairs. Just think of it: he was talking about making a room with lights under there for people to judge the colour of cloth by gaslight – an underground passage that would have joined hosiery to curtains! And he's furious, because he can't accept that an old crock like me should stand in his way when everyone is on their knees before his money! Never! I won't do it, and that's that! It could be that it will destroy me. Since I've had to contend with the bailiffs, I know that the rascal is trying to find out my debts, no doubt so that he can play some trick on me. It makes no difference. He says yes, I say no, and I shall go on saying no, by God, even when I'm nailed up between four planks like that girl over there.'

When they reached the Boulevard de Clichy, the carriage drove on faster; you could hear the mourners getting out of breath and feel the unconscious haste of the cortège, in a hurry to get it over. What Bourras did not admit openly was the deep poverty that had overtaken him; his head was reeling with the troubles of a small shopkeeper who obstinately hangs on while his business is going under in a hail of writs for non-payment. Denise, who knew how things stood, finally broke the silence and said in a pleading voice:

'Monsieur Bourras, stop being so stubborn. Let me arrange things.'

He interrupted her, with a violent gesture.

'Be quiet, this is nobody's business. You're a good little girl and I know you're giving him a hard time, that man who thought you were for sale, like my house. But what would you tell me, if I advised you to say yes? Huh? You'd send me packing. Well, if I say no, then don't go sticking your nose in.'

The carriage had stopped on the road for the cemetery, so he and Denise got out. The Baudus' family tomb was in the first avenue on the left. The ceremony was over in a few minutes. Jean had led away his uncle, who was staring at the hole with a dazed expression. The file of mourners spread among the nearby graves, where all the faces of these shopkeepers, drained of blood in the depths of their unhealthy ground-floor shops, took on a painful ugliness beneath the mud-coloured sky. As the coffin gently sank from view, blotchy faces turned pale, noses pinched with anaemia were lowered and eyelids, yellow with bile and bruised with staring at figures, turned aside.

'We should all jump into that hole,' Bourras told Denise, who had stayed close to him. 'It's the whole neighbourhood we're burying with that girl. I know what I'm saying: the old kind of trade can go and join those white roses they're throwing in with her.'

Denise took her uncle and her brother home in one of the funerary carriages. It had been a day of gloom and sadness for her. In particular, she was starting to worry about how pale Jean was, and when she learned that it was another affair with a woman, she tried to keep him quiet by offering him some money; but he shook his head and refused. This time it was serious, she was the niece of a very rich patissier who wouldn't even accept bouquets of violets. After that, in the afternoon, when Denise went to fetch Pépé from Madame Gras, she announced that the boy was getting too big for her to look after from now on – another worry: they would have to find him a boarding school and possibly send him away. And finally, when she took Pépé to kiss the Baudus, her heart was rent by the melancholy grief of the *Vieil Elbeuf*. The shop was shut, her uncle and aunt were at the back of the little room, and had forgotten to light the gas, despite the utter darkness of the winter day. They were all that remained, left face to face in the house that had slowly been emptied by financial ruin; and their daughter's death plunged the corners deeper into obscurity, like a final crack that would bring down the old beams rotted with damp. In his dejection, her uncle could not stop walking round and round the table, with the same step as in the funeral cortège, silent and unseeing, while her aunt, too, said nothing, slumped in a chair with the pallid face of a wounded person whose blood was draining away drop by drop. They did not even weep when Pépé planted a large kiss on their cold cheeks. Denise was choked with tears.

That same evening, Mouret called for Denise to discuss a child's garment that he wanted to launch, a cross between a Scottish kilt and a Zouave's trousers.[1] Still shuddering with pity and outrage at such suffering, she could not restrain herself. She dared first of all to mention Bourras, that poor, beaten man who was about to have his throat cut. But at the name of the umbrella merchant, Mouret flew into a temper. The old halfwit, as he called him, was ruining his life, spoiling his triumph, by his ridiculous obstinacy in not wanting to sell his house, a disgraceful shack which soiled *Au Bonheur des Dames* with its crumbling walls – one small corner of the huge block that resisted conquest. It was turning into a nightmare; if anyone other than Denise had spoken up for Bourras, she would have risked being thrown out, so strongly was Mouret tortured by an unwholesome desire to kick the shack to pieces. So what did they expect of him? Could he leave this heap of rubble right beside the store? It had to go, the shop had to go ahead. So much the worse for the old nitwit! And he recalled his offers: he had gone as high as a hundred thousand francs. Wasn't that reasonable? Admittedly, he wouldn't bargain, he would give what was demanded of him; but if the man would only have a bit of sense and let him finish his work! Did people try to stop the locomotives on the railways? She listened to him, her eyes lowered, finding only sentimental arguments. Bourras was so old, they could have waited until he died, a bankruptcy would kill him. At this he announced that he was no longer even in a position to interfere with events. Bourdoncle was looking after it, because the board had decided to get it over. She had nothing to add, much though it pained her and moved her to pity.

After an awkward silence, Mouret himself raised the subject of the Baudus. He began by commiserating deeply with them in the loss of their daughter. They were very good, very honest people, who had been hounded by misfortune. Then he returned to his argument: underneath, they had brought it upon themselves; it was wrong to insist in that way on remaining in the worm-eaten shack of old-fashioned trade, so it was no surprise that it was collapsing around their heads. He had predicted it twenty times; even she must remember how he told her to warn her uncle against a fatal disaster if he persisted in his ridiculous, outdated ways. Now the catastrophe had arrived and no one could prevent it. They could not reasonably demand that he should ruin himself in order to spare the neighbourhood. In any case, if he were to be foolish enough to shut down *Au Bonheur*, another large store would grow up by itself next door, because the idea was everywhere in the air: the seeds of success of the centres of labour and industry had been carried on the wind of the times which was blowing away the crumbling edifice of the past.[2] Gradually, he warmed to his subject, defending himself eloquently and with feeling against the animosity of his unintended victims, the clamour that he heard around from the little shops in their death throes. You could not cling to your dead, you had to bury them – and with a gesture he despatched underground, swept aside and cast into the paupers' grave the corpse of old-fashioned trade, the mouldy, diseased remains of which were becoming a blot on the sunny streets of the new Paris. No, no, he felt no remorse, he was simply doing the work of his time, as she very well knew, being someone who loved life and had a passion for grand schemes carried out in the full light of publicity. Reduced to silence, she listened to him for a long time, then left, troubled in her mind.

Denise hardly slept at all that night, turning in her bed, nightmares interrupting her insomnia. She thought that she was a little girl again in their garden in Valognes, bursting into tears when she saw the warblers eating spiders, which themselves ate flies.[3] Was it true, then, that the world must necessarily grow fat on death, in a struggle for life that raised creatures in the charnel-house of endless destruction? Later, she saw herself standing by the vault into which Geneviève was being lowered, then her uncle and aunt, alone in their dark dining room. A dull sound of falling masonry rumbled in the deep silence of the dead air: it was Bourras' house collapsing, as though worn away by floods. The silence returned, more sinister still, broken by the shuddering sound of another crash, then another, and another: the Robineaus, Bédoré and Sister and the Vanpouilles were each cracking and tumbling down in turn, the small traders of the district of Saint-Roch falling to an invisible pickaxe, with the sudden thunder of an emptying cart. At this, a great feeling of sorrow woke her up with a start. Oh, Lord, what agony! Families weeping, old men driven on to the street and all the poignant dramas of financial ruin! And she could not save any of them; she knew that it was good and that this dunghill of miseries was essential to the health of the Paris of tomorrow. When day came, she grew calmer, a great, sorrowful sense of resignation keeping her eyes open and turned towards the slowly lightened window panes. Yes, it was the debt of blood: every revolution needed martyrs and one could only go forward over the dead. Her fear of having been a bane to them, of having participated in the murder of those close to her, now dissolved into a pitying sense of regret at these unavoidable ills which are the birth pangs of every generation. In the end, she looked for what solace was possible and in her goodness she sought what might be done at least to save her own family from the final crushing disaster.

Now Mouret rose up before her, with his passionate face and caressing eyes. Surely, he would not refuse her anything and she was sure he would agree to any reasonable compensation. Her thoughts wandered, trying to judge his character. She knew about his life and was aware how calculating he had been in the past with his affections, how he had continually exploited women, taken mistresses in order to advance his career, become involved with Madame Desforges solely in order to keep a hold on Baron Hartmann, and all those others, the Claras he had picked up, the pleasure he had bought, paid for and cast back on the street. Yet these first experiences of an adventurer in love which amused the gossips in the shop were eventually only an aspect of the man's genius and his victorious charm. He was seduction. What she could never have pardoned him was the deceit that he used to practise, the lover's coldness beneath the play-acting gallantry of his little attentions. But now that he was suffering because of her, she felt no resentment. His suffering had made a bigger man of him. When she saw him in torment, paying such a heavy price for his contempt for women, he seemed to have expiated his sins.

That morning, Denise got Mouret to agree to the compensation that she felt was fair, whenever the Baudus and old Bourras finally gave in. Weeks passed and she went to see her uncle almost every afternoon, escaping for a few minutes to bring her laughter and her youthful optimism to cheer up the dark shop. She was especailly worried about her aunt, who had stayed in a blank stupor since Geneviève's death; her life seemed to be seeping away hour by hour and when anyone spoke to her, she replied with an air of astonishment that she was not in pain, but just weary. The neighbours shook their heads: the poor woman would not long be pining for her daughter.

One day, Denise was coming out of the Baudus' when, turning into Place Gaillon, she heard a loud shout. A crowd was running, driven by panic – the breath of fear and pity that suddenly blows along a street. An omnibus in brown livery, one of those that go between the Bastille and Batignolles, had run over a man at the entrance to the Rue Neuve-Saint-Augustin, opposite the fountain. The coachman had risen up on his seat in a surge of fury and was restraining his two black horses, which were rearing. He was uttering a flood of curses.

'For God's sake! For God's sake! Look where you're going, you clumsy oaf!'

The omnibus had now stopped and the crowd surrounded the wounded man; a constable happened to be on the spot. The coachman was still standing up, calling on the passengers to witness; they, too, had got up and were leaning out to see the blood, while he put his side of the story with gestures of exasperation, mounting anger making him almost speechless.

'It's not possible . . . What have I done to deserve such a fellow? He was standing there calmly, I shouted at him and he just chucked himself under the wheels!'

At this a workman, a house painter, ran over with his brush from a nearby shopfront and said in a high-pitched voice, amid the excitement:

'Don't get so worked up about it! I saw him: he jumped under the wheels, honest he did! Here, he dived forward like that. Another one who was tired of life, I suppose.'

Other voices rose up and they agreed that it had been a suicide attempt, while the constable took down the particulars. Ladies, very pale, got down quickly and went off without looking back, taking with them the horror of the soft shudder which the omnibus had sent through them as it passed over the body. Meanwhile, Denise came up, impelled by the active sympathy that made her become involved in all accidents: crushed dogs, horses brought down or workmen falling from roofs. And, on the roadway, she recognized the victim, senseless, his frock coat spattered with mud.

'It's Monsieur Robineau!' she cried out, in pained astonishment.

At once, the constable began to question the young woman. She gave his name, profession and address. Thanks to the coachman's quick reaction, the omnibus had swerved and only Robineau's legs had fallen under its wheels, though it was to be feared that both were broken. Four public-spirited volunteers carried the wounded man to a pharmacist in the Rue Gaillon while the omnibus slowly proceeded on its way.

'Damn it all!' said the coachman, cracking his whip at the horses. 'I've had enough for one day.'

Denise followed Robineau to the pharmacist who, while waiting for a doctor that no one could find, announced that there was no immediate danger and that the best thing was to take the patient home, since he lived near by. A man went to the police station to ask for a stretcher. At this, Denise had the good idea of going on ahead, to prepare Madame Robineau for the shock; but she found it very hard to get into the street through the crowd pressing around the door – a morbid crowd that was growing minute by minute. Children and women went on tiptoe and resisted all the shoving and pushing, while each new arrival invented his or her own accident: by this time, Robineau was a husband who had been thrown out of the window by his wife's lover.

In the Rue Neuve-des-Petits-Champs, Denise saw Madame Robineau from a distance at the door of the silk shop. This gave her an excuse to stop and chat for a moment, while looking for some way to deliver the dreadful news. The shop had the disordered atmosphere, the sense of a lost cause that comes over a dying business. It was the expected outcome of the great battle between two rival silks in which Paris-Bonheur had routed the competition after a new fall of five centimes: it was now being sold at four francs ninety-five, so Gaujean's silk had met its Waterloo. In the past two months, Robineau had tried every expedient and was living through hell in an attempt to avoid a declaration of bankruptcy.

'I saw your husband on the Place Gaillon,' said Denise who had finally come into the shop.

Madame Robineau kept looking out towards the street, with what seemed like a vague sense of anxiety. She said quickly:

'Oh, yes, just now, I expect? I'm waiting for him, he should be here. Monsieur Gaujean came this morning, and they went out together.'

She was still charming, delicate and high-spirited, but she was tired, being in the later stages of pregnancy, and more confused and uneasy than ever when it came to business, which her gentle nature was unable to grasp and which was going wrong. As she often said, why were they going through this? Wouldn't it be nicer to live quietly in a little home, with nothing to eat but bread?

'My dear girl,' she said, with a sad smile. 'We have nothing to conceal from you. Things are going badly and my poor darling is losing sleep over it. Only today, that Gaujean was bothering him over some late payments. I've been worrying myself to death, all alone here.'

She was turning back towards the door when Denise stopped her. She had just heard the noise of the crowd in the distance and guessed that they would be bringing the stretcher, together with the flood of onlookers who had attached themselves to the accident. So, even though her mouth was dry and she could not find the consoling words she wanted, she had to say something:

'Don't upset yourself, there's no immediate danger . . . Yes, I did see Monsieur Robineau, something has happened to him. They're bringing him home, but please don't worry.'

The young woman listened to her, pale-faced, not yet clearly understanding. The street was full of people, cab drivers were cursing and the men had put the stretcher down outside the shop, so that they could open both sides of the glazed door.

'He's had an accident,' Denise went on, determined to conceal the suicide attempt. 'He was on the pavement and slipped under the wheels of an omnibus. Oh, it's only his feet. They're looking for a doctor. Don't worry.'

A great shudder went through Madame Robineau. She gave two or three inarticulate cries, then said nothing more, but sank down next to the stretcher, pushing back the curtains with trembling hands. The men who had brought it waited in front of the house to take it away when at last a doctor had been found. No one dared touch Robineau who had regained consciousness and was in terrible pain at the slightest movement. When he saw his wife, two large tears ran down his face. She kissed him and was weeping and staring at him. Out in the street, the pushing and shoving continued, with faces pressed together as if in a theatre, with shining eyes. Some girls out of a workshop were threatening to break the windows so that they could see better. To escape from this feverish curiosity – and considering in any case that it was not appropriate to leave the shop open – Denise had the idea of lowering the metal shutter. She went to turn the handle herself; the mechanism gave a plaintive squeak and the sheets of metal came down slowly like a heavy curtain lowered across the dénouement of Act Five in a play. When she came back inside, after shutting the little round door behind her, she found Madame Robineau still distraught, clasping her husband in her arms, in the murky half-light from two star shapes cut out of the metal. The ruined shop seemed to be sliding towards the void, only the two stars shining on this swift and brutal catastrophe of the Parisian streets. At length, Madame Robineau was able to speak again.

'Oh, my darling! Oh, my darling! Oh, my darling!'

These were the only words she could find, while he choked at the sight of her kneeling, bent over, with her pregnant belly pressed against the stretcher; and, in a fit of remorse, he confessed. When he did not move, he could feel only the burning, leaden weight of his legs.

'Forgive me, I must have been mad. When the solicitor told me in front of Gaujean that the notices would be posted tomorrow, it was as though flames were dancing and the walls were on fire. And then, I don't remember anything. I was going down the Rue de la Michodière, and I thought that the people of *Au Bonheur* were mocking me and that great whore of a house was crushing me. So, when the omnibus turned the corner, I thought of Lhomme and his arm, and threw myself under it.'

Horrified by this admission, Madame Robineau slowly sank to the floor. My God! He wanted to die! She grasped the hand of Denise, who had leaned towards her, quite overcome by the scene. The wounded man, exhausted by his emotions, had once more lost consciousness. And still the doctor did not come! Two men had already searched the neighbourhood and the concierge had set off to look for him too.

'Don't worry,' Denise said mechanically, also sobbing.

So Madame Robineau, sitting on the ground, her head level with the stretcher and her cheek against the straps where her husband was lying, poured out her heart.

'Oh, if I were to tell you . . . It was for my sake that he wanted to die. He would say to me continually: I've robbed you, the money was yours. And at night he dreamed about those sixty thousand francs, he would wake up in a sweat, saying that he was incompetent. When you had no head for business, it was wrong to risk other people's money. You know he's always been nervous and a worrier. Eventually, he was seeing things that scared me. He would see me in the street in rags, begging – when he loved me so much and wanted to see me rich and happy . . .'

When she looked round, she saw that his eyes were open again and went on in her faltering voice:

'Oh, my darling, why did you do it? Do you think I'm so unkind? You see, I don't mind if we are ruined. As long as we're together, we won't be unhappy. Let them take everything. Let's go off somewhere, where you won't hear about them ever again. You can work whatever happens, you'll see how good things will be again.'

Her forehead was close to her husband's pale face and both of them were silent now, in the tenderness of their sorrow. In the quiet, the shop seemed to be sleeping, drowsing in the murky light of dusk while, behind the thin metal shutter, they could hear the noise of the street, the life of broad daylight going past in the rumbling of carriages and the crush of the pavement. Finally, Denise, who had been going minute by minute to look out through the little door that opened on the entrance hall of the house, came back calling: 'The doctor!'

He was a young man with bright eyes, shown in by the concierge. He preferred to see the wounded man before he was put in bed. Only one of the legs, the left one, was broken, above the ankle. It was a simple break and there was no need to fear any complication. They were getting ready to take the stretcher behind the shop to the bedroom when Gaujean appeared. He was coming to report on one last attempt he had made – though, in fact, it had failed: a declaration of bankruptcy was unavoidable.

'What is it?' he asked. 'What's happened?'

Denise told him, briefly. He was embarrassed. Robineau said weakly:

'I don't hold it against you, but all this is partly your fault.'

'Blast it, my dear fellow,' Gaujean replied. 'It would have taken stronger men than us. You know, I'm in no better state than you are.'

They lifted the stretcher and the patient still found the strength to say:

'No, no, stronger men would have given way even so. I can see why those stubborn old ones, like Bourras and Baudu, stick to their guns; but we were young, we accepted the new order of things! You see Gaujean, it's the end of a world.'

They carried him off. Madame Robineau embraced Denise, carried by an impulse almost of joy at being finally rid of the worry of business. And, as Gaujean was leaving with Denise, he admitted to her that the poor devil Robineau was right. It was crazy to try to fight against *Au Bonheur des Dames*. He personally felt that he was lost unless he could get on the right side of them again. Only the day before he had made a secret approach to Hutin, who was about to leave for Lyon; but he held out little hope and tried to get Denise on his side, aware no doubt of her influence.

'My goodness!' he went on. 'Too bad for manufacturing! They would laugh at me if I ruined myself struggling any more for the sake of others, while those fellows are arguing over who should make the goods at the lowest rate. Heavens, as you used to say, industry has to follow progress by organizing itself better or using new methods. It will all come right, as long as the public is happy.'

Denise smiled and said:

'Go and tell that to Monsieur Mouret . . . He'd be glad to see you and he's not the man to hold it against you if you offer him a profit, even a centime a metre.'

It was January when Madame Baudu died, on a clear, sunlit afternoon. For the previous fortnight, she had not been able to go down to the shop, which was looked after by a daily help. She was propped up in bed with pillows at her back. Only the eyes still lived, in her white face; and with her head held upright, she would turn them obstinately towards *Au Bonheur des Dames* opposite through the little curtains on the windows. Baudu himself suffered from this obsession, from these desperately staring eyes and sometimes tried to draw the large curtains. But she would make a gesture entreating him to stop, determined to look until her last breath. Now the monster had taken everything from her: her house, her daughter . . . She herself had gradually faded with the *Vieil Elbeuf*, her life slipping away with its customers; on the day of its death rattle, her breath went. When she felt herself dying, she still had the strength to demand that her husband open the two windows. It was mild and the bright sunshine fell pleasantly across *Au Bonheur*, while the bedroom in the old house was shivering in the shade. Madame Baudu's gaze remained fixed, filled with this vision of a triumphal monument and the clear windows behind which millions of francs poured by. Slowly, the colour drained from her eyes and the darkness came in; when they were extinguished by death, they stayed wide open, still looking and drowned in heavy tears.

Once more, all the ruined small businesses of the neighbourhood joined the funeral procession. There were the Vanpouille Brothers, livid from their December bills, which they had paid with a supreme and unrepeatable effort. Bédoré and Sister leaned on a stick, racked with such worries that his stomach trouble was getting worse. Deslignières had had a stroke; Piot & Rivoire walked in silence, heads bent, like beaten men. No one dared ask about those who were not there. Quinette, Mademoiselle Tatin and others who went under, from one day to the next, knocked down, carried away in the flood of disasters – not to mention Robineau, lying on his bed with his broken leg. But they did point out, with interest, the shopkeepers newly stricken by the plague: Grognet the perfumer, Madame Chadeuil the milliner, Lacassagne the florist and Naud the cobbler, still standing, but infected by their fear of the disease that would sweep them away in their turn. Baudu walked behind the hearse with the same step, like a stricken bull, with which he had accompanied his daughter; while at the back of the first funerary carriage you could see Bourras' eyes shining in the undergrowth of his eyebrows and hair, white as snow.

Denise was dreadfully worried. For the past fortnight, she had been worn out with anxiety and tiredness. She had had to put Pépé in boarding school and Jean was leading her a merry dance, so much in love with the patissier's niece that he had begged his sister to ask for her hand in marriage. On top of that, her aunt's death – these successive catastrophes – had finally overwhelmed her. Mouret had once more offered to help: whatever she did for her uncle and the others would be fine. Once again, one morning, she had a talk with him, at the news that Bourras had been thrown out on the street and that Baudu had to shut up shop. Then she went out after lunch, hoping at least to bring relief to those two.

Bourras was standing in the Rue de la Michodière, on the pavement opposite his house, from which he had been evicted the evening before after a clever trick which the solicitor had dreamed up: since Mouret owned some bills, he had had no difficulty in having the umbrella merchant declared bankrupt, then he bought the lease for five hundred francs in the sale of assets organized by the receiver, so that the obstinate old man had given up for five hundred francs what he had not wanted to sell for a hundred thousand.[4] After that, the architect, who arrived with his demolition crew, had had to call in the police to throw him out. The stock was sold and the rooms stripped, but he hung on in the corner where he slept and they did not dare drive him from it, out of a last shred of pity. But the demolition men started to take the roof off above his head. They had removed the rotten slates, the ceilings were crumbling, the walls were cracking and he stayed there, under the old bare beams in the midst of the ruins. Finally, when the police arrived, he left. But the very next morning he was back, on the opposite pavement, after spending the night in some furnished lodgings near by.

'Monsieur Bourras,' Denise said softly.

He did not hear her, his blazing eyes eating into the demolition men whose pickaxes were starting on the façade of his shack. Now, through the empty windows, you could see the interior, the pitiful rooms and the black staircase where no beam of sunlight had penetrated for two hundred years.

'Oh, it's you!' he replied at last, when he recognized her. 'They're making a fine job of it, aren't they, those thieves?'

She dare not say anything, touched by the pathetic sadness of the old house and unable to take her eyes off the mildewed stones as they came down. Upstairs, on a corner of the ceiling in what had been her room, she could still see the name in shaky black letters: Ernestine, written with the soot from a candle; and the memory of her days of poverty came back, filling her with emotion for all that she had suffered. But the workmen, wanting to bring down a whole wall at once, had decided to attack it at the base. It was shaking.

'If only it could crush the lot of them!' muttered Bourras, savagely.

There was a dreadful cracking sound. The terrified workers ran into the street. As it fell, the wall broke up and carried the whole of the ruin with it. The shack could not hold, of course, with all its cracks and subsidence, so one shove was enough to split it from top to bottom. There was a pitiful landslide, the flattening of a mud hut, soaked by rain. Not a wall remained standing and there was nothing on the ground but a heap of rubble, the rubbish of the past thrown out by the side of the road.

'My God!' the old man exclaimed, as though taking a blow to the guts.

He was left speechless, not believing that the end could come so quickly. And he was looking at the open gash, the space at last freed in the side of *Au Bonheur des Dames*, relieved of the wart that had shamed it. It was the crushing of the gnat, the final triumph over the blazing obstinacy of the infinitely small, the whole island invaded and conquered. Passers-by stopped to talk in loud voices with the demolition men, who were complaining about these old heaps and how dangerous they were.

'Monsieur Bourras,' Denise kept saying, trying to lead him away. 'You know that we won't abandon you; you will have all you need.'

He pulled himself up.

'I have no needs. They have sent you, haven't they? Well, you can tell them that old Bourras can still work and that he will find employment where he wants. Honestly! It would be too convenient if they could give charity to the people they murder!'

She implored him.

'I beg you, take it, don't make me so unhappy.'

But he shook his grey head.

'No, no, goodbye, it's all over. You be happy, while you're young, and don't prevent us old ones from clinging to what we believe.'

He gave a last glance at the heap of rubble and then walked laboriously away. She watched his back moving through the crowd on the pavement. Then the back turned the corner of the Place Gaillon and was gone.

Denise stayed there for a moment, staring into space. Finally, she went into her uncle's. The draper was alone in the dark premises of the *Vieil Elbeuf*. The cleaner only came in the mornings and evenings to do a little cooking and help him to take down and put up the shutters. He would spend hours alone like this, often with no one troubling him for the whole day, but panicking, unable to find the goods, if a customer did still venture inside. There, in the silence and the half-light, he walked constantly with the heavy steps of his funeral processions, giving way to an unhealthy need for these obsessive forced marches, as though trying to ease and relieve his pain.

'Are you better, Uncle?' Denise asked.

He stopped only for a second, then set off again, going from the cash desk to a dark corner of the room.

'Yes, yes, very well, thank you.'

She looked for some consolation, some optimistic words, but found none.

'Did you hear the noise? The house has come down.'

'Why, it's true then,' he said quietly, with a look of astonishment. 'It must have been the house. I felt the ground tremble. When I saw them on the roof this morning, I closed my door.'

He gave a vague gesture, implying that these things no longer interested him. Every time he came back to the desk, he looked at the empty seat, the chair with its worn velvet on which his wife and daughter had grown up. Then, when he came to the other end of his constant tramping, he looked into the shadows at the shelves where a few pieces of cloth were in the final stages of decay. The house was bereaved, those that he loved had gone and his business had come to a shameful end, while he alone remained to carry his dead heart and broken pride in the midst of the catastrophe. He looked up at the dark ceiling, listened to the silence that emerged from the darkness in the little dining room, that family corner which he had once loved even down to its musty smell. There was no longer a breath in the old house, only his heavy, regular footsteps making the old walls ring, as though he were trampling the tomb of his affections.

At last, Denise came to the reason for her visit.

'Uncle, you can't stay like this. You must come to a decision.'

He answered without stopping:

'Of course, but what do you want me to do? I've tried to sell up, but no one came. My God! One morning I'll just shut up shop and leave.'

She knew that there was no danger of bankruptcy. Faced with this relentless series of misfortunes, the creditors had preferred to come to an understanding. With all his debts paid, her uncle would simply be out on the street.

'But what will you do then?' she asked, trying to find a way to suggest an offer that she did not dare put into words.

'I don't know,' he replied. 'Something will turn up.'

He had changed his route: now he was walking from the dining room to the front windows; and on each round he cast a melancholy glance at those pathetic, neglected displays. He did not even look up at the triumphal façade of *Au Bonheur des Dames*, its architecture extending to left and right towards either end of the street. It was utter annihilation and he no longer had the strength to feel angry about it.

'Listen, Uncle,' Denise said eventually, with embarrassment. 'There may be work for you . . .'

She paused, then stammered out:

'Yes, I've been asked to offer you a job as inspector.'

'Where?' Baudu asked.

'Well, of course, over there, with us opposite. Six thousand francs, not tiring work.'

He had suddenly stopped in front of her, but instead of losing his temper as she feared, he went very pale, succumbing to a painful feeling of bitter resignation.

'Over there, over there,' he stammered, several times. 'Do you want me to work over there?'

Denise herself shared his feelings. She remembered the long struggle between the two shops, the funeral processions of Geneviève and Madame Baudu, and she could see before her the *Vieil Elbeuf*, beaten down, its heart ripped out by *Au Bonheur des Dames*. And the idea of her uncle working over there, walking around in a white tie, made her heart weep with pity and anger.

'Come now, Denise, my girl, is it possible?' he said simply, crossing his poor trembling hands.

'No, no, Uncle!' she cried, all her sense of justice and decency rising against it. 'It would be wrong. Forgive me, I beg you.'

He had resumed his walking, his footsteps once more shaking the sepulchral emptiness of the house. And when she left him, he was still walking, driven by the obstinate need of great despair when it turns in on itself, unable to find a way out.

That night, Denise was once more unable to sleep. She had just realized how powerless she was. Even for her own family, she could not find any solace; she would have to watch right to the end the invincible working of life which requires death to engender its renewal. She no longer fought against it, but accepted this law of struggle, though her woman's soul filled with anguished compassion and sympathetic tenderness at the idea of suffering humanity. For years, she had been caught up herself in the cogs of the machine. Hadn't she bled? Hadn't she been beaten, driven out and insulted? Even today, she was sometimes appalled at feeling she had been chosen by the logic of events. Why her, when she was such a puny little thing? Why did her hand suddenly count for so much in the workings of the monster? And the force that drove all before it took her in its turn, even though her arrival was meant to be a revenge. Mouret had invented this machine for crushing people, the brutal operation of which outraged her. He had strewn the neighbourhood with ruins, dispossessing some and killing others; and she loved him despite it all for the greatness of what he was doing, she loved him more and more at each excess of his power, despite the floods of tears that swept over her when she witnessed the sacred suffering of the vanquished.

CHAPTER 14

Brand new, with its chalk-white houses and the last scaffolding of some delayed building work, the Rue du Dix-Décembre lay beneath a clear February sun. A stream of carriages went past, in a broad march of triumph, down this trench of light cut through the damp shades of the old quarter of Saint-Roch. Between the Rue de la Michodière and the Rue de Choiseul, there was a riot, the press of a crowd excited by a month of advertising, eyes turned upwards and jaws hanging before the monumental façade of *Au Bonheur des Dames*, which was being inaugurated that Monday on the occasion of the Great White Sale.

Fresh and joyful, this vast, many-coloured architectural pile with gold highlights, prepared one for the din and brilliance of the sales floors inside, attracting the eyes like a vast display in the brightest colours. At ground-floor level, so as not to outshine the materials in the windows, the décor was restrained: at the base, made of sea-green marble; the corner pillars and the supporting pillars dressed in black marble, its severity lightened by gilded cartouches; and, for the rest, plate glass panels in iron frames – nothing but glass, which seemed to open the depths of the galleries and the halls to the broad daylight of the street. But as one rose up the window displays, so the colours became brighter. Around the frieze of the ground floor were mosaics, a garland of red and blue flowers, alternating with marble plaques, on which were engraved names of goods, extending into infinity, all round the colossus. Then the lower part of the first floor, in enamelled brick, once again supported the plate glass of the wide bays right up to the frieze, which was composed of gilded shields bearing the coats of arms of French towns and terracotta motifs, with enamel repeating the clear tones of the base. Finally, at the very top, the entablature burst out like a brilliant flowering of the whole façade, the mosaics and ceramics reappearing in warmer tones while the zinc of the guttering was carved and gilded, and along the upper plinth stood a whole tribe of statues representing the great industrial and manufacturing cities, their slender silhouettes outlined against the sky. Most of all, the bystanders marvelled at the main doorway, as high as a triumphal arch, also decorated with a profusion of mosaics, ceramic tiles and terracotta, surmounted by an allegorical group shining in new gold – Woman clothed and embraced by a merry flock of little Cupids . . .

Around two o'clock, a police picket had to get the crowd moving and supervise the parking of carriages. The palace was built, the temple raised to the extravagant follies of Fashion. It dominated the neighbourhood, covering it with its shadow. Already, the scar left on its side by the demolition of Bourras' shack had healed so well that one could search in vain for the site of this vanished wart; the four façades extended along the four streets without a gap, in magnificent isolation. On the other side, since Baudu had gone into a retirement home, the *Vieil Elbeuf* was shut and walled up like a tomb behind shutters that were never raised. Little by little, the wheels of passing cabs spattered them, posters buried them and stuck them together in a rising tide of advertising, which was like the last shovel of earth on the coffin of old-fashioned trade. And, in the midst of this dead shopfront, dirtied by the splashes from the street and blotched like the rags of the Parisian mob, hung an immense yellow notice, brand new, like a flag planted over a conquered empire, announcing in letters two feet high the great sale at *Au Bonheur des Dames*. It was as though the colossus, after its successive expansions, seized by shame and repugnance for the dingy district in which it had its humble birth – and which it subsequently slaughtered – had just turned its back, leaving behind the mud of these narrow streets, and offering its parvenu's face to the noisy, sunlit avenue of the New Paris. Now, as the print on the advertisements depicted it, it had grown fat like the ogre in the fairy tale whose shoulders threatened to break the clouds. First of all, in the foreground of this print, the Rue du Dix-Décembre, the Rue de la Michodière and the Rue Monsigny, full of little black figures, were unnaturally widened, as though to make room for all the customers of the world. Then there were the buildings themselves, of exaggerated size, seen from a bird's-eye view with their roofs showing the positions of the covered galleries and their glass-roofed courtyards suggesting the halls beneath – the whole infinity of that lake of glass and zinc shining in the sun. Beyond that, Paris – but a Paris reduced, eaten up by the monster: the houses near by were like mean little cottages, while beyond that they were scattered about in a vague dusting of chimney pots; the monuments seemed to melt away: on the left, two lines for Notre-Dame, on the right, a circumflex accent for the Invalides, in the background, the Pantheon, shamefaced and lost, no larger than a lentil. The horizon crumbled away, reduced to no more than an insignificant frame for the picture, as far as the heights of Châtillon and into the vast countryside with blurred distances suggesting its inferior status.

The crowd had been growing since morning. No shop had ever stirred the town with such a burst of publicity. Now, *Au Bonheur* was spending nearly six hundred thousand francs every year on posters, newspaper advertisements and announcements of every sort; the number of catalogues sent out had reached four hundred thousand and more than a hundred thousand francs' worth of materials were cut up for samples. Newspapers, walls and the ears of the public were comprehensively invaded, as if by a monstrous brass trumpet constantly blowing the news of great sales to the four corners of the earth. And now on this façade, in front of which people pushed and shoved, had become a living advertisement, with the gilded and multicoloured ostentation of a bazaar, its wide windows for exhibiting the entire poem of the female garment and its multiplication of painted, carved and sculpted signs, from the marble plaques of the ground floor to the leaves of cast iron arching above the roofs, exhibiting the gold of their banners on which the name of the shop could be read in the most modish colours against the blue of the sky. To celebrate the inauguration, they had added flags and trophies; every floor was decked with banners and standards with the coats of arms of the main towns of France, while at the very top, the flags of foreign nations raised on masts were flapping in the wind. Finally, below, the White Sale, behind the windows, took on a blinding intensity. There was nothing but white: a full trousseau and a mountain of sheets on the left, curtains like shrines and pyramids of handkerchiefs on the right, to exhaust the eyes; and between the hangings of the door – lengths of cotton, calico, muslin, in waves like drifts of snow – stood fully dressed pictures on sheets of blueish card, where a young bride and a woman in a ball gown, both life-size and dressed in real materials, lace and silk, smiled with their painted faces. A circle of idlers kept forming constantly, while a feeling of desire rose out of the amazement of the crowd.

Something that aroused still greater interest in *Au Bonheur des Dames* was a disaster which all Paris was talking about, the fire at *Les Quatre Saisons*,[1] the department store that Bouthemont had opened near the Opéra, barely three weeks before. The newspapers were packed with details: the fire itself, caused by a gas explosion; the frantic escape of salesgirls in nightdresses; and the heroism of Bouthemont, who had carried five of them to safety. Apart from that, the huge losses were covered by insurance and the public began to shrug its shoulders, saying that it was superb publicity. But for the moment attention turned back to *Au Bonheur*, fuelled by the stories that were circulating and generally preoccupied to the point of obsession by these department stores which were coming to play such a large place in public life. What luck he had, that Mouret! Paris saluted his good fortune and flocked to see him upright when fire itself was taking the trouble to sweep away the competition. They were already calculating the season's profits, estimating the increased numbers that the closing of the rival firm would bring through his doors. For a while, he had felt uneasy, disturbed at the idea of having a woman against him, that Madame Desforges to whom he partly owed his success. Baron Hartmann's financial dilettantism, putting money into both concerns, also irritated him. But most of all, he was exasperated at not having had a brilliant idea of Bouthemont's: the self-indulgent *bon vivant* had just got the priest of the Madeleine, followed by all his clergy, to bless his shop – an astonishing ceremony, processing with all the pomp of the Church from silks to gloves, putting God among the women's underwear and corsets! This had not prevented the place from burning down, but it was worth a million spent on advertisements for its effect on a fashionable clientèle. Ever since, Mouret had dreamed of getting the Archbishop.

Meanwhile, three o'clock sounded on the clock above the door. It was the afternoon rush, with nearly a hundred thousand customers pressed into the galleries and the halls. Outside, carriages were parked from one end of the Rue du Dix-Décembre to the other and on the Opéra side another compact mass occupied the dead end which was to be the start of the future avenue. Simple cabriolets mingled with broughams, coachmen waited among the wheels, rows of horses neighed and shook their shining traces, lit up by the sun. The queues were continually reforming, amid cries from the grooms and the shoving of the animals who were closing ranks of their own accord, while new carriages constantly arrived to join the throng. Passers-by leaped on the traffic islands in terrified groups, and the pavements were black with people down the vanishing perspective of the broad, straight street. A wave of sound rose between the white houses from this human river rolling beneath the spreading soul of Paris, a vast, soft breath sweeping over you with its giant caress.

Madame de Boves, standing in front of a window, accompanied by her daughter Blanche, was examining a display of half-made costumes with Madame Guibal.

'Just look at that!' she said. 'These linen costumes for nineteen francs seventy-five!'

In their square boxes, the costumes were tied with a ribbon and folded so as to show only the trimmings, embroidered in blue and red, while at the corner of each box a picture showed the garment fully made up and modelled by a young lady who looked like a princess.

'Good Lord, it's not worth more than that,' Madame Guibal replied. 'As soon as you touch them they fall to pieces.'

They had become friends, now that Monsieur de Boves was confined to a chair with attacks of gout. The wife put up with the mistress, actually preferring it to go on in her own home, because she got a little pocket money which she could filch from her husband, who needed her indulgence.

'Well, let's go in,' Madame Guibal went on. 'We must see their sale. Didn't your son-in-law arrange to meet you inside?'

Madame de Boves did not answer, staring into space and fascinated by the line of carriages which opened up one by one and emptied out more customers.

'Yes,' Blanche said at last in her weak voice. 'Paul is to pick us up at four o'clock in the reading room after he leaves the Ministry.'

They had been married for a month and Vallagnosc had just gone back to work after a leave of three weeks which they had spent in the south. The young woman already had her mother's build, her flesh puffy and as though thickened by marriage.

'Look, there's Madame Desforges!' the Countess exclaimed, staring at a brougham which was just drawing up.

'Would you believe it?' muttered Madame Guibal. 'After all that business . . . She must still be regretting the fire at *Les Quatre Saisons*.'

Yet it was indeed Henriette. She saw the ladies and came across with a merry smile, disguising her defeat behind a façade of good manners.

'Good heavens, yes! I wanted to take a look. It's better to find out for oneself, isn't it? Oh, we're still good friends with Monsieur Mouret, even though he's said to be furious since I became involved with a rival firm. Really, there's only one thing I can't forgive him, which is to have encouraged that match, you know? That Joseph, with my protégée, Mademoiselle de Fontenailles.'

'No! Are they married?' exclaimed Madame de Boves. 'What a dreadful thing!'

'Yes, dear, and it's just to put one over on us. I know him: he was letting us know that our society girls are only good enough to marry his shop assistants.'

She was getting excited. All four of them stood on the pavement, amid the pushing and shoving around the entrance. Bit by bit, however, the flow took hold of them and they had only to abandon themselves to the current, passing through the door as if lifted up without realizing it, while still talking in raised voices so that they could be heard. Now, they were asking for news of Madame Marty. It was said that poor Monsieur Marty, after violent rows, had just been struck down by a fit of megalomania: he would extract the treasures of the earth by the handful, he would empty the gold mines and fill wagonloads of diamonds and precious stones.

'Poor old fellow!' said Madame Guibal. 'And to think he was always so threadbare and humble, like the little tutor that he was! What about the wife?'

'She's devouring an uncle now,' Henriette replied. 'A decent old fellow, who retired to live with her when his wife died. Anyway, she should be here, we'll see her.'

Something stopped the ladies in their tracks. The shop extended before them, the largest such emporium in the world (as the advertisements said). Now the main gallery reached from end to end, opening on the Rue du Dix-Décembre and on the Rue Neuve-Saint-Augustin, while to right and left, like the aisles of a church, the narrower Monsigny gallery and Michodière gallery also stretched the length of the two streets, without interruption. At intervals, the halls expanded like crossroads amid the metal framework of the hanging stairways and the flying bridges. The arrangement of the interior had been reversed: now the reduced-price goods were on the Rue du Dix-Décembre, silks were in the middle and gloves at the back in the Saint-Augustin Hall; and from the new main entrance hall, when you looked up, you could still see the bed linen, removed from one end of the second floor to the other. The number of departments had reached the enormous figure of fifty; several brand-new ones were to be inaugurated that very day, while others, which had grown too large, were simply divided, so as to make selling easier; and because of the constant growth in business, the staff too had been increased for the new season to three thousand and forty-five employees.

What gave the ladies pause was the stupendous Great White Sale. Around them first of all was the entrance hall, a hall of clear glass with a mosaic floor, where displays of cut-price goods attracted a greedy crowd. Then the galleries led away in dazzling whiteness, a boreal vista, a whole landscape of snow, extending to infinity in steppes hung with ermine like glaciers heaped and shining under the sun. The whiteness of the outside windows was repeated, but here rekindled, colossal, blazing from one end of the huge building to the other with the white intensity of a burning fire. There was nothing but white: all the white items from every department, a riot of white, a white star that at first blinded one with its fixed radiance, so that the details were indistinguishable in this unrelieved white. Then, after a while, the eyes grew accustomed to it: on the left, the Monsigny gallery displayed the white headlands of linens and calicos, and the white rocks of sheets, towels and handkerchiefs; while the Michodière gallery on the right, occupied by haberdashery, hosiery and woollens, displayed white constructions in mother-of-pearl buttons, a great décor built out of white stockings and a whole room covered in white flannelette, lit from afar by a shaft of light. But the chief source of light was the central gallery, with its ribbons and scarves, gloves and silks. The counters vanished beneath the white of silks and ribbons, gloves and scarves. Around the little iron columns rose ruffles of white muslin, tied here and there with white headscarves. The stairways were decked with white drapery, alternating draperies of piqué and dimity which spread along the ramps and surrounded the halls up to the second floor; and these whites rising took wings, hurried on and were lost, like a flight of swans. Then the whiteness fell back from the vaults in a shower of down, a snowy fall of large flakes; white blankets, white quilts flapped in the air, hanging like pennants in a church; long jets of guipure lace crossed back and forth, seeming to support swarms of white butterflies, humming motionlessly; lace fluttered on all sides, suspended like gossamer in a starry sky, filling the air with their white breath. And the real wonder, the altar of this white religion above the silk counter in the great hall, was a tent of white curtains descending from the skylight. Muslin, gauze and fine lace poured in light streams, while very rich embroidered tulle and lengths of oriental silk dotted with silver served as the background to this giant décor, suggesting something between a bedroom and a temple. It looked like a great white bed, vast and virginal, awaiting the white princess of the fairy tales, the one destined to come at last, all-powerful, wearing her white bridal veil.

'Oh! How extraordinary!' the ladies exclaimed. 'Incredible!'

They could not get enough of this song of white, performed by all the materials in the shop. Mouret had never done anything so immense before: this was the masterstroke of his genius for display. In the outpouring of this whiteness, in the apparently random placing of the cloth which seemed to have tumbled by chance out of the emptied shelves and boxes, there was a single harmonic phrase, whiteness sustained and developed in all its tones, appearing, growing and flowering with the complex orchestration of a masterly fugue which, as it develops, carries the soul away on a constantly expanding flight. Nothing but white, yet never the same white, all whites, lifting each other, contrasting with each other, complementing each other and attaining the very radiance of light. It started with the flat whites of calico and linen, the dull whites of flannel and cloth; then came velvets, silks and satins, a rising scale, white little by little catching fire, to finish in small flames on the edges of the folds; and the whiteness took flight with the transparency of curtains, becoming pure clarity with the muslins, laces and, most of all, the tulles, so light that they were like the last, fading note, while the silver on the lengths of oriental silk sang highest of all from the back of the giant alcove.

Meanwhile, the shop was alive. The lifts were besieged by people, there was a crush in the buffet and in the reading room; a whole nation was travelling through these expanses covered in snow. And the crowd looked black, like skaters on a Polish lake in December. On the ground floor there was a dark surge ebbing back, in which you could see only the delicate, delighted faces of women. Then, between the ribs of the iron banisters of the stairs and on the flying bridges, there was a constant line of little figures climbing, as though wandering among snow-covered peaks. One was surprised, considering these icy heights, by the suffocating, hothouse atmosphere. The hum of voices made the huge sound of a passing river. On the ceiling, the profusion of gold, the windows with their gold niello and the golden rose mouldings, shone down on the Alps of the Great White Sale.

'Come, now,' said Madame de Boves. 'We ought to move on. We can't stay here.'

Since she had entered, Inspector Jouve, standing near the door, had kept his eyes fixed on her. When she turned round, their eyes met. Then, as she began to walk away, he gave her a short start and followed her from a distance without any longer appearing to be concerned about her.

'Look!' said Madame Guibal, stopping again at the first cash desk, despite the pushing. 'That's a nice idea, those violets!'

She was talking about *Au Bonheur*'s latest free gift, an invention of Mouret's which he had widely advertised in the papers: little bouquets of white violets, bought by the thousand in Nice and given to every customer when she made even a small purchase. Near each desk, liveried boys handed out these presents under the supervision of an inspector. So, little by little, the clientèle was flowered and the shop filled with these white wedding bouquets, all the women parading a pervasive scent of flowers.

'Yes,' Madame Desforges agreed, enviously. 'It is a good idea.'

But just as the ladies were about to leave, they heard a couple of salesmen laughing about the violets. A tall, thin one was expressing surprise: would it really happen, this marriage between the boss and the buyer from ladies' wear? And a little fat one answered that no one knew, but that even so the flowers had been bought.

'What's this?' Madame de Boves exclaimed. 'Is Monsieur Mouret getting married?'

'It's the first I've heard of it,' Henriette replied, feigning indifference. 'Anyhow, it has to end with that.'

The Countess had quickly glanced at her new friend. Now the pair of them both understood why Madame Desforges had come to *Au Bonheur des Dames*, despite the unpleasantness of breaking up: she must be giving way to an invincible desire to see and to suffer.

'I'll stay with you,' Madame Guibal told her, her curiosity aroused. 'We'll meet Madame de Boves again in the reading room.'

'Very well, let's do that,' Madame de Boves answered. 'I have to go to the first floor. Are you coming, Blanche?'

Up she went, followed by her daughter, while Inspector Jouve, still on her tail, took a nearby staircase so as not to attract her attention. The other two were swallowed up by the dense crowd on the ground floor.

Amid the mad rush of the sale, every department was again talking about the one topic of the boss's affairs. For months the sales staff had been delighted by Denise's long resistance and the matter had quite suddenly come to a head: the day before, they learned that she was to leave *Au Bonheur des Dames*, despite Mouret's pleas, on the grounds that she urgently needed rest. Opinions were divided: would she go or not? From one department to the next, they were betting a hundred *sous* on it happening next Sunday. Some clever ones had bet a lunch on the outcome eventually being marriage, but others, who thought she would leave, would not risk their money either, without good reason. Certainly, the young lady had the strength of a beloved woman who is withholding herself; but the boss, for his part, was powerful in his wealth, his happy widowerhood and his pride, which one final demand might drive to exasperation. In any event, all agreed that the little salesgirl had conducted the affair with the skill of a debauched genius, and that she was now playing the last hand by offering a simple choice: marry me, or I go.

Denise, meanwhile, was not thinking about such things. She had never made a single demand or a single calculation. The situation that had decided her to leave was in fact the outcome of the judgements that others formed about her behaviour, to her constant surprise. Did she ask for all this? Had she been wily, flirtatious or ambitious? She had arrived, simply, and was the first to feel astonished that anyone could love her in that way. Now, once again, why did they think it was a ruse on her part, if she decided to leave *Au Bonheur*? Yet it was so natural! She was getting in a state of nerves about it and suffering unbearable anxieties, what with this constant gossip in the shop, with Mouret's burning obsessions, and with her own struggles against herself; and she preferred to go somewhere else rather than risk giving in one day and regretting it for the rest of her life. If this was a clever ruse, she was unaware of it and wondered in desperation what she had to do if she was not to appear to be running after a husband. The idea of marriage now got on her nerves and she was determined to say no again, and always no, if he were to take folly to the point of asking her. Only she must suffer. The need for a separation drove her to tears, but she repeated, with that great courage of hers, that it had to be, and that she would have no rest or happiness, if she were to act otherwise.

When Mouret got her resignation, he remained silent and apparently cold in his efforts to contain himself. Then he said simply that he would give her a week to think it over before letting her do anything so stupid. After a week, when she returned to the subject, declaring her formal intention to leave after the great sale, he did not lose his temper either. He pretended to be talking common sense to her: she was throwing away her chances, she would never find another position such as the one she had here. Did she have another offer? He was quite ready to give her whatever advantages she thought she might obtain elsewhere. But she replied that she had not looked for another job, that she intended first of all to rest for a month in Valognes, thanks to the savings she already had. He asked what was preventing her from coming back to *Au Bonheur*, if it was only a matter of her health that induced her to leave. She said nothing, finding this questioning a torture. So, he guessed that she would be going to meet a lover, perhaps a husband. Had she not admitted to him one evening that she did love someone? Since that moment he had carried this admission, made in a moment of stress, like a knife plunged into his heart. So, suppose this man was going to marry her, she was giving everything up to be with him; that explained her obstinacy. It was over. He merely added in an icy voice that he would not keep her, since she would not confide the real reason for her departure to him. This conversation, hard, with no anger, upset her more than the violent scene that she had feared.

During the week that Denise had left at the shop, Mouret remained rigid and pale. When he walked through the departments, he pretended not to see her. Never had he seemed more detached and more engaged in his work; and the bets were on again, only the bravest daring to risk a lunch on the marriage card. However, beneath this cold exterior, which was so unlike him, Mouret was concealing a dreadful crisis of indecision and suffering. The blood would rush to his head in a fury: he saw red, he dreamed of grasping Denise in his arms and holding her there, stifling her cries. Then he would try to reason with himself and look for practical means to prevent her from going away, but he came up constantly against his own impotence, raging against the uselessness of his power and money. However, one idea did appear among the mad schemes and came to dominate his mind, despite his resistance to it. After the death of Madame Hédouin, he had sworn not to remarry: he owed his first opportunity to one woman, and he was determined henceforth to make his fortune from all of them. For him, as for Bourdoncle, it was a superstition that the director of a large department store should be a bachelor, if he hoped to preserve his male empire over the diffuse desires of his woman customers: to introduce a woman would be to change the atmosphere and drive the others away with her smell. So he fought against the irresistible logic of the facts, preferring to die rather than give in, seized by sudden feelings of anger against Denise, knowing full well that she was their revenge and fearing that the day he married her he would fall defeated on his millions, broken like a straw by the eternal feminine. Then, gradually, he would weaken again and argue against his revulsion: what had he to fear? She was so mild and so reasonable that he could abandon himself to her without fear. Twenty times an hour, the battle recommenced in his ravaged being. Pride irritated the wound and in the end he started to lose his mind a little, when he considered that, even after he had made this last concession, she might say no, still no, if she was in love with someone. By the morning of the great sale, he had still not made up his mind, and Denise was leaving the next day.

As it happens, that day when Bourdoncle came into Mouret's office at about three o'clock as usual, he discovered him with his elbows on the desk and his hands over his eyes, so distracted that Bourdoncle had to touch him on the shoulder. Mouret raised a face damp with tears, they looked at one another and their hands reached out in a sudden clasp between two men who had engaged in so many commercial battles together. In fact, over the previous month, Bourdoncle's attitude had entirely changed: he had given in to Denise and was even quietly urging his boss to get married. This was no doubt a tactic to avoid being swept away by a force that he now recognized as superior, but one might also have detected behind the change the reawakening of an ancient ambition, a timid and gradually expanding hope that he might in turn devour Mouret, before whom he had so long bowed down. It was part of the atmosphere of the place, this struggle for life, with its constant massacres driving sales up around him. He was carried along by the workings of the machine, seized by the appetite of others, by that voracity which from top to bottom drove the lean to exterminate the fat. Only a kind of religious fear – the religion of luck – had so far prevented him from closing his jaws. Now the boss was reverting to childhood, drifting towards an idiotic marriage, about to kill his luck and ruin his charm over the customers. Why should he dissuade him, when afterwards he might so easily take up the succession to this beaten man, who was falling into the arms of a woman? So it was with the emotion of a farewell and the pity of a long-standing comradeship that he grasped his superior's hands and said again:

'Come, now, bear up for heaven's sake! Marry her, and have done with it.'

Mouret was already ashamed of his moment of weakness. He got up, protesting:

'No, no, this is too silly . . . Come on, let's do our tour of the shop. It's working, isn't it? I think it's going to be a marvellous day.'

They went out and started their afternoon inspection, in departments that were full of customers. Bourdoncle gave him sidelong glances, worried by this last burst of energy and watching his lips to detect the least sign of pain.

The sale was pounding on, shaking the building with its infernal progress, like the shudder of a great ship proceeding at all steam ahead. On Denise's counter, a band of mothers was pressing with hordes of little girls and boys in tow, buried beneath the clothes they were trying on. The department had got out all its white garments and here, as throughout the shop, there was a riot of white, enough to clothe in white a whole flock of shivering cupids: white woollen jackets, dresses in white piqué, light cotton or cashmere, white sailor suits and even white zouaves. In the middle, for decoration, even though it was the wrong time of year, there was a display of first communion wear: the dress and veil in white muslin, the white satin shoes, a light blossoming erupting there like a huge bouquet of innocence and candid enchantment. Madame Bourdelais had her three children, Madeleine, Edmond and Lucien, sitting in order of height, and was scolding the last and smallest of them because he was fidgeting, while Denise was trying to put a little woollen jacket on him.

'Keep still! Mademoiselle, don't you think it's a little tight?'

She had the frank expression of a woman who isn't to be cheated and was weighing up the cloth, assessing the cut and examining the stitching.

'No, it's all right,' she continued. 'It's such a business when you have to dress this tribe. Now I need a coat for this big girl here.'

Denise was having to work on the floor, because of the crush in the department. She was looking for the coat when she gave a little cry of surprise.

'What! Is that you? What are you doing here?'

In front of her was her brother Jean with a parcel in his hands. He had been married for a week and on Saturday his wife, a little brunette with a delightful, worried look, had spent a long time doing her shopping at *Au Bonheur des Dames*. The young couple was to accompany Denise to Valognes on a real honeymoon, a month of holiday among childhood memories.

'Would you believe it?' he told her. 'Thérèse has forgotten a whole mass of stuff. There are things to be changed, others to get . . . So, as she's busy, she sent me with this parcel. I'll explain . . .'

But she interrupted, having noticed Pépé.

'What's this? Pépé too? What about his school?'

'Oh, well,' said Jean. 'After Sunday dinner yesterday I couldn't bring myself to take him back there. He'll go this evening. The poor child is miserable enough about staying shut up in Paris while we are having a good time there.'

Denise smiled at them, worried though she was. She handed Madame Bourdelais over to one of her sales girls and went back to Jean in a corner of the department, which luckily was starting to clear. The little ones, as she still called them, were now quite big lads. Now twelve Pépé was already taller and bigger than she was, but he was still quiet and needed to be hugged: there was an appealing gentleness about him in his school uniform. As for Jean, he was square-shouldered and a good head taller than her, but he still had his blond hair, artistically wind-swept, which gave him a feminine beauty. She herself had remained slim, no larger than a skylark, as she said, but preserving the anxious authority of a mother towards them, treating them as children who had to be cared for, buttoning up Jean's frock-coat so that he did not look like a rake and making sure that Pépé had a clean handkerchief. On this occasion, when she saw the younger boy's tearful eyes, she gently lectured him.

'Be sensible, dearest. You can't leave your school work. I'll take you when the holiday comes. Is there anything you need? No? Would you rather I left you some money, then?'

Then she turned round to the other one.

'And you, little rascal, you're giving him ideas, making him think we're going to have a good time! Try to use your head a little.'

She had given the elder boy four thousand francs, half of her savings, for him to set up home. The younger one was costing her a lot to keep in school, so all her money went to them, as before. They were her only reason for living and working, since once again she swore never to marry.

'Anyway,' said Jean, 'here we are. First of all, in the parcel, there's the brown jacket that Thérèse . . .'

Then he stopped. Denise turned round to find out what had impressed him and saw Mouret standing behind them. For a moment, he watched her acting the little mother between these two large lads, scolding and hugging them, turning them round like babies having their nappies changed. Bourdoncle had stayed a little way off, appearing to take an interest in the sale, but keeping an eye on what was going on.

'These are your brothers, aren't they?' Mouret asked, after a pause.

He spoke in his icy voice, the severe attitude that he used with her now. Denise herself made an effort to appear cold. Her smile faded and she answered:

'Yes, Monsieur . . . I have married off the elder one and his wife has sent him to me for some purchases.'

Mouret kept looking at the three of them. Eventually he said:

'The younger one has grown a lot. I recognize him. I remember seeing him one evening in the Tuileries, with you.'

He spoke more slowly, with a slight trembling in his voice. Feeling a lump in her throat, she bent down, pretending to rearrange Pépé's belt. The two brothers, both blushing, smiled at their sister's boss.

'They look like you,' he went on.

'Oh, no!' she exclaimed. 'They're much better looking than I am.'

For an instant he seemed to be comparing their faces. But it was more than he could manage. How fond she was of them! He started to walk away, then came back to whisper to her:

'Come up to my office, after the sale. I have something to say to you before you leave.'

This time, Mouret did walk away and continue his inspection. His inner struggle was starting up again, because he now felt irritated at having given her the appointment. What impulse possessed him, seeing her with her brothers? It was crazy, since he could no longer find any strength of will. When it came to it, he would just say goodbye. Bourdoncle, who had rejoined him, seemed less uneasy, but still examined him out of the corner of his eye.

Meanwhile, Denise had come back to Madame Bourdelais.

'And the coat, does it fit?'

'Yes, yes, very well. That's enough for today. They cost a fortune, these little creatures!'

Then, managing to slip away, Denise listened to what Jean had to say and accompanied him to the various departments, where he would otherwise surely have lost his head. First of all, it was the brown jacket, which Thérèse, on reflection, wanted to exchange for a jacket in white linen, the same size and style. So Denise took the parcel and went up to ladies' wear, followed by her two brothers.

The department had put out its clothes in soft colours, fancy knitted or light silk summer jackets and mantillas. But the sale was centred elsewhere and there were relatively few customers. Almost all the salesgirls were new. Clara had vanished a month earlier, carried off according to some by the husband of a buyer, or (others said) walking the streets. As for Marguerite, she was finally going to take over the little shop in Grenoble where her cousin was waiting for her. Only Madame Aurélie was still there, immovable, in the round armour of her silk dress, with her imperial mask, which still had the yellowish complexion of an antique marble bust. However, her son Albert's misdemeanours tormented her and she would have retired to the country had it not been for the holes made in her savings by that ne'er-do-well who even threatened to eat away bit by bit their house in Les Rigolles. It was like a judgement on them for their broken home, the mother having gone back to her elegant ladies' parties, while the husband went on playing his horn. Bourdoncle was already looking at Madame Aurélie with a dissatisfied air, surprised that she did not have the decency to retire: too old for selling! That bell would soon toll, carrying off the dynasty of the Lhommes.

'Why, it's you!' she said, seeing Denise, with exaggerated warmth. 'So? You want to change that jacket? Of course, at once . . . Ah! These are your brothers. Real men now.'

Despite her pride, she would have gone down on her knees to get on the right side of Denise, whose departure, in ladies' wear, as in all other departments, was the one subject of conversation. The buyer was quite overcome by it, because she had been counting on her former assistant's protection. She lowered her voice.

'They say you're leaving us. Come now, is it possible?'

'Yes, it is,' the young woman answered.

Marguerite was listening. Since they had settled her marriage, she had been going around with a still more distasteful look on her sour face. She came over, saying:

'You're quite right. Self-respect before everything, no? I'd like to bid you farewell, my dear.'

Customers were coming. Madame Aurélie severely instructed her to look after them. Then, seeing that Denise was taking the jacket herself to get the slip for it, she protested and called over an 'auxiliary': this happened to be something that Denise herself had suggested to Mouret, women helpers who were responsible for carrying purchases, so easing the burden on the salesgirls.

'Go with Mademoiselle,' the buyer said, giving her the parcel.

Then, coming back to Denise, she went on:

'Do, please, reconsider. We're all so upset at your going.'

Jean and Pépé, who were waiting with smiles on their faces among this pressing crowd of women, followed their sister. Now they had to go to trousseaux, to get six chemises like the half dozen that Thérèse had bought on Saturday. But at the lingerie counter, where the White Sale was tumbling down from every shelf, it was stifling and very hard to get through the crowd.

First of all, people had gathered in corsetry to watch a small disturbance. Madame Boutarel, who had arrived from the south this time with her husband and daughter, had been searching the shop since morning to find a trousseau for the girl, who was getting married. The father was consulted and it looked like going on for ever. The family had finally come to rest in lingerie and while the young lady was deeply engaged in studying some underwear, the mother had vanished, distracted herself by a sudden desire for a corset. Monsieur Boutarel, a great ruddy-faced man, abandoned his daughter in panic to go in search of his wife and eventually found her in a fitting room, in front of which he was politely invited to sit. These rooms were narrow cells, with frosted glass doors, from which men, even husbands, were barred, because of the management's exaggerated sense of propriety. Salesgirls came in and out of them quickly, each time giving a glimpse, in the swift opening and closing of the door, of ladies in blouses or skirts, with bare necks or arms, fat ones whose skin was pallid and thin ones with a complexion like old ivory. The men sat waiting on a row of chairs, looking bored. Monsieur Boutarel, when he realized what was going on, lost his temper and shouted that he wanted his wife and that he intended to find out what they were doing to her. He would certianly not let her get undressed without him. They tried in vain to calm him: he seemed to imagine that improper things were going on in there. Madame Boutarel emerged while the crowd was arguing and laughing.

This allowed Denise to get by with her brothers. All the feminine linen, the white underclothes that are hidden, was displayed in a series of rooms, divided between different departments. Corsets and bustles were on one counter, with stitched corsets, long-waisted corsets, boned corsets and above all corsets in white silk, with fans of colour, which had been the subject that day of a special display – an army of headless, legless dummies, with only their torsos and their flattened dolls' busts under the silk, with the disturbing lewdness of cripples; and near them on other stands, bustles of horsehair and dimity rounding off these rods with huge, taut buttocks which looked from the side quite ridiculously indecent. But after that came the attractive intimate wear, pieces of it scattered over the huge rooms as though a group of pretty girls had been undressing themselves from one department to the next down to the naked satin of their skins. Here were the items of fine lingerie, white sleeves and cravats, fichus and white collars, an infinite variety of light, frilly things, white foam emerging from its boxes and piling up like snowdrifts. Here were camisoles, little bodices, morning dresses, dressing gowns, linen, nansouk, lace, long white clothes, free and thin, in which one could feel the stretching and yawning of idle mornings after amorous evenings. Then the underclothes appeared, arriving one by one: white petticoats of every length, the petticoat tight around the knees and the petticoat that drags its train along the floor, a rising sea of petticoats, in which one's legs were lost; bloomers in cambric, linen and piqué, wide white bloomers in which a man's hips would have room to dance; and finally the underblouses, buttoned up to the neck for the night, revealing the bust by day, held only by narrow straps and made of simple calico, or Irish linen, or cambric, the last white veil slipping from the breasts across the hips. In trousseaux, it became an intimate unwrapping, woman laid open to view from underneath, from the petty bourgeoise with her uniform linen to the rich lady smothered in lace – a bedroom open to the public gaze, where the hidden luxury, the pleats, the embroidery and the lace, became a sort of sensual depravity, the more it poured out in its expensive fantasies. Then, woman was dressed again, the white wave of this cascade of linen slipped behind the quivering mystery of skirts, the chemise stiffened by the dressmaker's fingers, the cold bloomers keeping the folds from their box, all this dead percale and dead muslin, scattered across the counters, thrown aside, and piled up, was about to come alive with the life of the flesh, warm and redolent with the smell of love, a white cloud sanctified, bathed in night, the slightest flutter of which, to reveal the pink glimpse of a knee in the depths of this whiteness, would devastate the world. Then there was another room, baby clothes, in which the voluptuous white of women eventually became the pure white of the child: an innocence, a joy, in the mistress who is awakening to motherhood: infant clothes in fluffy piqué, flannel bonnets, chemises and caps as small as toys, and christening dresses, and cashmere shawls – the white down of birth, like a soft rain of white feathers.

'You know, these are like chemises at the theatre,' said Jean, beside himself with delight at this déshabillé, sinking into a flood of chiffon.

In trousseaux, Pauline ran over at once when she saw Denise and, before even asking what she wanted, whispered to her in great excitement about the rumours everyone in the shop was talking about. In her department, two assistants had even fallen out over whether Denise would or would not leave.

'You'll stay, I bet. What would become of me otherwise?'

And when Denise said she was leaving the next day:

'No, no, you think that, but I know the opposite. My goodness, now

I've got a baby, you've got to promote me to under-buyer! Baugé's counting on it, dearest.'

Pauline smiled, with a look of certainty. After that, she gave them the six chemises and when Jean said they were now going to handkerchiefs, she called over an auxiliary to carry the chemises and the jacket brought by the auxiliary from ladies' wear. The girl who appeared was Mademoiselle de Fontenailles, who had recently married Joseph. She had just obtained this lowly post as a favour and was wearing a large black overall marked on the shoulder with a number in yellow wool.

'Go along with Mademoiselle,' said Pauline; then, coming back and lowering her voice again: 'I'm under-buyer, that's agreed, huh?'

Denise promised with a laugh, going along with the joke. Then she left, going down with Pépé and Jean, all three of them accompanied by the auxiliary. On the ground floor, they came into woollens, part of one gallery entirely decked out with white flannel and flannelette. Liénard, resisting his father's efforts to get him back to Angers, was chatting with the handsome Mignot, who had become a broker and had the effrontery to reappear in *Au Bonheur des Dames*. They must have been talking about Denise, because both of them fell silent before greeting her attentively. There were whisperings: people said she looked triumphant and there was a new swing in the betting, with renewed bets of Argenteuil wine and fried fish on her. She had started down the gallery of whites, to get to handkerchiefs at the far end. White went by: the white of cotton, of heavy calico, of light calico, of dimity, of piqué; the white of nansouks, muslins and tarlatans; then came the linens, in huge heaps constructed of alternate pieces like stone building blocks, heavy linen, fine linen, of every width, white or unbleached ecru, from pure flax bleached on the meadow. Then it began again, department after department for every type of linen: household linen, table linen, scullery linen, a continuous outpouring of white, bedsheets, pillowcases, and every different style of towel, table cloth, apron and napkin. The greetings continued, with people stepping aside to let Denise pass. Baugé had hurried into linens to give her a smile, acknowledging the benevolent queen of the shop. Finally, after going through blankets, a room decked with white banners, she arrived at handkerchiefs, where the crowd was bowled over by the ingenuity of the décor:

there was nothing here but white columns, white pyramids, white castles, an architectural fantasy built solely out of handkerchiefs, in lawn, in cambric, in Irish linen, in Chinese silk, monogrammed, embroidered in raised satin stitch, trimmed with lace, with hem-stitching and woven patterns – a whole town in an infinite variety of white bricks, silhouetted like a mirage against the white heat of an oriental sky.

'Another dozen, you say?' Denise asked her brother. 'Cholets?'

'Yes, I think so; like these ones,' he answered, showing her a handkerchief in the parcel.

Jean and Pépé had not left her side, pressing against her constantly as in the old days when they first disembarked in Paris, exhausted by the journey. This huge store where she was so much at home had eventually started to disturb them, so they found shelter in her shadow, putting themselves back under the protection of their little mother in an instinctive reversion to childhood. People watched them go by, smiling at these two big lads following close behind this slender, serious-looking girl, Jean all bewildered with his beard and Pépé quite distraught in his tunic, all three now with the same fair hair, which made people whisper as they went by from one end of the store to the other:

'They're her brothers . . . They're her brothers . . .'

However, while Denise was looking for an assistant, there was another encounter. Mouret and Bourdoncle had come into the gallery and as Mouret stopped once more on seeing her, though without saying anything, Madame Desforges and Madame Guibal went by. Henriette controlled the shudder that went through her whole being. She looked at Mouret and she looked at Denise. And they looked back at her: it was like the silent dénouement, the banal end to a big romantic drama, a glance exchanged through a crowd. Mouret had already moved away, while Denise was disappearing into the back of the department, together with her brothers, still looking for a free sales assistant. Then Henriette, who had recognized the auxiliary who was following them as Mademoiselle de Fontenailles, with the yellow number on her shoulder and her coarsened, pasty, servant's face, relieved her feelings by saying to Madame Guibal, in an irritated voice:

'See what he's done to that unfortuante. Isn't it upsetting? A marchioness! And he forces her to go following like a dog after those creatures whom he picked up off the street!'

She tried to calm herself, adding on what she tried to make a tone of indifference:

'So let's go and see their display in silks.'

The silk department was like a great love nest hung in white to satisfy the fancy of a woman in love who wished her own snow-white nakedness to compete with it in radiance. All the milky pallors of a loved one's body were there, from the velvet of the back to the fine silk of the thighs and the glowing satin of the breasts. Lengths of velvet were hung between the columns, while silks and satins stood out against this background of creamy white as a drapery of metallic white and china white; and there were also arches of silk poults and Sicilian grosgrains, light foulards and surahs which varied in tone from the heavy white of a Norwegian blonde to the transparent, sun-warmed whiteness of a redhead from Italy or Spain.

Favier was just measuring out some white foulard for the 'pretty lady', the elegant blonde, a regular customer of the department, whom the assistants described only by that name. She had been coming here for years, and still nothing was known of her, her life, her address, or even her name. In any case, no one tried to find out, though all of them would speculate whenever she made an appearance, if only for something to talk about. She grew thinner or fatter, she had slept well or else she must have gone to bed late the night before . . . and every little fact about her unknown life, events outside, dramas in the home, thus had a sort of repercussion which was extensively discussed. That day, she seemed very pleased with life, so when Favier came back from taking her to the cash desk, he told Hutin what he thought:

'Perhaps she's getting remarried.'

'Is she a widow, then?' the other man asked.

'I don't know. But you must remember that time she was in mourning . . . Unless, of course, she's made some money on the Stock Exchange.'

There was a pause. Then he concluded:

'It's her business. Suppose we were to get friendly with every woman who comes here?'

Hutin, however, was thinking hard. Two days earlier, he had had a sharp exchange with the management and he felt the outlook was grim. After the great sale, he would surely be sacked. For a long time, his position had been shaky; at the last stocktaking, they had criticized him for failing to meet his preset sales target, and in addition to that – most of all, in fact – there was the slow, steady pressure of appetites trying to devour him in his turn: that hidden war in the department was driving him out, as part of the very operation of the machine. You could hear Favier working away in the dark, a loud grinding of jaws, muffled underground. Favier already had a promise that he would be appointed buyer. Hutin, who knew all this, instead of slapping his old friend's face, now considered him very powerful. Such a cold one, with that obedient air that he had used to get round Robineau and Bouthemont! The surprise he felt was not without a certain amount of respect.

'By the way,' Favier went on. 'Do you know she's staying? The boss has just been seen giving her the eye. There'll be a bottle of champagne in it for me.'

He was talking about Denise. From one department to the next, the gossip had been flowing faster and harder, through the constantly rising stream of customers. Silks in particular were in turmoil because there was a lot riding on the outcome here.

'By golly!' Hutin exclaimed, as though waking from a dream. 'How silly I was not to sleep with her! I'd be in clover now!'

Then, seeing Favier laugh, he blushed at this admission and pretended to laugh as well, trying to repair the damage by adding that the girl had undermined his position with the management. However, he was overcome by a need to express his anger, and eventually lost his temper with the assistants, who were being routed by the assaults of the customers. But suddenly he began to smile again: he had just seen Madame Desforges and Madame Guibal slowly walking across the floor.

'Do you need anything today, Madame?'

'No, thank you,' Henriette replied. 'You see, I'm just walking around. I came here solely out of curiosity.'

After stopping her, he lowered his voice. A plan was starting to take seed in his mind. He flattered her, disparaging the firm: he had had enough of it, he would rather leave than put up any longer with such chaos. She listened to him with delight. She was the one who thought that she was taking him away from *Au Bonheur*, offering to have Bouthemont engage him as buyer in silks when the *Quatre Saisons* reopened. The deal was done and the two of them whispered quietly while Madame Guibal was looking over the display.

'Might I offer you one of these bouquets of violets?' Hutin said aloud, pointing to three or four of the free-gift bouquets which he had got from one of the desks for personal presents.

'Oh, no, certainly not!' said Henriette, shrinking away. 'I don't want to join in the party!'

There was an understanding between them and they separated, laughing again and exchanging knowing glances.

Madame Desforges went to look for Madame Guibal and exclaimed in surprise when she found her with Madame Marty. The latter, followed by her daughter Valentine, had spent two hours being carried around the shop in one of those spending manias from which she would emerge exhausted and confused. She had trodden through the furniture department, which a display of white lacquered pieces had transformed into a huge bedroom for a young girl, then ribbons and fichus, where white colonnades were hung with white awnings, then haberdashery and soft furnishings, with white fringes around ingenious shields carefully made up of button cards and packets of needles, then hosiery, where the crowd was tightly packed this year, to see one motif of the huge décor which was the name of *Au Bonheur des Dames*, magnificent, in letters three metres high made up of white stockings on a background of red ones. But Madame Marty was chiefly excited by the new departments. They could not open a department without her coming to inaugurate it; she would dash in and buy something regardless. She had spent an hour in fashions, installed in a new room on the first floor, having them empty the wardrobes, and taking the hats off the rosewood hat stands laid out on two tables, trying them all on herself and her daughter: white hats, white bonnets, white toques. Then, she had gone back down to the shoe department, at the end of a gallery on the ground floor, behind ties, a department that had only opened that day; she had ransacked the window displays, seized by unhealthy desires for white silk slippers trimmed with swansdown, and shoes and boots in white satin on great Louis XV heels.

'Oh, my dear!' she stammered. 'You can't imagine! They have an extraordinary choice of bonnets. I chose one for myself and one for my daughter. And what about the shoes? Huh, Valentine?'

'Unbelievable!' the girl said, as brash as a grown woman. 'There are boots for twenty francs fifty – but such boots!'

An assistant was following them, dragging the inevitable chair, already under a heap of purchases.

'How is Monsieur Marty?' Madame Desforges asked.

'Not too bad, I think,' Madame Marty replied, alarmed by this sudden question unkindly breaking into her shopping fever. 'He's still away, my uncle was to go and see him this morning.'

But she broke off to exclaim in delight:

'Oh, just look! How lovely that is!'

The ladies, who had been walking along a bit, were now in front of the new department of flowers and feathers, which had been set up in the main gallery between silks and gloves. Under the bright light from the glass roof, there was a vast floral display, a white bunch as tall and wide as an oak tree. The lower part was decorated with small bouquets of flowers: violets, lily-of-the-valley, hyacinths, daisies, all the delicate whites of the flower-bed. Then, larger bouquets climbed up: white roses, softened with a hint of pink, large white peonies, barely touched with carmine, and white chrysanthemums in light sprays flecked with yellow. And still the flowers went upwards: great mystic lilies, branches of spring apple blossom, clusters of scented lilac – a continued movement of opening, surmounted at the level of the first floor by plumes of ostrich feathers, white feathers that were like the breath rising from this tribe of white flowers. A whole corner was full of trimmings and wreaths of orange blossom. There were metal flowers: silver thistles, silver ears of corn. Among the leaves and petals, in all this muslin, silk and velvet, where drops of gum were made to look like beads of dew, flew tropical birds for hats, purple tangaras with black tails and septicolores whose plumage shimmered through all the colours of the rainbow.

'I'm buying a branch of apple,' said Madame Marty. 'Don't you think it's delightful? And do just look at that little bird, Valentine. I'll have it, too.'

Meanwhile, Madame Guibal was getting bored, standing still while the crowd was moving all round. Eventually, she said:

'Well, then, we'll leave you to your purchases. We're going upstairs.'

'No, no, wait for me,' the other woman cried. 'I'm coming too. Perfumery is up there, I must go to perfumery.'

This department, only just set up, was next to the reading room. Madame Desforges was speaking of taking the lift to avoid the crowd on the stairs, but they had to abandon that idea since there was a queue for the apparatus. Finally, they got there, passing in front of the public buffet where the crush was such that an inspector was now having to restrain people's appetites by only admitting the hungry customers in small groups. And from the buffet the ladies had already begun to smell perfumery, a penetrating scent of trapped perfumes drifting along the gallery. The customers were fighting over a soap, the *Bonheur* soap, the house speciality. In display cases and on glass shelves were pots of pomades and creams, boxes of powders and paints, phials of oil and toilet water; while fine brushes, combs, scissors and pocket flasks were kept in a special cupboard. The sales staff had gone to great lengths to decorate the display with all their white china pots and all their white glass phials. The most delightful thing, though, was a silver fountain in the middle, with a shepherdess seated on an abundance of flowers, and a continuous thin stream of violet water running from it and tinkling harmoniously into the metal basin. An exquisite scent hung all around it, while ladies dipped their handkerchiefs as they passed.

'There!' said Madame Marty when she had taken her fill of lotions, toothpaste and cosmetics. 'That's everything; now I'm all yours. Let's go back to Madame de Boves.'

But on the landing of the main staircase, she was stopped once more by Japan. This counter had expanded since the day when Mouret had the amusing idea of risking a small bargain table at this point offering a few shopsoiled goods, never imagining what a huge success it would be. Few departments had had such modest beginnings, yet now it was overflowing with old bronzes, old ivories, old lacquer and had a turnover of fifteen hundred thousand francs a year. He scoured the whole of the Far East, getting travellers to rummage for him in palaces and temples. Moreover, the number of departments kept on growing. There were another two new ones in December, to fill the gaps in the winter off-season: a book department and one for children's toys, which were surely destined to expand and sweep away some more businesses in the district. Four years had been enough for Japan to attract all the art connoisseurs in Paris.

This time, Madame Desforges herself, despite her bitter vow that she would buy nothing, succumbed to a delightfully fine carved ivory.

'Send it to me,' she said quickly, at a nearby cash desk. 'Ninety francs, isn't it?'

Seeing Madame Marty and her daughter deeply involved in trying to choose between various pieces of cheap porcelain, she led Madame Guibal away saying:

'You'll find us in the reading room. I just have to sit down.'

In the reading room, the ladies had to remain standing. All the chairs were taken around the large table covered in newspapers. Some plump men were reading, sitting back, exhibiting their bellies, without the kind thought of giving up their seats ever entering their heads. Some women were writing, heads down, as if hiding the paper beneath the flowers on their hats. In any case, Madame de Boves was not there and Henriette was losing patience when she saw Vallagnosc, who was also looking for his wife and mother-in-law. He greeted her and finally said:

'They must surely be in lace, you can't get them out of there. I'll go and see.'

And he was gallant enough to get two chairs for them before he left.

The crowd in lace was increasing minute by minute. Here, in its most delicate and expensive whites, the Great White Sale reached its apotheosis. This was the sharpest temptation, the maddening desire that made all women lose their heads. The department had been changed into a white chapel. From above hung tulles and guipures, forming a white sky, one of those veils of cloud that make the morning sun pale behind their fine web. Lengths of Mechlin and Valenciennes fell around the columns, a ballerina's white skirts unfurled down to the ground in a shimmer of white. Then on all sides, on every counter, a snowfall of white: Spanish lace as light as breath, embroidered Brussels lace with large flowers on fine mesh, needlepoint and Venetian point with heavier designs, Alençon points and Bruges lace of royal, almost ecclesiastical richness. It was like a white tabernacle to the god of lace.

Madame de Boves, after walking around for a long time with her daughter, prowling among the displays and feeling a sensual need to plunge her hands into the materials, had just made up her mind to get Deloche to show her some Alençon lace. First of all, he brought her some imitation, but she wanted to see real Alençon, and was not satisfied with little trimmings at three hundred francs a metre, demanding instead high flounces at a thousand francs, and handkerchiefs and fans at seven and eight hundred. The counter was soon covered with a fortune in lace. In a corner of the department, Inspector Jouve – who had not let go of Madame de Boves, despite her wanderings – was standing motionless in the midst of the pushing crowd, with an air of indifference and his eyes constantly on her.

'Do you have any round collars in needlepoint?' the Countess asked Deloche. 'Let me see them, if you would.'

The assistant, whom she had been occupying for the past twenty minutes, dared not object, so grand was her air, with her little waist and voice like a princess. Even so, he did hesitate, because sales staff were advised not to let precious lace pile up like that, and ten metres of Mechlin had been stolen from him the week before. But she overawed him, so he gave in and left the pile of Alençon needlepoint for a moment while he turned round and took the berthe collars she had requested out of a drawer behind him.

'Look here, Mamma,' said Blanche, beside her, rummaging in a box full of little pieces of inexpensive Valenciennes. 'We could have this for the pillowcases.'

Madame de Boves did not reply. So the daughter, turning her soft face towards her, saw her mother, with her hands in the pile of lace, making some flounces in Alençon point vanish up the sleeve of her coat. She did not seem surprised, but was moving forward instinctively to hide her when suddenly Jouve rose up between them. He leaned over and whispered politely in the Countess's ear:

'Madame, would you follow me?'

She objected briefly.

'But, Monsieur, why?'

'Please follow me, Madame,' the inspector repeated, without raising his voice.

Her face distorted with anxiety, she quickly glanced around, then resigned herself and resumed her haughty attitude, walking beside him like a queen who has deigned to allow an aide-de-camp to take care of her. Not one of the customers packed into the room had noticed what happened. Deloche, coming back to the counter with the collars, watched her being led off, open-mouthed. What, her too? Such an aristocratic lady! Did you have to search them all, then? And Blanche, left free, followed her mother at a distance, pausing in the midst of the flood of shoulders, very pale, torn between the duty to stick by her and the terror of being detained with her. She saw them go into Bourdoncle's office and decided to hang around outside the door.

As it happened, Bourdoncle was there; Mouret had just managed to get rid of him. Usually, he was the one who decided in this kind of theft, involving respectable people. Jouve had long kept him informed of his doubts about this one, whom he was watching, so Bourdoncle was not astonished when the inspector briefly told him the circumstances; anyway, such extraordinary cases passed through his hands that he declared a woman capable of anything when carried away by her passion for cloth. Since he knew that the director was socially acquainted with the thief, he behaved with the utmost urbanity himself.

'Madame, we forgive such moments of weakness . . . I beg you, however, to consider where you might end up, forgetting yourself like this. Had someone else seen you slipping that lace . . .'

She interrupted him indignantly. She, a thief! Whom did he take her for! She was the Countess de Boves and her husband, inspector-general of the Stud, attended at court.

'I know, Madame, I know,' Bourdoncle said calmly. 'I have the honour to be acquainted with you. Could you first of all return the lace that you have on you . . .'

She protested again, not letting him say another word, splendid in her anger, even drawing on the tears of an insulted grande dame.

Anyone except him would have been shaken, fearing some unfortunate misunderstanding, because she was threatening to take him to court to make up for this insult.

'Take care, Monsieur! My husband will go right up to the minister.'

'Come now, you are no more sensible than the rest,' Bourdoncle said impatiently. 'We must search you, as there's no other way.'

She still did not falter, but continued with her proud air of self-assurance:

'That's right, search me; but I warn you, your firm is at risk.'

Jouve went to look for two salesgirls from corsets. On his return, he informed Bourdoncle that the lady's daughter had been left by herself and had stayed by the door: should he bring her in, too, even though he did not see her take anything? Bourdoncle, proper as ever, decided that they should not make her come in, for the sake of morality, so as not to oblige a mother to blush in front of her child. Meanwhile, the two men retired to an adjoining room while the salesgirls searched the Countess and even took off her dress, so as to examine her bust and hips. Apart from the flounces of Alençon lace – twelve metres at a thousand francs, hidden in a sleeve – they found, flattened and warm, in her bust, a handkerchief, a fan and a scarf, in all around fourteen thousand francs' worth of lace. Madame de Boves had been stealing like this for a year, driven by a wild, irresistible need. The crises got worse and worse, until they became a sensual desire necessary for her existence, overcoming all the arguments of common sense and procuring a pleasure that was all the sharper in that she risked, in the full view of everyone, losing her name, her pride and her husband's high office. Now that he allowed her to empty his wallet, she went stealing with her pockets full of money; she would steal for the sake of stealing, as one loves for love's sake, driven by desire, in the neurotic sickness that her unsatisfied desire for luxury had earlier produced in her through the huge, crude temptation of the department stores.

'It's a trap!' she exclaimed, when Bourdoncle and Jouve returned. 'Someone planted this lace on me, I swear before God!'

Now she had slumped back into a chair and was weeping tears of rage, stifling in her badly fastened dress. Bourdoncle sent the salesgirls away and then said in his calm manner:

'We are happy, Madame, to hush up this unfortunate business, out of consideration for your family. But first of all you must sign a declaration to this effect: "I stole some lace from *Au Bonheur des Dames*," then details of the lace and the date. Moreover, I shall return this paper to you, as soon as you bring me two thousand francs for the poor.'

She had got up and declared in one last protest:

'I shall never sign that, I should rather die.'

'You will not die, Madame. However, I must warn you that I am going to send for the commissioner of police.'

There was a dreadful scene. She swore at him, stammering that it was cowardly of men to torment a woman thus. Her Junoesque beauty and her tall, majestic body dissolved into the fury of a fishwife. Then she tried to appeal to their feelings, begging them in the name of their mothers, talking about kneeling at their feet . . . And, when they still remained immovable, hardened by familiarity, she suddenly sat down and wrote with a trembling hand. The pen spat out the words: *I stole* . . ., written with furious pressure, almost tearing the thin paper, while she repeated in a strangled voice:

'There you are, Monsieur, there you are, Monsieur . . . I am giving way to force.'

Bourdoncle took the paper, folded it carefully and shut it away in a drawer in front of her, saying:

'You see, it's in good company, because you ladies, after talking about dying rather than signing, generally forget to come and pick up these love letters. In any case, I shall keep it at your disposal. It's for you to judge whether it is worth two thousand francs.'

She had done up the last buttons on her dress and recovered all her arrogance, now that she had paid.

'May I leave?' she snapped.

Bourdoncle was already busy with something else. At Jouve's report, he had decided to dismiss Deloche: the man was stupid, he constantly let himself be robbed and he would never have any authority over the customers. Madame de Boves repeated her question and when they nodded for her to go, gave both of them a murderous look. From the stream of expletives that she was repressing, one melodramatic cry rose to her lips:

'Wretches!' she said, slamming the door.

Meanwhile, Blanche had not gone far from the office. She was disturbed by not knowing what was going on in there and by the coming and going of Jouve and two salesgirls, which suggested gendarmes, the assizes and prison. Then she was struck dumb: Vallagnosc was in front of her, this husband of one month who still embarrassed her when he called her *tu*; and he was asking questions, astonished by her bewilderment:

'Where is your mother? Are you lost? Come on, say something, you're worrying me.'

No adequate lie sprang to her lips. In her distress, she whispered:

'Mamma, Mamma . . . She stole . . .'

What! *Stole!* At last, he understood. His wife's puffy face, this pallid mask distraught with fear, appalled him.

'Some lace, like this, in her sleeve,' she was stammering.

'Did you see her? You were looking?' he said, horrified to think she might be an accomplice.

They had to stop talking because already people were turning round. For a moment Vallagnosc remained motionless, uncertain, full of anxiety. What should he do? He was just making up his mind to go into Bourdoncle's office when he saw Mouret crossing the gallery. He instructed his wife to wait for him and clasped his old friend's arm, informing him of the situation in a few brief phrases. Mouret hurried him into his office and set his mind at rest on the possible outcome, assuring him that he had no need to interfere and explaining how matters would undoubtedly be arranged, while not himself appearing to be at all surprised at the theft, as though he had foreseen it long ago. But Vallagnosc, once he no longer had to fear an immediate arrest, could not treat the affair with such splendid calm. He had sunk into the bottom of an armchair and now that he was thinking clearly started to lament his own fate. Was it possible? Now he had joined a family of thieves! A stupid marriage that he had messed up in order to please his father! Surprised by his friend's outburst, like that of a weak child, Mouret watched him weeping, but recalled his former pose of pessimism. Had he not heard him a dozen times argue the ultimate emptiness of life, in which only evil seemed to offer him some slight distraction?

So, to take his mind off it, Mouret amused himself for a moment by preaching indifference to him, in a tone of friendly banter. Suddenly, Vallagnosc lost his temper: he was definitely unable to recover his now compromised philosophy: all his middle-class upbringing welled up in virtuous indignation against his mother-in-law. As soon as experience intruded on him and at the least brush with that human misery which, otherwise, he treated with contempt, this sceptical braggart collapsed in agony. It was atrocious, they were dragging the honour of his race in the mud; the world seemed to be falling apart.

'Come now, calm down,' Mouret said eventually, feeling sorry for the man. 'I shan't tell you again that everything happens and nothing happens, because that doesn't seem to be consoling you at the moment. But I do think that you should go and give Madame de Boves your arm, because it would be more sensible than causing a scandal. I'll be damned! You were the one who used to preach phlegmatic contempt for the vileness of mankind.'

'Yes,' said Vallagnosc naively. 'When it affected other people!'

Meanwhile, he had got up and was following the advice of his former schoolmate. The two of them were going back into the gallery when Madame de Boves emerged from Bourdoncle's office. She graciously accepted her son-in-law's arm and when Mouret greeted her with respectful gallantry, he heard her say:

'They apologized to me. Honestly, it's appalling that they make these mistakes.'

Blanche had rejoined them and followed behind. Gradually, they vanished into the crowd.

Mouret, alone, thoughtful, once more walked through the shop. The scene, which had taken his mind off the inner conflict that was tearing him apart, now increased his fever, deciding him for the final struggle. In his mind, a whole series of vague connections arose: that miserable woman's thieving, the last folly of his conquered clientèle lying subject beneath the feet of the tempter, evoked the proud, vengeful image of Denise, whose victorious heel he felt against his throat. He paused at the top of the central stairway and looked out for a long time down the central nave, into which his nation of women was packed.

It was almost six o'clock and the light, fading outside, was falling in the covered galleries, making them already dark, and paling in the halls, which were slowly invaded by shadows. And, in this still unextinguished day, electric lamps lit up one by one, their opaque white globes scattering constellations of bright moons across the distant reaches of the store. It was a white light, dazzling and fixed, spread out like the reflection of a colourless star, killing the dusk. Then, when they were all alight, there was a delighted murmur from the crowd, as the Great White Sale took on the magic splendour of an apotheosis in this new light. It seemed that the immense overabundance of white was also burning and becoming light itself. The song of white rose up in the fiery whiteness of an aurora. A white radiance shimmered from the linens and calicos of the Monsigny gallery, like the bright band which first lightens the sky in the east, while along the Michodière gallery, haberdashery and soft furnishings, fancy goods and ribbons glowed with the sheen of distant hillsides, the white brilliance of buttons in mother-of-pearl, of silver-plated bronze and pearls. But the central nave above all sang of white dipped in flames: the white muslin ruffles around the columns, the white dimity and piqué hanging on the stairs, the white blankets hung out like banners, the white guipure and lace flying through the air, all opened on a dream heaven, a window into the dazzling whiteness of a paradise celebrating the wedding of some unknown queen. The tent in the silk hall was the vast bridal chamber, with its white curtains, gauzes and tulles, their brilliance shielding the white nudity of the bride. There was only this blinding white, a light in which all whites dissolved, a shower of stars falling against a brilliant white sky.

Mouret was still looking at his nation of women, amid this conflagration. The dark figures stood out sharply against the pale ground. Long shudders ran through the crowd, the fever of this great sale day passing like a swoon, rolling along the disordered mass of heads. They were starting to leave, the counters were littered with lengths of cloth and gold pieces rang in the tills, while the customers, despoiled, violated, were going away half undone, with the satisfied lust and vague shame of a desire slaked in the depths of some shady hotel. He was the one who possessed them in this way, who held them at his mercy, by his continual heaping up of goods, lowering of prices and profits, his charm and his advertising. He had conquered even the mothers, he reigned over all of them with the brutality of a despot, whose whim would destroy families. His creation was introducing a new religion, and while the churches were gradually emptied by the wavering of faith, they were replaced in souls that were now empty by his emporium. Women came to him to spend their hours of idleness, the uneasy, trembling hours that they would once have spent in chapel: it was a necessary outlet for nervous passion, the revived struggle of a god against the husband, a constantly renewed cult of the body, with the divine afterlife of beauty. If he had closed his doors, there would have been a riot outside, the frantic cry of pious women denied the confessional and the altar. Despite the late hour he saw them, in their luxury which had increased over the past ten years, obstinately following the huge metallic framework along the hanging stairways and the flying bridges. Madame Marty and her daughter, carried up to the highest point, were wandering among the furniture. Madame Bourdelais, held back by her children, could not tear herself away from novelties. Then came the group: Madame de Boves still on the arm of Vallagnosc and followed by Blanche, stopping in every department, still daring to look at materials with her arrogant air. But out of all the mass of customers, out of this sea of bodices bursting with life, heaving with desire, all decked with bouquets of violets as though for the public wedding of some sovereign, he could eventually distinguish nothing but the bare bosom of Madame Desforges, who had stopped in gloves with Madame Guibal. Despite her jealous rancour, she too was buying; and for the last time he felt himself to be the master, holding them at his feet under the glare of the electric light like cattle from which he had made his fortune.

With a mechanical step, Mouret walked along the galleries, so lost in thought that he abandoned himself to the flow of the crowd. When he looked up, he was in the new fashion department, where the windows looked out over the Rue du Dix-Décembre. And there, his forehead pressed against the glass, he paused again, looking at the exit. The setting sun was casting a yellow glow over the roofs of the white houses and the sky, blue from this fine day, was growing pale, cooled by a great breath of pure air, while in the dusk that was already spreading across the roadway, the electric lights of *Au Bonheur des Dames* cast the fixed light of stars on the horizon at the end of day. Towards the Opéra and the Stock Exchange stretched the three rows of stationary carriages, now in shadow, though their harness still had some flashes of bright light, the glow of a lantern or the spark of a silver bit. At every moment, there was a cry from a liveried boy and a cab came forward or a brougham moved out, picked up a customer, then went off at an echoing trot. The queues were getting smaller now, six carriages would move away together, from one side of the street to the other, amid the banging of doors, cracks of the whip and the hum of pedestrians spreading out among the wheels. It was like a continual expansion, a fanning out of the clientèle towards all points of the city, emptying the store with the roaring din of a sluice gate. Meanwhile the carriages of *Au Bonheur*, the tall gilt letters of their signs and their banners raised to the sky, still blazed in the fire of the setting sun, so colossal in this oblique lighting that they recalled the monster of the advertisements, the phalanstery whose extensions, constantly expanding, were eating up whole districts right out to the distant woods of the suburbs. And the swelling soul of Paris, a vast, soft breath, was falling asleep in the serenity of the evening and ran in long, tender caresses over the last carriages as they made their way down a street little by little emptied of its crowd and lapsing into the blackness of night.

Mouret, staring into space, had just felt something great pass through him; and while his flesh quivered in this shudder of triumph – Paris devoured and Woman conquered – he felt a sudden moment of weakness, a failure of his will which pushed him back in his turn before a superior force. There was an irrational desire to suffer defeat in his victory, the senselessness of a warrior bending to the whim of a child after his conquests. He, who had struggled for months and who that very morning had sworn again to stifle his passion, suddenly gave way, seized by vertigo, happy to do something that he considered folly. His decision was so swift and had demanded such energy from one minute to the next that it seemed to him the only thing that was useful or necessary in the world.

That evening, after the last service of dinner, he waited in his office. Shaking like a young man who is about to risk all his happiness, he could not stay in one place, but returned constantly to the door to listen to the noise from the shop where the assistants were cleaning up, buried up to their shoulders in the debris from the sale. Whenever he heard footsteps, his heart beat faster. Then he dashed forward with a start because he had heard in the distance a dull murmur, gradually growing louder.

It was Lhomme, slowly approaching, carrying the takings. That day, they weighed so much and there was so much copper and silver in the cash received that he had got two boys to go with him: behind him, Joseph and one of his colleagues were bowed down under the bags, huge bags, thrown over their shoulders like sacks of cement, while Lhomme, walking ahead, brought the notes and the gold, a portfolio swelling with paper and two small bags dangling round his neck, the weight of which was pulling him to the right, towards his missing arm. Slowly, sweating and panting, he came from the far reaches of the shop, surrounded by the growing excitement of the sales assistants. Gloves and silks had laughed and offered to relieve him of the burden, drapery and woollens hoped for him to trip and spill gold in every direction across the department. Then he had to go upstairs, cross a flying bridge, go up further and make his way around the girders, followed by the eyes of white linen, hosiery and haberdashery, wide with delight at the vision of this fortune travelling through the air. On the first floor, ladies' wear, perfumery, lace and shawls were lined up devoutly as at the passage of the Host in a religious procession. From one to another, the clamour rose and swelled to become the roar of a people acclaiming the golden calf.

Meanwhile, Mouret had opened his door. Lhomme appeared, followed by the two boys, staggering along; and breathless as he was, he still managed to cry out:

'One million, two hundred and forty-seven francs, ninety-five centimes!'

At last, the million mark had been reached, a million taken in a day – the figure that Mouret had dreamed about for so long! But he made an angry gesture and said impatiently, like a man waiting for something and bothered by an intruder.

'A million? Well, put it there.'

Lhomme knew that he liked to see large takings on his desk before he put them in the central counting-house. The million covered the desk, crushing his papers, almost knocking over the inkstand. Gold, silver and copper flowed from the sacks, burst out of the little bags making a large pile, a pile of raw takings just as they came from the customers' hands, still warm and alive.

Just as the cashier was leaving, annoyed at the boss's indifference, Bourdoncle arrived, happily exclaiming:

'So! We've done it this time! We got the million!'

Then he noticed Mouret's feverish preoccupation, realized what it meant and calmed down. His eyes were lit up with joy. After a brief silence, he went on:

'You've made your mind up, haven't you? Good heavens, I think you're right!'

Suddenly, Mouret placed himself in front of him and, in the fearful voice he kept for moments of crisis, said:

'What's this, my lad – you're a bit too pleased. Huh? You think I'm finished, don't you, and your teeth are bared. But just you watch it: no one eats me!'

Taken aback by this onslaught from that devil of a man, who could read one's thoughts, Bourdoncle stammered:

'What? You're joking, surely? When I admire you so much!'

'Don't lie,' said Mouret, still more savagely. 'Listen, we were idiots, with our superstition that marriage would be the end of us. Is it not the necessary health, the very strength and order of life? Well, yes, my friend, I'm going to marry her and I'll show you all the door if you make a move. Precisely! You'll go to the cash desk like anyone else, Bourdoncle!'

He motioned for him to leave. Bourdoncle felt he was doomed, swept away by this victory of womankind. Just as he was leaving, Denise entered and he bowed deeply, his head reeling.

'It's you at last,' Mouret said softly.

Denise was pale with emotion. She had just suffered one last blow: Deloche had told her of his dismissal and when she tried to keep him, offering to put in a good word, he persisted in his misfortune, wanting to disappear: what was the sense in staying? Why should he get in the way of others' happiness? Denise had said goodbye to him like a brother, tears in her eyes. Did she, too, not yearn for oblivion? Everything was about to end and she asked no more from her exhausted strength than the courage to part. In a few minutes, if she was brave enough to stifle the feelings of her heart, she could leave alone, go far away and weep.

'Monsieur, you asked to see me,' she said calmly. 'I should have come in any case to thank you for all your kindness.'

As she entered, she noticed the million francs on the desk and was hurt by the display of all this money. Above her, as though looking down on the scene, the portrait of Madame Hédouin in her golden frame kept an eternal smile on her painted lips.

'Are you still determined to leave us?' Mouret asked, his voice trembling.

'Yes, Monsieur, I must.'

At this, he took her hands and, in an outburst of passion, after his long period of self-imposed coldness:

'And if I were to marry you, Denise, would you leave then?'

But she had withdrawn her hands and was struggling as though oppressed by a great pain.

'Oh, Monsieur Mouret, I beg you, don't say that! Oh, do not make me still more unhappy! I can't, I can't! God is my witness that I was leaving to avoid just such a disaster!'

She continued to protest in broken phrases. Had she not already suffered enough from the gossip in the store? Did he want her to appear in other people's eyes and in his own as a whore? No, no, she would be strong, she would stop him from committing such a folly. He, tormented, listened to her, savagely repeating:

'I want to . . . I want to . . .'

'No, it's impossible. What about my brothers? I swore not to marry; I can't bring you two children, can I?'

'They will be my brothers, too. Say yes, Denise.'

'No, no. Leave me alone! You're torturing me!'

Bit by bit, he was losing hope, this last obstacle was driving him mad. What, even at that price did she still refuse? In the distance he could hear the noise of his three thousand employees, turning over his royal fortune in armfuls of money. And the ridiculous million that he had there! It was so ironic, he wanted to throw it into the street.

'So leave, then,' he shouted, in a flood of tears. 'Go and join the man you love. That's the reason, isn't it? You did warn me, I should have realized and not tormented you any further.'

She had remained dumbstruck by the violence of his despair. Her heart was bursting. So, with the impetuosity of a child, she threw her arms around his neck, sobbing herself and stammering:

'But Monsieur Mouret, you are the one I love!'

A last rumble rose from *Au Bonheur des Dames*, the distant acclamation of the crowd. Madame Hédouin's portrait was still smiling with its painted lips. Mouret had slumped onto the desk and was sitting amid the million which he no longer saw. He would not let Denise go, but clasped her desperately to him, telling her that she could go now, that she would spend a month in Valognes – which would shut everybody up – and that he would then come to fetch her himself, to bring her back from there on his arm, all-powerful.

NOTES

CHAPTER 1

1. *forty-five centimes . . . a franc . . . five sous*: the basic unit of French currency, under the Second Empire as now, was the franc, divided into one hundred centimes. There were copper coins for values from one to ten centimes, silver coins for twenty-five centimes to five francs, and gold coins for twenty and forty francs. In normal conversation people often still referred to an obsolete unit of currency, the *sou*, worth five centimes (in modern colloquial French the term is still used to refer to 'money' in general, or to a small sum). The standard rate of conversion was twenty-five francs to the pound sterling, so a *sou* was about one halfpenny, fifty centimes about five pence and five francs about four shillings.

2. *faille*: a type of silk cloth.

3. *familiar form*: the second person singular *tu* ('thou'), which is used with close family members, rather than the more formal *vous*.

4. *degeneration*: Zola's cycle of novels was built on the idea that physical characteristics, including acquired ones, could be passed on from one generation to another. Madame Baudu and her daughter are examples.

5. *army*: the French Army was in Mexico from 1862, supporting the Archduke Maximilian as emperor. Maximilian was shot in 1867 and a republic proclaimed.

6. *Seine-et-Oise*: the *département* which once covered most of the greater Paris region outside Paris itself. It ceased to exist in 1964 when it was subdivided into the three new *départements* of Yvelines, Essonne and Val d'Oise.

7. *Lyon*: the town has always been famous for its silks.

8. *Octave Mouret*: the son of François Mouret and Marthe Rougon, born in 1840, he is the central character in Zola's previous novel, *Pot-Bouille*, a figure of great energy and charm, whom the author sees as in many ways the epitome of his time.

9. *invest their money with him*: Aristide Boucicaut, founder of the *Bon Marché*, got his employees to invest in the firm and paid them interest on their savings.
10. *sell it dear*: the very opposite of Mouret's philosophy.
11. *the old ways*: Baudu, with his old-fashioned honesty and one weakness, has much in common with the eponymous hero of Honoré de Balzac's *César Birotteau* (see Introduction).
12. *saltpetre*: a form of calcium nitrate which occurs on damp walls.

CHAPTER 2

1. *rep*: a material with a finely corded surface.
2. *struggle for survival*: Mouret is applying a Darwinian principle to the relations between his employees, and this 'scientific' approach explains his success.
3. *Port-aux-Vins*: the little town of Chablis in Burgundy is famous for its white wines, so it is not surprising if Lhomme came up to Paris by river and found himself at the Port-aux-Vins on the Quai Saint-Bernard, where wines were unloaded.
4. *Auvergnat*: the people of the Auvergne have a (surely unjustified) reputation for meanness.
5. *Constantine*: a town in Algeria, captured by the French in 1837.

CHAPTER 3

1. *the familiar form*: she addresses Mouret using the formal *vous*. See note 3 to chapter 1.
2. *the Stud*: Zola wrote to a civil servant whom he knew inquiring about the salary of a teacher in a lycée (like M. Marty) and an inspector of the Stud – another example of his painstaking research into the background of the novel.
3. *four rules of arithmetic*: adding, dividing, multiplying, subtracting.
4. *Rue du Dix-Décembre*: later renamed Rue du Quatre-Septembre; the first name commemorates Napoleon III's proclamation of himself as Emperor in 1852. The chronology of Zola's account of the purchase of the land is inaccurate in some details.
5. *known prices*: as opposed to the old system of bargaining, which had been common in shops well into the nineteenth century.
6. *guipure*: a type of heavy lace where the elements of the pattern are joined by threads, not supported on net.

CHAPTER 4

1. *wearing hats*: in other words, relatively rich ladies from across Paris, as opposed to the hatless neighbours who were seen earlier.
2. *Delacroix*: the painter Eugène Delacroix (1798–1863) was known for his paintings of North African or oriental subjects.

CHAPTER 5

1. *work that would have finished many men*: Zola had been struck by an article in the periodical *Gil Blas* (16 January 1882) on the hardships of shop workers.
2. *twenty-nine sous*: a *sou* was five centimes, so this is one franc forty-five centimes. See note 1 to chapter 1.
3. *Batignolles*: a district in northern Paris.
4. *toque*: a small hat with no brim, popular in the late nineteenth century.
5. *phalanstery*: this is the first of several references in the novel to the Utopian Socialist theories of Charles Fourier (1772–1837), who proposed a social organization based on largely self-sufficient and self-governing communities ('phalansteries') living and working together for the common good, and designed to satisfy all the individual members' basic needs. Experimental Fourierist communities were founded in both France and America.
6. *Cotentin*: a peninsula in Normandy.
7. *Gymnase*: the Théâtre du Gymnase, in the Boulevard Bonne-Nouvelle, was reputed for vaudeville and comedies, especially those of Eugène Scribe (1791–1861).
8. *Drown . . . Sink and drown*: the original cries were: '*Les caboulots, à l'eau, à l'eau!*' (a *caboulot* was a kind of café, but here implies that the students haunt such places, or that they are well-off, like their owners) and '*Les calicots, à l'eau, à l'eau!*'; the derivation of *calicot* (from the variety of cloth) for a shop assistant is more obvious.
9. *marriages*: Zola's extensive notes on the *Bon Marché* do in fact point out that the store had a good reputation for morals and that marriages between staff were not uncommon there.

CHAPTER 6

1. *thirty sous*: one franc, fifty centimes. See note 1 to chapter 1.
2. *au gratin*: topped with grated cheese and baked in the oven.
3. *the Gaîté*: the theatre in the Square des Arts et Métiers which specialized in melodrama and also, increasingly, as here, in operetta.

CHAPTER 7

1. *ruining French industry*: Zola's information came from a man called Schneider, who supplied a note at the request of another of Zola's sources, Léon Carbonnaux (19 June 1882).
2. *zanella*: an Italian term for a type of light material, similar to satin, chiefly used for linings.

CHAPTER 8

1. *the Rue du Dix-Décembre*: on internal evidence, the chapter takes place in February 1867. The new Opéra was started in 1862 (though not finished until 1874). The street, later renamed Rue du Quatre-Septembre, would be opened in 1869. The expropriations mentioned in the next sentence were not in fact applied for until late in 1867 and early in 1868.
2. *Les Halles*: the huge central market of Paris, the setting for Zola's novel *Le Ventre de Paris*. It was demolished in 1971 and the market moved outside the city, to Rungis.
3. *electric lights were set up*: the building of the Hôtel du Louvre was the first time that electricity had been used for this purpose.
4. *against my conscience*: once more, Baudu's scruples make him comparable to César Birotteau, in Balzac's novel. See note 11 to chapter 1.

CHAPTER 9

1. *the new age*: Zola is here drawing particularly on the ideas of Frantz Jourdain, an architect who wrote to him in March 1882 sending a detailed plan for a new department store and insisting that 'stone should be used very sparingly in the

construction . . . The result will be more space, more air and more light.' However, the buildings in Paris that most clearly reflect these ideas are not those put up at the time when the novel is set (the late 1860s), but those built around 1900, at the time of the Exposition Universelle, for example the Grand Palais and the Montparnasse railway station (now the Musée d'Orsay).

2. *petty bourgeoises and women in bonnets*: the latter would be the wives of working men, the former wives of a slightly higher social group (e.g. shopkeepers).

3. *Orleans*: an English woollen cloth.

4. *Le Moniteur*: the newspaper, founded in 1789, which was the main journal of record and had a monopoly until 1869 for the publication of parliamentary debates and government decrees.

5. *straight lines across the void*: this description of the architecture of the store is in fact more consistent with the interior of the Parisian department store at a later date, for example *Le Bon Marché* as shown in a picture by Fichot for *L'Illustration* in 1880 (reproduced in Rachel Bowlby, *Just Looking: Consumer Culture in Dreiser, Gissing and Zola*, New York/London: Methuen, 1985).

6. *There were foulards . . . corahs from India*: all these are different kinds and qualities of silk.

7. *and classified them*: Zola here uses information that he obtained in his research at the *Bon Marché* and the *Louvre*.

CHAPTER 10

1. *which had to be finished that evening*: Léon Carbonnaux, a head of department in the *Bon Marché* and one of Zola's main sources for information about working conditions there, was his chief informant on the stocktaking.

2. *as their situation improved*: the staff in a large department store were hard to place in the social hierarchy, since most came from humble origins, while their job brought them into close contact with the upper classes and obliged them to adopt manners 'above their station'. Of course, the whole question has a direct bearing on Denise's feelings about Mouret, and vice versa.

3. *'Le Roi Dagobert'*: a popular comic song about one of the early kings of France.

4. *the last of the Fontenailles*: this decayed aristocratic family is another variation on the theme of class in this chapter.

5. *Bullier*: a dance hall in the Latin Quarter.

CHAPTER 11

1. *the King of Prussia's visit*: Wilhelm I visited Paris for the Exposition Industrielle in 1867.
2. *those young avenues*: the ones created by Baron Haussmann. See Introduction.

CHAPTER 12

1. *trade unions of the twentieth century*: the passage has been taken to throw light on Zola's own views about socialism, suggesting that he favoured something closer to a syndicalist, paternalist model, rather than a revolutionary, Marxian one; and the following paragraph reinforces this idea of change coming through the actions of an enlightened employer. Marguerite Boucicaut, wife of the owner of the *Bon Marché*, is credited with inspiring the changes that took place there in the 1870s, including a library for the staff, and lessons in music, languages and fencing and, eventually, an insurance scheme for employees with more than five years' service.
2. *trictrac*: a game similar to backgammon.

CHAPTER 13

1. *a Zouave's trousers*: the loose trousers worn by the French colonial troops.
2. *the crumbling edifice of the past*: Zola's vision of the future and of this dialectical struggle between the old and the new was to play an increasing part in the Rougon-Macquart novels.
3. *which themselves ate flies*: Denise's Darwinian nightmare shows that she has an instinctive understanding of the struggle for survival, tempered by compassion for its victims.
4. *sell for a hundred thousand*: Zola referred to a lawyer, Émile Collet, for help in finding the mechanism by which Bourras is finally destroyed. Collet replied with a letter suggesting how Mouret could trick the old umbrella-maker out of his lease.

CHAPTER 14

1. *the fire at Les Quatre Saisons*: a reference to the fire which destroyed *Le Printemps* on 9 March 1881 and drew attention to the living conditions of the shop workers.

THE STORY OF PENGUIN CLASSICS

Before 1946 …'Classics' are mainly the domain of academics and students, without readable editions for everyone else. This all changes when a little-known classicist, E. V. Rieu, presents Penguin founder Allen Lane with the translation of Homer's *Odyssey* that he has been working on and reading to his wife Nelly in his spare time.

1946 *The Odyssey* becomes the first Penguin Classic published, and promptly sells three million copies. Suddenly, classic books are no longer for the privileged few.

1950s Rieu, now series editor, turns to professional writers for the best modern, readable translations, including Dorothy L. Sayers's *Inferno* and Robert Graves's *The Twelve Caesars*, which revives the salacious original.

1960s The Classics are given the distinctive black jackets that have remained a constant throughout the series's various looks. Rieu retires in 1964, hailing the Penguin Classics list as 'the greatest educative force of the 20th century'.

1970s A new generation of translators arrives to swell the Penguin Classics ranks, and the list grows to encompass more philosophy, religion, science, history and politics.

1980s The Penguin American Library joins the Classics stable, with titles such as *The Last of the Mohicans* safeguarded. Penguin Classics now offers the most comprehensive library of world literature available.

1990s The launch of Penguin Audiobooks brings the classics to a listening audience for the first time, and in 1999 the launch of the Penguin Classics website takes them online to a larger global readership than ever before.

The 21st Century Penguin Classics are rejacketed for the first time in nearly twenty years. This world famous series now consists of more than 1300 titles, making the widest range of the best books ever written available to millions – and constantly redefining the meaning of what makes a 'classic'.

The Odyssey continues …

The best books ever written

SINCE 1946